Approaching the Speed of Light

Approaching the Speed of Light

A Novel

VICTORIA LUSTBADER

A TOM DOHERTY ASSOCIATES BOOK
NEW YORK

APPROACHING THE SPEED OF LIGHT

Copyright © 2013 by Victoria Lustbader

A Forge Book
Published by Tom Doherty Associates, LLC
175 Fifth Avenue
New York, NY 10010

www.tor-forge.com

Forge® is a registered trademark of Tom Doherty Associates, LLC.

Book design by Nicola Ferguson

Library of Congress Cataloging-in-Publication Data

Lustbader, Victoria.
    Approaching the Speed of Light / Victoria Lustbader.—First edition.
        p. cm.
    "A Tom Doherty Associates book."
    ISBN 978-0-7653-3490-9 (hardcover)
    ISBN 978-1-4668-1896-5 (e-book)
    1. Self-actualization (Psychology)—Fiction.   I. Title.
    PS3612.U79A88 2013
    813'.6—dc23

                                                    2012043863

Forge books may be purchased for educational, business, or promotional use. For information on bulk purchases, please contact Macmillan Corporate and Premium Sales Department at 1-800-221-7945 extension 5442 or write specialmarkets@macmillan.com.

First Edition: August 2013

Printed in the United States of America

0 9 8 7 6 5 4 3 2 1

For Eric, my one and only

You know quite well, deep within you, that there is only a single magic, single power, a single salvation...and that is called loving. Well, then, love your suffering. Do not resist it, do not flee from it. It is your aversion that hurts, nothing else.

—HERMANN HESSE

Approaching
the Speed
of Light

Prologue

OBSERVER EFFECT

*. . . as applies to the quantum thought experiment
known as Schrödinger's cat, in which a (theoretical)
living cat is sealed inside a box, at potential risk of
death by poisoning. The cat cannot be considered
either alive or dead until it is observed to be one or
the other. Until that moment, there is only
potentiality: everything is possible; all things that
might be, are. Thus, the unobserved cat in the sealed
box must be considered both alive and dead.*

*One might say, then, it is not a cat's own curiosity
about the world that determines its fate. Rather, it is
the curiosity of the world about it that determines
whether it lives, or whether it dies.*

IT'S LATE ON A FRIDAY afternoon in August of 1988. Seventeen-year-old Jody Kowalczyk is working at Marley's, the snack shack on the Great Cove dock in Bay Shore, where the ferries leave to cross Great South Bay for Fire Island. Jody looks more mature and behaves more adultly than a teenager should; he's been working summers at Marley's, off the books, since he was fourteen. He's in the kitchen, loading up a tray with their home-made doughnuts, items of legend along the southern shore of Long Island. They sell them as fast as they can make them. The dough-nuts are still hot and Jody is nearly stupefied by the heady aroma of fried dough. His hands, elegantly shaped and overlarge like a puppy's paws, as if he has yet to grow into them, are warm. His fingers, with their coating of liquefying sugar crystals, are as sweetly tasty-looking as caramel.

Jody doesn't know yet that this will be his last summer at Mar-ley's, his last summer in Bay Shore. He's on the other side of the sturdy kitchen wall so he hasn't seen her come through the restau-rant's door. He can see through a certain kind of wall—the kind that he constructs himself, with his mind—but this isn't one of those kind. It's a common kind, made with tools and hands, of wooden beams, lath, and plasterboard. Layers of paint and years of greasy fingerprints.

This afternoon, while still on this side of the wall, Jody expects to start a year of vocational school in September, then find a job in Bay Shore. He could have set his sights higher. His high school grades were decent and he's a natural-born athlete. But the ques-tion of whether or not attending vocational school is what he wants to do is not even another matter. It is of no matter. Jody doesn't think in terms of what he wants or doesn't want. Wanting things requires at its foundation a concept of consecutive tomorrows and an inner vocabulary to muse upon the concept. Jody does not possess either, concept or vocabulary. He lives one day at a time. He tries to keep his balance. Awareness of too much space behind or ahead of him would make that very difficult.

He grasps the enormous stainless steel tray in his able hands, puts his back to the swinging door, and makes ready to push himself out of the kitchen. Once he is through the kitchen door and materializes on the other side of the wall it will take less than three minutes for him to get bumped off the seesaw and find that his expectations have changed.

*

JODY TURNS INTO THE CROWDED room. He heads for the end of the long counter closest to the bay-side windows, where there is a space awaiting the tray of doughnuts. Squiggly waves of vapor rise from the tray and melt into the rays of light that stripe the air inside the snack shack. A customer is approaching the counter from the opposite side. Jody looks up and, through the waves and the rays, sees a statuesque woman illuminated in a searchlight beam of afternoon sun. She stands amid the crowd uncertainly, unsure where to look or whom to talk to. Her nose twitches. She turns her head in Jody's direction, in the direction of her nose's interest. She discovers the tray of doughnuts, then raises her eyes to Jody's face.

Her loose, abundant hair is sparking red-gold. It forms a visible aura of pure rosy light around her pale face and neck. Her eyes are the color of tender spring leaves, limpid yellow-green. A march of faint freckles dusts the fair skin of her cheeks and nose. Nestled and sparkling in the hollow of her throat is a violet-blue sapphire on a thin gold chain, and below smolders the rich burnt-orange silk of her blouse. Jody tosses his head to get his straight dark hair out of his eyes so he can see her better. He stares at her; he can't

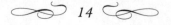

stop. She is a fantasy creature sprung to life from his own memory, from the forgiving and sheltering heart of a work of art he saw once and only briefly, on a school trip to the Cloisters when he was eleven, but never forgot—a sunstruck, gem-hued, shimmering panel of centuries-old stained glass. He had stood in front of it, oblivious to the bored jostling of his classmates, mesmerized by its radiating light and unpeopled serenity, and felt his leaden spirit stir and struggle to rise.

For a moment she fills the entirety of Jody's ageless and timeless universe. When her eyes meet his and hold there, Jody feels a sick, electric thrill in his gut. His heart rate jumps, his focus sharpens and narrows, his hearing dims, and time slows. Just the way it all used to happen, too often, when he was a child; the way it does now when he's on the ball field, the soccer field, or the hockey rink; when he's making love.

Despite his apparently calm, conscious control over himself, Jody is in fact largely ruled by his forever-vigilant unconscious, which has long been hyperattuned to the minutest vibrations of all living things beyond the borders of his being while remaining fiercely unreceptive to his own. In the blink of an eye it collects and analyzes a wealth of information about the woman, inputted to him in bits by her posture, the tinge of color in her face, the movements of her head and hands, the subtle array of fleeting expressions that dart among the new green leaves, and that arrange and rearrange her features.

She's overheated; she's overcautious; she's more respectful of the people around her than they are of her; she has a placid surface but there is something restless swirling in the deep. She's considerably older than he is, which Jody notes although it is a piece of information of no particular meaning or interest to him. And, she's in the grip of a serious hunger. He puts it all together and concludes he needs to give her a doughnut. He has nothing else to give her. He smiles at her, balances the tray with one hand, and with the other he makes his offering.

"You should have one. Here. On the house. On me."

Her spring green eyes grow huge. They fix on his mouth, on the baffled, lopsided curve of his full lips, on his hesitant smile. She stiffens, as if riveted to the sticky wood floor beneath her feet, her sun-pink cheeks go ashen. Her eyes seem to flicker at him, to warm and darken. She blinks. She exhales a held breath, smiles unconvincingly, then drops her lids, reaches out her hand, and lets Jody place his gift into her palm.

A New York City man with fine features and dressed in brand-marked khakis and polo shirt has crowded close behind her and is frowning over her shoulder. Her eyes go still and cool. Jody senses her discomfort as a startling wave of superheated air pushing at him, and he takes a small, involuntary step backward. The man, his tanned brow furrowed beneath a New York University Hospital sun visor, says, "Jesus, Ella, you're an animal. A doughnut after that lunch we had?" He pats the womanly swell of her hip with dishonest tenderness. "Let's go, sweetheart. The ferry's loading."

He doesn't wait for her, but dematerializes once more into the milling crowd. Her lids close slowly while she takes a breath. She opens her eyes again and Jody sees the turmoil behind their controlled stillness. She says, so low he can't quite hear her, he has to read her lips, "Thank you." The pink of embarrassment has recolored her cheeks.

"You're welcome." He doesn't smile at her now. That would be a mistake. If he did, she'd think he thought that all she wished to thank him for was the actual doughnut.

She hesitates, then raises the doughnut in the air like the prize it is and repeats herself, in a stronger voice. "Thank you." This time they smile at each other and Jody nods. The conflict in her eyes slowly morphs into a different sort, an outer-directed sort that makes the sick, electric feeling in Jody's gut want to spread. Her eyes quiver and slide off his face as she says, "Good-bye," and he nods at her again as she turns to leave.

He puts the tray down and watches her thread her way through the crowd, voluptuously eating her doughnut as she goes. At the door, she stops and looks urgently over her shoulder but he is already moving toward the window and she cannot stand in place long enough to find him. He watches her cross the dock, board the ferry, the sleek city man like a bodyguard by her side.

Her name is Ella. She lives in the city, she likes doughnuts, but doesn't like the man she's with.

The ferry pulls away and she's gone, but she has left her imprint in Jody's space. He works through the afternoon and evening, in and out of the kitchen, filling and bagging orders, taking money, making change. Every time he steps back into the main room he sees her, as a pulsing rosy glow in the air above and beyond the counter, like the light that blooms over the horizon heralding sunrise. He sees green and gold traces all over the room, wherever her eyes traveled, trails that promise spring, hope, and rebirth.

The promise of hope, rebirth. Jody has no inner vocabulary for concepts such as those, either, no more than for wanting or for tomorrow. He has advanced through his life by submitting to the forces that converge and descend on him, that herd him from one situation to the next. Which isn't to say that Jody has never wanted. Or has never invested himself in hope. He did, quite naturally, once upon a time. He doesn't anymore, and so his wanting to see Ella again, his hope that someday he might, shape-shifts into an inarticulate, seemingly casual decision to move away from Bay Shore at last, to move into the city and find work there. Any kind of work.

✳

TIME PASSES; THE MEMORY OF her sunrise aura fades. The unacknowledged hope fades, too, the way hope has always faded inside Jody. Soon enough, when he wanders the streets of the city, or walks through the door of a new place, he will no longer unconsciously scan the air for a rosy glow. What converged and descended on him for those three minutes had their way with him for a short while, but he was able to find his balance again. He has learned to neither think too much and feel too little nor think too little and feel too much. It is natural to him, as natural as breathing, to come back to that place where he both thinks and feels as little as possible.

Part One

SINGULARITY

A black hole is a spherical, three-dimensional region of space-time that has at its center a singularity, an anomalous place with such density of mass that its gravitational pull captures anything that crosses the "horizon" of the sphere. Events that may be happening inside the black hole cannot be seen by observers outside the event horizon, and escape to the outside universe of anything trapped inside is impossible.

One

ON THE MORNING OF THE first day of my final chance at a life, I got woken up by Einstein. My dog. I'd had three chances before, and it's not that they all were bad, but they were false starts. They found me, were handed to me, unasked. This one I chose, inasmuch as I believe anyone ever really chooses anything. If either of us, man or dog, knew what the day was going to turn out to be, we would have tried to start it with something more meaningful, something with a little more dignity than dog saliva on my face. After all, we were both pretty smart in our own ways, though it was hard to tell from just looking. Our smarts were below the surface, invisible to the naked eye, like a lot of essential things in this world.

Einstein didn't usually wake me up, even if she had to go out. But when I made that noise in my sleep, no matter what time it was, if I made that noise Einstein came running from wherever she was in the apartment and jumped onto the bed, right on top of me, licked me, and pushed at my face with her paw until I stopped. I heard the noise from inside my head, from inside the dream where I was making it, so I didn't know what it sounded like from the outside. If I was with someone, the noise would wake her up and she'd shake me hard, all upset, and say my name loud. Yell it. *"Jody!"* I'd apologize, tell her to go back to sleep. One of my girlfriends once said it was the scariest sound she'd ever heard, like some freaked-out spirit screaming to get out of hell. To me it wasn't even a sound, more a feeling, like I was choking, like I couldn't breathe and I couldn't yell, even though I was trying.

Every time, there was this taste in my mouth, my tongue was thick and my throat ached so bad, I knew there was a sound even though I couldn't hear it. I'd go to the sink and rinse my mouth with cold water until the taste was gone and there was enough room there for my tongue again.

After I got Einstein, maybe a year after, and had the dream a few times, right near the end of it I started hearing her nails fast clicking on the wood floor, a signal to say she's coming, that it's okay, I'm going to wake up *now*. I loved that sound. Einstein would get to me faster than any girl, as if she knew when I was having that dream even before the freaked-out spirit scream hit.

I had a sneaky new version of that same dream every few months. I must have had other dreams, but that was the only one I ever remembered. It had been like that since I was nine. I knew it wasn't normal, but I've always known I wasn't normal—at least I hoped to God I wasn't—so I was fine with it. I didn't want to remember my other dreams. One time I tried to imagine what they might be, but it didn't take long before my remembered dreams of dying started looking really good, and I never tried that again. I'd have preferred not to remember a lot of things, but there were still ways my mind worked that were the same as anyone else's. So I remembered. But since everything is relative, including damage, including memory, I spent a lot of time repositioning my memories, having to figure out where they fit, relative to who, where, and when I was at the moment I remembered something.

It wasn't easy, keeping track of myself in the world other people lived in. It was just something I had to do. I'd known that since I was nine, and was fine with it, too. It didn't provide happiness, but happiness was just a joke and I'd stopped looking for it even before I'd stopped remembering my dreams. I read somewhere that Buddhism says the nature and purpose of life is to seek happiness, that that's what life is, an arrow in flight, aimed at happiness. I thought that was an astonishing, even enviable, point of view, since I saw life more like a fixed-finish, pointless race to outrun annihilation. But there was another thought, I didn't know where it came from, that since we have no clue what we're really looking for or what we want, our best shot at finding what we were looking for was to stop looking for it. And in the end that still seemed right to me because I wasn't looking for Tess, I didn't know I needed her to hold my secrets, and I wasn't looking for Ella, I didn't know I wanted her to love me, and I wasn't looking for peace, I didn't know that's what *I* was aimed at, but I found them anyway.

✳

THAT DAY. I LAY THERE for a bit after Einstein pawed and licked me. Even after I understood that I was breathing and not dying, the dream always left me feeling like I couldn't move. She waited, next to me on the bed. I had cold cereal for breakfast, Einstein some Purina, and we left for work by seven.

I walked to work, or at least to where my day started, at the office and warehouse of Citywide Glass and Mirror. I'd worked there since I came to the city at the beginning of 1989, when I was just eighteen. Nearly eleven years. The owners, Stan and Billy Dudek, made me an installation foreman after three years. It was hard physical work and I was good at it. And I was good with the measurements. That sort of stuff, math, pure and precise, I could do in my head. Many times, the other guys had me do the measurements for their jobs because I never screwed up, not even by a fraction.

The Citywide mother ship was down under the Williamsburg Bridge, at Delancey and Columbia streets, an excellent location. Queens was right over the Williamsburg; the Bronx straight up the FDR Drive; Brooklyn over the Manhattan, Williamsburg, or Brooklyn bridges. The location of my apartment was another story. I lived in a top-floor walk-up in the East Village, on Tenth Street, between Avenues A and B, about twelve blocks north of Citywide. It was one of the only neighborhoods I could afford ten years ago, but it was also the perfect place for me, packed in shoulder to shoulder with the addicts and drunks and homeless, the nuts and freaks and idiots and arty oddballs. I knew it bothered my family, my choosing to live there, but there was nothing anyone could do about that.

Once, I thought I might like to live in Greenwich Village when I made enough money. It was the East Village's counterpart west of Fifth Avenue, the other side of the mirror. The pretty, civilized side. But when I walked through the clean streets with their fancy brownstones and window boxes full of flowers, everyone with smart eyes pricking at me, even the little kids pouring in and out of their special schools, I knew I didn't belong there. I'd just make a mess, bleed all over their pretty, civilized world. I liked the pressure of ugliness around me, like a tourniquet to keep it all together. And there were too many men who stared at me too long and too hard. That wasn't something I could deal with day after day. The East Village teemed with weirdos whose internal shit was smeared all over their skin and whose eyes looked in. Maybe all that chaotic psychic radiation interfered with mine, with whatever it was about me that people thought they saw, because there I became transparent.

So even though by now I had the money to live somewhere better, I wouldn't. And besides, the East Village was sort of glacially cleaning up from its X to an R rating so it could make it into the new millennium with the rest of the city and not get turned back at the gate for

Excessive Violence and Gratuitous Depravity when that ball dropped in Times Square. Even Tompkins Square Park, across from my building, which used to be three square city blocks of filth and mayhem, and where there were riots between the homeless and the police in the summer of '88, was a lot safer and pretty these days, with a dog run where I sometimes took Einstein. It was a good place to pick up girls, the dog run, and I did it a few times, but I stopped because it just got unpleasant after I broke up with them.

※

RIGHT . . . THAT DAY. BY EIGHT I was behind the wheel of a company truck, a day's worth of glass strapped to its sides, heading deep into Brooklyn to start the job I'd prepped for all spring. Replacing windows and mirrors in the Parkside Home for Seniors. It was in a six-story former apartment building, built sturdy in the thirties. Some of its original glasswork was still there, some of it even still good. And some had been replaced twenty-five years before, when the building was converted. But now half the mirrors were clouded over or cracked, a lot of the windows, too, or their frames leaked air and water. I did the first look-see, then asked for the job. I said to Stan, "The people who live there, they're going to die there. They should be able to see things right."

Orlando rode next to me, Hector and Frank in the back with Einstein at their feet. I usually left her to wander around the warehouse and get spoiled rotten by the girls in the office, or with the loudmouthed, stone-eyed, mush-hearted Israeli guys, probably ex-Mossad agents all, from Sabra, the twenty-four-hour car service company next door, but, when I could, I took her with me. Mrs. Jacobs, Parkside's administrator, saw how good and obedient she was and said as long as I was careful it was okay for me to bring her. There were almost always other dogs there. Mrs. Jacobs told me they were therapy dogs; their owners brought them to spend time with the residents because interacting with animals was good for the elderly and the sick. She was seriously eyeing Einstein while she talked, taking her measure, and I could tell she thought Einstein would make a good therapy dog. I thought so, too. I'd found her abandoned on the street three years ago, scrawny, scabby, and shaking. She was maybe eight months old, with a dislocated back left leg, broken ribs, a collapsed lung, and an infection in her eyes. She could recognize loneliness and fear.

It was funny, but after seeing Mrs. Jacobs's face while she was looking at Einstein, it seemed to me that Einstein started looking at me sometimes that same way, as if she was thinking that *I'd* make a good therapy dog, too. As if she was thinking, *Come on! We could do it together! Aren't you good and obedient? Don't you recognize loneliness and fear?* But I knew it wasn't that simple. Sure, I was good and obedient. I recognized loneliness and fear. But I didn't recognize them the way other people seemed to, as bad things, things to be paid attention to, things that should be fixed. I simply recognized them; damp clingy particles floating in the air as familiar and natural to me as the motes of dry dust.

※

I LEFT THE GUYS TO unload, went to tell Mrs. Jacobs we'd arrived, then headed back to the dining room, where we were going to start. A group of women was walking down the wide hallway toward me, coming from breakfast. Old women, walking slowly, close together, a little battalion, murmuring. I was keeping close to the right side wall, but I got even closer, until my arm touched the wall, and I slowed down, so I wouldn't startle or disrupt them when we passed each other. They looked small and frail, like you could blow them over as easily as blowing out a candle. When they went by, they turned their heads and stared at me, but in a good way, the way old people look when they look at babies. As if they were petting me with their eyes. They smiled at me and I smiled back.

"Good morning, ladies."

One of them said, "Good morning, young man," and the others all nodded, agreeing with her, their smiles all serious now.

They moved on, turned their heads away. Except the one who'd spoken. She was still looking at me. A space grew between her and the rest as she came to a stop and they kept going. There was a quick pang in my stomach; the lifeboat was pulling away and leaving her behind. I tilted my head and scooped my eyes in the direction of her friends, to get her going again, but she didn't go. Instead, she crossed the width of the hallway until she stood in front of me. Up close like that, she didn't seem frail, although she was on the small side and slender. I was just over six feet, she had to bend her head back a bit to look at me. Her silver hair was pulled into a bun at the nape of her neck, and the shape of her face, turned up to me like that, was a seamless oval. No forehead peaks or chin juts, but a perfect oval with no beginning or end.

She said, "Matt?" Her eyes were an unusual shade of brown, a living warm green-brown, like the inside of a tree. But they were strange, too shiny, off in infinity somewhere. She was clutching a picture frame against her body, so hard it was like she wanted to push it right into her heart. Her fingers were like claws around it, you'd need pliers to take it away from her. "Mattie?" Her voice was breathy. It faded away into a happy bewilderment on the final syllable.

The hallway we stood in was windowless, lit by fluorescent bulbs overhead. The light that filled the corridor was bright, bright enough for people who had to be careful how they walked. It was hard, breakable light and I didn't want to be stuck inside it. But right where I stood, me and this woman with the oval face and spacey eyes, the light was different. Soft and gentle, and we were wrapped up in it together. It was her. Her face was lit from inside, as if she had a luminescent layer between her smooth milky skin and her flesh. I moved away from the wall, deeper into that soft light, so she could see me more clearly, see that she'd confused me with someone else.

"No. I'm not Matt. My name's Jody. Jody Kowalczyk."

Her eyes searched my face, side to side and up and down, and they slowly lost that strange shine. "Oh."

She didn't sound happy anymore, just confused, and I felt guilty, like it was my fault I wasn't who she wanted me to be. Matt. "Yeah, I'm sorry. I'm Jody. Sorry."

She tried out my name. "Jody. Jody." She shook her head. "Are you sure?"

I listened to the beat of my heart, a sudden gallop inside the locked corral of my chest, before I said, "Yes. I'm sure."

Her eyes filled with tears. "Oh, my goodness. Forgive me. What a foolish thing to say." She looked so sad. "Jody. Such a sweet name. Do I know you?"

She had an accent, from a long time ago. I thought I recognized it, that I'd heard it before, but I wasn't sure, it was so faint. I should get to the dining room, but I didn't want to leave her. Her milky skin and her sad eyes and her gentle light. Her wanting me to be someone else.

"I don't think so. I mean, we've never met. Maybe you've seen me here before, though. I've been in and out over the last few months."

"No, I didn't see you before. But I see you now. Why? Why are you here? You don't belong to anyone. Why are you here now?"

"I'm going to be working here for a while, putting in new windows and mirrors."

I answered her odd questions as if I heard them the same way any-one else would hear them. To look at me, no one could ever tell that her questions didn't seem odd to me, that I didn't exactly hear them. I felt them, the same way I felt but didn't hear the strangled cries that woke me from my nightmares. I felt them creep through my brain like radioactive dye hunting for a buried hot spot.

Her gaze hadn't left my face and now her light brown eyes, completely clear, fastened on to mine. "New windows and mirrors. That's good. We certainly need them." She smiled. Her voice was hushed and kind when she said, "Jody. *Hai gli occhi di un angelo.*"

She spoke in Italian. *Hai gli occhi di un angelo.* That was the accent. She spoke to me in Italian. The words punched a tiny hole through one of those walls in my head and there was a bright flash behind my eyes. My throat constricted. *You have the eyes of an angel.*

I was aware of her walking around me and away from me. As if from a great distance I heard someone call out, "Tess? Are you coming? Tessie!" By the time I could hear and see again, the hallway was empty. She had vanished. I was all alone again in the present, in the hard breakable light. I looked wildly in both directions, but I couldn't see which way she'd gone. Whether it was into the past or into the future.

※

I GOT HOME A LITTLE before seven after laboring like a convict all day. I'd worked as hard as I could and I was tired, but I wasn't worn out. It took a lot to wear me out, so I had to keep moving. I needed to be worn out, to be too tired to think.

It was the middle of August, there was still plenty of daylight left so I changed into gym shorts and a T-shirt, grabbed my Rollerblades, and me and Einstein went out again. I zigzagged west, skating through the traffic, six long ugly avenue blocks till I crossed Fifth Avenue and coasted into Greenwich Village. I kept on toward the river down Eleventh Street, like I always did, so I could skate slowly past the double-wide red-brick town house with the color-crazy little garden in front and the piano visible through the floor-to-ceiling first-floor windows.

When I reached the Hudson and the riverside bike path, I took off,

flying over the pavement. Einstein raced beside me on a long leash, panting hard, a sleek shadow at my side, her wagging tongue bright pink against her black muzzle. She ran with her head cocked, her big ears up, her chocolate eyes fixed on my face with that look in them.

The sun was a huge glaring ball sinking beyond the river, behind the Jersey skyline. It was brutally hot and humid, and my legs and lungs caught fire fast. I didn't mind; I loved it. I knew what to do with physical pain, how to use it. With each thrust and push of my muscles, each pounding beat of my heart, I patched up the hole in the wall. I skated to the Battery, past my brother Brendan's apartment and the twin towers of the World Trade Center, jutting up into the sky like a challenge to the gods of destruction, and back up to Fourteenth Street again and again, maybe six miles each round trip. It was full dark by the time I skated home.

I detoured to John's on East Twelfth Street and got a small pizza, extra cheese. I sat sweaty at my kitchen table and wolfed it down in nonstop little bites practically without breathing, finished all six slices in ten minutes. I still ate too fast when I was alone. I fed Einstein. I took a shower. The new book I was into was on my bed, but I didn't try to read. The marks on the page would only slide around under my eyes, I wouldn't understand the words. I wouldn't be able to read for days, not until I could get everything inside my head configured right again. Instead, I watched part of *Blade Runner*, just started it from where I'd stopped it the last time. I could always count on its sodden gritty future world, all that rain, anger, and desperation, to blot out all the past and present worlds of my own existence. That night, it turned out to be the last part, the end.

"I've seen things you people wouldn't believe. Attack ships on fire off the shoulder of Orion . . . All those moments will be lost in time . . . like tears in rain. . . . Time to die."

Hai gli occhi di un angelo. Why did she say that? Of all the millions of things she could have said to me, why did she say that?

Brendan had called while I was out, left a message. "Hey, baby bro. Call me. We have to talk about next weekend." I didn't call him. I went to bed and because I was finally worn out, I lay awake for only a few minutes, sifting and cataloging and placing every sound and every shadow movement, before I fell asleep. And then I slept the way I usually did when I finally got there, up and down, one minute out like a dead person, the next awake watching shadows again. I didn't dream; I didn't scream. Einstein stayed in the living room.

Einstein lay down on her round pillow bed next to the couch, but she didn't stay there, like Jody thought. She listened to him move around the bedroom. She heard the bed groan faintly when he finally lay down, heard the click of the bedside lamp when he finally turned it off. She waited a few minutes, then softly padded across the floor in the dimness, back up the hallway, careful that her nails not tick on the clean polished wood, and reverentially settled herself just outside his door. She wanted to be close, keep vigil, because although he didn't often scream in his sleep two nights in a row, tonight the energy that emanated from him and encased his form, while never calm or light, was a frightening mass of dark and muddy movement, like it always was when he did scream in his sleep. She'd done this many times before, whenever he went dark like that, and like most of those other times he slept quietly after all, and in the morning came into the living room in all innocence to find Einstein passed out on her bed, twitching in the throes of a dream of her own. It was really too bad she was a dog and couldn't understand or answer him when he talked to her in words. Because there were a lot of important things she would have wanted to say.

Two

TESS. THE STRANGE OLD LADY. I couldn't stop thinking about her, about the light that radiated from her, and the warmth of her eyes and her voice, even in her disappointment that I wasn't who she wanted me to be. About her sadness. And the things she'd said to me. She'd disturbed me, but still, I was sorry when I didn't see her again all that first week.

We'd been eating our lunches in the truck in the parking lot, which was about as much fun as picnicking on Venus since the truck had no air-conditioning. Orlando and Hector didn't care. They were hot-blooded Dominicans, they ran for their hoodies and two pairs of socks if the temperature dipped below eighty. But Frank and Einstein and I were dying. The park was cool and green across Prospect Park West, but going in there would've taken up too much time.

Toward the end of the second week, Mrs. Jacobs noticed we were coming in more limp than before our lunch break and took pity on us. She looked like she'd be all business—long horsey face, thin and sharp as a new number-two pencil, clothes like a prairie schoolmarm—but Mrs. Jacobs was one of the nicest ladies you could ever meet. I think what got to her was the pitiful sight of Einstein with her tongue down to the ground, her ears droopy, and her eyes hanging on to Mrs. Jacobs's face with a look of imminent expiration in them. Einstein was a girl who knew how to get what she wanted. Mrs. Jacobs gave us permission to use Parkside's inner courtyard garden during their lunch hour.

The courtyard was a good size, with packed-earth walkways connecting umbrella-shaded tables set on circles of blue slate. Long teak benches, some in the sun, others in the shade of honey locust, ginkgo, and pear trees that gobbled up the city's carbon dioxide and soot like it was fertilizer. Neat beds of shrubs and flowers planted in the spaces between the lanes. We stood in the shade of the building's red brick wall, white paper lunch bags from the deli in our hands, Einstein's in her mouth, while I looked around for a place to sit where we wouldn't be in the way of any fast eaters or staff. I chose a bench along the ivy-covered wall opposite the building's double glass doors. It was mostly in the sun, but there was a decent breeze, and I figured better us, dark-skinned and too stupid or nihilistic to give a rat's ass about melanoma, than the oldsters who were working at staying alive.

About twenty minutes later I was bending over, picking up the wrapper from Einstein's chicken cutlet, when Einstein's head and ears swiveled toward the doors like a weathervane pushed by a blast of wind. I raised my head and saw Tess come out of the building with two other women and a man. She looked right at me and when our eyes met, her face lit up, like that layer beneath her skin ignited at the sight of me. Something lit up inside me too then, and a fool smile took over my face.

Her friends headed for a table near our bench. One of the ladies put a small tote bag on the table and unpacked two decks of cards, a pad fat with use, and a pen. But Tess kept coming on toward us, holding on to that silver picture frame just like the last time. As she got closer, Einstein barked once and made to go to her. I hooked a finger under Einstein's collar to hold her, but Tess started up with the coos, clucks, and come-hither pats on her thigh. So I let her go. She offered up a paw and Tess took it, gave it a shake.

"Oh, aren't you a*dor*able! You are the *cut*est dog!"

Einstein had that effect on people. She was part indiscriminately affectionate black Lab, part something smaller and more thoughtful—the vet thought maybe there was some border collie in there somewhere. She was friendly and trusting even after the miserable condition I'd found her in, with the most noble face in all of dogdom and eyes that lowered your blood pressure fifty points just by looking into them. I could never get my head around how someone could have hurt her and left her on the street like that. She pointed her snout at the old lady's face, and the tongue went out. I figured that was enough. I'd promised Mrs. Jacobs my dog wouldn't annoy anyone and, cute as she was, not everyone enjoys a wet tongue on the nose. I stood up.

"Einstein!"

"It's all right. Stay there. I'll bring her." She gave Einstein a scratch under her chin.

"Tessie! Are we playing cards or what?" It was the man, sitting with his hands together in front of him pleading with her, his furry eyebrows lifted. Like he'd been trying and failing for years to get her not to do this all the time, wander off when they were supposed to be doing something.

"I want to chat with the gentleman who names his dog Einstein."

The man turned his head. "Sonny, does your dog play rummy or is it too busy pondering the nature of the universe? We could use a reliable fourth here."

"If it's anything like fetch, I guess she could hold her own."

Tess smiled at me. "Just start without me, Abe. I won't be long."

One of the ladies called over, "Hold on to your hat, young man!" She looked at Tess with a lot of love in her eyes and laughed, but she was for sure half-serious, because as it turned out you needed something to hold on to when you were around Tess. At least I did.

She put her back to the others and let out a sigh. "Oh. I'm happy to see you."

"It's nice to see you, too. How are you today?"

Tess had to be near eighty, but she had that spark that makes lots of old people these days seem younger than they are. She stood straight, looked healthy, and was dressed more youthfully than Mrs. Jacobs, in a turquoise polo shirt and white pants, white canvas Keds on her feet.

"Better now." She lowered her voice, moved closer. "I was afraid I'd imagined you. I can get a little mixed-up sometimes, about where I am, what I'm seeing. It's not that I forget exactly, but . . . I get a little lost. I'm so sorry, I hope I didn't upset you."

"It's okay. You don't have to apologize. I can get a little lost too sometimes."

She studied me with her green-brown eyes. She nodded. She didn't look mixed-up, or off in space. She looked pretty damn sharp. "Yes. Reality and memory can be difficult to sort out. Time is such a fluid thing, so hard to grasp, isn't it?"

Her eyes were on mine and it was as if she was seeing right down through them, into a part of me no one was meant to see, the part that knew more than a little about the fluidity of time and sorting out reality and memory. And I let her, I didn't look away, or bring the curtain down. It was unsettling, how good it felt to be seen like that. I didn't like being unsettled. I got hold of myself, started fussing with Einstein, picking nonexistent mucus out of her eyes.

"I guess so."

I could feel Tess's gaze linger another moment on my bent head, then pull away.

"What do you think, Einstein?" Tess teased. At the sound of her name, Einstein barked twice and shimmied her rear end. "She agrees. And she should know, yes, all about reality and time?" Tess leaned over and patted Einstein between the ears. Then she patted my hand and smiled. "You call your dog after perhaps the smartest man who ever lived. Why? Do you think your Einstein is smarter than you?"

It was obvious from her tone that Tess didn't, but my opinion on the matter, why I named her that, the things she did understand better than me, was complicated. "Of course not, but if one of us ever comes up with a unified field theory, I guarantee it won't be me."

She laughed. "Well, maybe she is smarter than you. Why aren't you wearing a hat, and sunglasses? What's wrong with you? Don't you know how to protect yourself?"

"I like the feel of the sun on me and I don't burn. You're the one who should be wearing them."

She shook her head. "My eyes still see everything. And my skin, it doesn't matter now. They say it's the damage from when we're young that's the danger." Her all-seeing eyes drifted down to the scar at the left edge of my mouth. "Past damage we can't do anything about."

I didn't know how to answer her. Everything she said seemed to have a hidden meaning, as if she had suspicions about me and was trying to draw out a confession. I grew up surrounded by people who were experts in making you feel that way, like you were lethally wrong about whatever you thought was right a blink ago. Like the murder of squat nosy *nonna*s in black dresses camped out in the park near my grandfather's house, hairs springing from their chins and upper lips, eyes like coals and stares like lightning bolts when they thought you'd been wicked, which was always. The *nonna*s would have tagged Tess *chiaroveggente*, clairvoyant, someone who could see things beyond the senses. Then they'd have all crossed themselves. But I didn't care how good Tess's eyes were. She couldn't have seen anything, she didn't know anything about me, she was just a little off-center and I was just being paranoid.

I put my hand on Einstein's rump and looked out past Tess's shoulder, at the thick brick walls of the building. I counted the windows on the wall where the glass doors were. By the fifth floor, the numbers piling up on each other pushed her words to the background.

"Now I *did* upset you. Jody? That is what you said your name was, yes? Jody?"

"Yes. Jody Kowalczyk, and no, you didn't upset me. But I've got to finish my lunch and get back to work. And your friends are looking a little impatient over there."

She glanced back at the table. They were playing without her, but Abe noticed Tess looking and gestured for her to come. She gestured back, *In a minute.*

"We play Brooklyn rummy. We made it up years ago. We forget the rules, we make up new ones. Two can play, six can play, it doesn't matter. That way, we die off but the game lives on. I've been winning for five years. I didn't really want to talk to you, I just wanted to give them a head start." She grinned like a mischievous little girl.

That made me laugh.

"What a lovely sound. Why do I think you don't do that often enough?"

"I don't know." She was right. I didn't laugh a whole lot. "Why do you?"

"Because I think you're someone for whom life is not funny. But yes, it's time to let you go. And if we don't run into each other next week, you come see me. My name is Tess Fischer, and my room is on the second floor." She put her hand on my right forearm. "Don't be afraid, Jody. First try to let yourself give me one simple thing, all right? How is it you call yourself by a landlocked Polish name when you have island eyes and Mediterranean skin?"

Give me. Not tell me. As if she already knew the reason, and that what was important wasn't the reason itself but me recognizing her as the person I was meant to pass it on to, pass all the reasons on to, before it was too late.

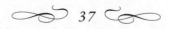

She drew her hand down my arm and gripped my wrist. "And such skin. Like honey in the sunlight."

Good thing it wasn't my left arm. That would have added up to more than all the windows in the whole damned building could have handled.

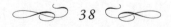

MRS. JACOBS WAS UNDER THE awning at the back entrance looking over the parking lot when we came out with the last of the week's debris to cart away.

"Mr. Kowalczyk. How did you all enjoy the garden? A little better than your truck?" Mrs. Jacobs patted Einstein's head, which had coincidentally appeared right under her hand.

"Please, call me Jody. I keep looking for my dad when you say Mr. Kowalczyk. Yeah, the garden was great. Thanks. I hope we didn't disturb anyone."

"I'm sure you didn't. The buzz in the dining room is that *those window boys* are as neat and quiet as mice and unfailingly polite at every turn. For which I thank you." She dipped her head and smiled. "And having young people around lightens everyone's spirits. Not to mention *you* . . ." She went nose to nose with Einstein and fell into that lovey-dovey way of talking that makes dogs want to flop onto their backs for you. "*You* could never disturb *any*one."

"Mrs. Jacobs? Could I ask you about one of the ladies here?"

She tore herself away from my dog to answer me. Like most women I met, she was probably going to end up liking Einstein better than she liked me. "Of course. Which one?"

"A lady named Tess Fischer?"

"Oh, Tess . . . Tess is one of my most adored people. I'm glad the two of you have met. What do you want to know about her?"

"Well, for one thing, was she born in Italy?"

"Ah, you have a good ear. Yes, in Rome, but she's lived in New York for most of her adult life, since she was in her mid-twenties. I've known her since I was a child, actually. She was a piano teacher in Yorkville, on the Upper East Side, where I grew up. I must have been her worst student, but she made me feel like I had all the talent in the world. She could do that."

"I can imagine." I wondered what it would have felt like to be little and sit on Tess's lap and play "Come Back to Sorrento." "But I guess what I really want to know is, is she okay now? Her mind, I mean?"

Mrs. Jacobs didn't immediately ask, what are you talking about? She just looked at me, and her bony face softened. "Jody. You are such a nice young man. And the answer to your question is yes, Tess's mind is fine. She was always, how should I put it . . ."

"A little bit spooky?" I smiled.

She laughed. "Yes, I suppose you could say that. But I prefer to think of Tess as being *different* rather than spooky. She's connected to an older, more spiritual world than the modern pragmatic one most of us dwell in. I've always found her very reassuring to be around. Sometimes we need to believe there's more to life than what we can see."

"Yeah, I would agree with that."

"But why did you ask? It happens that summer is a painful time for her, and she can get a little lost in the past. Did she say or do something odd?"

I couldn't even say what I'd wanted to know; maybe that Tess was just garden variety demented and not *veggente* at all. "I don't know, nothing really. She's so nice, and she seemed a little mixed up the first time she saw me is all. She thought I was someone named Matt."

"Oh. Oh my . . ." She narrowed worried eyes at me, as though she was honing her vision, trying to see what Tess had seen.

"It was just for a couple of seconds. Probably just a trick of the light or something. Who is he?"

"I think I should let Tess tell you about Matt." She gave me a good-bye smile. "Have a good Labor Day weekend, Jody. I'll see you bright and early Tuesday."

※

THE GUYS WERE FINISHED LOADING the truck and I was about to get behind the wheel when I heard Hector draw in his breath and Orlando murmur, "*¡Hola! ¡Hay una mujer guapa!*" They were both married, with seven kids between them, but scoping out sexy women seemed hands-down to be the Dominican male's lifelong favorite sport. On a clear day those two could spot one twenty-five miles away. Frank and I tended to keep our eyes to ourselves, but we didn't mind reaping the benefits. I looked over to see what had got their attention just as a full-bodied woman, a mane of curling red-gold hair tumbling over the shoulders of her gauzy ivory dress, emerged from the sea of parked cars like something from a Renaissance painting, and Mrs. Jacobs lifted her arm in a wave and called out, "Ella!" My hand slid off the truck's door.

There's a warehouse full of pictures, snapshot memories, trapped inside my head. Mostly they stay where they are, until something, a smell or sound or sight, riles them up and then whammo, I'm time-traveling like I've been shot out the back end of a cannon, sailing through a million out-of-order images, hunting for the connection so I can make sense of what's in front of me. Every time it happens, and the link gets made, the memory snapshot changes a little because I'm seeing it through the eyes I have now, not the ones I had the last time I saw it. The past and the present collide, merge bits of themselves, and neither is ever the same again. That's what I meant before, about my memories being relative to the moment, and me having to figure out all over again where things fit.

Most of the images orbited around and around each other, part of the cloud cluster of memory particles in the way-back of my brain. If the link turned out to be to one of them, I might bang into it when it popped to the front, but I'd almost always stay on my feet. It was the others, the toxic ones shut away in lead-lined boxes, that I had to watch out for. And it was hard to be vigilant while you were falling through space, hard to determine whether what was coming at you was dangerous or not. There were times I couldn't slam the lid down fast enough.

I saw the red-gold hair. I heard "Ella." The memory reared up so fast it nearly took the top of my skull off, made me light-headed and nauseous. August 1988, Marley's, a woman who broke apart into waves of guilty love when she saw me staring at her, as if I had somehow become the prism of her unwanted emotions. She left me wanting to gather that guilty love into myself, not let it scatter through the ragged holes in me, hold it until she wanted it again and had to come back to me to get it. Even gone cool, her sea green eyes were deep and clear, like an infinite, peaceful pool, and I'd seen myself diving straight down into it as if off a high cliff. It was the same quiet pool of my last dream, the one I had on a night long ago, before I stopped remembering my dreams. I'd dreamed of swimming in that pool forever, of peacefully drowning in it, but then the shark appeared, and then I woke up and got eaten alive. I couldn't shake her, she kept getting hung up in my twisted passages, and finally I had to conjure up a box strong enough to contain her and big enough to hold so much loneliness, and force her into it.

"Hey, Jodee. Come on, man. Lez go." Orlando was sweating at me from the passenger seat. It was hotter than Hades in the truck.

Mrs. Jacobs and Ella had turned in our direction. Mrs. Jacobs was talking and gesturing, and then Ella started to walk toward us. I stood there like a cornered rabbit and watched as her long red-gold hair lifted and swayed in the warm afternoon wind.

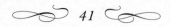

"Ai, Madonna. Today our lucky day." Orlando vaulted into the driver's seat and peered over my shoulder, all cool as a cucumber.

I took a few steps away from the truck. Ella came up to me and held out her hand.

"Jody? Hi. I'm Ella Landreth. Helen tells me that you've made friends with Tess. I just wanted to say hello, and thank you."

She was unchanged, exactly how I remembered her. My fingers closed around her hand, hers closed around mine, our palms came together. I couldn't feel where my hand ended and hers began, it was as if our two hands had always been one. My palm tingled and a warm slow shock flowed up my arm to the top of my head, as though we'd blown open a pathway for a dammed-up current when we touched. I felt the warm asphalt of the parking lot through the soles of my work boots, but what ground I was standing on was a mystery to me. Wherever it was, at least my mouth still worked there.

"We've talked a couple of times. She's a sweet lady. Are you a relative?" I didn't want her to be. That they were connected at all was heavy enough. That they might be that close, tied to one another that way, weighed too much, left me weighing too little.

"Sort of. She's been like a mother to me for a long time."

The friendly *Hi, I'm Ella* look on her face was already crumbling and her smile had slipped to half-mast. But her hand stayed where it was, and her fingers tightened a little. Her green eyes traveled over my face and then went still. Her smile faded to quarter-mast. I felt her pulse flutter faintly in my palm.

"Did Tess really call you Matt?"

"She did." I smiled my confusion at her. "So, who is he?"

Her eyes dropped to my mouth as hard and fast as shot birds to the dirt. Her smile evaporated.

"Matt is Tess's son."

She pulled her hand away and that flow stoppered up inside me.

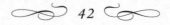

My mouth opened and I started babbling just to relieve the pressure. "Oh. So if Tess is like your mother, I guess that means Matt's like your brother?" Like me, Irene, and Brendan. *Like* a mother, *like* a brother. Better maybe, but not the real thing.

Ella didn't answer. She just looked at me with a suspended expression, like she was hibernating while I figured out how to not be a raging nitwit.

"Okay. So . . . what? Do I look like him? When he was young or something?"

"No. You don't look like him. But I can see how you might remind her of him."

Ella was staring at me and backing away. She realized she'd seen me before. Her mouth opened, as if she were about to speak, but she didn't. I wanted to ask her, *Do you still like doughnuts? Are you still with that rude guy? What is this connection, you, me, and Tess?*

But all I said was, "Yeah? How?"

She glanced behind her. Mrs. Jacobs was waiting under the awning. "I'm sorry, I have to go now. I'm giving a piano recital and a class, I'm going to be late—" She cut herself off in midsentence with a shake of her head, was silent for a few long beats. "I'm here twice a week, for another month. We'll see one another again." She stood very still. "Jody." She said it quietly, and as if to herself, not to me. Just my name, but there were more words attached to it, I could hear them as clearly as if she'd said them, too. *So that's who you are, that's your name, the boy who gave me a doughnut. Jody.*

The pressure eased up a little and I smiled at her again. She drew in her breath, turned away, started walking back to Mrs. Jacobs.

"Ella?"

She stopped and looked at me over her shoulder.

"Are you still with that rude guy?"

I thought she wasn't going to answer me, the way her face closed down again, but she said, "No. We divorced several years ago." Her eyes stayed on me. After another minute she said, "You cut off all that beautiful hair."

"Long time ago." When I came to the city, I got rid of my mass of suburban eighties hair in favor of a shorn black skull-hugging cap.

She smiled. "It suits you. And I can see your eyes." She made a last measured study of my face, then turned and walked away.

Orlando was gawping at me through the driver's window, Hector and Frank from the open rear door. I didn't trust myself to drive so I headed for the passenger seat and said to Orlando, "You drive." He put his hand on my shoulder and gave me the same look he gave his kids when they were sick. He didn't say a word, not even some lewd wiseass crack. That was a first. I think that's when I really got it that something serious had just happened.

Three

"**H**EY, IGGY. YOU UP OR did I wake you?"

It was eight o'clock Saturday morning. You'd think after twenty years my brother would have noticed that I didn't sleep past six, maybe seven on the rare day. The last time I did was the last time I was in the hospital, and I didn't think that should count since I was nine years old and in a three-day coma at the time. I might stay in bed to read, or fuck, or lie paralyzed in a cold sweat, but I didn't sleep.

"No Brendan, you didn't wake me up. Here, listen." I walked the phone back to the kitchen table and crunched a mouthful of granola into the receiver.

"Christ, what are you eating? BBs? You're going to pick me up at ten, right?"

I usually worked Saturdays, Labor Day weekend no exception, but since there were visitors and activities at Parkside on weekends, Mrs. Jacobs had asked us to work only five days. So today I was going with Brendan to visit our folks. I hadn't been in months. It wasn't that I didn't like seeing Karl and Irene. I just didn't like being in that part of the world.

Brendan was fourteen when Karl and Irene brought me home to live with them. He was waiting at the door, pudgy and eager, sweat

45

darkening his blond crew cut. I was skinny, dark, and cold. He took me by the hand and led me up to his room. He'd taken one look at me, decided I needed a protector, and declared himself it, laid his eternal loyalty down around me like a human moat. He's never known there wasn't anything left for him to protect me from. But his protection came with his friendship, and I needed that. He'd been my only real friend ever since, so I forgave him twenty years of his checking up on me all the time to make sure I hadn't accidentally stepped off the competency cliff while he wasn't paying attention, and about fifteen years of calling me Iggy, which evolved from his original nickname for me of Jody the Idiot Genius, to the Idiot Genius, then I.G., then just Ig, or usually Iggy.

"Uh-huh. And you'll be happy to know I'm going to wash and vacuum the car before I come get you."

Brendan, the actual genius of the family, a computer whiz with a six-figure salary and a two-bedroom, two-bathroom apartment in Battery Park City overlooking the river and the Statue of Liberty, had an overengineered toy that was paying for a mechanic's time-share in Aspen. Me, I was still driving the '87 Corolla I'd moved into the city with. The only way that car was ever going to die was if I took it out and shot it. Its only fault was that its backseat was currently upholstered in dog hair.

"Ah, yeah, about that. I'd be even happier if you maybe left the doggie home."

"Absolutely, can't see why not. I'll leave her a key so she can take herself out for a walk. And a Baggie for her poop. What's the matter? You like Einstein. She's the only girl you're not afraid of."

The doggie, the girl, was standing at the kitchen doorway with her leash in her mouth, watching me. I turned my back to her and put my dish in the sink.

"Very funny. Just because I don't have a revolving door in my bedroom doesn't mean I'm afraid of girls. You go for quantity, I go for quality."

Brendan wasn't afraid of girls, I was just being obnoxious, but he'd always been afraid of scaring them off, seeming too interested in what all guys were interested in. He was too nice, he presented himself as friend, not boyfriend, material. He was slow to believe someone might honestly be into him. I was basically the opposite and I think for a while, when we were younger, he envied me my steady stream of girls. He didn't understand what was really going on with me, that we needed different things, and that he was the one who'd end up in the enviable place.

"Yeah, whatever. So what's the deal?"

"I'm bringing somebody with me, and she's not wild about dogs. But I know you can't leave her, forget I asked. I'll sit in back with Einstein and Fern can sit in the front."

"Who's Fern?"

He cleared his throat. "She's . . . a woman I've been seeing for . . . well, for a few months."

"A few months? Why haven't I heard about her until now?"

In the past ten years Brendan had rarely gone on more than two dates with anyone without telling me all about her—his intense new lawyer, investment banker, commodities trader, software engineer girlfriend—and wanting to show her off to me and my "captivating bimbette du jour," as he jokingly referred to my happy worker-ant girlfriends.

"Look, Jody, I'm sorry. It's just . . . I like her. A lot. She's a little high maintenance, but she's so beautiful and sweet and smart. She's the head of I.T. for the bank we're doing the Y2K compliance work for. I'm crazy about her. I wanted to be sure we were in the same place before I exposed her to the Kowalczyk clan, you know?"

A little high maintenance. About as oxymoronic a concept as being

a little fucked up. Either you were or you weren't. Brendan's women were all high maintenance. Once a protector, always a protector.

"Wow. This sounds serious."

"It is. She's the one. I'm going to ask her to marry me. Holy cow, can you believe it?"

"Wow. No. I mean, yeah, that's great. Wow."

"I'm sorry, man, really. I know it's a lot to lay on you all at once."

I was in fact pretty stunned. "No, it's cool. I totally understand. I can't wait to meet her."

"Her last name's Kaplan, she's Jewish . . . do you think mom and dad will have a problem with that? I haven't told them. Christ, I hope not. She's a Polish Jew, though. Man, listen to me, I'm a wreck, I can't think straight."

"Calm down, Brendan. You know they won't care. At this point as long as whoever either one of us brings home isn't a serial killer, it's party time." That got a chuckle out of him.

"The voice of reason. Thanks. So, listen, do me another favor, Igman, and don't be too fucking charming today, okay? I sort of want her to say yes."

Igman. That was new.

He was laughing, but it didn't make the new version of my nickname sound any friendlier. I felt like crap to think that anything like that might still be on his mind. Mostly, Brendan's girlfriends and I got along fine. They'd meet me, find out a few facts, then treat me with the thoughtless sympathy people show for likeable unfortunates who won't ever make it far in life. Sort of the way the recent ones treated Einstein after they heard her story. But years ago, someone he was dating came on to me practically in front of him. She must have misplaced her brains, imagined she wanted to go slumming. Brendan knew I'd never do anything, but I didn't see much of him for a few months and he didn't introduce me to his next couple of ladies. It was not a fun time.

Better not to go there. I laughed back at him. "She'll say yes. She'd be a fool not to."

I had the tuner on in the living room, set to an FM classic rock station. The Rolling Stones' "Under My Thumb" was playing while we talked. If I had a more cinematic mind, or if I hadn't been consciously avoiding thinking about omens and connections so I wouldn't have to deal with the fact that I was not going to come up with a reason or a solution or a defense for Tess and Ella showing up in my life together like they had, I might have known to listen, I might have heard it.

※

FERN DISLIKED ME ON SIGHT. The minute we met the whole of her itty-bitty being recoiled in self-defense, like I'd caused an instant allergic reaction, a huge fat sneeze. I guess it was a chemical thing, I hadn't even said a word to her.

She and Brendan were waiting on the sidewalk, and I pulled up and got out of the car to say a proper hello. She took a step toward me and her polite smile turned cold when she actually looked at me, which she did only briefly, and with an expression that looked a lot like horror. She said hello when Brendan introduced us, but managed to not shake my outstretched hand, squinting up her eyes and turning away to rummage like a madwoman in her bag for her sunglasses like she'd just been warned about an imminent nuclear whiteout. Brendan was in his own world with her, he was seeing love everywhere, he didn't notice.

I'd been all set to like her, but so much for that. I saw why Brendan did, though. The sweetness I was going to have to trust him on, but she wore her braininess like a sandwich board, it was plastered all over her averted face, her crisp clothes and hundred dollar haircut. And Brendan was right about the other thing, too. She was beautiful. In a fragile, tubercular way, never my type, but I could see it. Shoulder-length black hair, enormous black eyes, flawless pure white skin. She stood up straight as a dancer, which gave a taller impression, but she wasn't much over five feet, thin and narrow, wrists and ankles so tapered I could have wound my fingers around them twice over, the knobs of her shoulders and collarbone standing out underneath her white top more noticeable than her breasts, hips and ass like a teenager's. Definitely not my type. She looked like one of those round-eyed girls you see in all the Japanese cartoons—stark, startled, helpless. She looked like she needed to be shielded from everything, but somewhere inside she was tough enough to make it in a profession dominated by men. She was Brendan's ideal woman. I got the unhappy feeling I was looking down the long barrel of a *very* not fun time.

"Okay then. We should get going, there's probably going to be heavy holiday beach traffic. Fern?"

I gestured to her as I walked around the car and opened the front passenger door. She stayed on the sidewalk. Her eyes went from the hood to the trunk with a pause for a quick assessment of Einstein, who had her head out the half-open back window, taking it all in. Fern turned to Brendan and cooed at him.

"Brendan, love, you sit up front. You and your brother have things to talk about, I'm sure. I'll be fine in the back. I didn't sleep too well last night, I wouldn't mind taking a little nap." She'd reconsidered her options and made her choice—dog bad, me worse.

Brendan put a beefy arm around her shoulders, she cozied herself into his side. He was a square-built, medium-height blond bear of a guy, tucked up together like that they were as seamless a fit as a yin/yang symbol. I was on the other side of the car from them, and suddenly my '87 Corolla didn't feel like the only thing between us.

"Babe, are you sure? You don't like dogs, I don't want you to be unhappy." I could see that Brendan wasn't happy, he was confused, didn't know if he'd be protecting her better by telling her how swell she and her offer were or insisting she sit up front.

"I'm sure the dog can be made to stay on his side. Can't he, Jody."

It wasn't a question. It was a command. *Do it*. Her head turned toward me and my breath solidified, I couldn't draw it in or push it out. I looked at the two of them together. It wasn't dislike I was feeling for her, it was fear. She wasn't going to treat me with mindless sympathy. She wanted Brendan to herself and she'd already decided I was in the way.

"Einstein's a she." I opened the rear passenger side door, leaned in, showed Einstein my palm, and said, "Stay." I backed out. "She knows when someone doesn't want her near them. She won't bother you."

Traffic on the Southern State Parkway wasn't bad and we made it to Bay Shore in ninety minutes. Fern didn't say much. She was sitting behind Brendan. I could see her in the rearview mirror. She'd taken off her glasses and was resting her head and cheek against the window. Her eyes were closed, and I thought she really was napping. But at one point, when Brendan asked if I was still seeing Brianna and I told him no, and he joked was I trying to set an end-of-millennium record, going through girls the way I'd been this year, I felt Fern's eyes on the back of my head and when I looked into the mirror she was staring at me, in an emotionless way, nostrils flared in distaste, coolly gathering more damning data. Then she turned back to the window, closed her eyes again, curled herself up against the door. My girl was behind me, sitting up tall, her muzzle half out her window. I snatched a glimpse of the two of them like that, wedged into their corners, giving each other the cold shoulder. If life were a cartoon, it would've been funny to see. But it wasn't funny, and I paid attention because this was one of the ways Einstein was smarter than me. She knew how to manage herself around people and I didn't, history had taught me nothing. She knew what to do about Fern. Leave her alone, stay out of her way.

Brendan looked back at Fern every five minutes, and after a few times it struck me that with all their *love*s and *babe*s and how wild they were about each other, there wasn't any heat between them. It was like she really was a fern, too delicate to be exposed to too much light or heat, and Brendan, everybody's brother, was there to shelter her, make sure she didn't burn up and turn to ash. It worried me. Everything needed some heat and light, even ferns, or they wouldn't uncoil and grow at all. They'd just wilt. Lay down in the dark and cold all closed up and die.

✳

I COULD NEVER BRING MYSELF to call Irene mom. If she was disappointed she never let me see it. I did come close once, though. I was still sharing Brendan's room. There was a spare bedroom, but Brendan didn't want me to be alone at night. I didn't want to be alone either but I didn't say anything. I never wanted to cause anybody any trouble, have them look at me too closely, expect me to look at them too closely. I took care of myself. Irene never had to pick up my socks, make my bed, or wash my dishes; Karl never had to help me clean my skates or teach me to drive. I never asked where my mother was or what they'd done with Scott's body. So Brendan just did it himself, announced to everyone that I was sleeping with him until I was down to no more than once a week of waking up squealing like a stuck pig during the night, his description, which took about a year. After a few months he learned to sleep through it, so the first thing he'd say to me every morning was, "Jody, did you have that dream last night?" It wasn't until I was fourteen myself that I really appreciated the sacrifice he'd made for me, giving up his bedroom privacy. I guess even then it made Brendan happier to be a friend than a lover.

At any rate. Every night, Irene came in to say goodnight to us. And every night, Irene sat on Brendan's bed and kissed his forehead and he hugged her around the neck. They'd said goodnight like that since he'd been a baby. Then she'd do the same thing with me, but I didn't move or even look at her. I didn't pull away, or ask her not to touch me, I just lay there holding my breath, waiting for it to be over. One night, she's bending over me and I'm already feeling her hand moving my hair away and her soft lips on my forehead and I don't plan it or think about it, but my arms fly up and I'm grabbing her around her neck. She lifted me right off my pillow and held me, for a long time, she held me and rocked me until I fell asleep and let go of her. The next morning I came down to breakfast all ready to say, *Hey Mom, what's for breakfast?*— specifically, I remember stopping to practice on the stairs, imagining the look on her face when she'd turn from the stove. But when I walked into the kitchen and saw her there I knew I couldn't do it. I had a mom, somewhere, and even though she never wanted me to call her that, that word belonged to her; it wasn't transferable.

I NEVER CALLED KARL DAD, either. For the entire ten years that I lived in the Kowalczyks' house, until the day I loaded the Corolla and drove to Manhattan, there wasn't a moment when I stopped being afraid of him. At first it was enough that he was built like a linebacker, liked to get all up in your grill when he talked to you, and had guns in the house. It didn't take long though for me to see that even after all the awful human misery and ugliness he'd seen, his compassion was still intact. I came to trust that Karl would never hurt me. But I was still afraid of him. For ten years I cringed inside like a man on his knees waiting to be shot whenever Karl was near me. He'd been the one who'd found me. He was in that house that morning, he carried me out and maybe he talked to me to try to wake me up, and I don't know what I maybe said from wherever I was then, falling and falling deeper into a hope and belief that I'd never wake up. But even if I said nothing, he saw everything and he'd been a cop for thirty years, and he was really smart. He could follow all those little tributaries to where they emptied into my private slimy sea. So from the day I opened my eyes in the hospital and saw him there looking at me from the foot of the bed, and I understood who he was, from that day on, when he watched me from across a room, or walked toward me, or said my name, or put his hand on my shoulder, my brain and blood turned to ice and I'd know in the pit of my stomach that he'd figured it out. He knew what I'd done and this life, this good chance, was over. It had hit the wall and gone splat, as impermanent and pointless as everything that had brought me there.

It never did happen, Karl figuring out my sins. What happened instead was in a way worse. He got tired of me shutting him out and gave up on trying to be a father to me. One morning I overheard him and Irene talking in the kitchen. "The kid's a puppy that's been whipped one time too many. He'll never let me near him," he said. And she said, "He is what that monster made him. Just be there, Karl. That's all anyone can do now." There were tears in their voices. I heard the rustle of her hands on his shirt when she hugged him. I wanted to be inside that hug, I didn't want to be a dog that made people sad, I wanted to be a real person who could scream I'm sorry loud enough for them to hear me, loud enough to open a space between them big enough for me to fit inside. But obviously Karl knew what he was talking about, because as I recall I crawled back up the stairs on all fours and hid under my bed like a you-know-what in a thunderstorm.

AFTER LUNCH I EXCUSED MYSELF and went out for a drive. Irene walked with me to the car.

She linked her arm through mine. "You've been so quiet. Are you all right, Jody?"

"Sure, I'm fine." Irene had been an emergency pediatric nurse, she'd never forgotten how we first met. "I promised Brendan I'd give you and Karl time with him and your future daughter-in-law." That got her mind off me.

"Oh, my goodness! I had a feeling, the way he's been talking about her. Finally!"

"He hasn't asked her yet, but he told me this morning he's going to. They look like a done deal, though, don't they?"

"They do. She seems lovely. A bit reserved, but very lovely. Do you like her?"

"I just met her." I always could lie like a rug. Irene worried about me as it was, I didn't want her worrying about anything going wrong between me and Brendan. "I don't think we have much in common, but if Brendan loves her, I'm sure she's great. I just want him to be happy."

She stretched up and kissed my cheek. "I know you do. And when are you going to bring someone home?"

Irene never asked me about my relationships. Her question caught me off guard and for a second I was in the parking lot again, immobilized by the thrill of Ella's hand in mine.

"Jody?"

I shook my head and tried to free my arm. Irene held on, looked up at me with her bright blue eyes wide and her mouth open, waiting for me to drop my answer in there like a honeyed gift.

"Well, there is this older woman . . ."

"Yes? You know, I've always thought someone older would be good for you. And who is she?"

I put on my best somber face. "A really nice woman at the place I'm working. Her name's Tess. She's around eighty. You think maybe that's too old?"

Irene looked exasperated, then laughed and pushed me away. "You devil. That's what I get for asking."

Yes. That's what you got for asking.

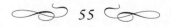

I DROVE DOWN TO THE water. I thought I'd say hello to the folks at Marley's—I had good memories of that place, the first place where I was only Jody, no baggage trailing me, just Jody Kowalczyk, Idiot Genius kid who worked like a horse and balanced the till in ten minutes—then kill time watching the ferries come and go.

The shack was packed. I accepted a round of hugs and *how-you-doings?* as well as a bag of doughnuts to take back to Karl and Irene, and left. I watched a ferry headed for Ocean Beach recede toward the distant sliver of barrier island. When it grew so small you could barely make it out, I was overcome with the sense that I was receding, too, shrinking to a dot on the horizon, and that soon I'd vaporize into a puff of smoke and be reconstituted in a galaxy far, far away. I was about to get manhandled off my two-decade-old default temporal/spatial plane, the one I'd been standing on alone and balanced until two weeks ago. I could feel the tremors underfoot. Frankly, I'd just as soon have had it the old-fashioned way and not known about it until I found myself naked and huddled on the new plane, but for once I was being warned to get ready. I doubted if that was really possible, but I got back in the car and headed inland.

I HADN'T LAID EYES ON the block or the house at 901 Trestle Road since I was five, but I'd been to and from the marina with my grandfather so many times, his Chevy Corvair impregnated with the stink of fish, that the route was permanently stored in my internal GPS. I pulled up across the street.

I let the car idle and watched a boy shoot hoops in the driveway. Not good, but persistent. After a couple of minutes his mom came out of the house, suspicious eyes on me as she crossed the street.

"Can I help you?" Her arms were crossed over her chest.

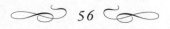

I put both hands on the steering wheel where she could see them. "Sorry to bother you. I used to live here. A long time ago."

"Oh." She relaxed her arms, glanced back at her house. "I'll bet it's changed a lot."

"Yes and no." I smiled at her, like we both understood what the hell I meant by that.

She smiled back. "Hmm. You seem like a nice young man, but I'm sorry, I don't feel comfortable inviting you inside."

"No, that's okay. I don't want to come in. I just wanted to see it again for a minute." The kid missed the basket for like the fortieth time in a row. "Tell your son not to just push the ball at the hoop like that. He's got to feel it in his whole hand, guide it with his wrist and fingers when he releases it—like this . . ." I gave her a demo.

She looked impressed. "Would you show him? He'd be so thrilled."

I shrugged. "No. Not me. His father should do it, that's what he'd want."

A room had been added above the garage, the gray-white aluminum siding replaced with pale yellow vinyl, the chain-link fence with a line of boxwoods. In the back, where my aunt's rose garden and the two red maples outside our window used to be, there was an above-ground pool surrounded by bright green, heavily fertilized lawn. I could see the footprint of the house I remembered, but it wasn't the same anymore. It looked like a house where happy people had always lived. You could do that with some houses, paint over, rip out, replace, uproot what used to grow and live there, make them fit to inhabit again. Other houses the only thing to do was burn them to the ground.

*

A FOR SALE SIGN SWUNG from a post stuck into the parched lawn. The metal links and grommets that attached the sign to the post were rusted; it had been swinging there for a while. Weeds had over-

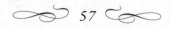

run the cracked flagstone path from the sidewalk to the door. There was a new screen door, already warped, new storm windows, a new roof already missing some shingles, sad signs that somewhere along the line someone thought a Band-Aid was all you needed to stem a gushing artery. The place looked derelict and felt emptier than my mother's heart, even from the street. If someone told me no one had lived there since the morning of July 6, 1980, I'd believe it. I walked around the garage to the back. The doghouse was gone. Where it had been no grass grew, there was just dead dirt. That was about right. I squatted down, picked up a dusty handful. It was dry now, but on that hot sunny morning it had been wet. I looked back at the house. The kitchen screen door was hanging open just like then. A roaring silence filled my ears, images spun from spiderwebs bloomed in the air around me. I squeezed my eyes shut and paraded notes and numbers across the insides of my eyelids. I don't know how long I stayed there like that, until sound came back, a bird call, a cicada, the click of a heel on the sidewalk beyond the house, and when I stood up my knees were stiff.

A black lady in her early sixties was standing by the Corolla, curious to see who it was looking at the house. It took me no time to recognize her. Mrs. Williams. Mother of Duquan, another aspiring driveway hoopster. I remembered him having talented hands, a soft touch. Watchful eyes. Good manners. She walked straight up to me.

"Sir, I trust you are not considering buying that house?"

"No, ma'am, I am not. I don't like the look of it." Everyone, even six-foot-five Mr. Williams, would *Yes, ma'am,* and *No, ma'am,* Mrs. Williams. This was not a lady you got casual with, no ma'am. Clever Scott *ma'am*'ed her six ways from Sunday every chance he got and she thought he was the loveliest junkie she'd ever met. Marian, Our Lady of the Perpetual Tactless Tongue, called her Clarisse and then whined about being the only living creature on the block Clarisse Williams didn't like.

Mrs. Williams's head bobbed up and down. "I'm glad to hear it. That house is no good. It's full of ghosts. No one has lived in it more than two or three years since . . . Well, never mind."

"I don't see any ghosts, just an ugly old house. But thanks for the warning." Like a rug, my friend. Like a rug.

Mrs. Williams squinted at me as I got in the car, her eyes following after me as I drove away. I wondered how surprised she'd have been if I'd said, *Hey, by the way, ma'am, how's Duquan doing?* But really, everyone was so careful to not see me then, why would they stop being careful now?

*

FERN WAS A DOLL WITH Brendan and Irene and Karl, but for the rest of the day she barely talked to me, didn't look me in the eye for more than two seconds at a time. She ignored me so pointedly she had me imagining it was me she was in fact paying the most attention to, if that makes any sense. It was nerve-racking. And then, right before we left, she pulled a Jekyll and Hyde on me. She and Brendan were saying good-bye to Karl and Irene in the entryway, I'd snuck into the den to take a last look at the family photos crammed onto a big table there. I wasn't aware of her coming into the room, but suddenly Fern was next to me in the semidarkness, so close I could feel her narrow shoulder at my elbow.

"Why are there no baby pictures of you?" She turned her face up to me, searched out my eyes in the dull yellow light from the table lamp.

Even if she hadn't avoided me like toxic waste all day, it would still have been a jarringly intimate question. I was thrown by it, by the way she asked, simply, no hostility or mockery, and by the intrusive curiosity in her huge dark eyes. Before I could think, I slammed her full bore with a *Fuck you, where the fuck did that come from?* look. She drew back, blinking furiously, as though I'd raised a hand to her, or a torch to her face, and I thought again, too much heat and light and she dies. I took a breath.

"I'm sorry. You, uh, startled me." I tried to calm down. I wanted us to get along. I gave her a weak grin and she sort of grimaced back.

"It's all right. I should have announced myself." She moved closer again.

"The Kowalczyks adopted me when I was nine." I pointed to the earliest shot of me. "That's me five months after I got here, blowing out the candles on my tenth birthday cake. I thought Brendan would have told you."

"He did. But it's still surprising not to see any evidence of your previous life anywhere. Didn't you bring things with you?" She was talking quickly and quietly, as if she'd been told not to talk to me at all.

I almost said to her, *I'm the evidence.* "I travel light."

Fern didn't bother to look at me. She heard the case-closed tone of my voice. I saw her nod, saw her throat move as she swallowed.

"Well, you look happy."

I peered at the photo. "What do you know. So I do." I did look happy. From the outside, numb and happy are hard to tell apart, and anyway, people tend to see what they expect to see.

She glanced at me with a tiny smile. There was a weird vibe coming off her, like she was now scared of me for some reason, and it made me more scared of her. I tried to deflect it by seeing her tiny smile and raising her a bigger one.

Brendan called to us from the hall. Fern jumped. She moved behind me, put a feathery hand on my back, speed-whispered at me. "My parents were children in the Treblinka concentration camp. Their families died there. They're gone now, too, and there are no photos of them from before, either. Their childhoods are just a big black hole. The baby pictures they took of me could fill Madison Square Garden and every time I look at them I feel myself getting pulled down. I feel as if I don't understand or deserve anything." She slid her palm down and spread her fingers across the small of my back. "You were a gorgeous child." She took her hand away and scurried out of the room, wiping at her eyes.

I stood there for the minute it took to get her words out of my head, her touch off my body. I didn't know why she told me that and I didn't want to know, she was trying to make some connection between us but whatever it was I wanted no part of it. The only other thing she said to me after that was good-bye.

CHRISTOPHER IS STANDING IN THE doorway of Marian and Scott's bedroom in Scott's house on Superior Street in Bay Shore. He's watching her ransack drawers and plow through the closet, throwing her stuff behind her in the direction of the unmade bed where her big green suitcase is propped open, yawning up at the ceiling like the maw of a crocodile waiting for a myopic seagull to dive into it. He knows what's happening. She and Scott don't even bother to fight anymore. She doesn't come home for days at a time and when she does she trails a sharp, leathery smell wherever she goes, a smell Christopher recognizes as a man smell, one that's not Scott's. He knows what's happening, and he's rigid up to his eyelids, afraid to let her out of his sight for even the blink of an eye.

There's an ache in Christopher's chest that's been there forever, and while he watches her dismantle the room, it erupts like a volcano inside him, bathes his heart in boiling lava. She's going to leave and never come back. He knows, but still he says,

"What are you doing?"

"What does it look like I'm doing, dummy."

He doesn't respond, and after a few seconds she turns around and looks at him in a way he doesn't recognize, like she's actually seeing him. She laughs. "God, you look grim. Lighten up, pest. It's every man for himself."

She starts shoveling clothes into the suitcase. She's singing that Donna Summer song from last year, "Hot Stuff," the hit song of 1979 that he taught himself to play on the piano in an hour because it's her favorite. She's swinging her hips around as she packs.

He whispers, "Don't go. Please, Mommy. Don't go."

She doesn't hear him. Or she pretends she doesn't. Either way. It's all the same.

The lava scorches through him. He takes a blind step into the room and says it again. "Don't go. Please, Mommy. Don't go."

This time, she hears him. She doesn't stop packing or turn to face him, but she says, "It wouldn't matter. It wouldn't change anything."

"Then take me with you. I'll be good, I promise. Don't leave me here."

"Don't be a retard for once, please, huh? I can't take you. I can't take care of you. You know that already, for God's sake. Christ, I can't even take care of myself."

She keeps packing. After a minute she stops what she's doing to turn and look at him again. She looks for a long time, then walks up close and stares down into his face. "Fuck. You're actually one fucking pretty kid. I think you look like him, you know, the one with the mouth. He kept trying to kiss me. As if." She shakes her head and sneers. Her arm shoots out and she clamps Christopher's jaw in her hand, wrenches his head from side to side while she examines him, like he was some farm animal she was thinking of buying. "Yup, you definitely look like him. So I guess that was your father. Good for you. The other two were butt-ugly."

Christopher is immobilized with incomprehension. Who is she talking about? What is it that he's supposed to know? It's him who's butt-ugly, and he thought Jesus was his father. At least that's what Aunt Marie always told him and no one ever told him otherwise—even Scott, when Christopher asked him if it was true, smiled at him and said, "Sure, why not?" He's thinking so hard, his brain is banging inside his skull. Never before, never ever, has he heard Marian say those two words: *your father*. Your father, like he might be an actual person. He wants to ask a million questions, but he doesn't say a word. He knows she wouldn't answer him, but maybe,

maybe, if he just stays quiet, the way she likes, she might keep talking, say something more. About the one with the mouth. His father. He can tell she's high as a kite, and she never shuts up when she's that high. She blathers on to Scott for hours, and he'll let her yap, yap, yap until his ears bleed rather than cut her off and piss her off more than she's already always pissed off at him.

But Scott's not there that afternoon. He took his black gym bag and his Walther PPK and went out to make deliveries. There's only Christopher.

"He told me his name. The jerk. Like I cared. What the hell was it? José? Jorge? No, wait. Oh man, Angel!" Her low-brow Long Island palate can't handle the elegant guttural sound of a Spanish *g*, or *j*, and on her tongue the melodic names come out toneless, unlovely: Hoezay, Horehay, Onhell. "He had these purple-blue eyes. Elizabeth Taylor eyes. Light and dark at the same time, like yours. I remember thinking it was weird for a Puerto Rican and then he said his name was Angel and I thought, Oh yeah, angels' eyes are supposed to be all strange and blue! Right, pest? *Gli occhi di un angelo.* I cannot believe I just remembered that. God, the incredible shit we have stuck in our heads!"

Christopher doesn't know any Elizabeth Taylor. He knows a Jonelle Taylor, a jumpy black girl in his class whose dark brown eyes carry the same hard squeeze behind them that he feels in his own eyes, the squeeze that's the exit point for the constant twisted knot of his stomach.

Marian lets go of Christopher with a rough swipe across his jaw, prances back to the bed, continues loading the suitcase. Christopher is paralyzed where he stands. He can't even move his eyes so he has no choice but to watch her bent and swaying back while she rabbits on.

"He wasn't so bad. Angel." She snickers. "Maybe I should've told

him about you, huh, pest? He was nice. He probably would've taken care of you better. Well. Such is life."

She's really on a roll now. She looks over her shoulder and smiles at him. She twirls a little in his direction, cants her pelvis, sets her fists on her protruding hipbones. Her eyes and lips go sly. She drawls, "'His mother should have thrown him away and kept the stork.' Hey, blank face, come on, that's funny, that was Mae West." She laughs. "I wanted to abort you—you know, get rid of you right away?—but your grandfather and that jack-off priest of his, Father Assface, wouldn't let me." She sucks her lips into a fleshless line and frowns. "'You have sinned, Marian, but all life is sacred.' Yeah, right. While he's got mousetraps all over the fucking church. Why's a person more important than a mouse, who says mice don't have souls, huh? And you weren't even a person, just some stupid blob of cells. Who would have missed you if you'd never been born? Life is sacred, my ass. You think you and me are living sacred lives, pest? I don't. No one loves you. No one loves me, either."

"I love you!" he blurts. That's all he cares about, that she knows he loves her. That he loves her and she can't leave.

She makes a raspberry sound and cackles. "You have to, dummy. You don't have a choice. I loved my mother, too, before she left. Now I hate her. What are you now, nine? You'll hate me before you're ten, and believe me, it's better that way. Don't bother loving anyone, 'cause they won't love you, they'll just hurt you."

He almost laughs, that's how wrong he knows she is. He's figured it out. When somebody really hurts you, it's *because* they love you. Marian doesn't love him. She ignores him.

His logic all worked out, he says, "You're wrong. Scott loves me."

She nearly screams with laughter. "Jesus. I thought you were smart! Yeah, he loves you. He loves you so much he'll probably kill you some day. Actually, that wouldn't be so bad. You should definitely pray for that. I think you'd go to heaven. I mean, you didn't do anything wrong. Forget what Father Assface says, born in sin and all that crap. Then you really would be an *Onhell!* Cool."

She snaps the suitcase closed. A horn blares from the street below; there's the sharp leathery smell, the new boyfriend. Marian opens the bedroom window, leans out and yells, "Shut up with that! I'm coming." She starts lugging the suitcase toward the door. "Hey, pest. I've got a great idea. If Scott doesn't kill you, you could kill him. One day, when he's passed out. You could stab him. Or you could drag him into the garage and turn on the car. Or you could mix some Comet or something into the horse. Why didn't I think of that before? You'd get away with it, just cry a lot, who's gonna put a pathetic little kid like you in jail. Hey, you gonna stand there, or you gonna help me with this fucking suitcase?"

What she said about Scott he doesn't hear. The words turn to gibberish somewhere in the air between them. All he hears is the last thing, her asking for help with her suitcase. He can see himself running to help her, can even feel his legs bend and straighten, his hands tighten around the cracked plastic handle. But he doesn't move. He can't. He'll do anything for her, things she asks and things she doesn't. He'll try to remember to not call her Mommy, he'll be as quiet as death while she's asleep, he won't try to take her hand when she's near him, he'll pretend it's okay that she doesn't love him and because he understands how important it is to pretend, he'll even forgive her for pretending not to know what Scott does to him when she's not there.

He'll do all that for her, and more. But not this. He won't help her leave him forever.

She maneuvers past him and the suitcase bangs against his stiff legs. At the top of the stairs, she turns to him and says, "You'll be all right, Christopher. You're a tough kid, you'll be all right. You go be an astronaut, fly off to the stars and never look back." She hesitates, then bends awkwardly over her suitcase and places an inept kiss on the top of his head.

Shock throbs his eardrums. Through the reverberations Christopher hears the syncopated thumping as she makes her way down with the heavy bag, the creak of the door as it opens and closes, and now her voice rising from the street, the slam of a car trunk, the vroom roar of a souped-up engine as the car pulls away. He hears all those noises of her leaving, and it sounds like endless blackness raining down on him. He tries to hold in his head the sound of her voice speaking his name, finally, and the thought that maybe he's not nothing to her after all if she knows his dreams. *Fly off to the stars and never look back.* But it's so little, so late, her voice and the words, the brush of her lips, won't stay. They melt like ash in the black rain.

She left her white vinyl boots on the bed. He takes them up, holds them against his chest. He stumbles downstairs with them in his arms. He doesn't know where to go, what to do. It's slate-gray outside, and freezing cold, but he's burning up, the lava fear is pumping away in him. He goes out the back door and crawls into the rotting doghouse.

WHEN SCOTT COMES HOME TWO hours later, he finds Christopher shivering on the frozen dirt floor, curled up around his mother's boots, whispering with blue lips all the things he should have said that might have kept her from leaving. Scott kneels down, peers in at him over the metallic rim of his dark glasses, and says, "So the bitch is gone. It's just you and me now, buddy. Just you and me. Feel like pizza?"

Four

I MADE IT BACK TO my apartment around ten, not in the best frame of mind. Tess and Ella and now Fern were frothing up my brain like an unseen storm out on the ocean pushing waves to the shore, rocking my boat inside its snug harbor. I tried listening to music, tried to read. Then I tried *Blade Runner* again, and while it was always easy enough to believe I was something along the lines of one of the replicants, the creation of a self-absorbed, amoral mind, something very much like but not quite human, it was a stretch to convince myself that my memories had been borrowed from someone else. Instead of calming me down, it made things worse. For me, the rewards of being fully present in the moment were not all they were cracked up to be.

At eleven thirty I left Einstein snoring, galloped down the stairs and out the door. I started walking, east on Tenth, north up Avenue B, west on Fourteenth, in the opposite direction from where I really wanted to go, because I knew I shouldn't go there. My plan was to walk fast and far enough to escape the pull of Tess and Ella and the itchy feeling Fern had left beneath my skin, to release the clawing in my chest, and let me hold out until Wednesday night, when my Lower East Side hockey team played the Hell's Kitchen guys. I'd board or cross-check McBurney, he'd do a respectable job of beating my brains in with his stick, I'd go contentedly vacant for a few days while my reset function did its job. Life the way it's supposed to be.

I made it as far as Broadway when my throat closed up and I caved. I had only one trick left in my puny bag, but I knew it was the one that would work. I needed to be in bed with someone soft and warm. I needed to go somewhere deep and far away, even if I ended up there alone. I turned around and in less time than it takes to say, You're a flaming asshole, I was right where I shouldn't be, sitting in a booth at the Coronet, the twenty-four-hour café around the corner from me, opposite the park on Avenue A between Ninth and Tenth Streets, nursing a cup of chamomile tea and flirting with Arwen. I was going to make a mess with her no matter how hard I tried not to, I knew it, but what else could I do?

Arwen waited tables at the Coronet four nights a week, the four to midnight shift. I'd seen her take flak for her name more than once from awkward guys who confused making fun of her with good pickup technique. She never batted an eye. She loved that her apparently unrepentant middle-aged flower children parents named her after the elf-girl in *Lord of the Rings*, the one who gives up her immortality to stay behind and pour her elfish light and love on her lover King Aragorn while all the other heaven-kissed elves sail off to the Undying Lands and leave Middle Earth to the cloddish mortals. Arwen had been working at the café less than a year but already no one could remember the place without her.

The Coronet's elf-girl had long tawny hair and dark brown eyes and a cute little layer of baby fat padding out her curves. She wasn't stupid, but not the brightest bulb in the array either, pretty much the same as how most people saw me, and she was young, in her early twenties, which made her an easy girl for me to be with. Not as in shooting-fish-in-the-barrel easy. I was a wrecking ball of a boyfriend, but I was no predator. It was just that, attracted as I often was to them, I couldn't be with a smart mature complex kind of woman. I had long since concocted explanations for the scars—I couldn't hide them even from a blind woman—but smart mature women weren't satisfied. They noticed too much, the squirminess behind my lying eyes and amusing stories, and asked too many questions, "Really? A dare? You burned yourself there on a dare?" Girls like Arwen stopped asking questions after the first round. Who knows, maybe they were the smart ones.

"Hey, Jody. My shift's almost over. Do you want anything else?" She was back at my table refilling the teapot with hot water.

"No, thanks, just the check. I wouldn't mind some company, though. Are you too tired to sit and talk to me for a little while?"

"Of course not. I'll be back in a few minutes."

She looked like she'd just won the lottery. Eyes round with stunned disbelief, breathless, cheeks tinged pink. Of course for some people, winning the lottery only fucked up their perfectly fine lives. Ditto sleeping with Jody Kowalczyk.

To be honest, I guess there was an element of the fish-in-the-barrel with me and the girls I took up with, but only in the sense that I didn't make a move until I was as sure of what kind of response I was going to get as I could be. I couldn't afford to make mistakes. I couldn't afford to misread people. I needed to get a thing right the first time, no matter what it was. The measurement thing with the windows and mirrors, my being able to see numbers, dimensions, spatial relationships, I was born with that. The girl thing, judging their interest in me, I taught myself.

I started feeling better as soon as Arwen sat down and we started talking. She was definitely her parents' daughter, set at everlasting cloudless noon on a dual-sunned planet. I couldn't see any shadows on her anywhere. Staying focused on her, on her flat unmysterious landscape, was like raising a flaming crucifix to the fanged face of the vampire angling in toward your neck. It kept things at bay.

"So, you're not going to be a waitress all your life, are you?"

"No way. I've got plans." She raised her chin and straightened her back, a little show of defiant pride. Sweet. "I'm going to be attending the Fay Teller Institute in January?" She registered my dumb look and clarified. "I'm going to be a cosmologist?"

Now it was my turn to look like I'd been poleaxed. I had this wild image of her sitting cross-legged on my bed, a pair of glasses on the bridge of her adorable nose, and said nose in my copy of Hawking's *A Brief History of Time,* or an Einstein book (Albert). "What?"

"Omigod. What did I say?" She slumped, put her hands up to her cheeks. I could practically feel the heat coming off them. "A cosme*tolo*gist! I'm going to be a cosme*tol*ogist—facials and things, you know? Oh. What did I say?"

"No biggie, you just lost a syllable there. A cosmetologist . . . okay. That's great. You'll give out-of-this-world facials."

She rolled her eyes. "Someday, I hope. I need practice. Maybe I can practice on you sometime? I mean not that you need it!" Indignant, as if it was offensive to even think I'd need one. "You have perfect skin." Her big eyes went to my throat, down the length of my arms, back to my face. "Really, you do. It's the most awesome color. Like . . . like, I don't know, like . . . warm toast or something." She wasn't blushing anymore.

"I think you've been serving too many BLTs."

She didn't even crack a smile.

I let my eyes drift away from hers and waited out my flare of anger. It wasn't that she'd said anything wrong, but it made me uncomfortable when people talked about me that way. It passed, I looked at her again, touched her hand with the tip of a finger. "Would you maybe want to take a walk with me?"

She nodded, but I saw the hint of doubt in her eyes.

I smiled. "You know how I am, Arwen. Not good for anything serious. You can say no. I won't be mad or anything."

"I don't want to say no. I'm a big girl. Don't worry, I don't expect anything."

This was one of those moments when I hated myself more than usual, because I should have told her to forget it, go home, but I didn't. I took her up to my apartment, and took her to bed even though I knew she was lying to herself. Of course she expected something. Why shouldn't she? Nice girls deserved better than to be used as sedation. I did care about their feelings, all the nice girls who were so good to me. I wanted very much to please them, and I wanted them to know it, to feel it when they were with me. Any woman who was nice enough to be there when I needed her, to let me fumble around for a while in her pretty make-believe world and lose myself in the real-world beauty of her body, deserved at least that. I was never going to shower them with love, but I could be counted on to all but drown them in gratitude.

✳

FOR MOST PEOPLE, SEX WAS an end in itself. For me, it was a vehicle. The perfect vehicle. A slow-burning rocket headed toward the white well of infinity, with flames hot enough to torch my memories and acceleration strong enough to lift me off a barren blasted earth and point me toward the possibility of paradise. The longer the journey, the longer the flames burned, the better it was. If I could have made it last forever, if I could go and never come back, if I could be incinerated, that would be best.

At some point, Arwen fell away from me like a spent booster rocket. She didn't notice, none of them ever did, that we hadn't both come to ground when we were done. We were tangled up together in my bed, panting into each other's faces like a pair of cheetahs at the end of a kill sprint, our hearts pounding against one another, so how could she tell that she was just imagining me, that I wasn't really with her at all, I was still out there, clawing at the void for something solid to hold on to so I wouldn't have to come back.

I LISTENED TO ARWEN'S SLEEPING breath, tried to slow my breaths to match hers so that maybe I'd sleep, too. I usually slept better when someone was with me, had the dream less often, but that didn't equal me wanting someone with me. It wasn't that simple a fix. In my world, much as I respected mathematics, two plus two didn't always equal four, so even though I'd had regular girlfriends from the time I was sixteen, I slept alone more often than not. It was safer for everyone, a speed bump on a treacherous road so things wouldn't move too fast. I wanted to stay with someone at least a few months before the L word reared its head and I started shutting everything down, one switch at a time. There was no shutting anything down now, my brain and heart wouldn't stop zooming. I'd fallen back to earth and landed in the Tess Fischer haystack of strange questions. For over an hour I'd been lying there unsuccessfully trying to avoid the needle pricks. When my clock radio read 2:30, I eased myself off the bed and out of the room, closed the door as quietly as I could.

I went into the living room. I wedged myself into the corner, on the floor, into the space bounded by the wall on one side and the side of the sofa on the other, beneath the bottom shelf of the bookcases I'd hung. Unless some wily cockroach with a carpentering yen hung out there when I wasn't around, I was the only one who knew what the underside of those shelves looked like. I'd studied it as thoroughly as I'd studied the ceiling of the doghouse in the backyard of Scott's house.

I'd woken Einstein. She came and sat in front of me, watched me with an intensity that made her whole body quiver. It made her so unhappy when I derailed. These sad, tight, high-pitched whinnies seeped out of her. It turned my stomach to hear them. I watched her eyes and little by little I slowed down. I put out my arm and said, "Einstein. Come." She slid over and tipped against me. I stroked her between her ears. If she could talk, maybe she could tell me who or what I was, but when she was near me at least I could believe I *was.*

Einstein was roused from sleep by an odd yelping sound. She came to a crouch, ears flattened against her skull, a low growl in the back of her throat, ready to defend her domain and her master against any and all intruders. The sound came again, and she recognized it as a human sound, animal-like but human, of the kind that signaled that Jody was not alone. She rose fully and sent her senses questing. The scent and timbre of voice was of the female human who inhabited one of the places where Jody often went to find food. The female human with the unbroken stream of light coursing around her. Einstein gathered her senses into herself, twitched her ears, shook herself from head to toe, releasing the wary tension in her muscles. He probably wouldn't need her tonight. He didn't usually scream, or even slide in and out of wakefulness, when he wasn't alone. She circled in place a few times, following the trail of her tail, then settled down onto her bed and closed her eyes.

She came awake again sometime later, roused this time by his presence in the living room. She cracked an eye and watched him cross the room and lower himself to the floor in the corner beyond the far end of the couch. It was never good when he did that. She got up, padded past the sofa and sat on her haunches in front of him. She whined. She stared at him, unblinking, straining toward him but not moving, and he stared back, blinking and breathing rapidly, then breath and eyelids gradually slowed, until he sat quietly, his forearms resting on his tented legs. She maintained a placid pose, she never let him feel her fear for him, for herself, that something might happen to him and she'd be without him

again. He held out an arm and made the noise she'd been waiting for. She went to him, put her head on his knee. His hand fell between her ears. He made more noises, and every time she heard the one that was her name, her tail thumped softly on the floor.

※

"SO. THE NICE DITZY LADY wants to know why I have a Polish name. Should we tell her? Hm, Einstein? Should we tell her it's no simple thing, that it's everything?"

Einstein lifted her head and licked my hand.

"I'll take that as a qualified yes." She licked my chin. "Aha. I'll take that as a definite yes. You think if I could really give it to her, get rid of some of it, that it would make a difference?" She nuzzled her head into my palm, looked me in the eyes. "Tess. She's not like anybody we've ever met before, is she? You think we can trust her?" A heavy paw landed on my knee. "Yeah, easy for you to say."

My downstairs neighbors were shouting at each other, I couldn't make out the words but the anger and hatred rang out clear as a bell. They argued like that a few times a week, always in the wee hours. I found it reassuring, especially if it coincided with a visit to the corner. I took my hand away, lay my cheek on the flat hard plane of Einstein's skull and listened to them fight for a while. Then I crawled over to my desk, got a lined yellow pad and a pen, and crawled back under the shelves. Then I got up and sat on the sofa. Then I got up and sat at my desk. Then I got up and went into the kitchen. Einstein was already there, waiting next to my chair. I held out the pen and pad and said, "Maybe you want to write it, smartass?" She gave me a disdainful look and settled down on the floor. She was so smart, she didn't have to pretend to know what she didn't know.

I didn't want to write it, either. I didn't even know what *it* was that I didn't want to write. Those images in my head all had captions, riots of words I'd kept as heavy a lid on as the pictures themselves. Whole bunches had been yelling at me for days now. I really wanted them to shut up and go away, but clearly I wasn't as good at making them do that as I'd been in my salad days. Back then, I'd driven at least three very canny therapists to fantasies of early retirement by my zombielike refusal to write, draw, or say anything.

I sat there with the pen in my hand and tried very hard to think about nothing. Thinking about nothing can be a dangerous thing to do, however, because the brain can't stand not thinking about something and if you let go of your control it's going to do whatever the hell it wants. Like say to you, *Hey, Jody, lookie here, these four women who just crowded into the limited space of your paltry life? Their names are Fern, Arwen, Tess, and Ella? They spell FATE man! Can you believe it? Oh wait, actually, they also spell FETA. Ha, ha, gotcha moron, got you believing maybe it's the Meaning of Your Life, but it's only a plate of dry crumbly cheese! Or . . . they also spell FEAT, as in Herculean, as in the hardest thing you'll ever do in your life. So perhaps it's time to get off your cowardly ass.*

I wrote *For Tess, from* and stopped. I didn't know who from. I ripped the page off, tossed it to the floor, started again.

For Tess When I

I froze. My fingers, my lungs, paralyzed. Spots danced in front of my eyes like when I was a kid. I pushed away from the table so hard the chair skidded and nearly tipped over. I lunged forward, tore the page from the pad, crumpled it, and pitched it into the sink like it was a sizzling basketball in my hands. Not good enough. I ran to the sink, retrieved it, ran into the bathroom. I stood over the toilet bowl, shredded it into tiny pieces, and flushed it, kept my eyes on the water until it and my gorge stopped rising.

Again.

For Tess When Christopher was

Still no good. Right to the toilet this time. Einstein was getting a little agitated, following me, skidding on the kitchen floor. I sat down one more time, tried to clear my head and let the right words come. I closed my eyes. I thought about music. Einstein put a paw on my leg. I opened my eyes and started to write.

For Tess It's night. He's not quite five years old.

I waited, pen hanging over the pad. My ass stayed in the chair. I kept going.

I flipped back to the first page and titled it. *Trestle Road.* It was a story, after all, and all stories want a title, their essence whittled down to a word or a phrase, once their essence is known.

I didn't read it. There were a lot of pages. I put them in a drawer of my desk. I was a little dazed, a little chilled. A lot of pages filled with my handwriting. But not my words. I'd never said or written words like that in my life. The time on the oven panel read 5:30. It was light outside. I'd been writing for three hours. I didn't remember them. I had the uneasy but not wholly unpleasant feeling of having been slipped a mickey. I didn't touch alcohol or drugs, it had been a long, long time since I'd felt anything like that. Einstein looked pretty blitzed, too. She was lying on her bed on her back, legs splayed, out cold.

I went back into the bedroom, slipped into bed. I thought Arwen was asleep, but she right away moved to touch me.

"You're so cold. Come here. I'll warm you up. I know what you need."

She put her arms around me, slid her body over mine. I could tell she'd been awake, I didn't know for how long, but she'd been awake and hadn't needed to come looking for me. She'd been okay leaving me in private with whatever had kept me from sleep. I held her head and kissed her. Her breath was pure and clean but all I could taste was the bitterness of remorse. She was a girl worth loving and I was going to waste her.

For Tess

TRESTLE ROAD

It's night. He's not quite five years old. Forty-one inches tall. Measured that morning against the kiddie height-chart taped to the wall near his bed. There are smiling animals up and down the sides of the chart, watching his progress. He's past the frog and a rabbit. Today there was a dolphin right by his head. The chimp awaits up in a tree.

It's night. It's late. The dolphin's asleep. He was, but he's not anymore. He slides out of bed and cracks his bedroom door, stands in the narrow slant of light coming from the hall. It's not really his bedroom, it's his aunt Marie's. There's no other place for him in the house. There are only two other bedrooms, his grandfather's and his mother's. He doesn't re-member ever sleeping in his mother's room. He doesn't remember ever sleeping anywhere near her.

There isn't a lot of extra space in Aunt Marie's room, just enough for his single bed, a chair. Some shelves for his clothes, his books. An old milk crate for his toys. A small scarred desk that once belonged to his mother, hauled up from the basement for him about a year ago. Aunt Marie's bed is a single, too, neat as a nun's across the room from his. A painted wooden crucifix hangs on the wall over her pillow. She lets him climb up on her bed sometimes and touch it. It's old and chipped, but there's some gold paint still on it and whenever there's any kind of light in the room, it pulls the light right to it, like a magnet. Aunt Marie says that only the light of Jesus can remove the terrible stain of sin he was born with, the stain that lives inside him. He thinks she means the light he sees around the crucifix, he doesn't understand that there's another kind. He thinks it must be a kind of magic, a light that can go right into a person and erase his badness. He doesn't know how it works, Aunt Marie doesn't say anything about that, but he figures that as long as the light is there, there's hope for him. He looks over his shoulder for a second to see if the Jesus magic is working now. The crucifix is glowing against the shadowed wall.

He stands in the triangle of hall light. His eyes are at the level of the doorknob. His left hand is wrapped around the knob, to hold himself up. He's awake now, but he's sleepy. He rests his head on his hand. His right hand hangs useless at his side, plucking at the leg of his pajamas, last year's flannels. There's no carpet on the floor, just the same old worn linoleum as the kitchen and it's cold. Summer's over. The pajamas are too small for him and the cold floats up around his uncovered ankles.

He's listening to his mother and grandfather fighting. The screech of their voices woke him up. They fight nearly every night and there are words they use that are so powerfully bad they can travel from any starting place in the house, into the hallway, through his door, to his bed, into his ears. He doesn't know what they mean but he knows they're bad. They have a different sound from the words he does understand. They're sharp, they vibrate on a wavelength that he picks up like it's sonar and he's got the world's biggest receptor embedded in the center of his brain. Whore. Tyrant. Bastard. Fuck you. His mother's husky roar sends a gobble-dygook combination of Fuck you, tyrant flying into the air. He suddenly thinks, the whore that roared, like it's a Dr. Seuss book, one he's not old enough to read.

When the words hit his brain his right hand forgets about his pajamas and makes a beeline for his mouth. He shoves his thumb in and starts sucking. He waits for what always follows and it comes, the sound of her boot heels thumping toward the front door. It's only been since breakfast yesterday that she's been gone, but it feels like he hasn't seen her in forever. He scurries down the stairs, along the hall, takes his thumb out of his mouth and says, Mommy? He doesn't whine, he's careful about that, she doesn't like him when he whines. She keeps going all the same. She doesn't look at him. She doesn't like him even when he doesn't whine. She says, What did I tell you about calling me that? Get back to your room, but she's not even really talking to him. He watches her start through the door, Marian, his twenty-year-old mother with her warm olive skin and dark brown eyes, in her high-heeled knee-high white plastic disco boots and white plastic skirt practically up to where no one's supposed to see and he thinks in a panic, she'll be cold, she'll get sick. He rushes her, grabs onto her leg. No Mommy, you go be cold! She pulls away, laughs. His love is funny to her. No, dummy, Mommy no go be cold. Get back to bed before your grandfather sees you. He tries to hold on, tries to plant just a quick little kiss on the back of her knee, but she shakes him off. Don't go, Mommy! I going back to bed now! Look! He backs fast down the hallway, waving his arms. He's desperate. She doesn't close the door when she walks out. Her boots are like white strobe lights flickering on and off through the red and yellow leaves that cover the cement walkway.

Sal charges to the door from the kitchen, running like a blotto crab on short bandy legs, wrapped in a filthy apron and carrying a smeared knife. He cringes against the wall, his thumb back in his mouth, as Sal screams out another word he doesn't understand. Puttana! Like your puttana mother! Don't come back here no more! You hear me? Tomorrow I change the locks! Sal slams the door and runs back into the kitchen without seeing him.

His cheeks are wet, but his throat is Death Valley dry and he needs water in the worst way. His heart is thumping against his ribs as hard as Marian's boots against the floor and he wants his aunt Marie. Water and aunt are both in the kitchen and he thinks if Sal didn't see him in the hallway then maybe he won't see him there, either. Barely over the threshold, he starts feeling sick. Things look normal—Sal is at the counter by the sink, cleaning the fish he caught in Great South Bay that afternoon. Aunt Marie is sitting at the kitchen table with her head in her hands—but it feels like a bomb went off in there, shock waves are bouncing off all the hard surfaces.

He tries to retreat, but Aunt Marie raises her head and sees him. She looks like she wants to go to sleep. What do you want, child? It's not an inviting question. He doesn't want anything anymore except to get back to his room. Sal turns around. Your aunt she ask you a question. Sal's face is bright red. The shock waves are coming from there, from the middle of Sal's red face. Get that stupid thumb outta your mouth and answer her then getcha ass back to bed. His thumb is stuck, it won't come out, his teeth and lips won't unclench. His feet won't move.

Sal's got the gutting knife in his right hand. The fish is on the kitchen counter, a big striped bass, its bones and blood and guts dripping onto the floor. Sal takes a few steps, waves the knife in his face and yells, Hey, shit for brains, what I just say? Aunt Marie shakes her head. Sal. _Il ragazzo ha un nome. Non è stata colpa sua._ The boy has a name. It's not his fault. Her eyes are pecans behind her glasses, bulging, dark, and polished. They look like his feel, stretched and aching. Sal says without looking at her, Shut up, Marie, I'm talkin' to my _puttana_ daughter's butt-ugly bastard. Take that goddamned thumb outta your fat mouth. I see it there one more time I cut it off. He and Sal stare at each other and then Sal hooks his thick left index and middle fingers like a lobster claw around his wrist and yanks. The thumb pops out. Sal hauls him across the room by the wrist, yanks his arm up and pins his hand to the slippery counter, the goddamned thumb forced out to the side. Sal raises the knife high in the air. Aunt Marie jumps to her feet, cries, _Non gli fa male!_ Don't hurt him. The knife slices through the air, his whole body bucks like he's being electrocuted, he shrieks, his heart explodes up into his throat. The knife stops an inch above his thumb. Sal drags his hand like a rag through the stinking fish gore, coats his fingers with it, says, Here, half-breed, suck on this, and forces the slimed thumb into his mouth again.

He gags on the slime and his own terror, pouring sour into his mouth, but he's so freaked about what Sal might do if he pukes on the kitchen floor that he swallows it. Sal lets him go and he spits out his thumb and somehow ends up on the wet floor, curled up like a stepped-on slug and wailing to beat the band. Maybe he skidded on the fish's insides. Maybe his brain went dead for a minute and he lost the use of his legs. Who knows. Who cares. Sal turns back to his fish. Marie sighs, helps him off the floor and takes him upstairs to the bathroom.

He throws up into the toilet bowl. He sits on Aunt Marie's lap and cries while she cleans him up. She tells him that Sal doesn't really mean the things he says and does. She even tells him Marian's coming back. Aunt Marie only means to make him feel better. She's too old to remember that four-year-olds can know things. That they know lies when they hear them.

Back in their bedroom she makes him kneel next to her by her bed. She doesn't look at it while she prays, he thinks because she's afraid, like he is, that Jesus will be angry with her for bothering him, but she talks to the crucifix and asks for her brother Sal and her niece Marian to love each other. She tells him to pray for them, too, and to pray for himself, to ask to be forgiven for making his grandfather angry and for all his other many sins. So that's what he does. He says whatever Aunt Marie says.

In bed he wants to cry again, he wants to call out for his mommy. He's dying to put his thumb in his mouth to stop the tears and mommy from coming out, but as soon as his right arm starts the move toward his face he gets nauseous. He twists his arm up and tucks it under the small of his back so it won't go anywhere. He can't be a baby anymore, pucker up like a suckerfish every time someone yells at him. Babies are weak and weaklings are a lower form of life, lower than ants' balls. Even Jesus probably can't stand them. He's got to be strong. He prays to Jesus some more. But this time, even though he's very afraid, he asks for something different. He's sure it must be a terrible thing to ask for because it's for himself and you're not supposed to ask for anything for yourself, except to be forgiven for all your sins, and now he's adding another one to his, but at least it's the truth and he hasn't learned yet how mean-ingless that is. He promises that he will never suck that goddamned thumb again and he asks if Jesus would please then let him disappear from this place.

With no thumb, the big strong not-quite-five boy doesn't sleep so well. He wakes up too early the next morning, with the birds. He stays in bed with his eyes closed, picturing the birds—crows and robins that hang out all year in the maple trees out back. The crows always sound tough and the robins always sound happy and he struggles to hear them through the snores coming from Aunt Marie's side of the room. He has no trouble hearing the front door open and close. Sounds that come from inside the house are so loud compared to sounds the rest of the world makes, it's like they're amped by microphones and wires hidden in the walls and floors. The door closing means Sal's leaving for work. He hears the car start, Sal revs the engine a few times. He doesn't move until he can't hear even the tiniest humming memory of the car's tires on the pavement. Then he gets up and real quiet he goes down to the kitchen.

Sal's espresso cup and a plate with crumbs on it are in the sink. The aluminum espresso pot is on the stove, the burner is off. He loves espresso but Aunt Marie doesn't let him drink it. She says it'll stunt his growth. He heads to the refrigerator for some juice, but then he sees there's already something at his place at the table. An espresso cup, half filled, the black coffee with a thin brown foam on its surface, two small lumps of sugar, and a piece of lemon peel on the edge of the saucer. An espresso spoon, little like his baby spoon, on one side of it, a paper napkin on the other. Neat. Waiting for him. The coffee still warm.

He kneels on his chair so he's the right height at the table, and stares at the cup. His heart is pounding, like it was last night, and every few seconds he looks fast all around the room to get rid of the pressure behind his eyes from trying to figure out what he's supposed to do. The cup of espresso is under his nose. The gutting knife is on the drain board. He thinks really hard, but he just can't find enough information anywhere in the universe to tell him what the right answer to this kind of test is. He's tried before. He touches a fingertip to the coffee, and it's gone cold. The only thing he can see to do is to change the universe back to where this didn't happen so he can't do the wrong thing.

He climbs down and pushes his chair over to the sink. He goes back to the table, puts the sugar and lemon peel in his mouth and eats them. He carries the cup and saucer and spoon to the sink. He climbs onto his chair and puts them next to Sal's. He memorizes where Sal's stuff is, then he takes it out of the sink and puts it on the counter. He pours the cold espresso down the drain, rinses the cup and saucer and spoon, dries them and puts them away. He puts Sal's dishes back into the sink, just where they'd been, wipes up the counter. Pushes his chair back to the table.

He's sitting at the table drinking his juice when Aunt Marie comes in. He watches her with Superman x-ray vision. She's pretty easy to read, and he's sure she doesn't notice anything. He still doesn't know what would've been the right or wrong thing to do, but at least this time, whatever the wrong thing was, he didn't do it.

Autumn, 1975. His last fall on Trestle Road, beneath the sheltering roof of his grandfather's house and the watchful eye of Jesus. A few images from his baby album. There aren't any of the regular kind. Only these. His memories. Come on—smile for the camera, shit for brains. Click.

The human brain doesn't lay down real memories until around the age of six—that's what the experts say. So maybe these things didn't actually happen this way. Maybe things like them happened, a hundred times over, and he's got them all jumbled up together. But what do the experts really know? And what does it matter? Who gets to say what real is, what a real memory is? We all live alone inside our own heads. Whatever a person remembers, that's what's real for him.

Five

THREE O'CLOCK TUESDAY AFTERNOON. HECTOR and I were in the music room on the first floor, taking down an entire wall of old mirror. We'd been wrestling with it since eight that morning. Whoever hung it must have used the same glue that held atomic particles together. An excellent opportunity to learn a few colorful new Dominican curses. It was okay, I needed the distraction.

By Monday evening my desk had started looking to me like a lit stick of dynamite and that morning, while she was at breakfast, I'd slid what I'd written under Tess's door. I hadn't seen her yet and had been flinching at white-haired strangers all day. On top of that, Mrs. Jacobs mentioned that Ella was due back at five and was looking forward to seeing me again. Why? I was a Neanderthal who'd given her a doughnut once, King Kong slobberingly handing Ann Darrow a flower.

"Ah. There you are."

I was up on a ladder, hacking away at the dried adhesive between the glass backing and the drywall. I climbed down. I didn't know what to call Tess to her face, so I opted for the respectful and polite name she deserved and said, "Hey, Mrs. Fischer." I held my breath.

Tess glanced at Hector, up on another ladder ten feet away, imitating a man minding his own business. Not an Oscar-winning performance.

"That was a lovely gift you left for me." She kept her voice low but I knew it was pointless, Hector had hearing like a cat. "Can you come by before you leave so I can thank you properly? I'll be in my room between five and six."

"Sure."

I waited a few minutes before risking leaving the floor and climbing the ladder again. Hector was giving me the hairy eyeball the whole time. I ignored him. Finally, he couldn't take it anymore. When it came to poking around in other people's lives, he and Orlando operated by a set of rules that could have come from *The Demented Dominican's Guide to Social Misconduct,* for all the logic in it.

"Awww. Jody sweet on the soft old lady. What you give her, man, an engagement ring?"

"She seemed sad last week. I brought her a box of chocolates. Jerk."

Hector chuckled. It amused him royally that I didn't use bad language. He gave me a deep black-eyed look. It was not candy-toting weather, and besides, if I'd been carrying around a box of candy he'd have seen it. The envelope I'd been able to stick into the waistband of my jeans, under my T-shirt. He knew I was lying but he didn't say anything else. I'd been working with these loco Latinos for ten years. We'd seen a lot of each other, literally. We didn't know anything about each other below the skin of those ten years, but we all knew when to bend our private loco rules and butt out.

※

TESS'S ROOM WAS ACTUALLY A cozy apartment, with a bedroom, bathroom, living room with a kitchenette in one corner, a sink and microwave, no stove. The apartment wasn't too big or too small. It was just right. It felt like her, neat and elegant and a little old-world foreign. There was a tall plant in a brightly painted ceramic pot on the floor of the bedroom that needed turning. I rotated the pot so that the stunted side would get the strong morning light. The bedroom window faced east, out over the avenue into Prospect Park. There was an armchair positioned beneath it, and on the seat lay a medium-sized sketch pad and a couple of charcoal drawing pencils.

"You've got a great view. Is that what you draw?" I gestured toward the pad.

"That, and other things. The view is lovely, though, isn't it? I like to sit in my chair in the mornings and watch the sun lift up over the trees. I imagine I'm in the bedroom of my childhood. My family had a villa near Frascati, a hill town outside Rome. My window looked out over acres of olive groves and vineyards."

She made it sound like Eden, except she'd left it. Or been kicked out. I estimated she would have grown up under Mussolini and the coming of World War II, which couldn't have been much fun.

We sat together on the couch in the living room. My opus was on the table in front of us. My head felt light as a balloon. Tess took my hand. She didn't say a word, just surrounded my rough brown hand with both of her delicate white ones. Her fingers were swollen with arthritis. Her skin looked ancient, fragile, worn thin by time. An old ache radiated through my chest. It was all there in her touch, that she'd read my story and accepted that we didn't need to talk about it, that what had been done couldn't be understood any more than it could be undone.

"There are going to be more stories. We should decide now what to do with them, yes?"

Like I had a clue. "You decide."

There were going to be more, she was right. I'd gone to sleep in one coherent piece and woken up with the rock-hard frozen core of me booming and cracking and I didn't know how to stop it. A buried mountain of words was pushing up through the cracks. Overnight, those silent, black-and-white snapshots of my past had become saturated with color and noise. They'd become movies.

"These are your memories, Jody. Do you want to keep them, or let them go?"

Clueless again. Those were both basically impossible options as far as I could see. "I wouldn't mind *un*doing them."

She patted my hand and chuckled. "Ah, well then. Maybe we should trade memories. Then someday I will forget your memories for you, and you will remember mine for me."

That was about as good an offer as I was ever likely to get. Too bad Mr. Spock wasn't there to do the Vulcan mind meld on us.

"Well, that would be good for me. But we can't do it because it wouldn't be good for you. Before you forgot, you'd have to remember and I don't want you to have my memories. I like you."

"Your memories can't harm me, Jody. Someone needs to know them. I'll take them from you, take them with me when I go." She stood up. "But all right. This is what I think. For now, we exorcize them, we burn them and flush them away." Her eyes swept the room. "Matches. We need matches . . . I don't . . ."

"It's okay. I have a lighter." I kept a Zippo in my pocket for work purposes and for burning ticks off Einstein, who had yet to meet a bush she didn't like.

"Ah, good."

"Are you even allowed to burn things in here?" There was a smoke detector on the ceiling and a carbon-dioxide detector by the door.

"No, of course not." She picked up the pages. "Too bad. Come." She marched into the bathroom, turned on the fan. Closed the door behind me.

We stood at the sink. Tess put the pages into the bowl and said, "Would you like to do the honors?" I flicked the lighter and watched

Trestle Road go up in smoke. The paper curled and turned to ash. Tess turned on the cold water and together we pushed the ashes down the drain. An interesting sensation, watching them go. My memories declined to go with them, however. Surprise.

"The boy in the story, he was a very brave little boy. Did he have a name?"

I didn't answer. I didn't know if my mouth could form that sound anymore. We looked at each other in the mirror.

"You must work so hard to keep people from seeing you. Especially since nature designed you to be looked at, so powerfully beautiful, like a leopard."

I kept my eyes on her. Looking at myself in the mirror was not something I enjoyed doing. I didn't get angry, though. I couldn't, not at her. "More like a wildebeest." God's mistake people called it, designed by committee, thrown together from all the leftover parts on the animal junk heap.

"Funny boy. As you wish. You're not beautiful. You make your eyes into mirrors to shield people from your ugliness, not so that you can see out without them seeing in." Tess glanced down at my hand. I had the Zippo in a death grip. "You might want to put that away before you break it. Wait here. And breathe."

She was back in a jiffy, with the photo in the silver frame. She held it up near my face, expectant eyes all over my reflection, and now there were three people in the mirror.

A big good-looking boy, late teens early-twenties, broad-shouldered and rangy, with long wavy red-brown hair and light brown eyes. He's sitting at a grand piano in a windowed corner of the living room of a high-floor city apartment. Half a Scandinavian-modern couch against the wall bleeds off the right-hand edge of the picture. The boy is wearing black jeans and a blue-and-orange tie-dyed T-shirt, dirty sneakers with undone laces trailing on the floor. His feet are on the pedals. He seems loose and relaxed but his fingers and eyes give him away. The fingers are tensed, arched like talons above the keys, and his eyes are blazing off the glossy paper. He's looking back over his shoulder at whoever it is taking a picture of him and you can tell it's someone he loves and is preparing himself to lose, his eyes are swimming with it, with a gigantic love about to be interrupted. There's a helpless lopsided smile on his mouth, something disturbing about it, like his confusion has gotten the best of him. And even though he doesn't look even remotely like me, and there's no reason why she should have, I know that this is the person she thought I was. This is Matt. And I know that this is one of the last pictures ever taken of him. Because he's dead.

There was a fizzing sensation behind my breastbone. "What happened to him?" The question came out despite my not really wanting to know the answer.

"He died. But he is not at rest and I don't know what happened to him after. Where he went. You see, don't you? Why I get confused when I look at you, who you are?" She hoisted the picture right smack up next to my face. "He's missing. Like you are missing." She turned and touched her palm to my cheek. "Like you are not at rest." Her eyes were filling with tears. "You both disappeared and no one knew where you went or how to find you. Do you see now? Why I know you? Why you know me?"

I did. That fizzy sensation raced all through me, like a horde of ants fleeing a bombarded anthill. It took over my nerves and muscles, and like when my arms went by themselves around Irene's neck, now they went around Tess and hugged her. She shook like a baby bird against me, wracked with silent crying. I lowered my head to hers. "The boy in the story, his name was Christopher. *Mi chiamava Christopher.*"

When her crying stopped I relaxed my arms. She stepped out of my hold. "Ah. Christopher. Cristoforo. And you're Italian. You're not

Polish. I knew it." She made a face that said any cretin looking at me would know I wasn't Polish and let's just stop kidding ourselves.

"Yeah, well, don't look so smug. Only half of me is."

"Your mother. And the other half? Your father?"

I shrugged. A fat-lipped, blue-eyed, very nice, nonpig, not butt-ugly SOB of a Puerto Rican named Angel who was let-me-at-it down with gang-banging a stoned fifteen-year-old girl. Unless of course I was the second coming, the other undiscovered virgin birth, which my aunt certainly preferred to think, and Marian hallucinated angels during the blessed event and then made up a devilish story guaranteed to make me feel worse about myself than I already did when she left, like she hadn't done enough for me.

"I never knew my father."

"You are so angry."

"No, I'm not. I'm not angry. These things happen. Who should I be angry at?" I wanted to go home. I'd sent the guys ahead with the truck and Einstein, told them to leave her with the Israelis. "It's six. I've got to go." Tess followed me into the living room.

"It will get easier, Jody, I promise."

What was it about people, making all sorts of promises they had either no intention or no power to keep?

I kissed her on the cheek. "Come on, Mrs. Fischer. If you're ready, I'll walk you down to dinner."

She linked her arm in mine. When we reached the top of the staircase to the ground floor I looked down and thought, *Oh right, like anything ever gets easier.* Ella was at the bottom, looking up at us. Even in that cold hard hallway light, she was the warmest softest thing I'd ever seen.

SHE TOOK UP TESS'S OTHER arm and we bookended her on down the wide bright hall. Tess didn't need anybody's support, really, but

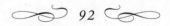

you could tell how happy she was, Ella on her right, me, the Matt substitute, on her left. She hugged our arms to her sides, kept looking, back and forth, back and forth, like she was zigzag stitching us all together.

Ella turned to me and said, "Hello, Jody." There was something different, purposeful, about her tone and her look that made my insides churn. I grunted something, the faculty of speech at that moment appearing to be an instinct I'd been born without.

"I hoped you'd come to the music room this afternoon, Tess. Not everyone plays, you know. It's fun just to listen." Ella's voice was mellow, measured, and melodic. She didn't need an instrument to make music.

"Maybe next time, *cara*."

Ella sighed. "All right, maybe next time. I know we have a date for Sunday, but I wanted to see you for a moment at least before I ran home." With her free hand, she reached over and cradled Tess's gnarled fingers. "Tess was the best teacher I ever had. I learned more in her house than I did at Juilliard."

I beat back an immediate impure urge to put my hand in there, too. I wanted to let Tess know I was sorry she'd lost her ability to play the piano, but mostly I wanted to know the feel of that comfort, the heat and press of Ella's fingers burrowing into my own skin.

"You are as good as I ever was. Do you play the piano, Jody?"

"No."

"You should, it's very meditative, very therapeutic. Let Ella teach you, you need something to do on Saturdays."

"No offense to anyone, but no thanks. I don't play the piano, I play sports."

"Ella, you have time on Saturday, don't you?"

My joke-as-deflecting-device routine was clearly nonoperational around here. I turned to Ella with a smug smile, all set to laugh with her across the top of Tess's head. But Ella looked at me with this ultracalm sincerity and said, "I *do* have time actually."

And then I realized what the difference about her was, in her tone and her look. They were missing the turmoil that had been there when we'd met before. It was like she'd pondered some questionable or problematic aspect of me since last week and made her peace with whatever it was that had riled her up, made her peace with what she wanted with me. That put her way ahead of me. I was still suffering brain cramps when I saw her and not understanding why. But once I figured out what it was she wanted with me, I'd know what I wanted with her, or what was okay for me to want. I'd know what to do.

One of Tess's friends was by the dining room doors, arm and hand reaching out as we got near, like a relay racer set up for the baton. Tess disengaged from Ella and moved me out of earshot. "Let Christopher have his name, and tell him I look forward to hearing from him again. Tell him I will cherish and hold private all his stories. And both of you can call me Tess."

She went off with her friend. She waved at us over her shoulder, called out, "*Ciao, bambini.* Have fun, children." A tricksy swoop and lilt to her voice, the last stitch, the tying of the knot, making sure Ella and I stayed sewn together without her in the middle.

I HAD TO WAIT OUT a couple of raggy heartbeats before I turned back to her. Ella was calmly watching me, a touch of color tingeing her cheeks when my eyes caught hers, but no quiver and slide away of her eyes, no breaking apart. I stood there, mute, not believing it possible, but feeling it nonetheless, that the time had actually come. She was ready, and I'd been dropped into her path again so she could get it back, that heavy load she'd left with me ten years ago, her guilty love.

She smiled, her mouth just barely trembling and her liquid eyes green oceans of heartache. Her face was a picture worth a million words, but the only one I could read was *Matt*. She was the one who'd taken that picture of him. Ella, his soon to be lost beloved. It was all about long-dead Matt for her, too. It had to be.

She began walking along the corridor that led to the back entrance. I'd been planning to go out the front. When I didn't move, she stopped and held out her hand. She didn't walk back to me, she didn't say, *Come here,* she just held out her hand. I took it.

"I thought you'd gone home for the day. I saw your truck leaving as I came in."

"The other guys left. I stayed to visit with Mrs. Fischer. Tess. I'll catch the subway."

"I noticed a Lower East Side address on the truck. I'm driving to the Village, over the Manhattan Bridge. Where do you need to go? I can drop you."

"It's way east on Delancey. You're going west. I don't want to put you out."

"It's a short detour. The subway won't even get you close. It's a good offer." She smiled, a sturdy smile this time, and tilted her head, lifting her pale eyebrows. *What do you say?*

We arrived at the back doors. I was aware that we weren't having a conversation at all, I mean, yeah, words were being spoken and ultimately either I was going to take the lift or I wasn't, but that wasn't the important thing. We were dancing, the whole exchange was a subtle series of steps, just the same as when she held out her hand. I was resisting, backing away from her, and she was pursuing me. Not by coming after me. By staying exactly where she was and waiting for me to decide, to move, to step to her. Need I say that this was not a place I was used to being in relation to another person. In my experience, people were either coming at you with the speed of an avalanche, rocks hurtling, or showing you their departing back, grown to the length and breadth of the Great Wall of China. For crying out loud, all she was asking me to do was say, *Yeah, thanks, I'd love a ride,* why did it feel like inching across the prison yard in full view of the guard tower?

And it's not like I didn't want to say yes.

"Matt. What happened to him?" Even a few more of those million words I'd seen on her face would help. Something more than just *Matt.*

She nodded, exhaled, as if she'd been yearning to answer that question since the beginning of time. "He was reported missing in action in Cambodia, in June of 1970. No trace, no witnesses ... He was just ... gone from the face of the earth. Ten days after he got there. He was twenty years old."

That stopped me cold for a second. I didn't know what I'd imagined from seeing that one shot of him, a kid with a heart full of love and eyes full of unanswerable questions—a suicide, a knife to his chest trying to stop a mugging—but definitely not that. Definitely not the universe turning away and letting him slide through the wrong door *there,* a door meant for someone who maybe wasn't supposed to come home.

"He was your boyfriend."

"Yes. He was my boyfriend."

There was an incomplete truth if ever I heard one, but since I could already hear all the lies and half-truths I was going to have to tell her, it wasn't like I was offended or disappointed.

"I'm really sorry."

"Thank you." She squeezed my hand.

Anyway, it was enough, enough for me to get a good idea of what she wanted with me, which was her version of what Tess wanted. For me to be Matt. I still didn't understand what it was about me that screamed *Matt* to Ella, but I didn't need to. After all, I was only a shell, I guess they'd both been blasted enough to recognize one when they saw it, and if they wanted to pour their memories of this boy they'd loved into it, and make like I was him, get what they could out of that now, who was I to tell them not to. It was all right with me. It was a hell of a good offer, actually, and unlike Tess's memory swap, it didn't require superior alien neurosynaptic abilities to make it happen. Just some good old-fashioned camouflage technique, one of my particular specialties.

"Okay then. Yes. I'd appreciate a ride into the city. Thanks."

Ella ran the music program at a private Village grade school and gave lessons at home evenings and weekends. By the time she dropped me at Citywide I had an appointment for my first lesson. Saturday at eleven. She'd done it again, put it out there without pushing, let me feel how much she wanted me to say yes but without any hint that she'd be angry if I said no. I didn't want to take piano lessons. I'd never expected to touch a piano again in my life, but now that I knew what she wanted, I knew what I wanted. I wanted to make her happy, do what pleased her, buy myself permission to be near her. If it meant playing the piano for her, how hard could that be, how much could it cost?

She wrote down her address and phone number, gave me the folded paper as I got out of her car. I didn't look at it until I got home. She lived on West Eleventh Street. I recognized the number of her building. It was a double-wide red-brick town house with a color crazy little garden in front and a piano visible through the floor-to-ceiling first-floor windows.

Six

I MADE MYSELF SOME EGGS and bacon for dinner, then biked up to Central Park and slipped myself into the last hour of a softball game at the Heckscher Ballfield. The field still had a few years restoration ahead of it, same as the fields up at the North Meadow, but they weren't the mess they'd been when I first came to the city. I knew all the guys that played, and I could handle any position so there was always a spot for me. Brendan and I were regulars for years, Sunday afternoons from May through September. He'd been a no-show all summer, blowing off my questions with lies about his time-consuming role in averting global financial chaos come the witching moment. It had nothing to do with making sure we still had our bank accounts the morning of January 1, 2000. It was that Fern probably liked softball about as much as she liked dogs.

When I got back home, I locked my bike in the vestibule of my building and headed to the Coronet to tell Arwen we were going to be friends, to end it with her while things were still easy between us. I felt good around her, a lightness-of-being elf girl in a troll-dominated world. I didn't want to have to never talk to her again one day. I stopped at the bodega on Avenue A to get her a dozen break-up roses. This was undoubtedly my ticket into the *Guinness Book of World Records* for mind-boggling male selfishness, and we all know how stiff the competition is, but I was kind of tickled to be bringing the ax down on someone for a reason other than that her love had become intolerable to me—not that I'd ever said anything close to that to any girl. As I crossed the avenue, I could almost believe I was an ordinary, healthy, caring guy about to do the right thing.

She saw me through the plate glass window and came running out. Before I had a chance to say a word, she pulled me to her, kissed me long and hard. When she drew away, her eyes were as dewy and promising as the world's first dawn.

"I know what those flowers are for, Jody, but I'm not letting you end this. You don't believe it, I know, but I'm going to be good for you. I've been watching you forever, you need someone like me, someone who has faith in happiness." She didn't pause for a breath, or for me to get a contradictory word in. "Oooo, they're gorgeous." She relieved me of the roses. "I *love* them. Okay, I have to get back to work. I'll come over as soon as I'm done."

She kissed me again, then again, then rushed away, her nose in the flowers.

My brain did an immediate one-eighty. She wasn't the one I wanted, but what if she was the one I needed, all that lightness, all that unapologetic confidence? The good old Rolling Stones again, no radio necessary, apparent prophets of the coming apocalypse. Or at least of my personal one.

I didn't go after her. To set her straight. To do the right thing. I kept my feet firmly on the familiar path of least resistance—so familiar and comfortable it felt like I'd been plodding it through multiple lifetimes—turned around, and went home.

I HAD THE DREAM LATE in the night, came to with Einstein on one side of me, Arwen on the other, both of them all over me, trying to pull me out of it. Arwen a touch too wide-eyed. I throttle hissed, "I'm sorry."

"Don't apologize. It's okay. You're okay. It was just a bad dream. You're okay. Your girls are here."

That got what must have been a very scary-looking smile out of me, and a death-rattle-sounding attempt at a laugh. Arwen flinched.

The terror released me. I mumbled, "I'll be right back," eased out from between them, went into the bathroom, did my thing. When I came back, Einstein had yielded the bed to Arwen but gone no further than the bedroom door. I squatted down to pet her, to let her see I was all right, then stumbled back to bed.

Arwen was sitting up, watching me with an innocent's worried look, profound and ignorant, ready to do battle with evil as gamely as only someone who'd never been touched by it could be. "Do you want to talk about it?"

In the optimistic glare of that look I was the vampire, shriveling back into the darkness. I laid her down, flipped her onto her side, curled up behind her so I wouldn't have to see her face.

"There's nothing to talk about. It's just a dream I have once in a while. Sounds a lot worse than it is. Go back to sleep. It's late and I have to kick you out by seven."

Her skin gleamed like pearl. I licked her from her shoulder to her neck, just to feel the unmarred smoothness on my tongue. She turned her head, mouthed, "*I love you, Jody,*" craned up as if to kiss me. I shook my head.

"No, you don't. Go to sleep."

She giggled, wiggled her butt against my thighs. Purred. Drew my arm tighter around her. Closed her eyes. She smelled of roses.

※

I WROTE ANOTHER STORY FOR Tess. Got up to piss, wound up at the kitchen table.

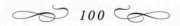

They *were* my memories and my words, I suppose. I should have felt something, but I can't say that I did, no more leastways than an observer's fascination with the process. I was the midway stop on the Underground Railroad for Revolting Recollections, blindfolded, secretly passing all these unclaimed words to Tess behind the back of a watchful, voyeuristic world. Tess would hold them, forever unspoken, and take them away with her when she went. To the primordial sea, the teeming void between the stars, the cosmic soul nursery, to wherever it was we all came from and returned to; to the place and time of all beginnings and all endings, where the fires of creation and destruction would reduce the words not to ashes, but to nothingness. And none of it would ever have happened.

✳

I WOKE ARWEN, MADE LOVE to her until there was nothing but daylight in the corners of my bedroom. I did need her, although not why she thought, not for any reason that could do her any good. I was about to attempt my first and final high-wire act and she was going to be my safety net. So I made love to her and bullshitted myself that the word was as false coming from her mouth as it was from my body. I bullshitted myself that her faith in happiness was unbreakable and would keep her safe and might even balance me, when I knew in my heart that if I wasn't careful I was going to end up catapulting her right off her side of the scale. Because sooner or later darkness wins and everyone is punished for the sinners' sins.

For Tess from Christopher

BEGGAR DOG

So now it's spring. He had a growth spurt somewhere over the winter, he and the chimp have met, and he's aiming straight for the snowy owl with the bright yellow eyes. On that entire chart, it's those eyes he's most fascinated by. They're the only eyes in the house other than his that aren't brown. He looks a whole lot more like the chimp but the eye thing's been making him wonder if he and the owl might be related. He still doesn't know exactly what bastard means, but he's figured out, from all the ways and times the word's been thrown around the house, that it's definitely not a good thing, and that he is one. It's got something to do with not being related to the people you live with, but they let you live there anyhow. Even though they don't really want you because you're ugly and no good. And it's got something to do with that stain inside him.

Bastard: a bad weird kid or dog or maybe cat—he's not sure about other animals—that doesn't belong to anyone and no one wants, so if you find it one day, bring it home and feed it and keep it because that way you'll go to heaven. You don't necessarily have to be nice to it.

His five-year-old interpretation of sin and goodness, mercy and charity, Jesus's love.

Okay, so he's wrong. But still, he's not a stupid kid. Aunt Marie even says he's smart and he thinks that she might actually be telling the truth this time because he can read. She's been teaching him. Not The New York Times or anything like that yet, but most of his books and a lot of other stuff he sees. None of the kids he plays with in the park can do that. None of them can put together puzzles as fast as he can. None of them know without having to think about it that if Mrs. Pinella brings two chocolate chip muffins for a snack and there are six kids there that day, she's got to divide each muffin into three pieces for everyone to have a share. None of them see the shapes and colors of words and numbers, know how to move them around and build things out of them in their heads. He does. It's an honest mistake he makes, believing he's smart, right? But he doesn't make the mistake of letting anyone see that he is. Aunt Marie and Sal tell him all the time no one will ever like him if he brags, shows off, makes like he's better than they are. So even though he really likes the idea that he might be smart, he likes even better the idea that he might be liked.

He's planning on reading for his mommy today. She comes around to see him every two or three weeks, during the day when Sal is at work, and whenever she comes he does tricks for her, like he's a dog, or a clown. He shows her the new thing he's learned to do or say, always pretty sure this is the one that'll prove he's worth her attention. He's not looking for so much, just for her to stay a little longer, come back sooner. Scratch him behind the ears. Whatever. Laugh at him. She doesn't even bother to do that anymore. The last few times she was there, all she did was talk about Scott, her boyfriend. She gives him orange lollipops when she leaves. He doesn't like orange, he likes cherry or chocolate, but he slurps and gobbles them down. He'd gum and gobble the sticks if Aunt Marie didn't pull them out of his mouth and throw them away. He hides the sticky wrappers, first in his pockets then under his mattress. At night, when he can't sleep, he works his hand in there and touches them, imagines that she's in the room with him, that her fingers are sticky and they're both laughing.

He plans to read _The Runaway Bunny_ for her even though it's an easy book. "Once there was a little bunny who wanted to run away." He plans to read it to her and then she'll leap up and cry, _Christopher, you're my little bunny, I will run after you_. But she won't, and his stomach turns into a steel fist when he tries to take it down from the shelf.

So he's going with _Goodnight Moon_ instead. It's safe. And it's impressive.

"In the great green room / There was a telephone / And a red balloon / And a picture of—" He's been carrying it around all morning. He can write, too, and before he reads he's going to show her where he's written his name on the inside of the cover. He's nervous and at breakfast he spills milk from his bowl of Frosted Flakes and smears part of his name.

When Marian comes, she's not alone. The boyfriend is with her. Scott. His speculations about the owl go into overdrive when he sees Scott. Scott has blue eyes. Not the same blue as his—Scott's are washed-out and watery behind his gold-rimmed half-frame rose-tinted granny glasses—but they're not brown and Mommy likes him so much she's living with him. Now he wonders if Scott and the owl might be related, since not only are Scott's eyes blue but his long hair is an ultralight blond, almost as white as the owl's feathers. He looks at Scott and like with Mrs. Pinella's muffins, his mind right away sees a solution to a question and he thinks, okay, if Scott and the owl are related, and he and the owl are related, then maybe he and Scott are related. If A equals B and B equals C then shouldn't A equal C? He doesn't look anything like him, but he gets stuck on the idea that maybe Scott's his father. Because he doesn't look much like Marian either, and she does seem to be his mother.

He's already half in love with Scott for no good reason, stupid drunk on the impact of all the possible meanings behind someone who looks even more different from everyone else than he does walking into this house attached to his mother. A male someone who isn't Sal. So when Scott grins at him and says, Hey, whatcha got in your hand there, buddy? while Marian just looks at him with a look like she's not sure <u>what</u> he is, forget <u>who</u> he is, he thrusts his eyes and the ragged copy of <u>Goodnight Moon</u> in the direction of Scott's mouth and says It's my favorite book. I can read it. I can read it to you.

Marian snorts and says, Yeah right. His eyes get wet and fall to the floor and he mumbles, I can, like he's talking to his toes. Scott does this amazing thing then. He says, If the kid says he can read, I bet he can read.

C'mon buddy, let's sit on the couch and you read to me. And then Scott's yellow-stained fingers land on the top of his drooping head, slip under his shaggy dark hair, and move like a soft wind over his scalp. He's never felt anything like it in his life. The soft wind feeling turns into a thick tingle that warms his whole body. He gets dizzy and nearly topples over. He falls against Scott's leg and Scott doesn't push him away. He nearly pees his pants, it feels so unbelievably good, it's as if Scott's spidery fingers and big hand are a net all around him, drawing him into the same human space as Scott. No one's ever touched him like that. Touched him just to touch him.

He lifts his head. Scott is backlit by the living room windows and there's a spooky second where Scott seems to glow pale and be looking down at him in the same deeply sad, tender way that Jesus looks down from the crucifix on the wall in his bedroom. It's just a trick of the light on white blond hair. Scott's grinning with bared teeth and pinwheeling eyes and giving off about as much wild energy as the sun. He grins back, he wants to show Scott that he's got wild energy in him, too, that no one's ever seen, but his grin is weak and sick, he can feel it from inside his face and now he knows he might as well actually be a dog, because he's so pathetic, nothing but a beggar.

After Scott and Marian leave, he can't calm down. He runs out the door, down the walkway, pushes through the gate in the chain-link fence and pogos around on the pavement, eyes popping out halfway up the street. He wants Scott to come back. He doesn't care if he is less than a dog, he just wants Scott to come back and take him away. Aunt Marie waddles after him and drags him back to the house. By the third time, she's breathing hard into the not so lamblike late-March wind and sweating into her heavy black dress. Her stockings are down around her puffy feet. She yells at him. Stay in the house! I can't run after you. She gives his behind a good wallop. The smack knocks the secret out of him, But Scott's my father! and he starts to blubber. Marie makes a clucking sound and shakes her head. *No, he's not. You don't have a father.* She pinches his cheeks. *You're a lucky little boy, Christopher. You're a child of Jesus.*

Aunt Marie takes the hand of the blubbering child of Jesus who doesn't quite get how lucky he is, and walks him over to the upright piano. His tears dry up on the way there. She does sometimes know how to make him feel better. She sits on the bench and he climbs onto her lap. He puts his right hand on the keys, his thumb over middle C. He knows where to find middle C on the piano. He knows where to find it on the pages of sheet music. Today it's "Come Back to Sorrento," Aunt Marie's favorite song. She puts her calloused right hand over his and moves his fingers, and together they play the melody while Aunt Marie hums it to herself. He's concentrating for all he's worth, hearing the next note in his head while he looks for it on the page and thinks about where his finger will go, so at first he doesn't notice when she goes quiet and her hand stops moving, grips his too tight and pins it under hers against the keys.

She makes a huge gasping noise and pitches backward and they fall off the bench together onto the floor. His hand is being crushed in her grip and he's flailing around on his back on top of her like one of the dying fish on the bottom of Sal's wallowing boat. Except Aunt Marie's not moving at all. He feels like the red balloon from <u>Goodnight Moon</u> is in his head, pushing out any brains he has. He doesn't know what's happening. He says, more like wails, *Aunt Marie? Get up. Let me go.* He struggles off her and pries his hand free. She's still not moving. Her eyes are open and so is her mouth. She's not making any noise.

On the kitchen wall, next to the phone, there's a calendar from the garage where Sal works. The number is on it but he's afraid to call Sal. He doesn't know where Marian is. He pushes a chair across the floor and climbs up. He dials <u>Q</u> and tells the operator that his aunt Marie fell down and isn't moving. The operator asks if he's alone. He says yes. She asks how old he is. He says five and a quarter. She asks his name. He says Christopher. She asks, What's your last name? He says, Cannavarro. She says, Do you know your address? and he says, Yes. She laughs softly, clucks, and says, What is it honey? Where are you? He says, 901 Trestle Road—and he spells it for her—in Bay Shore Long Island New York. She laughs a little and says, You're a smart little boy for five and a quarter. You just stay right where you are, someone will be there soon.

When the ambulance comes a nice black lady in a uniform sits and talks to him while two men kneel by Aunt Marie, then put her onto a stretcher, put a cover over her, over her face, and take her outside. The nice lady says, What's your name, sweetheart? He's a quick learner, he's prepared for the question and knows what to answer. Christopher Nicholas Cannavarro. He even throws in his middle name this time, just in case it's important somehow. She puts her arm around him and says, Who else lives here with you, Christopher? My grandfather. Did you call him? No, he'll be angry with me. He won't be angry. You didn't do nothing wrong. You did good. He wells up with tears. He can't even begin to tell the nice lady all the things he does wrong all the time that make Sal angry with him. She says, I'll call him for you, okay, Christopher? Okay, angel? She hugs him to her and she feels so soft, like Aunt Marie, he starts to cry. Don't cry, baby. You got a mommy? Yes. Where's your mommy at? I don't know. She lives with her boyfriend. Or all the things he does wrong all the time that make his mommy not want him near her. Well, we gotta find her for you. What's her name? Marian. What's the boyfriend's name? Scott. Scott what? I don't know. I don't want to live here anymore.

He's crying hard, he's sobbing and shaking, even though the nice lady keeps telling him not to. He's been really bad. He did do something wrong. He prayed every night to be disappeared from here. All this morning he was praying inside to be able to go live with Scott and Marian. He didn't know that prayers can come true. It's not like he's ever seen it happen before. But that's no excuse. He's not smart after all. If he was he'd have known how it works—that if you're nothing but selfish and greedy about what you ask for, Jesus will give it to you but only to teach you you shouldn't have asked. Now he can go live with Scott and Marian. His prayers killed his aunt Marie.

Asking for what you want most, for that thing that makes you hurt all over when you think about it, goes the way of thumb-sucking. Never again.

SAL ORDERS THE SPIC BRAT to go up to his room, close the door, and wait there until someone comes for him. But Christopher can't do that. It isn't really his room, it's Aunt Marie's, and he knows that if he sets foot in it, the light from Jesus on the cross over her bed will sweep him up like a tornado and scatter him all over hell for his evil prayers. He can see it happening in his mind, like on *Star Trek* when something goes wrong with the transporter beam and someone ends up in molecules, no one knows where, for all eternity. He gets sick just thinking about it. So he makes a lot of noise stomping up the stairs, slams the door to the bedroom, then tiptoes back down. Sal and Marian are in the living room, but Scott is coming up the hall from the kitchen holding a glass of water. He looks at Christopher and they both freeze.

"Please, I don't want to go up there." Christopher's voice is no more than a choked whisper. The cloying miasma of Aunt Marie's lilac powder has impregnated his corduroy shirt, from when he fell on top of her. It's creeping over his shoulders now like a wraith from the grave and doing its best to smother him.

Scott grins. "Afraid of ghosts, little buddy?" He mimes a Halloween kind of ghoul face and starts to laugh quietly, but stops when he sees tears spring into Christopher's eyes. Scott glances toward the entry to the living room. "Okay, Chrissie. Just stay here on the stairs." He holds up a warning finger. "Don't make a peep. Don't cry."

Christopher perches on the next to the bottom step and listens to the often heard sounds of his grandfather and his mother arguing, this time about what to do with him. He's so weak and frightened that he has to lay his side and head against the wall to stay solid, or else the loose feeling in his stomach might spread everywhere and he'll turn into dirty water, dribble down the stairs onto the floor, and ooze out the door.

"YOU GET HIM OUTTA HERE, now, tonight. I don't gotta have him here *no* more." Sal's voice is as cold and flat as a dead fish.

"Oh for Christ *sake*, Pop," Marian whines. "Ask Mrs. Zanfino to watch him while you're at work, she's already home with her litter of brats. What the hell am *I* going to do with him?"

"Put him out with the garbage. What do I care? I want him outta my house."

"I can't take him! I don't even know what to *feed* him! It's not like he's a real person!" Marian is about to start screeching, her voice is thinning with angry horror. "And we don't have furniture. I don't have a bed for him!"

"You don't got a bed? You don't got a bed?" Sal yells. "How 'bout the bed you whored in, you go get *that* one! I don't take care of your bastard no more, you understand me? You lucky I let Marie . . ."

"*Lucky?!*" Marian doesn't much care what her father calls the pest, but she never reacts well to him calling her a whore. "Fuck! You! I'd rather be a whore than a hypocrite, you miserable son of a bitch! If you think I'm a whore and the kid's a bastard, why didn't you just let me get rid of him, like I asked you to? He was a stupid fucking *accident,* a broken condom, I never wanted him! I *begged* you!"

"Go on! You want rid of him so bad, so get rid of him! Dump him, like your whore of a mother she dump you. But not here, not on me!"

Scott has been sitting on the couch, sipping his water, staying out of it, while his hot lunatic girlfriend and her righteous caveman father go at it. Every few seconds his eyes dart out toward the hallway. Now he stands up and hisses, "Marian, for Christ's sake, the kid's right outside in the hall. What the hell's the matter with you?"

She whirls on him with black gimlet eyes, shows him her fine

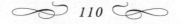

white teeth, and snarls like a hyena. "What the hell's the matter with *you?* He's not your goddamned kid."

"No," Scott snaps. "He's *your* goddamned kid. You don't throw away your kid."

Scott spins on the heels of his scuffed cowboy boots and stalks out of the room.

CHRISTOPHER IS HUNCHED UP, CHEWING on his lips, and sobbing into the wall. Scott kneels down in front of him, puts his bony hands on Christopher's shoulders, gives him a little shake.

"Hey, Chrissie, look at me."

Christopher turns his tear-soaked face to Scott. "Am I going into the garbage?"

Scott winces. "No man. You're coming home with me and your mom. Nobody meant that. They're just angry, and your mom's aunt just died . . . you know. But listen. Don't you worry, buddy. Everything's cool. Scott's going to take good care of you from now on, okay?"

When Christopher doesn't answer, just looks at Scott through puffy red and blue eyes, Scott shakes him again, says, "Okay?"

Christopher nods.

Marian is at the foot of the stairs, peering over Scott's shoulder. "Oh fuck me. Saint Scott." She heaves a dramatic sigh. "Okay. Let's get the hell out of here."

Scott lifts Christopher off the stairs. Christopher clamps his arms around Scott's neck, his legs around his waist, and clings fast.

Marian trails after them to Scott's vintage '64 Mustang. At the curb, she turns and shouts back at Sal, who's bristling in the doorway. "And I want that fucking piano! You hear me? It was my mother's. It belongs to me!"

Marian hurls herself into the passenger seat, whips around to-ward the back, and screams at Christopher, "What the holy fuck are you still crying about! Shut . . . up!"

"That's enough, babe. Calm down. Leave the kid alone."

Marian glowers at Christopher for one last maniacally satisfying moment, then deflates into the leather bucket seat like a spent bal-loon. He wants to do what she asks but he just can't stop crying, no matter how hard he tries. The best he can do is bury his face in his arms so she won't have to hear or see him.

Part Two

GRAVITATION

. . . the natural phenomenon by which objects with mass, living or non, attract one another.

Sir Isaac Newton posited gravitation to be one of the four fundamental cosmic "forces," its strength dependent upon the mass of the objects and their distance from one another. Two centuries later, Albert Einstein advanced Newton's theory of gravitation, hypothesizing that attraction is not a force, but rather an effect of the curvature of space-time on free-falling objects.

However one chooses to conceive or perceive it, as a natural force or a cosmic intervention, it is a fact that gravitation holds the universe and everything in it together. But, as with electromagnetism and so many other natural phenomena, no one can explain how attraction actually works. Or how, when we free-fall into love, we can blaze in the furnace of the sun and freeze in the coldness of space all at once.

Seven

A SNOOTY-FACED KID OPENED THE door. He had a white cable-knit sweater tied around his narrow shoulders over a pink polo shirt, like he was on his way to the yacht club, and was head to toe ridiculously overdressed for a warm September day. One hand was holding a book, that Harry Potter novel it seemed every single kid in the city was toting around since a few months ago, and he wore a pair of round black-framed glasses identical to the Potter character on the cover. He pushed his blond baby-yachtsman's hair off his forehead with his free hand, looked me over, and with a sour mouth and jutting jaw twisting up his pretty mug said, "Oh. Who are you?"

"I'm Ms. Landreth's eleven o'clock. You just leaving?" I smiled angelically. "Have a peachy day then, sailor . . ." I moved aside to let him out. I could live in a world without kids, no problem.

Ella materialized behind him, put her hands on his shoulders, her cheek against his temple. He wiggled his head away and turned red.

"Evan, this is Jody, my new . . . student. I told you about him the other day. He's a friend of Aunt Tess." She raised her head. "Good morning, Jody. This is my son, Evan."

Evan and I stared at each other. It was neck and neck as to which one of us was more alarmed. He was maybe seven or eight and had a kid's prissy equivalent of my mental *oh fuck* in his eyes. He had interesting eyes, actually, behind his trendy glasses. Amber colored, gooey soft like butterscotch, I could see him working them, trying to get them to harden up, form a shell, like mine, as he beetled up his brows and scowled at me.

"Jody's a girl's name."

Ella looked pained. "It can be either, Evan."

A horn sounded from the street. Evan's eyes popped, he peered past me, then wrenched himself from under Ella's hand, ran into the apartment, came back lugging a duffel, launched himself through the brownstone's door and down the stone stairs. Still holding on to that book.

Ella called out, "Hey, how about a kiss good-bye?" just as the man behind the wheel stuck his head out the window and yelled, "Move it, Evan, we don't have all day!" It was the rude guy.

The kid jerked to a halt, looked back at Ella like a deer trapped between dueling sets of headlights. She beamed at him, a smile big enough for two. "Go. Have fun. Call me tonight."

Evan staggered on down, ran to the car, started to open the rear door. The rude guy barked, "In the trunk, Evan, in the trunk!" Evan ran to the trunk, hoisted his bag inside, slid into the passenger seat, the car moving down the block before he'd even had a chance to buckle his seat belt.

I'd slipped into the entry hall while this show was going on. Ella closed the brownstone door, sagged against it. Her ex hadn't even glanced at her. She pushed herself upright, turned, walked past me. I followed her into the apartment, into the high-ceilinged front room, and shut the door behind me. There I was, on the other side of the windows I'd skated or biked by, slowed down to look through from the outside, maybe a thousand times over the past ten years. And there was the piano, a big gorgeous Knabe music room grand, its walnut finish gleaming as bright as it did thirty years ago. In Tess's photo of Matt. It was the piano he'd been sitting at when that picture was taken, but in a different room now.

The wood floor was mostly covered by a genteelly faded Persian carpet and the far wall by built-in bookshelves. Ella crossed the room and perched on the shelves' shallow waist-high ledge, hugging her arms to her body, looking like she wasn't quite ready to deal with me. I stayed by the door. Neither of us seemed to know what to say.

I went to the piano, ran my hand over the polished warmth of the wood. "Great piano."

"Thank you. It was Tess's originally. She gave it to me ten years ago, as a wedding present. She hadn't touched it in years. Her hands . . ." Ella held up her own hands, bent her fingers into sad soft claws.

I looked out the window, then around the room. "You know, I have to tell you, it's a little weird, being here. I live in the East Village but I like to skate or bike along the Hudson. I've been down this block so many times, seen your garden, and the piano, wondered who lived here. . . ."

"Well, I guess you were meant to find out."

"Yeah. Here I am." My fingers wandered down to the piano keys.

Now Ella looked out the window, then back at me. "Not the most relaxed way to start our first lesson, is it? I'm sorry you had to see that, and I apologize for Evan's rudeness. He's a lovely boy, he really is, but his father makes him frantic. Ronald was supposed to pick him up at ten thirty. *He's* half an hour late and he yells at Evan. He spends so little time with him as it is. He's such a jackass."

"Not the world's best parent, your ex, I gather."

"No. Not the best. He was so excited to be a father, but he is so intolerant, so unforgiving. Nothing Evan does is ever good enough. He reads too much, he's clumsy, he's a sissy, he's too small for his age, like that's his fault, or mine. . . ." She was working up a real head of steam,

but stopped herself before she started to smoke. She dropped her arms and let her hands come together loosely on her thighs. "Well. I guess he can't help it, Ronald's exactly like his own father."

"Doesn't look like old Ronald's too pleased with you, either."

She twisted up her mouth and grunted out a laugh. "You think? Seven years—and he's been remarried to his perfect mate, the cold-blooded Cheryl, for five—and he's still angry with me for divorcing him."

Her jokey smile turned sad and serious.

"Anyway. I'm sorry. Just give Evan a little time, he has issues with adult males. He could use some kinder ones in his life."

"Whatever. I'm not all that comfortable with kids, maybe we should just stay out of each other's way."

The look on her face told me loud and clear that my solution was not the one she'd had in mind.

"What does that mean, you're not comfortable with kids? You're not that old, Jody, don't you remember what it felt like, wanting the approval of your parents when you were little? If you . . . if we . . . if you . . . think you might be . . . spending time here, you know . . ." We were both squirming where we stood, the question of why we were even in the same space together a ton lump of unformed clay in the middle of the carpet. "All I'm asking is that you be nice to him. I know I'm overprotective, and it's probably not always such a good thing. But he's only nine years old. Okay? Can you do that?"

"Yeah, sure, of course, you're right." What was I supposed to say? "And for what it's worth, I think it's a good thing, you being protective of him, I mean." I put my hand on the flat wood surface to the right of the piano's music stand. "It must make Tess happy that you have the piano now."

"Yes, it does. It makes me happy, too."

The area of wood surface was small and the edge of my hand fetched up against the frame of the photograph there. I bent to look

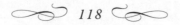

at it. It was a picture of Ella and Matt. It was taken on a beach, in sun but in cold weather, they're bundled up against a wind I could almost feel, blowing their hair around their adolescent faces, he's behind her, his arms full and hard around her, she's melting into him. They're not smiling, but two more blissed-out people never existed.

"I should never have married Ronald. It was so unfair to him. He's right to be angry." Ella had come up alongside me. Her soft voice was practically in my ear.

"I can see why. I'm really sorry."

"You notice things, don't you?" There was the trace of a smile on her lips. "Behind those wary eyes of yours, you notice everything."

"Oh yeah. I notice things. Like I notice I'm not learning to play the piano yet."

She laughed. "All right, I can take a hint. This hour is now devoted to you. So. A-I-S, mister."

"What's that?"

"Ass In Seat. Step one of every lesson."

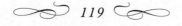

I WAS SURPRISED BY MY feet banging against the pedals. The last time I sat at a piano, my feet didn't reach the floor. I adjusted the bench and then let my fingers come to rest on the keys. They fell into place, right thumb on middle C, just like that. It was weird, how familiar it felt, even with my fingers now able to stretch a full octave, and more, easily. There was a yellow-covered Schirmer primer of beginners' Haydn sonatas open on the stand. Even after all these years, I could read it, I could read the notes, I could hear them in my head, and while Ella rifled through the stack of music books on the shelves for *Piano for Dummies,* or whatever she used for the likes of me, I started to play, slow and unsure, picking my way, my hands and fingers stiff and clumsy. But I was playing.

I'd forgotten how being inside music is pure and beautiful the way being inside math is pure and beautiful. Intervals and beats and rhythms and null spaces in between and relationships between notes and the layering of chords and making everything fit like putting together a seemingly silent puzzle and then it all falls into place and you've got the music of the spheres in your ears, in your head. The truth of the cosmos.

"Soften your wrists, Jody."

Ella was behind me, a little to one side, looking over my shoulder. I willed my muscles to loosen up, but they wouldn't, not with her so close, watching me.

"Don't think. You're rusty, but the memory is there, in your body. Just relax and let your fingers remember. Here."

She reached around me, took my right wrist in her right hand, her thumb on top, at the juncture of my wrist and hand, her fingers underneath, spread across my palm. She moved my hand up and down, to release the tension there. It was only what she undoubtedly did with every beginner she'd ever taught, using her hand as a teaching tool, but I felt her fingers tremble on my skin, and my pulse throb beneath her fingers. The memories let go and the stiffness in my wrist gave way.

She stepped back. "That's better. Start from the beginning now."

After a few minutes, she sat down on the end of the bench. "How long has it been?"

"Twenty years. A little more."

"Why did you say you didn't know how to play?"

"I didn't say I didn't know *how* to play. I just said I didn't play."

She smirked at me. "Congratulations. You're multitalented. You can play sports, piano, spot-the-rotten-parent, and word games. Let's try again. Why didn't you say you could play?"

I put my head down on my arms and laughed. "I don't know. It was a long time ago, I forgot. It wasn't something I thought I'd ever do again. Why do you want to teach me?"

"Because Tess suggested it for you, and I trust her instincts about what people need."

Tess had suggested it for both of us, if you were going to be accurate, but I *noticed* Ella didn't say that.

"Oh yeah? You do? So, did Tess suggest you marry Ronald? Is he what she thought you needed?"

I seemed to be doing an uncharacteristic amount of all manner of things without thinking lately. My blood was yammering in my ears and when the muscles in her jaw bunched so did my stomach. But then her mouth turned up in a touché kind of smile.

"Hardly. She told me to wait for someone who made me feel the way Matt had. Sometimes I think she gave me this piano so I'd be reminded of that daily. She has her ways, that woman."

"That she does." I tilted my head toward the windows, toward the lingering meanness of the morning's scene just outside. "I guess she was right. Why didn't you wait?"

"Because it was never going to happen. I didn't want to love anyone the way I'd loved Matt, I just wanted him back, and I couldn't bring myself to get over it. But I . . . something happened when I was in my thirties and I . . . I wanted a child . . . and Ronald was . . ." She faltered, faded off into some private memory. She played her fingers over the keys up there in the high treble zone, they moved like water leaping over shallowly covered stones, and the sound was like something dancing stars might make. "It wasn't all bad, Ronald can be quite charming and we had a lot of interests in common. And now I have Evan. But yes, she was right." She stopped fooling with the piano and looked at me. "I'm glad you decided to do it, to take lessons."

"Me too." I smiled.

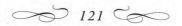

Her face changed, became defenseless, like the face of the girl in the photograph. "You have his smile. You realize that, don't you, you saw it in the photo in Tess's room? As if someone has just confused you, or frightened or thrilled you so deeply you don't know whether you're going to live or die."

An astonishingly accurate summation of my state of mind for half my life, present moment included. As succinct and jolting as a crack across the face. And the minute she said it, I felt my smile for the first time the way it must really look, that same disturbing smile of Matt's on my own mouth.

I tried to even it out, form it into something jolly. "Yeah, I'm not all that smart, I get confused fairly easily."

Her eyes flashed. "Don't do that. Don't talk about yourself that way, it's not funny."

"I'm sorry." I looked away, took my hands off the keys, stayed still. Now I really had angered her.

I stretched out my left arm to futz with the music book. Ella was on my right. She blinked fast a few times, then her eyes opened wide and made a slow sweep from my hand to my shoulder, took in the crooked fingertips and dented nail beds, scar bundle on the inside of the wrist, long ragged scar on the forearm, crescent of pink puckered flesh barely peeking out the sleeve edge of my black T-shirt. She was adding it all up, in her smart mature complex-kind-of-woman brain.

"Why did you stop playing? You have a gift for it. And you enjoy it, I can tell."

"I did, enjoy it, but then I stopped enjoying it so I stopped playing." I hunched over the keyboard, put my hands between my knees.

"Jody, I'm sorry. I had no right to criticize you before, about Evan. Maybe you actually understand him better than you let on . . . ?"

She wasn't angry with me. The vise around my chest unscrewed and I took a breath.

She waited, but when I didn't give her anything more she said, "In any case, I spoke thoughtlessly, and I apologize."

I lifted my head. "No, it's fine. You were right. I remember what it felt like." I longed to wade out into the green ocean of her eyes until the surface was miles above me. It wouldn't do for her to see that. I looked past her, at the picture. "How did he end up over there?"

She watched my face a moment, then followed my eyes. "Because he wanted Steven—his father—to be *proud* of him." More than a little hint of bitterness there. "Steven was in World War Two." She turned back to me with a quick bright smile, the diverting memory of something nice in her eyes. "That's how he and Tess met. Steven was with the American army forces that liberated Italy. He was wandering around Rome one afternoon, and got lost, and Tess saw him poring over a map and asked if he needed help. She told him later how handsome and heroic he looked to her. How reassuringly American." She laughed. "And he, he was struck dumb the moment he saw her, hit by the thunderbolt." She sighed. "He loved to tell that story. He must have told it to me a hundred times after Matt died. In any case, he'd been a willing soldier, he thought men should be men. Not poets, not pianists . . ."

I looked closer at Matt's image in the photo, his face, his eyes, his body language, imagined that now I recognized the tension, the shadow of resignation, the anticipation of collapse behind his bliss.

"Yeah, sons will definitely do stupid things to please their fathers. I guess you and Steven didn't get along all that well."

"No, we got along fine. I know how that sounded, but Steven was really a very dear man. He worshiped Tess and Matt, and I think what he loved most about them, although he could never have said so, was how different they were from him, from the entire culture of America after the war. Tess with that indescribable otherworldly spirituality of hers. Matt with his passion for his music, and his moodiness. Steven lived in the present. He was a pragmatist and a patriot. An optimistic, modern-thinking businessman, the proud owner of Fischer and Sons Appliances of Yorkville."

Ella's affection for him came through the mockery, but even if he was a good guy, I couldn't see Tess married to someone who didn't get what made her her. Like I couldn't see Ella married to Ronald. Tess hadn't been able to, either, and I'd have bet the farm it was because Steven hadn't been the love of Tess's life. I hadn't seen any pictures of him in her room.

"So what happened? Matt enlisted so his father would think he was man?"

"No." Ella shook her head, like she still couldn't believe what she was about to say. "Matt was drafted, in the 1969 lottery. His birthday was December seventh, and December seventh drew number twelve. December eighth came up a hundred and five. He was born at eleven thirty-three p.m. If he'd waited just half an hour more to come into the world, he'd have been safe, he'd still be alive. It was bad luck, cruel Fate, who can ever know. Tess and I wanted him to go to Canada. With me. And he would have, except he believed his father would hate him for running away. Steven never encouraged him to enlist, but once he was drafted . . . It was so sad, really. Steven lost his faith in everything after Matt died. He just . . . faded away. He lived another ten years, but he was never the same." She turned to me with a wry smile. "I should have tried harder, I should have forced him to go with me." There was a miserably helpless shimmer in her eyes and all I could do was look at her glassy-eyed. "What? Jody, what's the matter?"

"His birthday was December seventh?"

"Yes. Why, what . . ."

Confused, frightened, and thrilled unto the brink of death. Was Tess right? *Was* I him? Or even partly him?

"That's *my* birthday, too. December seventh. I was born the night of December seventh, nineteen seventy, eleven-oh-eight." I barked out a laugh. "Bizarro, right? I mean, not that it means anything. It's stupid. Forget it. It's nothing. What happened to him, that's what's important. Don't blame yourself. You couldn't have forced him. I'm not just saying that. It's true."

Her mouth opened but all that came out was an involuntary gasp. Our eyes locked. We'd unconsciously moved closer, our knees were touching. I wanted to kiss her. I wanted to rest my head on her breast. I wanted to do both. I couldn't know what she wanted, what she was feeling, my own fear and desire were so strong they were all I could see in her eyes.

The doorbell rang.

It was her next pupil, an excited little girl with a cute friendly face, in baggy denim overalls and a red I Heart Poodles shirt. She was holding her father's wedding ring–less left hand and levitating out of her sandals, and her handsome father was smiling at Ella with irritating familiarity, and like he wanted to take a big juicy bite out of her. He introduced himself and his daughter as we crossed paths on the stoop. Dr. Alex Chase, of the firm slow handshake and steady observant dark trust-me eyes that took their time assessing me and seemed to radiate an immediate understanding of who and what I was, and Kaylee. I could spot therapist types, everything and anything from psychoanalysts to chakra aligners, with the same accuracy and from about the same distance as my Dominicans and their hot women. Dr. Chase was a psychiatrist. He appeared to be a warm, genuinely reassuring kind of guy and I'd bet a month's salary that he was great at his job. I had no reason not to like him, but I can't say that I did.

Eight

ELLA'S APARTMENT WAS A DUPLEX, the bed-
rooms on the second floor. When she let me in the next Saturday, Evan came clattering down the stairs. On the way
over, because Ella had asked me to, I'd given myself a pep talk regard-
ing my lack of rapport with small two-legged creatures. At least with
regards to this particular one. She must have told Evan to do the same
with me. We gave each other cautious hi's, and he came out of the apartment into the entry as I took off my Rollerblades. I asked him if he liked
to skate. His lower lip vanished; he shook his head and pushed his
glasses up his nose. Ella was behind him. She waved her hands in distress, got an anxious look around her eyes, and mouthed, *"Ronald tried
to teach him. He fell and . . ."* She shook her head.

He stayed in the room with us the whole time, curled into a big
chair in a corner, making like he was reading that book. He'd have
been more convincing if he'd turned a page once in a while. His eyes
darted around like goldfish at the slightest movement of my head in
his direction. It was pretty obvious he was sizing me up, but not with
that same feeling as last time, like why else would I be there except to
steal the silver. Maybe he was just trying to make sense of me as a
friend of Tess and his mother. Understandable. Whatever the reason, I
didn't mind it, and with him there Ella and I had to concentrate on the

music. There wasn't a lot of conversation, which suited me fine, just her close to me on the bench, our arms and legs touching, our fingers gently bumping, and the music we made together.

Evan hung in the doorway while I sat on the top step of the stoop and put my Rollerblades back on. He said, "I'm sorry I said that about your name."

"It's cool, I could see you were under pressure."

"Yeah." His voice timid, a little up at the end, half a question, like the pressure was still on him and did I have any suggestions on how to get it off. I did have one, but although an adult person thought it okay to suggest it to me as a way of rectifying less-than-stellar parenting when I was about his age, I had since concluded it was a bit extreme and not really the kind of thing you want to suggest to a kid unless you were a minion of the devil. "But, you know, I did hear my mom tell someone on the phone that you had eyelashes like a girl." He was trying every which way to let me know how sorry he was.

I stood up and grinned down at him. "Yeah, I've gotten that a few times. Or like a giraffe. Which do you think?" I stretched my neck and eyes, pushed my ears out with my fingers. Suddenly, I was a comedian. But the kid really did look in bad need of entertainment and Ella was quietly watching us from the apartment doorway.

"A giraffe! A giraffe! A blue-eyed giraffe!!" He broke up laughing, so hard he fell against the side of the door. "Jody the Giraffe!" He hooted and flopped his way down to the floor, holding his sides.

Watching that was like taking a punch to the throat. On the other hand, it was the most, and most fun, conversation I'd probably ever had with someone under the age of sixteen.

I suggested then that maybe they'd come to Central Park the next afternoon, join the spectators for the softball game. Tess would be there, I was going to pick her up, and if they wanted to come early we could toss a ball or a Frisbee around for a while, have dinner after. Evan stopped laughing, twisted up his puss again, and said, "Whatever," but Ella came out onto the stoop, smiled, and said, "Thank you, Jody, we'll be there." She put her hand on my shoulder and kissed me on the cheek and if Evan hadn't been there, gawking up at her like she'd budded a second head, I might have done something stupid.

Kaylee arrived just as I was about to push off, this time delivered by her also unringed mother. When Kaylee saw Evan, she scrambled up the stairs like there was a pot of gold at the top, calling out, "Hi, Evan!" then stood there worshiping at him. Evan was so flustered he turned into his dad on the spot; he frowned at her and grunted something that sounded vaguely like her name, then stomped into the apartment. Kaylee trotted after him, unfazed, bright-eyed, chirping away about some school thing.

✳

I PUT THE CAR IN a garage on Central Park South and we walked into the park at the Seventh Avenue entrance, just south of the ball fields. I juggled my gear and a folding chair and umbrella for Tess while she took charge of Einstein, who without needing to be told—ahead of me again—had tucked away her hunter's instinct to chase every squirrel in sight gibbering up a tree and was walking patiently by Tess's side. Apparently it wasn't too late for either of us to lift ourselves from the murk of our involuntary urges and take on some new civilized behaviors.

It was a perfect day for softball. For anything. Warm sun, cool crisp air, the smell of autumn decay on the wind, sweet and wistful. The diamond light etched clean lines around everything, every leaf, every blade of grass. On the far north field, orange-shirted junior high school kids chased a soccer ball over the emerald lawn. They stood out so clear it was as if you were seeing them through a telescope. In that light, the softball was going to seem the size of a small sun and spin in slow motion and I was going to hit or catch anything thrown or batted at me.

My muscles were already firing. It was going to be one of those rare out-of-your-skull days. And Ella was there to see me.

There'd been another Sunday like this one soon after I'd moved into the city, an amazing fall day here on this same field. I was playing in a fast and rough soccer game, and toward the end, as things got wild and messy, I got tripped up and went down hard with two guys on top of me. I couldn't see anything past the dust particles churning around my face, into my mouth and eyes. My ears were ringing and a headache was blooming in my right temple. I lay in that familiar daze, waiting for my body to reassemble itself, and in that moment, for the first time, I realized something I hadn't in ten years with the Kowalczyks. I realized that I'd survived. I was alive. I wasn't a child anymore. I was free. My body did only what I told it to do. Scott was gone, no one was ever going to hurt me that way again. I was two months shy of nineteen. Time had always moved so slowly for me I had no sense of what nineteen translated to in human terms and I couldn't conceive of living another ten years. All I knew was that I was as whole as I needed to be right then, whole enough to get up off the ground, kick the winning goal, and go home with one of the girls arrayed on the lawn every week like flowers there to be plucked.

I hadn't thought about that moment since, but it came spinning back to me as Tess and I crossed onto the southern edge of the fields and I saw Ella and Evan hurrying in from the west side, Ella waving. Then all at once I saw Arwen and another Coronet waitress giggling in from the east, Arwen waving. I heard a shouted "Jody! Wait up!" from behind me, and turned to see Brendan, who hadn't said a thing about coming to the game when I'd had dinner with him on Tuesday, and Fern passing the playground, Fern waving.

I stopped, caught in the crosshairs of too many magnified eyes, then seemed to see, coming toward me from the north where there'd been no one but the soccer kids in the distance, a shadowed specter of myself, of the unimaginable me I was going to become on December 7 when I turned twenty-nine, the age Scott was when he started with me. And I felt myself splinter, fragment into an infinity of funhouse mirror images, no real me among them. It had happened often enough before, and it lasted no more than a second—by the time everyone converged on me I'd reassembled into a working image—but this time I knew myself to be anything but as whole as I needed to be.

BRENDAN AND FERN WERE FIRST to reach me by a nose, and spared me the potential pitfalls of having to introduce anyone— as in, Ella, I'd like you to meet Arwen, who I swear is not my girlfriend although she's going to say she is because I'm sleeping with her; Arwen, this is Ella, the woman I've been moving toward my entire life but I'm afraid I'll never get near enough to and that's the only reason I'm sleeping with you. Yeah, that would have gone over really well—because Brendan dropped his bag, opened his arms wide, shouted out, "She said yes!" and bear-hugged me. "It's a miracle, Jody. She said yes!" His throat was clotted with emotion.

"Didn't I tell you she would? It's no miracle, you're a great guy. Just be happy with her." I held on to him for a while. I wanted this to be a good thing. Even with the bond between us weakening, him shifting his protective allegiance to Fern, me accelerating past the Kowalczyks into a future their love couldn't alter any more than it could my past, Brendan would always be my best friend, my brother.

Fern let me hug her and didn't turn her head away when I kissed her cheek. She actually smiled, then raised her left hand. A diamond engagement ring with the relative-to-finger proportions of a Volkswagen Beetle sent shards of sunlight flying through the air and drew all the females into an oohing, aahing, barking circle around her, leaving us guys on the sidelines.

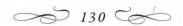

"Fern looks radiantly happy, or maybe she's just in shock at the thought of a lifetime with you." I squinted at her. She was flushed, her smile was sheepish, a little wacky, and her hair was disheveled. "I don't know her well enough to tell."

"She's a little drunk is what she is. We had some champagne to celebrate. She can't hold her liquor. It's so adorable. Doesn't she look cute drunk?"

"As a button."

Arwen had her back to me. She offered her hand to Ella. "Hi, I'm Arwen? Jody's girlfriend? And you are . . . ?" Ella gave her a stupendous smile and said, "Ah. I'm Ella. His . . . piano teacher." I tried to grab her attention over Arwen's head, shaking my head like mad, but Ella wouldn't look at me.

Fern lurched daintily to Brendan's side, linked her arm in his, reclined into him like he was a lamppost.

"Jody, Jody, Jody. We really must get to know one another now." The alcohol had done more than put some color in her face and poof up her hair. It had loosened her, stoked some ordinarily extinguished part of her, she was radiating sparks in the duck-and-cover way people who don't know they have any fire in them radiate sparks. "You'll come to dinner soon. The weekend after next. And you'll bring . . . Arlen, Arlene . . . ?"

"Arwen. It's a name from *Lord of the Rings*."

"Huh? But okay. Ar-wen. That's a pretty name. Bring her. She seems like she'd be a lot of fun." She sounded sincere, and her words were the right ones, but her glittery unblinking eyes and foxy smile said something different and made me think that Fern would have fun, slicing and dicing me and Arwen into a tasty main course, but it wouldn't be such a good time for anyone else.

"She'll be working, but I'll bring someone else fun. I've got an entire closet full." What the hell, it was only what she already thought of me.

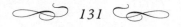

"Yes, go into your toy chest and pick out something sparkly." She shot me a look and went back to the ladies.

I didn't know what it was with us, but Fern and I definitely did not bring out the best in one another.

This time Brendan noticed, but typically, he noticed the way he wanted to. Wrong. "Wow, I'm so glad you two like each other. Fern's only funny around people she's really comfortable with. You're very quippy together. Like Tracy and Hepburn. Very amusing."

"We're a riot."

Evan had moved away; he was standing off by himself, looking at me. I mouthed, "Giraffe." His face cracked open and he clamped his hands over his mouth.

"Listen, Brendan, I'm sorry, but I had no idea, and I'm here with people. I promised that kid over there I'd play ball with him before the game starts . . ."

"Oh." Brendan hadn't even been aware of anyone but Fern and me. He looked at Evan, bent over giggling, then at the women still huddled together. "Oh, yeah, look at them all. Since when do you know that many people?"

I knew what he meant by that, it wasn't an insult or anything. "No kidding. Since a few weeks ago. I don't know if I like it."

"They look harmless. Who are they? Which is the one you're sleeping with?" Brendan laughed, nodded toward Tess. "Or, should I ask, which is the one you're *not* sleeping with. All the others are babes. What a surprise. Yeah, go on. I'll catch you later."

Tess had taken hold of Arwen's hand. "Hello darling! I'm Tess, Jody's godmother. I'm sorry, I don't remember him mentioning you. How long have the two of you been together?"

"We're kinda new. A couple weeks?"

Tess patted Arwen's hand the way the nice nurse does while the mean doctor jabs a humongous needle into your rear end, gave out with a loaded "Mmmm," and everybody got the message: *Oh well then, dear, you're not quite his girlfriend, are you?*

Arwen turned, disagreeing eyes searching for her constant Aragorn in shining armor to leap to her defense. Her eyes were blurred with tears. I looked right past her.

Tess's little act had got Ella to look at me. It was like the other week at Parkside, but this time neither of us could laugh it off, pretend we didn't understand what Tess was doing. *She has her ways, that woman.* She wanted us to be together, in some unspecified but very definite way, and she was asking us to trust her. Trust was not something I did particularly well. It was a wee tad more complicated than sports, or math, or even camouflage technique. Even when my head tried to tell me it was okay, I couldn't go there. I'd been wrong so many times, I couldn't trust myself.

EINSTEIN MADE IT TO EVAN before I did. She was howdy-licking his hand with monumental canine devotion and an equivalent amount of drool. He'd stopped giggling. He was rigid, afraid to move. He was probably scared of everything, what with a bully of a father and a worrier of a mother. I wouldn't have thought so, but maybe you could protect your kid too much.

"Hey, Einstein really likes you." I scratched Einstein's rump. "You can go ahead and touch her if you want, she loves people."

He held his breath and put a tentative wet hand on her head. She nuzzled into his leg. His whole skinny body seemed to melt. "Hi, Einstein."

He looked up at me. Behind their half-stunned, half-triumphant glaze his eyes were sunny puddles, spinning with happiness. It might have been me, my hand not on the head of a dog but on the cool metal of a brand-new green Schwinn. I shunted my gaze to Einstein's eyes, took a few breaths, and reminded myself how upset with me Ella would be if I bolted on him.

I gritted out the next twenty minutes, trying to explain to Evan that if he didn't look *away* from the ball like it was a car wreck about to happen every time it got lobbed at him, he might actually catch it. Of course I was doing the same thing with the loaded glances being lobbed at me by four sets of women's eyes. But then, I badly didn't want to catch anybody's attention and I had to assume Evan badly did want to catch the ball. In my life, I didn't remember ever praying harder for a softball game to get started. Not even that time in fourth grade, another dazzling warm fall day, when I made the rare mistake of forgetting and taking off my long-sleeved Yankees jersey, folding it and laying it on the bench, turning around to see Miss O'Reilly staring through her red bangs at the bandage on my left biceps, and having to melt into the long afternoon shadows, keep sliding away from her moist green-eyed pursuit for an endless fifteen minutes before we were finally allowed onto the field.

Nine

"IT IS EXHAUSTING, WATCHING YOU play ball."

"Really? Why? It's just a friendly game, I don't even give it my all."

Tess was having trouble wrestling the seat belt into its clip. Her weakened hands shook from the effort to hang on while she tried to fit the pieces together. I moved to help her.

"Stop that, I can do it." She slapped my hand away. "Yes, that's what I mean. I am *exhausted* from watching you reining yourself in." She poked a finger into four different spots on my arm, as if she was measuring the consistency of my flesh. "Where do you keep it? All the joy, all the skill? I know it's in there, somewhere. Exhausting. So now I'm famished. What are we doing for dinner?"

"Dinner? Am I nuts, or didn't you just tell everyone you were too tired for dinner."

"I had to rescue you. What should I have said? So sorry, but we have to leave, Jody is overwhelmed, he can't manage all of us at once?"

I'd given up getting rattled by Tess, by her excavations of the abnormalities and shortcomings of my personality, her pronouncements about the past and present, or even about the future. For one thing, she was always right. But also, there was something about the way her observations came out of her, unapologetic, no judgments attached, no explanation, that made the things she said feel like indescribably perfect gifts.

I laid my head against the headrest. "God. What is wrong with me?"

"*Niente.*" She touched the back of her hand to my cheek. Her skin felt dry and delicate as parchment, like a butterfly brushing against me. "The girl, Arwen. She's an angel, but you know she's not yours, leave her alone. That Fern on the other hand"—she tsked a few times—"she has demons with her, and your brother, he's not strong like you. Be careful." She took her hand away, settled into the seat. "I think maybe hot dogs, no?"

"Oh man, yeah. And fries. We need Nathan's." It was hard to beat a serious dose of fat, starch, and salt for managing your angels and demons. I straightened up and started the car.

Forty minutes later we were on a bench on the Coney Island boardwalk, looking south out over the deep powdery white sand beach at the darkening Atlantic, on the right the Jersey shore stretching away into invisibility, on the left the dream of far-off Europe, of an older maybe wiser world, hovering in the mists of an endless ocean. Cardboard boxes on our laps filled with the best hot dogs and fries in the city. We ate without talking for a while, as the eastern sky slowly became night, and the pink orange and gold of the setting sun torched the western shoreline, as the lights along the boardwalk and in Astroland started to blaze, and the seagulls dived for fish and crumbs of human food, their shrill screams not much different from the shrieks of the happily terrorized kids riding the Cyclone roller coaster a few blocks away. I'd bought plenty. We took turns biting off small pieces of meat and feeding them to Einstein.

Tess ate one last fry, wiped her fingers. "Thank you. The perfect dinner." I smiled my agreement. "*Bel ragazzo.* Beautiful boy. How did you get that scar at your mouth?"

"A hockey puck." Said with a *so it goes* grin.

My automatic response. I'd been asked that question so many times I didn't have to think about what to say. I'd played hockey since I was in grade school. Hockey was a dangerous game. Guys got slammed with pucks and sticks and skates all the time. You could get a scar that way. I could have gotten my scar that way. It had stopped sounding or even feeling like a lie a long time ago, but it felt like one when I said it to Tess and she answered with a rueful little smile. I didn't want to lie to her. I'd hammered it into insensibility, but I was still a few blows short of having clubbed to death my baby-seal desire to trust someone. I was going to tell her the truth sooner or later—there was a metallic taste on my tongue and the memory of that night was starting to imprint itself on the inside of my eyelids—just not yet, and not like this, not out loud.

"How about some ice cream to cut all this grease?"

She handed me what was left of her feast. "You are a very, very bad boy. Vanilla for me, *per favore.*"

When I got back with her dessert—mine had gone into the garbage after a bite; I loved ice cream but every so often it just wouldn't go down—Tess was sitting at the end of the bench, her head turned to the east, absentmindedly stroking Einstein's head. Literally absentmindedly it looked like. I took the lid off the paper cup, stuck the small flat wooden spoon in it, and put it on her lap. She looked down at it, then up at me. If you'd offered me a million dollars I still couldn't describe the look in her eyes.

"You were gone so long! I was afraid I'd lost you again."

I'd been gone about five minutes. "Tess? It's me, Jody. Where are you?" I put my arm around her shoulder. "Tess? You okay?"

I felt a tremor travel up her spine and neck. I saw her eyes change, saw her pull herself back to reality, and it was like watching myself, in the park, pulling the splintered pieces of myself back together. It was a relief, but sad because I could tell how much happier she'd been in that other place.

"Were you thinking of Matt?"

"No, not Matt. A boy from long before I was Tess Fischer. When I was still Tessa Parenti. His name was Teo. Timoteo Doria." She sang the name, like out of an Italian opera.

"Tell me about him." Timoteo Doria. Tessa Parenti. Italian names could be so pretty sometimes.

"Yes, you see, I told you, you give me your memories and I give you mine." She ate some of her ice cream. "Can Einstein have this?"

I shrugged. "Sure, life is short." She gave me the cup and I put it down on the ground.

"Teo." She shook her head and gave out a pained sound. "The last time I was with him was April of 1940. We'd gone for the day to Sorrento. We sat on a bench by the sea at sunset and kissed."

Tess's lost love.

She patted my knee. "Don't be scandalized; it was all right, we'd been engaged for a dozen years already. He'd woven a ring for me out of straw, one day when we were playing in the loft of his family's barn. We were eight. Even as a child, he had the most exquisite, dexterous fingers." She sighed, remembering. "We knew everything about each other. We planned to marry when the war ended. We were young, and ignorant, we thought love would keep him safe. He died that June, in the Battle of France. I woke up that morning, and I knew. That was the first time I'd ever known something in that way, something I could not possibly have known. It was as if Teo had reached out to me as he died and taken a piece of me with him. Ever since, there is an opening in me and I see things, feel things I cannot explain." She turned to look at me. She smiled. "You won't die in June."

I had the chance, once, to die at a moment when the air was hot

and the sun shone on green trees, but I blew it. I was going to die in cold and dark. "No, I don't expect to."

"Thank you." She lifted her shoulder and dipped her head to the side, touched her cheek to my fingers. "Love didn't keep Matt safe, either. I knew it wouldn't. Why did I let him and Steven have their way? Why didn't I fight harder? I have never said this to anyone, but I miss Teo more than Steven, my husband of thirty-five years. I think of him, and Matt, every day. Isn't that terrible of me?"

"No, it's not terrible. It is what it is. There's love, and then there's love."

Even when she wasn't talking about me, she made me understand things. That Scott and Marian were the ones who knew everything about me, were the ones I'd be thinking about at the end of my life. Like I'd said, there was love, and then there was love. I kept my arm around her shoulder while we both stared out to sea.

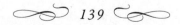

THE PHONE WAS RINGING AS I walked in the door. It was Arwen. My answering machine showed three messages and I knew they were from her, the way the red number blinked, wet-eyed and confused.

"Hey, Arwen. I just got in."

"Oh. Okay. Um, am I going to see you tonight?"

What Tess had said about her and me . . . I had to do the right thing now. I'd screwed up before, but it was too soon for it to be too late.

"Yeah. I think we should get together for—"

"I'm on my way."

"No. Don't come here. I'll come to you. Where do you live?"

"My roommate's here . . ." She said it in a dramatic, confidential whisper.

"That's all right. I just want to talk to you."

Nada.

"Arwen, give me your address."

﹡

I HAD SECOND THOUGHTS ABOUT breaking up with her when I walked into the twelfth-floor, rent-controlled, two-bedroom apartment in Stuyvesant Town that three successive generations of her family had lived in. An entire neighborhood called the Gashouse District had been demolished after World War II to build Stuyvesant Town and Peter Cooper Village, just to the north. The complex sprawled from Fourteenth to Twenty-third streets, from First Avenue to Avenue C and the East River. Fifty-six buildings, over eleven thousand apartments, miles of sidewalks, twelve parks, acres of grass, cavorting squirrels, mace- and pepper-spray-toting security officers. Twenty-five thousand people. You could think it was the world when you were in there.

The roommate scurried from the kitchen into her bedroom when I came in, cup of something hot in both her hands, flung a doleful glance at Arwen and a *how could you* glower at me as she passed through the living room.

I took Arwen by the hand and sat us down on the couch. The Empire State Building was framed in the living room windows. "Whoa. That's a view." It was pretty eye-popping, but on third thought, I decided I liked my grungy neighborhood and my view of Tompkins Square Park better.

She didn't even turn her head. She wasn't impressed. She'd looked out that window every day of her life. She'd be just fine without me. I held both her hands.

"Jody, don't. You're making a mistake." She was trying not to cry, her mouth was trembling and her eyes were wet, she looked so incredibly kissable, but I wasn't tempted. Whatever I was or wasn't with girls, I was nicer than that.

"No, it was a mistake not leaving things the way they were with you. I'm sorry. We're friends, Arwen, and I want us to stay that way. Okay? That's what I need you to be. My friend."

Tears started running down her face. "But I love you, Jody. I've loved you since I first saw you, for a whole year practically!"

"Arwen, come on. You don't, you don't know the first thing about me. Not really. Not anything important, anyway."

"What's so important to know? I know you're lonely, and you're sad a lot, and you have scary scars and bad dreams, and you're kind and funny and you don't drink or smoke, and you need someone to love. And you like well-done English muffins and chamomile tea and you're a good tipper." She bit her lower lip, dipped her head, gave me a meaningful look from under her lashes. "And a great lover. Did I miss anything?"

She was so earnest I couldn't help myself. I laughed, then raised her hands to my lips and kissed them. "Yeah, a few things."

"Things that that woman Ella knows? Why, because she's older? You don't have to be old to know things, Jody."

"No, that's definitely true."

"I know you could love me if you'd let yourself."

"That's not going to happen. And you have to trust me when I tell you that I am not what you need. Let's stay friends. Please. You toast the best English muffin and brew the best pot of chamomile tea in town. I don't want to have to go somewhere else."

"You'd better not!" She sat up straight. That defiant pride of hers was back. She hugged me. "Okay, for now we're friends. But I'm not wrong. You'll see."

For a second, I wondered if it could be as simple as that, with her. As letting myself believe that the things she knew were enough, that it wasn't important that she might know but never understand the things she couldn't see, the things that the scars and the dreams and the rest

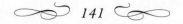

of it were made from. And maybe someone else could have done that, but not me. Because just like there was love and then there was love, there was knowing and then there was knowing. And with me, that space between knowing and understanding would crack us apart, like a fissure in the earth, with her on one side and me on the other. The only way for us to ever be on the same side would be if I made her understand, if I shoved her down into the crack and broke her.

*

I WOULD NEVER HAVE TO do that to Ella, there was no gap between knowing and understanding with us, there never had been. She'd been lying at the bottom of her own fissure since Matt died.

I stood on the sidewalk outside her brownstone, propped against a car, and watched her at the piano. Listened to the muted sounds that escaped into the night through the long windows. She was playing something from memory, eyes closed, head and shoulders dipping and swaying with the music. She had her hair piled carelessly on her head, out of her way, coppery tendrils curled around her face. I wasn't so knowledgeable about classical stuff, but I guessed maybe Beethoven, or one of those melancholy Russians, the music was big and soulful, deep in the lower register, even through glass the sounds vibrated inside my chest.

She stopped playing. Her eyes opened and her head turned toward the windows. She got up and looked out. I waved. She waved back. She walked out of the room, reappeared a moment later at the front door.

"Hi there. Content to peep, or were you planning on ringing the bell?"

I moved away from the car, into the circle of light from the street lamp. "I don't know. I didn't really have a plan. I just knew I wanted to see you."

We looked at one another, she on the brownstone's stoop, above me, lit from behind by the light spilling through the door, still as a marble sculpture of the goddess whose shrine I'd come to, to plead for my future, for my life. She didn't even seem to be breathing. I'm sure I didn't either.

"Okay . . . that's nice." She inhaled, nodded her head. "I was just going to make tea." She smiled. "Do you know whether you want some?"

I laughed. "I'm sure I'll figure it out by the time you make it." I came up the steps, into the light of her apartment.

She looked over her shoulder as I trailed her into the kitchen, and casually asked, "Where's Einstein?"

"Asleep in my living room. Where's Evan?"

"Asleep upstairs."

The rear of the apartment was a big open space divided by counters and furniture into kitchen, dining room, TV room, playroom. The far wall was almost all south-facing window, with a deep, cushioned bench underneath. In the left corner a door led out to a small deck. An outdoor light was on and I could see the short set of stairs down to her building's share of the gardens that ran between the facing backs of the brownstones on Eleventh and Tenth Streets. That was one of the great things about the Village, all that majestic sky and earth behind the buildings. All that silent and elemental green and blue air. Walking the screaming gray streets, you'd never know it was there.

I sat on a stool at the kitchen counter while Ella put up water, began to spoon loose tea from a canister into a glazed teapot that looked like it belonged in a museum. I watched her movements, as deliberate and flowing as the way she spoke, the way she played the piano. The pulse that had been beating in my stomach like a second racing heart ebbed to a throb, then faded completely. My eyes, suddenly too heavy for their sockets, rested on her slightly bent head, on the angled planes of her face. I couldn't believe how much I loved to look at her. The colors of her, like jewels on an ivory cushion, the wildness of her brilliant hair, the serenity of her features. She didn't look like anyone else in the world. And I loved that she didn't look or feel like a girl, that she had crow's feet at the sides of her eyes, a hint of heaviness along her strong jaw, a womanly roundness to her lower belly, and that while there might be a cocoon of sadness, or something deeper than sadness, around her, there was no confusion or chaos or anger firing out into the world through her pores. I wasn't all that calm with her, outwardly, but when I was near her I was calm in a place inside that I'd never had control over, a place inside me that had never known calm.

Her hand, holding a last spoonful of tea leaves, hovered over the pot. "Umm, you know, this is chamomile. Is that all right, or do you want something more . . . masculine?"

"No, I'm just a big wuss, chamomile is great. That's what I usually drink. With honey if you have some."

"Of course." She put the tea into the pot, and got mugs and honey out of the cabinets. "So, tell me about yourself. When and why did the big wuss leave Long Island for the big city?" She poured the boiling water.

"A few months after I saw you at Marley's. I was turning eighteen soon . . ." And soon after that I'd have been Jody for as many years as I'd been Christopher. ". . . and feeling like I had to *do* something. When I saw you, I knew I had to leave."

She cupped her hands around the teapot and looked at me in surprise. "Are you saying you left because of *me?* Why?"

"I don't know. I was kind of hoping you could tell me, that this all makes some kind of sense to you, you know, what happened then, what's happening now."

I'd been sitting up, with my hands in my lap, but now I put them on the counter and leaned into them for support. Ella's hands slid off the teapot and over mine. They were so warm, I whimpered, like a dopey baby.

"Jody."

The thumb of her right hand brushed upward across the inside of my left wrist, paused, then reversed direction. Her thumb's soft pad found and settled on the thickened knot of ruined flesh. The seeping warmth of her finger became the hot tug of a rusty razor and it was another time, a different kitchen, other hands on me. My left hand heaved under hers. She took her hands away and I put mine back on my lap.

Her eyes were warmer than her hands, but I was out of reach now, behind my cool mirrored gaze. "The tea should be ready, don't you think?"

After a moment's hesitation, she said, "I believe it should be, yes." She poured me a mugful, put it in front of me, poured some for herself, and stared down into the steam. "I don't know that there is any sense to be made of it. All I know is that when I saw *you* . . ." She gave me an uncertain smile. "Do you want to know this?"

"Yes."

"And then you'll tell me what happened when you saw me?"

"I'll try."

"Do you want to go sit over there?"

She nodded toward the big U-shaped sectional sofa. It looked lethally comfy cozy.

"No. I'm good here. But if you want to sit . . ."

"No. This is fine." She drank some tea. "This isn't so easy. I don't want to embarrass myself. Or you."

"You couldn't. Come on, I'll get the ball rolling . . . for some reason, I made you think of Matt, right?"

She took a deep breath, wrapped her fingers around her mug although they had to still be plenty warm, collected herself.

"That June, just weeks before I saw you, was eighteen years since Matt died. I was eighteen when it happened. I'd come to the moment

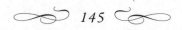

when he'd been dead for as long as I'd been alive when I lost him, and I'd been stumbling around for weeks, wild, trying to understand what it meant. It felt profound. And so, so awful. It was as if I was moving past him, past us, past everything that had ever been with him. My relationship to time had gone haywire. Oh, this is so hard to put into words. I must sound delusional."

"No, not even a little. My relationship to time is permanently haywire, I get those kinds of overlaps all the time. Go on, you're doing fine."

"Okay. I was looking for a sign, something to tell me where I was meant to go now. And then I walked into that shack where I'd never been before and would never be again—I don't even know why, I wasn't hungry, I didn't want anything—and I saw you.

"Physically, there was nothing similar about you, except I suppose your age and your height, and yet when I saw you I thought I was seeing Matt, the way he was during those last few weeks before he left for Vietnam. So frightened, so unsure of what he was doing, and trying so hard not to show it, not to feel it. But with me he couldn't hide it, he'd look at me and his fear of what was going to happen to him would come pouring out through his eyes, and his smile. You looked at me the exact same way. Frightened of something, wanting help, and not knowing how to ask for it, or how to take it." She fiddled with her mug a little while she studied my face. When she continued, it was with a smaller, sadder voice. "It was as if Matt had found me and was begging me to try again, to not let him . . . cross that time line and fade from my heart, from my life." Tears were pooling along the bottom rims of her eyes. She paused to collect herself. "At any rate, that's when I decided to marry Ronald. And to have a baby, a life I could hold and . . . protect. When I saw you." She found the courage to look at me again, although she was holding on to that mug like she was bracing for a lightning strike to her heart. "Was that TMI? Have I grossed you out totally?"

I shook my head. "No, I can't imagine you ever being gross. That was really . . . pretty amazing." But I'd gotten all tangled up in the idea of Ella equating me with a baby and that pulse in my stomach started up again, although I knew that wasn't what she'd said, exactly. I switched gears and concentrated on what she'd said about Matt. "That picture of Matt that Tess has . . . him at the piano? You took that, didn't you, sometime during those last weeks."

"Yes."

I zeroed in on my first impression of his face, his look, in that photo. "I don't think he was afraid of what was going to happen to him, not like in getting hurt or dying. You can't really imagine those things, and when they do happen, they feel like they're happening to someone else. He looked to me like what was real to him?, what he was afraid of?, was leaving you, and of what would happen to you if he never came back. Because you kept each other safe."

"What makes you say that?" But her voice broke apart around me, just the way her look had broken over me back then, split into colors of grief, guilt, anger, disbelief, hope.

"I don't know. I just . . . Because that's what I felt when I saw you, like there was someone in my head telling me that if . . . if a person was near you, maybe . . . maybe he'd be safe."

"A *person*?" She pushed the word back at me, but gently, a heart-imploding hint of a smile on her mouth. A tear hung at the inner corner of her right eye. "What kind of a person, Jody? A person who doesn't have to imagine what those things feel like? A person like you?"

I shrugged. "Yeah, I guess." I tracked the tear as it crept passed her nose. "Yeah. A person like me."

"And so you moved from the suburbs to New York City, to the East Village of 1988, looking for safety? Looking for me?"

"Well, believe it or not there were always more dangerous places than the East Village in the eighties, and no, I didn't look for you. How could I? I guess I was just sort of instinctively following your trail, the feeling seeing you left me with, that I had to get out of there."

She'd made no attempt to wipe the tear away, she just stayed with her hands around her tea, watching me while the tear continued on down to her upper lip. I reached out and caught it on my thumb, touched my thumb to my lips. I leaned over the counter and kissed her. She pulled back.

"No. Jody, don't. It's not right."

My head was swimming from that tiny taste of her mouth, the smell of her skin and hair. "Why? Why not?" Then I got it and my head cleared of anything even remotely pleasant. She didn't want it. For the first time since I was fifteen I'd fucked up, really bad. I hadn't just misread her, I hadn't remembered to read her at all, I'd stepped out into traffic without looking in *any* direction. My guts were trying to turn themselves inside-out. So much for my newborn calm. Or for the fantasy of ever being safe.

I got up, walked around the counter and behind her, put my mug in the sink. "I'm sorry. I'm an imbecile. I'll leave. I'm sorry."

She pirouetted around. "What? Why? I don't want you to leave. Jody, please. It's just that . . . For God's sake, have you looked at me? I'm old enough to be your mother."

There wasn't a lot of space for us both between the two counters. She shrunk back against the divider as I turned to face her. I'd looked at her. I'd been looking at her for a decade. I looked at her now.

"Believe me, you're not anything enough to be my mother."

But that was a lie. She *was* old enough to be my mother. In fact, she was older than my mother. Eighteen and eighteen and eleven makes forty-seven. Iggy the math wizard strikes again. Marian would be forty-four. Assuming she was still alive.

Ella shook her head. "I am. You're too young." She edged away from

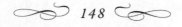

me, went over to the dining table, and started folding the acres of the Sunday *New York Times* spread out there.

I forced myself to center my brain so I could interpret her body language, the things her eyes and skin did without her even knowing. I mean, she hadn't said, *No, that's not what I want, how dare you.* And she didn't seem pissed off at me. Her eyes were downcast and she was blinking a lot, I could hear her breathe, her face looked hot, she couldn't get the folds right, her movements were uncoordinated. She wasn't behaving like someone who'd found herself on the receiving end of something distasteful. It might have been a long shot, but my money was on shame.

"I'm not like other people my age. I'm not young. You know I'm not. I think maybe you're getting youth mixed up with boorishness."

Her head snapped up. She was all set to hurl another *Don't talk about yourself like that* at me, but when she saw me grinning, she laughed. "Maybe I am. It's all too easy to do these days, don't you know." Her hands remained still. "No, you're not a typical twenty-eight-year-old, Jody. That much is clear to me, even without my knowing all the reasons why. But still, you are too young. And even if you weren't, I'm too old for this." She went back to misfolding the Arts & Leisure section. Her hands and her jaw were clenched and shaking and after a minute she threw the mess of newspaper onto the table and looked up at me with pink, feverish eyes.

This. Not *you.* Not, I'm too old for you. *This.* Shame.

"Okay. Really, I'm sorry. So . . . Thanks for the tea. I'm going to go. It's a school night, we've both got stuff to do . . ."

"You don't have to apologize. It was flattering, but . . ."

"No, I get it. It's fine."

She relaxed some, the tension deflated out of her in a long noisy exhale. "It *is* getting late. But I'm glad you came by, Jody. And I'll see you Saturday morning?"

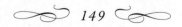

"Of course. And, listen, I was hoping that maybe the next Saturday, my brother and his fiancée want me to come to dinner, maybe you'd come with me?"

Her eyebrows went up. "You're not going to take Arwen?"

"I'm not seeing Arwen anymore." I slipped that in there, matter of fact, no comment required, kept going. "And also, for the sake of peace in the family, I want to finally make a decent impression on Fern. She thinks I'm the missing link; she's expecting me to show up with someone who can barely count her toes. You can be my beard. She won't know what to make of you. It'll be fun."

"Oh my. How can I pass up the chance to show off my toe-counting skills, and to a banker no less? And I just bought a new pair of sandals." She smiled. "They seem like nice interesting people. I'd be happy to go with you. Come, I'll walk you out."

The phone rang before she'd taken two steps.

"I know the way. See you Saturday."

From down the hall I heard her say, "Alex! Hi! I was just going to call you."

This. Maybe what she was ashamed of was feeling something she thought she'd wanted to bury with Matt. But more likely it was who she was feeling it for: a scarred-up low-life no one like me.

For Tess from Christopher

THE BIKE

In Scott's house, Christopher's got two things he's never had before, his own bedroom and a daddy. There's no crucifix on the wall above the bed. That got left behind. In this house, no one prays, and Christopher's God isn't Jesus Christ, it's Scott Hanson, a skeletal twenty-eight-year-old two-tour Vietnam medic with bloodshot eyes, the anemic blue irises nearly blacked out most of the time by dope-dilated pupils. Scott. All the second coming Christopher needs, the herald of a new life. Why shouldn't he think that? Scott's ways are as mysterious to Christopher as those of the Lord. He's lanky and limp and hangs above Christopher's head like a rag-doll saint. His hair is long. He can heal people, although he doesn't do it much since he got his coked-out thieving ass fired from his PA job at the hospital. Scott's tormented by the ugliness of the world, and by sins committed and observed. He careens around looking troubled and dreamy, in a state of bruised confusion, like he's already been hammered full of nails and he's trying to figure out what he's supposed to do with the pain.

For the moment he's experimenting with transubstantiation, turning pain into love for the unloved and unlovable, in this case a stone cold girl-child and her bastard boy-child. So the only differences Christopher can really see between Scott and Jesus are that Scott's a drug dealer, which Christopher is pretty sure Jesus never was, and he's a whole helluva lot angrier than Jesus ever seemed to be. Scott's as full of rage as he is of pain and love. Christopher is working on being like the mice in the basement that can turn themselves into gray pancakes and vanish into spaces you can't even see. He's going to flatten himself out and slip unseen beneath Scott's rage so he can cuddle up to those other parts, the ones he understands, to the pain and the love.

There's no height chart with smiling animals in Christopher's new

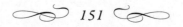

room. That got left behind, too. Some other kid is going to meet the yellow-eyed owl one day, not him. The thought of that makes him really sad, even though he knows it's stupid, that the owl's not real. Still, he gets sad the whole time he lives in that house when he thinks about the owl not ever knowing him. He was so close.

But, here, there's Scott. From now on, Christopher's growth is going to be measured against the towering emaciated length of Scott's body. No way he's ever going to reach the top, stand eye to eye, pale blue to dark blue. You never stand eye to eye with your God. Not until you're dead.

Christopher isn't used to so much space, ten by twelve feet all to himself. Along with the half-room's worth of stuff brought over from Trestle Road, there are things left behind by the family who'd rented the house before Scott kicked them out and moved back in. A dresser, a lamp on it with a parchment shade made to look like a sail. Cartons of books. An old wooden chest full of LEGOS, Lincoln Logs, Hot Wheels, and Matchbox toy cars. On the wall, instead of a height chart, posters of Rod Gilbert and Neil Armstrong.

Even with all those neat things around him, he doesn't feel good in his new room. He feels tiny, like he could get lost behind the furniture, or in the vacant areas in between things. He's lonely and he feels in pieces, not whole, like he's the tangled-up echoes and shadows of two different Christophers, the one from Sal's house and the one from this house, and even together they don't add up to anything real, to _him_.

At night he's in pieces, and scared, besides. He's not used to being alone in the dark, he misses his aunt Marie, and he can't forget, ever, that it's because he killed her with his thoughts that he gets to live in this house with Scott and Marian, gets to have this second life. She was good to him and he killed her. Alone in his room in the dark, no light of Jesus shining from the wall, it's all he can think about, that it was a sin and one day he's going to be punished for it. On top of being punished for the sin he was born with. It's the weight of all that sin and punishment pressing on him that's breaking him apart.

He only feels good, he only feels whole and safe, when he's with Scott.

Il ragazzo ha un nome. The boy has a name. Christopher. Since he's been living with Scott and Marian, he's started calling himself Christopher, not out loud, but in his head. Consciously, on purpose. He thinks, Christopher is hungry. Or, Christopher wants a New York Rangers T-shirt with Rod Gilbert's number 7 on it. Or, Christopher wants his mommy to stroke his head the way Scott does. He does it, thinks of himself by name, so he won't forget his name. He could, the way he's forgetting things about Trestle Road, because in Scott's house he hears his name even less often than he did in Sal's.

Marian sometimes calls him dummy or pest—that's all she's ever called him, along with an occasional vermin type of thing—but mostly now, even though she sees him some every day, she doesn't call him anything. He has no hint how she does it, but she manages to address him, tell him what she wants him to do, or what a pain in the ass he is, without the use of a whatever the hell part of grammar it's called, how you call someone. She just gets a Marian voice on and says Leave me alone, stop banging the fucking piano, get out of here, you smell bad, stop whining, don't touch that, you're a fucking filthy mess, no you can't have any more. Like that.

Christopher studies and analyzes that voice she uses, pulls its tones and cadences apart like he does with the songs he hears then picks out on the piano, but he can't find its equal in himself. He can hear notes in his mind, find them on the keyboard, but nowhere in his mind are there notes and tones to match the bitter hatred in Marian's voice when she talks to him.

✳

Marian works from five in the afternoon until two in the morning, six nights a week, at the Pussycat Lounge. It's in an old warehouse not far from the Bay Shore train station. She dances, alone in a round metal cage. Every day before she leaves the house, she smokes one of Scott's special cigarettes. Christopher makes sure he's near her when she does. For one thing, those few hours in the afternoons are the only times he sees her. Also, she gets a charge out of blowing the smoke in his face. It makes him dizzy and act goofy, and that makes her laugh. He closes his eyes and turns his face toward her so the smoke, warm from her breath, falls on him. He breathes it in and pretends she's kissing him with smokey lips.

Sometimes he's awake when she gets home but she doesn't know that. She never comes into his room. He stays in bed and listens to the quiet noises she and Scott make in the living room, matches being struck, bubbling sounds, air drawn in and let out in long deep tired sighs. Then silence, thick and dulling, like the blanketing fogs that roll in off the bay, menacing and comforting at the same time. He likes the quiet noises, but that silence makes a baby of him again. He sucks on his sheet to fall back to sleep because later, from their bedroom, the silence like fog he can't see through is going to be shattered by sounds he doesn't want to hear, sounds like the neighbor's cat makes, that make him think of sharp claws and bloody scratch marks.

Scott calls him Chrissie once in a while, but usually it's man, buddy or, the best, mongrel or mongrel boy. Then it's, Hey, mongrel, get your butt over here!, or, Mongrel boy! Bring me a beer! It's the best because Scott always grins and roughs his hair, or chucks him under the chin, or spins him around when he calls him that. It's not like when Marian would call him dummy or pest, stare all the way through him, and turn her back on him. Or when Sal would call him nigger-lips or spic brat and raise his hand in the air, maybe hit him maybe not, before he turned his back on him.

Mongrel is a good thing, it's a special nickname, a secret between them other people don't get even though they hear it. It's a code, the way Scott lets him know that he's his favorite kid in the world, that he already likes him better than he even likes Marian. Scott talks to him. Touches him. Plays ball with him, carries him on his shoulders to the playground, cleans and bandages his cuts and bruises. Takes him out for pizza. Gives him his bath, reads with him, puts him to bed at night, wakes up early to give him breakfast. Christopher spends five months glued to Scott's side, and when he starts school in September, Scott gets him dressed, holds his hand all the way to his seat in Miss O'Reilly's classroom, and doesn't leave until Christopher stops crying, and then he walks him to and from the school bus every single day. Scott never turns his back on him. Scott never hits him.

So Scott calls Christopher mongrel, and the mongrel giggles and comes running, every time, does whatever Scott wants. Eventually Christopher learns what it means, mongrel. But so what. He doesn't care. For one thing, he is one, right? Just like he's a bastard. It explains what he sees every time he gets caught in a mirror, why he looks so weird, a patchwork of colors and shapes, not all neatly one thing like everyone else he knows. For another thing, the most important thing, by the time Christopher learns what it means, mongrel already means something else to him. When Scott calls him mongrel, Christopher knows he really means son.

This is how he knows that. It's the end of July of that first summer—he's been living there maybe four months. Marian's at work, and after dinner, after Scott takes his vitamin shot and the powder medicine for his nose, while they're watching TV, Scott all of a sudden looks over at him. He looks for a long time and then he says, Pretty little mongrel boy, do you love me? Christopher's heart starts to trip, to expand inside his chest. He's been waiting for this since the first day he ever saw him, for his chance to tell Scott that he loves him, so he says Yes and smiles till his mouth hurts. Then Scott narrows his eyes, moves in close, and says, You're my boy, Chrissie. You want that, don't you, to be my kid? You want to call me daddy? Christopher can't even talk, he can't say a thing, he's got this huge heart-shaped lump in his throat. He can't even look at Scott. All he can manage—the triumphant mouse who sneaked in under the rage—is to scurry across the sofa and nuzzle into Scott's shirt and nod and nod. After that, almost every night, after his shot and his nose medicine, Scott finds him, comes close and whispers, Pretty little mongrel boy, who's your daddy? And Christopher whispers back, You are. And Scott says, Say it. And Christopher takes Scott's hand and kisses it and says, I love you, Daddy.

So mongrel is still a good thing to be called, it means Scott doesn't care what he is. It means Scott wants him to be his kid. It means Scott loves him back.

For Christopher's sixth birthday Scott gives him a bicycle, a real one, a six-speed apple-green Schwinn with thick tires and high handlebars and a round metal bell with a little tab you push to ring it set near one of the hand grips. It's got no training wheels. He doesn't need them. He'd ripped the trainers off his old bike when he was four. From the second he sees the Schwinn he loves it more than he's ever going to love anything again in his life. It belongs to him. And it's from Scott.

Marian doesn't give him anything. One Tuesday—her day off—a few weeks later, she does come downstairs before noon, though, says, Hey pest, what are you now, six?, and makes him a bologna sandwich. She dumps everything in her bag onto the table next to his plate and scratches through a wad of crumpled bills and cocktail napkins with men's names and phone numbers scribbled on them, until she finds a linty toothpick with red cellophane shreds wrapped around the top of it. She sticks it into his sandwich, like a birthday candle. She puts chips on his plate and pours him a Dr. Pepper. She goes back to bed and leaves all her crap on the table to keep him company while he celebrates.

He wants to take the bike out for a ride right away, but Scott says no, it's December and there are sheets of ice on the sidewalks and streets. He lugs it up the stairs to his room and waits impatiently for spring. It's not so bad being alone there at night after that. He can see the bike from his bed. The round metal bell glows in the dark, its light more radiant than Jesus.

Before he knows it it's March and the ice is gone. Scott watches him pedal like a fury and do killer wheelies on his new bike and he says, You're a natural, man, and you're fearless, mongrel, I love that. Scott watches him flipping and jumping and pirouetting on his scarred-up skateboard and says, You're a goddamned pint-sized magician on that thing, man.

When Scott's watching him, there's nothing Christopher can't do.

Lennie Cardoza is Scott's business partner. Lennie comes over every few days, usually after dinner. Christopher gets to stay up late and hang out with them and feel really grown-up, what with the important jobs they give him to do, like putting exact amounts of Scott's nose powder or vitamin pills into little plastic bags, or winding rubber bands around the hundred-dollar stacks of cash they make from a big messy pile of bills that appears on the floor whenever Lennie shows up. Lennie calls Christopher Mule Train—short he says for Mule in Training, and though Christopher has no idea what it means, of course he laps it up. Lennie doesn't pay him a lot of attention, but not in the same way Marian doesn't pay him attention. It's in an easy way that makes Christopher feel like he belongs there, with Lennie and Scott, doing whatever they do. Like when they smoke those sweet cigarettes they roll themselves and Lennie hands one off to Christopher at some point and Scott always has to say, Hey what the fuck? He's a fucking kid for fuck's sake! And Lennie always looks up startled, like he just woke up, and says, Oh, sorry, I keep forgetting. He takes the cigarette away and hands it to Scott. Then he stares real seriously into Christopher's face and says, Your daddy's right, Mule Train. You got yourself a fine brain, and that shit's no good for it. In the meantime, Mule Train's breathing that shit in right out of the air.

Scott and Lennie use more obscene words in one hour than Richard Pryor does in a year. It's just the way they talk. One time, they're talking about a customer who owes them money and Scott says, If that cocksucker doesn't pay up by Sunday, he better hightail it to the end of the earth, man, to the goddamned bumfuck North Pole, because anywhere else I'm going to fucking find him and rip him a new one. Cocksucker already has Christopher giggling like a guilty pervert when out comes the new and even better bumfuck, at which point he totally loses it and goes absolutely totally nuts. He starts to howl.

There's a kid named Jake in Christopher's class at school who turns to jelly whenever anyone farts, or even says the word fart. Jake gets sent to stand in the corner about six times a day because a couple of other boys in the class sneak up on him and say fart in his ear, or even better if they can actually fart in his ear, and Jake goes ballistic laughing. That's what happens to Christopher now with bumfuck. Scott and Lennie get it right away, and torture him for an hour using the word over and over, casually in their conversation, until Christopher can't take it anymore, his sides ache like they're going to cave in, and he crawls up the stairs into his room and collapses.

After that, Scott springs it on him without warning, bumfucking all over the place until Christopher can't breathe, tears pour down his face, he's sobbing he's laughing so hard. One afternoon while Marian's home,

Scott says to her, Hey, Marian, watch this. It cracks her up. They all crack up, hysterical laughing, holding their stomachs, screaming bumfuck over and over, Scott and Marian doubled over, pointing at Christopher bucking and writhing on the floor. For a second Marian even forgets she hates him. She kneels down and hugs him.

That's maybe the best moment ever. Ever.

Little by little he doesn't feel in pieces anymore, and there are nights when he doesn't think about Aunt Marie, or sin and punishment. School's a new world and he's gulping it down like it was chocolate milk. At home, he stays close to Scott and tries to keep out of Marian's way.

More than a year goes by.

It's a Saturday afternoon in the middle of May. It's warm and sunny and he's dying to ride his new bike and he's getting impatient, waiting in his room like he's supposed to for Scott to wake up from his vitamin shot. Scott needs the shots more often than he used to. If he waits too long he doesn't feel good, he gets wired and the anger tries to push up from wherever it is he keeps it.

Marian's not there to yell at him—she starts work at noon on weekends now—so Christopher humps his bike down the stairs and out the door and wheels it to the driveway. He starts pedaling in big ovals and figure eights, from the garage door to the street. The sun is shining on him, the air smells like wet earth, he's riding his green Schwinn, and his daddy's right inside on the couch. He feels a warm tingle from his head to his toes, like he did the first time Scott touched his head. This time, though, he knows what that feeling is. He's happy.

He's so happy and all that's missing is Scott there watching him, so he starts yelling and beating on that little metal tab, ringing the bike's bell to get Scott up and out. Christopher's delirious in love with the sound of the bell and his own voice, and with the strength of his legs pumping up and down. He wants to do this until the sun burns itself out of the sky, that's how much he loves it.

Scott comes out of the house, his shirt hanging open, no shoes on, a skinny cigarette in one hand. He's wearing sunglasses, but his face is still scrunched up from the shock of the brightness outside. Christopher grins at him and rings the bell harder. Scott grunts and tosses the cigarette into a puddle in the gutter, steps onto the driveway. He points his index finger at Christopher, his thumb sticking up at a right angle, like he's taking aim with one of the guns he keeps in his bedside table. Christopher thinks it's a new pretend game, and his grin gets huge and toothy like a baboon's, his mouth open wide as he yells. Scott tracks Christopher's circuit a couple of times, and Christopher pedals as fast as he can, showing off for his daddy. The third or fourth time around, just as he's about to give his loudest yell and sail by Scott, Scott straightens his arm stiff and hard as a rifle, says, I told you not to look at me, gook, then slams his clenched fist into the side of Christopher's head. He hits Christopher with such brute force that he gives him a concussion, knocks him clean off the bike and catapults him onto the cement. When Christopher lands on his left arm and it breaks in two places and bone pokes through his skin, he's so stunned and confused he hears the bones snap and his skin pop but he doesn't feel it. When the spinning bike falls on top of him, he's so stunned and confused he doesn't realize that the cloud shadowing his face is blood pouring from a two-inch gash gouged into his scalp by the sharp tab of the metal bell. When Scott walks over and kicks him in the back, steps on the bike, and pins him under it, he hears a thud and a crunch but doesn't know what caused them. When Scott looks down and says, Did I say you could ride that fucking bike? You only do what I tell you, you ugly gook monkey, you got it? he hears the words but doesn't understand them. And when he's lying there, alone, after Scott goes back into the house, Christopher is so stunned and confused that he can't understand what's wrong with him, why he fell off *his new bike or how he could have dreamed something so impossible, that his daddy came out of the house to play with him, but hit him instead. All he knows is that a minute ago the sun was shining on him, but now it's dark and he's in pieces again, broken and pressed into the ground by the unmovable weight of sin and punishment.*

THE DAY OF SCOTT HANSON'S transformation is a particularly lovely one. An unusually buoyant, mild, and meteorologically hopeful early May day in 1977. People should not do hellish things on days so naturally heavenly, but, sadly, man and nature are often out of synch.

When he emerges from the midday interior dusk of his shabby aluminum-sided house, where he has lived for far too many of his twenty-nine years, into the unwelcome light of a barely remembered sun, what is Scott thinking? What is he feeling? Are his overstimulated mind and undernourished body all atingle with a dislocating, titillating intimation that he is about to surrender his humanity to the Godlike power of destruction that resides in him and become something monstrous—the Divine Deformer of a dependent, powerless child who loves him, whose god he in fact already is? Does he see his new annihilator identity standing there on the sidewalk, waiting for him inside his previous passive form? Does he embrace it? Does he choose it?

Interesting questions to contemplate. Scott is not, after all, a psychopath; not even a sociopath. He's a relatively normal human being, and it's comforting to believe that this relatively normal human being might have a little conversation with himself in the seconds before he succumbs to the only Divinity he's ever personally had any faith in. A little conversation that might go something like this:

Whoa. Fucking bright fucking sun. So. Today I could go on pretending to understand Why Things Happen—and I mean Why Anything, no need to specify—and that I'm a success as evidenced by the fact that I make enough money to buy beer, food, cars, and guns and take care of my frigid bitch of a girlfriend and her little bastard kid, and that I'm an upstanding human being as evidenced by the fact that I love the kid even though he's not mine, or I could admit that I'm a marginal person, a glazed-brained drug addict who got the crap, trust, and love beat out of me daily by my alcoholic father, got my moral compass demagnetized in the antimatter Universe of Vietnam, and who has felt for pretty much as long as I can remember that there's an entire barrel of grenades about to explode inside my clueless head . . .

It's tempting to believe that such a conversation takes place in Scott's mind in the two or so minutes that pass between the moment he steps outside and the moment he knocks the kid he loves to the ground and kicks him where he lies, and to believe that Scott makes the choice to pull the pins on the grenades, to transcend his already marginal humanness.

It's tempting to believe that doing evil is *always* a choice, that the problem here is that Scott is weak or stupid or genetically flawed and fails the choice test. Tempting to believe that most people, we certainly, would pass.

Unfortunately, there's no empirical evidence to support that belief. All we seem to know for sure is that human beings are capable of doing terrible things, and that we regularly horrify and amaze ourselves by doing them. The why remains unclear.

＊

SO WHAT DOES HAPPEN THAT afternoon? Scott's a man, a guy barely holding it together, who is woken from a heavy heroin-induced sleep by a repetitive, invasive, metallic ringing noise and the sound of someone yelling. As he thrusts his sunglasses on to his face, lights a joint, and staggers outside, he has no intention anywhere in his mind or body of mitigating his own torment, his guilt and worthlessness, by inflicting torment on Christopher, so innocent and valuable. For Christ's sake, that's what he uses the drugs for.

And except for the people he'd killed in Vietnam, which isn't something he would have chosen to do if he'd had a choice—and even there his chosen job was to help people, not harm them—Scott Hanson has never hurt anyone in his life. And he really does love Christopher, more and more every day. If Scott ever did have a son, he'd want that son to be Christopher—smart, good-looking, strong, fearless, funny—and to love him the way Christopher loves him. Like no one in the world has ever loved him, not even Molly, the dog Scott had when he was a kid, that doe-eyed spaniel his father clubbed to death for shitting in fear on the backseat of his new car. Christopher makes Scott feel like that dog made him feel, but a million times better.

So what happens? What goes wrong in Scott's head, in his soul? Yeah, he's pissed off that the kid woke him up with his beating on that stupid bike bell, but he knows the kid only did it because the kid loves to be with him, so that's not the trigger. It has to be something else.

*

PERHAPS IT'S THAT VERY DEPENDENCE, Christopher's doglike unconditional love, that he finally can't tolerate. Scott is unworthy of such devotion, and he's always known it. His unworthiness squirms and pulses throughout his body, an undiscovered fifth humor among the known fluids that constitute his Being, as real and powerful as the blood that dictates his rash and quickly forgotten actions.

His heart expands with joy every time he sees the love in Christopher's eyes, but at the same time, all around his happy heart he feels that squirming fluid harden into a red-eyed, adamantine rage. The kid's look reminds him of the looks of his dying buddies, or of the tortured Viet Cong prisoners, silently pleading with him to save them. Or the look Molly would turn on him when his father beat her. Or his mother. Or his little sister. Scott has never been strong enough to hold another creature's life in his hands. He couldn't save any of them. Who the fuck did they all think he was?

✳

PERHAPS IT'S THE DEVILISHLY IRRESISTIBLE lure of the power itself, lyrically singing *Use me, abuse me,* a veritable aphrodisiac to a pent-up man who has never before in his life experienced a relationship in which he didn't feel inferior. Scott isn't even the equal of his best friend. They both pretend he is, always have, but the truth is that Scott is nothing but a remora, a basically useless suckerfish hitching a free ride on Lennie's sharklike negotiation of life's waters. Mighty hard to pass up the chance to finally *be* the shark.

✳

PERHAPS IT'S THE RAGE THAT inhabits Scott like a virus, a mindlessly canny virus that has lain dormant for years, and then, sensing its host's resistance fatally weakening, breaks free of its casing and comes virulently to life, feeding and feeding until there's nothing left of its human host but a six-foot-two bone-hard outer shell housing 158 pounds of rage. Viruses are evolutionarily compelled to endure by endlessly replicating themselves, and so the virus of Scott's rage has to go hunting outside the shell of Scott Hanson for something new to feed on. It doesn't have to go far. As if placed in Scott's orbit solely for the rage's comfort and ease is the delectable morsel of a human child, still growing, still forming, who can not only nourish and sustain the rage but can magically regenerate itself after each and every feeding, be plump and juicy and ready to be sacrificed anew by the next feeding time.

✳

PERHAPS IT IS A RESULT of a different sort of evolutionary compulsion, the sentient being's imperative to pass learned behavior on to the next generation. For what wakes Scott, actually, what gets through the murk in his head, is not the grating noise of the bike bell, but Christopher's unsullied voice, lately grown so confident, so demanding of him, calling out *Daddy! Daddy! Daddy!* So that in a single moment, after a year of playing at being Christopher's father, Scott abandons the game and starts taking his paternal responsibilities seriously. His intentions are probably good in that regard, but everything Scott knows about how fathers love, control, discipline, teach, and communicate with their children, how fathers prepare their sons for surviving a tough world, unfortunately comes from an outrageously God-awful manual.

※

BUT PERHAPS, ABOVE ALL, IT'S the love, the very real love that Scott feels for Christopher that is the catalytic factor, the one that binds together all other factors, ensures the permanence of Scott's transformation, and dictates its trajectory. A very real but warped love that provides the necessary barrier between Scott and his own horrific acts, that allows him to disown them and thus repeat them, over and over, without ever having to see himself as the monster he is. Because in the aftermath, when Scott returns from the house carrying a bowl of warm water and a cloth, kneels down and wipes the blood off Christopher's face with careful strokes, gently assesses his injuries and then says, with a rueful smile, "Hey, you fell off your bike there, little buddy. How did that happen? Looks like you did yourself some serious damage. But don't you worry, your daddy's gonna get you to the hospital, stat now," Scott feels a completeness inside him of such sublimity that he knows he has finally found the perfect physical expression, the only possible expression, for the intimacy that he and his pretty little mongrel boy share, an intimacy unique to both of them, craved and deserved for so long.

Scott's conviction of this is so strong he knows without having to ask that Christopher must feel it, too, this geyser of love that erupted after the delivering and receiving of pain; the catharsis, the release, the relief. Scott knows that beneath the red haze of his momentary suffering, behind the deathlike stillness in his deep blue eyes and the drowning-man scrabbling of his good right hand on Scott's arm as Scott tenderly carries him to the car, the boy is rejoicing in the beauty of his own consequent transformation. No longer merely Scott's chosen son, Christopher is now and forever more Scott's truest, secret partner. The line they have just crossed, the precipice they have fallen from, together, is already so far behind them it might never have existed at all.

※

IT IS MOST LIKELY THEN that there is no conversation, no words, no conscious thought in Scott's mind in the instant prior to his becoming a child abuser. There are just the grenades going off at last, as dazzling and mesmerizing as the grand finale of a stupendous fireworks display. Multihued emotions, past and present, all equally significant, equally weighty, shooting in all directions, firing his brain and his limbs, engraving into the night sky of his mind a clear image of his inevitable future self. A blueprint providing the guidance Scott has always needed, leading him to the unexpected place of release and relief from all his pain. Clear and simple. All he has to do is follow it.

Ten

YOU TWO ARE THE EXPERTS here. If you say planes are going to fall out of the sky, I don't know enough to argue with you. But from what I've read, there's a lot of disagreement about how bad this Y2K thing is really going to be."

"Planes may or may not fall out of the sky, Jody, but that date glitch could definitely cause millions of electronic records to be lost or scrambled . . . people aren't aware of how much information is organized electronically now." Fern tilted toward me, legs crossed like a contortionist, the ankle of her top leg wrapped around the back of the ankle of the bottom one, like she'd always wished she'd been born with a single leg, no between spaces, and was determined to undo nature. Her elbows were hugged into her sides, her fingers entwined and embedded into her thigh. "Imagine the chaos if the databases of governments, banks, hospitals, schools, all became unreadable, or irretrievable. The point is, we can't be certain of what's going to happen, so we simply must be prepared. Right, love?"

She turned to Brendan, who was sprawled in his chair with his eyes half-closed.

He mumbled, "Hmmm, absolutely. The babe is one hundred and ten percent right."

We were on the terrace of Brendan's apartment, winding down in

the mellow Indian summer darkness. We'd gotten into a discussion about what was going to happen come twelve a.m. January 1. It was hard not to. Three months to go, and it seemed the whole human race was burning up with apocalyptic fever. The topic lit Fern up like a Roman candle. She was quivering like an overbred greyhound.

Fern and I had made it through the evening in good shape, no tension, no sniping. I was sure my being there with Ella had a lot to do with it. Fern was a little in awe of her, I could tell. Every so often, while Ella was saying something wise and cultured, I'd see Fern's eyes move from Ella's face to mine and back again, a perplexed, almost annoyed crinkle to her nose. Halfway through dinner—which was fancy and yummy, Brendan was going to be fifty pounds heftier by the time he turned forty—I started thinking I could come to like her, and not just because she made my tank of a brother hover two inches above the floor.

"Okay," I said. "I can see how that part of it might be real, but not all this end of the world talk. Nothing in the universe cares that much about us. Besides, people can't even agree on when the millennium actually is, this year, or next, and man *created* clock and calendar time in the first place. So we wouldn't be late meeting our friends at Starbucks. No, you know, seriously, so mankind could agree on the when of things, feel like there was some order to existence, be able to get things done. Time doesn't exist on its own, not in the measurable way we think of it."

"As Einstein famously said earlier today," Ella chimed in, "quoting her namesake, 'Woof woof woof.' Or, as Albert originally put it, 'The only reason for time is so that everything doesn't happen at once.'"

I laughed.

Brendan snorted and said, "Next *time,* bring Einstein and leave Jody home. Then we'll really have some good conversation."

Brendan was three sheets to the wind and he was amusing the hell out of himself. He nearly slid out of his chair laughing. My brother had no greater tolerance for alcohol than his bride-to-be did—which had always worked for me since I wasn't going to be anyone's drinking buddy—but he'd gone for the wine at dinner, managed to add a good half bottle to his overall blood volume.

Ella's light eyes twinkled like stars. "No, translating for her would be too much strain. And moreover, I don't date girls."

Ella wasn't looking at me, her gaze was trained out over the terrace railing, on the fat orange moon suspended behind the Statue of Liberty, and the cool-fire ripple of its reflection in the river, but she tapped a sandaled, perfect five-toed foot against my shoe and the bubbles from my last sip of club soda tickled their way back up through my chest.

Fern showed no reaction to our sparkling witticisms. What she said next made it obvious she hadn't even heard them.

"Well, it may seem idiotic, but people are scared, and not just people who believe in a vengeful God, or in apocalyptic prophecy. No matter what you believe in, you can't help thinking about the sins of the world, and about your own sins, and wondering if this will be the moment of our genuine punishment. The world's moment, or our individual moment. Because it could be, couldn't it? If we believe in it strongly enough, it could come to pass. We don't know why things happen when or how they do, really, do we? So why not this, now?"

Fern's voice got thinner and more unsteady, until by the end she sounded more like an apologetic little girl, secretly talking about herself, than a grown woman with a couple of master's degrees under her belt and confidence in how to prepare for the unknown.

The three of us froze for a beat or two. Brendan looked like he was expecting his punishment within the next few seconds, and I didn't know what to say. When she put it in terms of sin and punishment like that, thinking the world was actually going to end still sounded idiotic, but awaiting some kind of retribution, in general, didn't so much.

Ella took hold of Fern's hand.

"I think you're absolutely right, Fern. When we feel overwhelmed by the things we're truly frightened of, it's easier to externalize them, and focus on this. I see it in Evan, my nine-year-old son. He comes home asking me questions about what's going to happen. He's anxious about the future, he says."

"A nine-year-old shouldn't even know what anxious *is,*" Fern muttered, then looked straight at me, with anger, like Evan's anxiety was my doing, and for the first time all evening I felt that prick of aggression from her, a feeling like she was attempting to bore through my eyes into the dank cesspool where I'd dammed up my part in some dark complicity between us.

"Come on, let's not end this on a downer." Brendan's eyes were open. He put his glass on the floor next to his chair, levered himself to his feet with merely a trace of the mechanical grace of the plowed. Either he'd learned to hold his liquor better than he used to, or something had sobered him up. "You ladies don't mind if we gents leave you alone for a few minutes, do you? Give you a chance to yak about us before we call it a night. That might cheer you up." He hooked a thumb in my general direction. "The family engineer volunteered to take a look at the bathroom mirror. I thought you might like a bigger one, better lights, love. He's gonna take some measurements, give us his opinion." He turned his deadpan *Follow my lead here* face to me, the face that had guided me through my first few years of living in the everyday world, until I'd gotten the hang of it.

"Why thank you. That's very generous of you, Jody." Fern raised her glass.

That was the first I'd heard of my own generosity, but I was on board with it. "Sure, my pleasure. You know me, a day without measuring something is like a day without sunshine."

I followed Brendan back into the apartment. Through the living room, down the hallway, through the master bedroom, into the en suite bathroom. He closed the door. Sat on the side of the bathtub, his elbows on his knees. He stared at the floor. He listed a little backward. I closed the lid on the toilet seat and said, "Hey, Brendan, maybe you should sit over here?"

He lifted his big head and turned his round face to me. "Don't worry, I'm not going to fall into the tub."

His smile was crooked. And the mirror and lights were as big and bright as a drag queen's dressing room.

I sat down on the lid. No use wasting it. "You know I don't have my measuring tape with me, right? Contrary to popular belief, I don't keep one permanently stashed in my briefs."

"You would put it like that. In your briefs. What's wrong with your pocket."

The crooked smile was joined by embarrassed eyes. I threw in his reaction to my briefs line and the still-no-sizzle between him and Fern, and I had my explanation for the wine and why we were as far from the terrace as you could get in twelve hundred square feet. Brendan wanted to talk to me about sex. It was the one area where I'd actually been of some return use to him. Starting the year we both lost our virginity, me first, at fourteen, a little early even for your brainless horndog adolescent, but the books say that's not unusual for someone with my history—there are other behaviors they say aren't unusual either, but I didn't care to think about them—then Brendan, nineteen, a few months later, out of bruised ego more than raging desire. It had been a long while, though, since he'd needed to bring up the subject.

"I remember that look, Brendan. What's going on? Is there a problem with you and Fern . . . ?" I tilted my head toward the door to the bedroom.

He barked out a gunshot of a laugh, but looked relieved at my cutting to the chase. "I'm worrying for nothing, Ig, I know it. I mean, physically, we're comfortable with each other and all, even though, you know, there's not a lot of . . ." He made a bursting open gesture with his hands, like fireworks. "Which is fine with me, I've never . . . you know. And she says she enjoys it, being intimate, even though she doesn't . . ." He made the same gesture again, smaller this time. "She's told me, straight out, that we're good exactly the way we are, she loves me, she trusts me, we're best friends, she feels safe with me . . . sex was never that important to her, either . . ."

"Okay. It sounds like you're on the same wavelength. Neither of you with a lot of need for it. Like you said, you've always been like that, there's nothing wrong with it, everybody's different, I suppose that's just the way you're wired. And she's telling you she is, too. That seems a good thing. Unless . . . so, what's the problem, do you not believe her?"

He shook his head hard enough to rearrange his gray matter. "No. Of course I believe her. I'm right for her, Jody, I give her what she needs, love, security, understanding. You know I'm better than most guys at the important things, the emotional aspects, the things that last. And she says it's not me, that she's never . . . with anyone, and it doesn't matter. It's just . . ." he made a mini cathedral of his fingers, pointed the spire in my direction ". . . help me out here, Ig, this brawn over brain stuff is your meat and potatoes." I smiled. We'd always been comfortable with each other's relative positions on the evolutionary ladder. "Should I be worried that . . . oh what the hell, that I can't make her come? I mean, we're talking a lifetime together, she's a beautiful woman, what if one day it changes and I'm not enough . . ."

"All right, a few things going on here. First, forget you not being able to make her come. If she's really never had an orgasm it's not about you or anything you're not doing right, it's about something with her. Second, she loves you, she wants to marry you, she's not a kid, you've got to trust her, that you're what she wants. Third, maybe she just needs time, with the right person, with you, for her to let go . . . I'm not saying to ignore it, but stop worrying about it. You're just going to create a problem you probably don't really have. Talk about it with her once in a while, make sure you're both still okay, or see if something wants to change." The thick muscles of his neck and shoulders softened. "Better now?"

Brendan blew out a breath and hauled himself off the tub. "Better. Thanks, Jody. I swear, you were the best thing Mom and Dad ever brought home."

I puffed up inside to hear him say that, but something was niggling at me, making me feel like I'd just given him a song and dance. I was picturing Fern on the terrace earlier, her hatchet body squeezed so tight there were no openings anywhere until you got to her mouth and eyes, open only as outlets for her intellect. I was picturing her a little drunk, at the softball game, uncontrolled sparks flaring like spontaneous brush fires. I stood up.

"You're welcome."

Brendan hung by the bathtub, smiling his kindly and rueful protector's smile, which came as a matching set with kindly and rueful crinkled up eyes. He swayed on his feet. His head drooped. Now that his tension had drained away, his wine high was flowing back in.

"The best thing. I loved having you as my baby bro. I loved that you needed me, man. Nobody else needed me. You don't need me anymore, I know, I know, you're all grown up, mister tough guy. But Fern does. She had a screwed-up childhood, too. I mean, not like yours, but it was scary. Bleak. Her parents did a number on her. They were Holocaust survivors, messed-up, distrustful, pessimistic, the whole nine yards. She's shy, she's hard to get to know, I know that, but so are you, right? You two, you're going to love each other, you'll see . . ."

"I'm sure we will, Brendan. Come on, the ladies are going to come looking for us."

He nodded. "In a sec." He peered at me with that smile still plas-

tered to his face and eyes gone narrow with curiosity. "Ella's something different for you. What's going on there?"

"As in what is she doing with a grunt like me?"

"Well, hell yeah, there's that. But really, what are you doing with someone like her? She's not the type you throw away after six months. Not to mention her being, what, ten, twelve years older than you?"

"Closer to nineteen."

"Wowza! She looks good." He lost his train of thought, stood there with his eyes wide, staring off into space, thinking, I assumed, about just how good Ella looked.

"And your point would be . . . ?"

"Oh. Yeah. No, I mean, *she's* the adult here, right? So you don't get to be all manly and adored and in control, you know? Like with your clingy little chicklets? I don't know, but I guess my point is, are you actually *dating* her, or is this something else? I mean, she's already got a son, right? And I thought you already had one mother too many in your life."

Something must have shown on my face, a reflection of the spasm of anger that knotted my stomach and jaw.

"Hey, Iggy, I just meant . . ."

"I'm not looking for another mother, Brendan."

"I didn't mean to say you were." Brendan never could lie as well as me, or maybe it was the truth and what he wasn't coming out and saying was the other obvious thing, that Ella wasn't so much out of an acceptable age range as she was out of my league. "I just don't want to see you get in over your head." Bingo. "But whatever you do, it's cool with me, you know that. Arwen, Ella, whatever makes you happy, Ig, I just want you to be happy."

"I know. I'm sorry. I shouldn't have jumped down your throat. Truth is, I don't know what she and I are doing with each other yet, but I like being with her. Could we go back now?"

"Actually, as long as I'm here..." He pointed to the toilet then grappled with his zipper. I lifted the lid and the seat for him and made my way back to the terrace.

✳

ELLA AND FERN WERE STANDING at the railing, deep into a serious-looking conversation, Ella particularly upright, Fern slanting in, her hands insistent on Ella's arm. It gave me a good feeling, watching them, thinking how the four of us might become friends. They were so intent, they didn't notice me at the open sliding doors between the terrace and the living room, and as I stepped through I caught Fern saying, "... ever leave Evan *alone* with him, do you? You know what they say about abused children becoming..."

I stumbled over a chair. She stopped talking, I stopped moving. When she saw my frozen stare, her shoulders stiffened and the shadow of a smile played across her face. In the moonlight, cool silver now, her eyes gleamed with hostility, with righteous guilt, with the nasty things she believed about me. They defied me to prove her wrong. I wanted to kill her. Rage rose up from the soles of my feet and swallowed me whole. I wanted to grab her by her swanlike neck and hurl her off the terrace.

I didn't even see Ella move, all I could see was Fern's granite face, but there she was standing in front of me, her tall, sturdy body half blocking me from Fern. She put her left hand flat and steadying on my chest, at my shoulder, and pushed at me, held me in place.

"Look at *me,* Jody. Look at me," she said quietly.

Fern turned her back to me, releasing me to move my eyes. I looked at Ella. I was clenching my jaw so tight my teeth were chattering.

"We'll talk about this outside. She didn't mean it the way it sounded. Try to calm down. I left my purse in the dining room, on the hutch. Why don't you get it for me while I use the bathroom, and then we'll say goodnight." She used her hand and the strength of her body to push me backward, off the terrace.

I somehow found the hutch, collected Ella's bag. When I turned around, Fern was standing in the opening between the dining room and living room, studying me like I was a lab experiment, a mutant in a cage. I erased the space between us so fast she had no time to retreat, got as close as I could without touching her, trapped her against the wall. There was menace in me, and a bolt of pleasure in seeing her jaw tighten and her taut throat wobble as her head fell back. Her round dark eyes goggled up at me.

I kept my voice low. "Look . . ." I paused. *Bitch.* Heavy on my tongue, pushing against my lips after lying in wait twenty years, since the last time I heard Scott refer to Marian as one, *the bitch is gone,* waiting for the right time and the right person to call it forth. But I held it in, I didn't say it. "Look. You and I don't have to like each other, but Brendan loves you and I love Brendan, and we're going to have to deal with each other for the rest of our lives, so do you think you could shove your contempt for me up your ass where no one has to see it so we can at least be in the same room together?"

I had to give her credit. She didn't flinch, or step away from me hulking over her, even when fear crowded out the other emotions in her eyes and her bones seemed to go slack inside her flesh. The anger flushed out of me, replaced by a strangling impulse to apologize to her. I heard myself say, "All right, let's just forget what either of us said." She nodded a couple of times, then turned away, blindly took me by the hand, and we walked together to the front door, where Ella and Brendan were waiting to say goodnight.

It was like nothing had happened. Fern and Ella hugged. Brendan and I hugged. Brendan and Ella hugged. Fern and I hugged. And she surged into me like a wave, a powerful undulation from thighs to throat, her hands busy exploring the muscles of my back, and her head turned and lifted and her lips were urgent and moist at the side of my mouth. Her movements all so small and quick no one else could have noticed. Then she peeled away, pecked me on the cheek, waltzed into Brendan's arms, and said, "Goodnight you guys. This was lovely, we'll do it again," and Brendan beamed, and Ella and I said, "Yes, yes we will," and then we were out of there.

Eleven

DO YOU MIND IF WE walk a bit?"

"Not at all." Ella tucked her hand into my elbow. "It's such a nice evening, I'm happy to walk the whole way if you want."

North along the riverside terrace, east on Harrison to Greenwich Street, then north again for the long haul to Eleventh. I concentrated on the slap of our footfalls on the pavement, the thud of my heart, the filling and emptying of my lungs, the gentle collisions of our arms and sides as we walked together. The blocks flowed by, and those steady rhythms slowed my careening thoughts, which were tick-tocking between Fern's hatred of me and her rubbing against me like a cat in heat. Gradually, the swinging pendulum settled into the still neutral center of my brain.

I could feel Ella waiting for me to say something more. She darted questioning glances at me, like Einstein when we ran together, but I had nothing to say. We were nearly through Tribeca before she pulled on my arm and broke the silence.

"She didn't tell me anything I hadn't already guessed, Jody. Looking at the pictures in Brendan's living room confirmed my suspicion that you were not born a Kowalczyk."

Brendan kept dozens of family photos on display, just like Irene. He was such a girl.

"You sounded just like Tess when you said that,"—proof that you didn't have to share genes with someone to become like them—"like there's never been a black-haired, blue-eyed, unusually tanned Pole in the history of humankind."

"Name one. But seriously, aside from your somewhat more . . . exotic looks, it just didn't seem possible to me that you and Brendan were children of the same parents. So as for her informing me that you'd been abused . . ." She had her hand tucked into my left elbow and she let one finger stray for a second to the scar on my forearm. ". . . I'd figured that out, too. What you overheard her say, it's nonsense, Jody. It's not that black and white, and no one who knows you would ever think such a thing. And whatever she said, it wasn't even about you. But maybe you already put that together. Did something happen while I was in the bathroom? You and Fern appeared okay at the door, saying goodnight. Or, you're such a good actor, was that just a show for your brother."

"I'm not that good an actor. I am a good retreater, though." I glanced at her and gave a wheezy laugh.

"One of the best I have ever met." She said it with joking pride and tightened her grip on my arm.

"But yeah, we ironed things out. We'll be fine. We need time to get used to one another, I guess. We're different. We'll figure it out."

"Can I say something, that might help?"

"You can say anything." I'd always been up for giving people the green light to say whatever helpful things came into their helpful heads. Couldn't hurt. Thinking they were being helpful made people happy. I wanted Ella to be happy.

"Okay. This is what I think. Obviously, Brendan and Fern are both very smart, very cerebral. Fern is also wound as tight as they come so it's easy to see how an easygoing mush of a teddy bear like your brother would ground and comfort her. You, on the other hand, are so much more . . ." she cleared her throat and fluttered her eyelids ". . . *masculine.* Next to Brendan, or to any man she'd be friends with, you must feel like a wild grizzly. You're her future husband's brother, of course she wants to get along with you, but she doesn't know how, she doesn't know what to do with you. I think you frighten her, the same way not knowing what's going to happen to the world frightens her. Does any of that seem right to you?"

It all seemed right. For sure, Fern was too delicate to ever befriend an ape, talk about brain versus brawn and relative positions on the evolutionary ladder. In fact, Ella's analysis was so psychologically impressive that I could only suppose she'd been spending quality time with the smooth Dr. Chase. That thought, plus the fact that I'd have cut out my tongue to avoid talking any more about what Fern had done and why, deflected me from obsessing about Fern long enough to turn pea-green jealous, and more offensive than Fern in her worst nightmare.

"Merely awesome. Where did you learn to analyze people like that, on psych one-oh-one date nights with Dr. Alex Chase?"

Ella very deliberately unwound herself from me and put her hands on her hips. "Very possibly. And how do you know he's a psychiatrist? He didn't say what kind of doctor he was."

"I have a nose for people who can't wait to tell you what your problems are."

"It must be twitching now. Shall I tell you what your problem with Alex is, or do you want to tell me?"

I shrank against the wall of the building at my back, my hands laced on top of my hanging head. I was such a moron. She was so out of my league. What made me think I could do anything but disappoint her? On a positive note, I'd gotten us off the subject of demon-woman.

"I'm sorry. He's perfect for you, I'm glad you go out with him. I'm sorry."

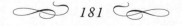

"You say that too much, Jody. You know that?"

"I know. I do. I know. I'm sor—"

She shook her head, I lifted mine, and we both laughed.

"Yeah, you know, actually, I once calculated that if I could go back one month for every time I'd said I'm sorry"—which was at least once a day but usually a lot more from the time I was two and a half to nine, then regularly with varying frequency thereafter—"I'd wake up somewhere in the twelfth century, maybe on a nice hillside in Italy with a friendly bunch of goats, and die peacefully of an infected boil or some such at the ripe old age of twenty-something."

"Nice friendly *lady* goats?" Ella leered and wriggled her eyebrows, Groucho Marx style, then sighed, pirouetted to my side and put her back to the wall. "Is this life really all that bad, Jody?" Suddenly, she laughed and pointed. "Look!"

On the steel security gate over a storefront across the street someone had artfully graffitied the line Repent Sinners, The End Is Coming, and under that some other joker had spray-painted *Don't worry about the world coming to an end today. It's already tomorrow in Australia.* Which was a line from Charles Schultz. I was a big Peanuts fan.

I turned my head until my cheek lay against the rough brick of the old warehouse wall and I could see her profile. "The world feels good right now. I wouldn't mind if it ended tonight."

A little poof of a laugh came out of her. She found my hand. "I have gone out with Alex over the past few months, a number of times. But I told him I can't see him anymore."

"Why?"

"Oh for crying out loud! You *doofus!*" She flung my hand away, flung herself off the wall like she'd been stabbed in the back, glared daggers at me through that shamed pink-eyed haze again. She spun around and flounced up the street, her hair bouncing between her shoulder blades, her uncovered arms and legs flashing white in the broken darkness.

A few quick strides and I was in front of her. She couldn't stop in time and bumped into me. I caught her by the shoulders, sunk my fingers into her hair, tilted her face up, and kissed her. This time, she didn't pull away. Her mouth softened and opened to me, her arms went around my back and she moved into me, like Fern had, but so utterly different, not like a storm-driven wave bent on destroying itself on a rocky coast, but like a warm wavelet marrying itself to a sandy shore. The kiss receded, but our lips held at kissing distance and when she said my name the sound rode the crest of our mingled breath all through me, and for the first time since I took that name for my own, I glimpsed the form of a Jody Kowalczyk who was real and solid, who was *me,* but the image didn't hold, it crackled and flickered and broke up, a momentary miracle transmission from outer space that no one would ever hear or see again.

Twelve

EINSTEIN PUSHED HERSELF PAST THE baby-sitter's legs into the doorway like a determined linebacker, her muscular upper body in the entry hall and her waggling rear in Ella's music room. She wedged her nose into my palm, gave a sniff and a sharp stealthy nip at my fingers, sniffed Ella's hand and lovingly licked her fingers—some major girl bonding going on there—then put herself in reverse and pointedly sat down below the dangling end of her leash, which I'd looped over the standing coatrack just inside the door.

Ella and I went out to monitor the sitter's trip home—three multimillion dollar town houses further west on Eleventh—and as soon as the girl waved goodnight and closed her door, Ella turned to me. With movements sensuous as taffy, she lifted her arms, rested one hand on the nape of my neck, caressed my head with the other. Small shocks rippled across my scalp and down my spine.

"Jody. Tell me this isn't crazy. Tell me we're right to trust what we feel."

I couldn't pretend to trust my feelings. Or anyone else's. Reassuring her that I did would be a whopper of a magnitude that was beyond even my capabilities. But she and I were an inevitability and, if I knew anything, it was that you couldn't avoid the inevitable. There was nothing for it but to slosh through the dread, trust or no trust, and hope you came out the other side. So I was able to say with some confidence, "This isn't crazy."

Her eyes wandered, slow as her liquid hand, over my face.

"It's true, what you said. You're not young. You never had time to be young. Life moved too fast." She pulled her head back. "You don't even look like a boy, not really, not beneath the surface, and you certainly don't feel like one. Matt didn't either." She brought her head close again and her eyes bored into mine. Her hands clutched my shoulders. "You feel so much like him. I don't know why, but you do. But I have no fantasies that you *are* him, Jody. Maybe Tess does, but I don't. It's important that you believe me. You're *you*. And *you* are the reason I told Alex I couldn't see him anymore. Because I didn't want to make the same mistake with him that I made with Ronald."

I could have told her why I felt so much like Matt to her, why I made her feel the way he had. I knew the reason. Because even though I was right there with her, I was already gone, the way Matt had always been already gone the whole time Ella loved him. That moment in Cambodia when he'd disappeared once and for all was rushing in to meet him from the second he was born, he'd been feeling it all his life, a searing wind in his face, and he'd been waiting for the instrument of his obliteration to reveal itself, terrified and exhilarated, while she remained ignorant and innocent, stunned when it happened. She wasn't ignorant or innocent now, and she felt it, deep in her right brain, how tenuously attached to this world I was, and how, for reasons no one could ever explain, any more than anyone could ever explain why Scott had done the things he did to me, I was meant to love her forever, same as Matt.

I could have told her to go ahead and be like Tess, let herself believe I *was* him, that that was really the only way we made sense, since all she was going to uncover of me in time were the absences, and the holes. And because like with Alex and Ronald, she thought she didn't want to make the same mistake with me as she'd made with Matt, but the truth was it was still Matt's life she wanted to save, the thread between her and Matt she wanted to keep from being severed.

I could have said all that, but it was better to leave it be, let her maneuver us as she wanted, into the darkest corner of the stoop, away from the open front door, the building's stone wall at my back, the wrought-iron railing at my thigh, her body so close to mine our magnetic fields merged and coursed around us, drawing us closer and closer, making a single entity of us, joined first at the hip, then the breast, the lip, at our hot, shaking breath.

"Come inside with me."

Her voice was a whisper. Her fingers a whisper gliding down my arms. She took my hands and floated backward, one purposeful step after another, pulled me after her into her apartment. I hooked a foot around the door and kicked it closed behind me. It shut with a loud click and a heavy thump, sounds of doneness, of finality. I looked into her eyes and saw there what I'd been feeling in every touch we'd shared. She wasn't going to be like anyone else I'd ever been with, she wasn't going to fall away from me, ever, leave me to keep traveling on my own. I wasn't going to find myself out in the airless timeless universe alone, having arrived at the end but with the journey unfinished again, and when I returned to earth she would be there with me, too. And I would have to be there with her. I would have to be real and whole, someone she could hold on to and feel not just in her arms but in her soul. That crackling fragmenting image of Jody Kowalczyk would have to hold together somehow and step, naked and uncontrollable, into the world with her. And there wasn't a synapse, a cell, an atom, a quark, a lepton anywhere in me that believed me capable of doing that.

Panic bloomed in me like toxic sludge exploding across the surface of a pond. It bellowed in my ears, tore at my nerves, drained the warm blood from my suddenly freezing fingers and toes. In the blurred periphery of my vision I saw Einstein rise to all fours, a low warning growl vibrating in her throat.

"Jody? What just happened?"

"What do you mean? Nothing happened. We forgot about Einstein. I need to walk her." My voice echoed in a hollow head. I'd been way too modest earlier, saying I wasn't that good an actor. I was fucking John Gielgud. I dropped Ella's hands, lifted Einstein's leash off the coatrack. "Right, girl? You have to go out?"

Einstein came to me, whining and squirming, her nose pointing alternately at me, then at Ella. I clipped on the leash, reached behind me for the doorknob. I had to look Ella in the eye and say something, and I didn't know how I was going to do that. My eyeballs and lips were numb, my brain was a fuzz of cotton candy.

Look at me when I talk to you, dirtbag! My autopilot switched on. It compressed and swallowed the panic from my eyes and mouth. I looked up at her and smiled. I opened her door, starting weaseling my way out. She didn't smile back.

"So, I'm going to go walk her?" I was in the entry hallway. Hand on the outside door handle. "And you know, I think then I'm going to just go home, okay?" I nodded, pretended I didn't see her standing there looking like at least one of us had tumbled down the rabbit hole, her head turning minutely side to side in denial. "Maybe you were right, before, and this isn't such a good idea. Too soon, too fast. Maybe you *are* too . . . , you know, if you think . . . I don't know." She exhaled a wounded breath. "Goodnight then."

I opened the front door, edged out onto the stoop. Einstein followed me, but her attention was still on Ella rather than where it should have been, on the patch of gutter up the block she'd weeks ago ID'd as her first pee stop.

"I'll talk to you during the week." It took everything I had to stay there long enough to get the words out, to not turn tail and run.

Ella calmly watched me self-immolate. She smiled a curious smile, eased her door closed and said, "Goodnight then, Jody. Safe home."

✳

EINSTEIN BARKED AND LAGGED AGAINST her leash right from the get-go. She stopped to pee for the fourth time before we'd even made it to Fifth Avenue.

"Come on, Einstein!" She ignored me. I pulled at her, lightly. She raised her head, barked some more, pulled back, lightly. I pulled a little harder. "Come. On." She gave me the stink-eye, but lumbered after me.

We stopped at the corner of Fifth. A city bus was barreling down the avenue, determined to make it through Eleventh before the light changed. There was a strain on my arm as Einstein sat herself on the sidewalk the full length of her leash behind me. The bus sped closer, its tires and diesel engine whirring like a circular saw. And I thought, *Why don't I just step in front of that bus? If I'm going to walk away from her, I might as well. Just end it now.* Because if I didn't go back now, there'd be no next time, and I'd never know if it really was Matt she was still trying to save, or if it was me after all. And if I did go back, and it *was* me, what then?

I stood half off the curb, paralyzed by an old familiar terror. Terror to move ahead, terror to go back, terror to stay where I was, terror that no matter what I did it wouldn't matter, I was going to get hit by the bus all the same. The wind of the bus's approach plucked at me and I leaned forward. The driver leaned on his horn.

Einstein pulled against her leash, hard enough this time to pull me back and off my feet. I whirled around. She was hunkered down on her rear legs, her front legs braced on the sidewalk, head tucked into her neck, teeth bared. In her eyes a *Just try and make me!* look I'd never seen before. She started barking again, big raspy booming barks, the sound scratching at my brain like chalk on a blackboard until my brain started to bleed and I don't know what happened but for a split second I went berserk. I took the leash in both my hands and yanked so hard I felt something pop in my upper back. So hard the leash bit into Einstein's neck and jerked her right off her feet. And then I screamed at her, shrieked my throat raw.

"God damn it, Einstein! Stop that! Stop it! Stop it!"

She yelped. One nearly supersonic, eardrum-piercing *Yip.* She stared at me for a nanosecond, eyes huge and black with pain or shock, I couldn't tell which, then her eyes and her body dropped to the ground as though she'd been felled by an ax blow to the head. She crouched in front of me like a whipped slave, whimpering and trembling.

Dark spots pulsed all around me. I almost threw up, right there on the smooth clean sidewalk. The bus blasted by behind me. It should have taken me with it, splayed against its massive front, smashed and broken. *Okay,* I told myself, *she's just a dog. You yelled at your dog. Get a grip.* But I couldn't get a grip. I couldn't see, couldn't breathe, my legs shook, worse than Einstein. I lowered myself down onto the cement, still warm from the day's heat, onto my knees next to her, and I stroked her and crooned to her, "I'm sorry, Einstein, please, I'm sorry. It's okay. I didn't mean it. Oh God, I'm sorry."

She stopped shaking, licked my face and hands like there was no tomorrow, little grunts of forgiveness and love rolling off her tongue. I'd rather she'd bitten my hand off.

After a few minutes, we both got up. She immediately started inching cautiously back down Eleventh, looking at me from a lowered head. I turned in the opposite direction, looked over to the far side of Fifth Avenue. Then I turned back and started running. Einstein leapt and ran after me.

I was all set to sit on Ella's bell like the bus driver on his horn, life and death, but she was already there, opening the door for me as I galloped up the stairs.

"I'm sorry." There were times when it wasn't possible to say that too much. "I'm sorry. I'm pathetic."

"You're scared." She cupped my face in her palms. "But you came back."

"I don't want to be scared. I want to come in."

She smiled. "You can do both."

Einstein's heart raced like a puppy's, hopping and jumping inside her chest. She hadn't wanted to do that to him, crack open his heart like that, make him think he'd hurt her, frighten him to his knees. But she had to make him stop, make him turn around. She'd tried to tell him, but he hadn't listened to her, he'd just gotten more and more scattered, kept moving in the wrong direction. She was strong, but he was stronger, and heavier, she couldn't drag him back to the woman who soothed him with her voice and absorbed his constant noise with her touch. She had to scare him back, it was all she could think to do, make him so unquiet that he'd have no choice but to go back or go lost. With every wet rasp of her tongue she tried to tell him she was sorry, that he'd done nothing wrong, that her cowering wasn't from hurt or fear of him but from shame for tricking him.

She slipped past them into the apartment, trailing her leash, lay down in the cavelike warmth beneath the piano, listened to the sounds they made, he and the woman speaking their alien language. His earlier quiet began to return, to push out the clamoring noise. She felt him grow lighter and quieter as he and the woman climbed the stairs together. Her shame subsided. She draped a forelimb over her eyes. Little by little, she sank into a happy exhaustion, and even when her heart regained its stately grown-up rhythm, it continued to beat with the joyfulness of a pup.

Thirteen

DAWN LIGHT SEEPED THROUGH THE tall windows like vapor, turning the air inside her bedroom pearly pink. Ella's scent and the smell of sex lined my nostrils, a delicious aroma the same pearly pink as the air I breathed. My lids and limbs were heavy, my brain and blood sluggish. The building's thick stone walls and double-hung windows smothered the sounds of the city, made it possible to believe that nothing on the outside had sharp edges or anything to do with us. An old Bradford pear tree in the back garden cast a long silhouette across the west wall. The shadows of its up-reaching limbs bled and bent onto the ceiling. Soon, the rising sun would bleach them out of existence. I lay there, staring up at the ceiling, studying the shadows as if they were a trail to the place Ella and I had never quite found during the night. She'd gone farther with me than anyone ever had, but not all the way, not to the stars. I didn't think I was wrong about her, though. The others had fallen away, used up and satisfied while barely out of orbit. But Ella had wrenched herself away, not fully spent, as though she didn't trust that she'd emerge intact from that final flame.

I couldn't have gotten more than two or three hours sleep, but I was up, it was nearly seven. Ella was sound asleep. She lay on her back, unmoving except for the rise and fall of her breath. The room was warm and she was uncovered, the comforter pushed aside and bunched between us. I drew it behind me, moved closer to her, propped myself on an elbow and let my eyes feast on her while she slept. She glowed like a ruby in the dusky light. The hair between her legs was the same curly red-gold as the hair on her head. Her skin was as creamy smooth as Arwen's, with trails and groupings of pale freckles that I would spend hours in the weeks to come mapping with my fingers and tongue. Stretch marks glinted on her breasts, on her hips and belly, reminders of Evan. My wandering gaze toppled into her navel, and into my muzzy brain came an image of a curled-up boy-child, living and growing in the vessel of Ella's body, being breathed and fed and held by her. An image of myself. That awful panic started to uncoil its tentacles in my own belly and it slithered me right back to earth, out of her bed, into my clothes, and down the stairs.

It was just as well. Ella hadn't had to ask me to be quiet or to be gone—for sure from her bed but better all together—before Evan woke up. I knew no kid needed to hear or think about what adults did in private and while I seriously doubted I was the only guy Ella had slept with in seven years, it was pretty obvious Evan had no reason to have become accustomed to such things. I wasn't particularly vocal during sex anyway—I liked it fine when a girl screamed her head off, but that kind of untamed expression wasn't my thing. Although, a couple of times during the night something raw and wild tried to get the best of me, and I was grateful for Evan sleeping down the hall, reminding me to keep the lid on myself.

I swung off the last step, into the front room, looked around for Einstein. She wasn't there, but her leash was, pooled on the piano bench. I had no memory of taking it off her last night, focused as I was on other things, and to my knowledge unclipping her own leash had not yet made it into her bag of tricks. Like a retard, I found myself peering at the apartment door. It was locked. Then out of the silence came a faint rustling from the back room.

Evan was nestled into a deep corner of that comfy-cozy couch, fanning the pages of his Harry Potter book, his feet tucked under Einstein's belly. Their heads lifted, both with round surprised eyes, and the three of us stared at each other like dumbfounded cartoon characters. Einstein yawned, jumped down off the couch, stretched herself awake.

"What are you doing up so early?"

Evan closed his book, using a finger for a bookmark. "Dunno. Just am." He extended a bare bone-white foot onto the coffee table, nudged the phone there with his big toe.

"You expecting a call?" I grinned at him.

The foot retracted like a released vacuum cleaner cord. He turned red, opened the book, and glued his eyes to it. "I let Einstein out into the garden before, is that okay?"

"Sure. Thanks. So . . . Evan . . . is my being here okay with you?" I had no idea if he was upset, knowing I'd spent the night with his mother, so I figured I'd ask.

"That's a stupid question. Grown-ups can do whatever they want, that's what my father says. My stepmother was always at his house, before they were married, and *he* never asked if I was *okay* with it."

His nine-year-old voice dripped with fifty-year-old scorn and he couldn't be bothered looking at me. Obviously, asking wasn't the way to go. I'd never learn how to talk to kids.

I whistled for Einstein, who was squished against the windows, mooning over a squirrel shimmying up the pear tree. "Gotcha. Tell your mom I'll call her later."

Squirrels played havoc with Einstein's loyalty to me. I had to go fetch her. When I turned back, Evan was up off the couch, blocking the hall to the front room.

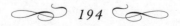

"You like French toast?" He was wearing a turquoise polo shirt with a Mamaroneck Beach & Yacht Club logo on it over his pajama bottoms. The shirt must have been his dad's, it was huge on him, hung down to his knees, and in the gaping sleeve his arm looked thin enough to snap just from him gesturing toward the refrigerator.

"Love it. Why?"

"I know how to make a special kind. Aunt Tess taught me. I was going to make some for breakfast. You can stay, if you want. I don't care. But if you're—"

The phone rang. Evan sprang off the floor like a kangaroo and dove, and I mean literally, catapulted himself headfirst over the back of the couch, slid onto the coffee table like an ace base-stealer, hand outstretched for the receiver. I thought he was going to crack his jaw but he held his head up and had that phone to his ear by the middle of the first ring. I was impressed. The kid had unexpected moves in him.

"Hello. I'm up. When are you coming?" He jockeyed himself to a sitting position, cross-legged on the tabletop, hunched over the phone, head bent. His back was to me.

The nasal voice on the other end was unmistakable. I couldn't make out the words, but it was Ronald, and whatever he was saying was ruining his son's day before it even started.

"But Father, you promised . . . I *didn't* tell her anything! . . . But you said we . . . I'm sorry, I didn't mean that, I know it's important . . . I'm not, I'm not crying! . . . No, I won't tell her . . . All right, Father, it's all right."

Evan hung up but didn't take his hand from the phone. His bony back and shoulders heaved as he tried not to cry. I'd gone cold where I stood, but there was a tiny spot near my heart that leapt hot with the urge to tear Ronald's throat out through the phone line.

I had nothing for him, but I couldn't just walk out, I couldn't leave him like that. "Evan. Hey, I'm sorry. Your daddy let you down, huh?"

He didn't turn around. "No, he didn't *let me down,* he has something else to do. And he's not my *daddy,* he's not some truck driver like yours probably is, he's a surgeon, he's my *father.*" His voice quaked, but he managed to put a healthy dose of sneer into it. "That's how people with class talk, in case you didn't know."

That stung like he meant it to, but I didn't take it personally. You stuck up for your father, your daddy, no matter what, I got that. "Okay, like I said before, tell your mom I'll call her later. And don't worry, I won't say anything."

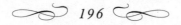

BY THE TIME I MADE the corner of Tenth and A, I was beyond starving. I didn't know about Evan's French toast, but the Coronet's was terrific. For a scruffy East Village hangout, their food was way better than it had any right to be. Plus, it was pooch friendly, and at that hour on a Sunday morning it was dead. Peaceful. Just Rasta-haired Nelson reading poetry behind the bar and a few regular customers. Hekyll and Jekyll, a pair of tattooed, pierced, black-and-chrome-clad punk lovebirds of indeterminate gender scarfing down *huevos rancheros,* and the Professor, a tweedy sixtyish guy with ink-stained fingers working the *Times* crossword over espresso and a croissant. Nicknames, compliments of yours truly.

Nelson waved. I heard the whirr of the juicer and muffled laughter coming from the kitchen. I took a corner booth, Einstein plopped herself under the table. I'd come for the French toast, but I scanned the menu out of habit, on the off chance that the undefinable thing I'd been wanting all my life to eat had miraculously appeared since I'd been there last.

"Hi, stranger."

Arwen didn't work Sunday mornings, but there she was, bruised eyes, spunky smile, and all. It's not that I'd been consciously avoiding her exactly, but we hadn't crossed paths in two weeks.

"Hey! What are you doing here?"

"I switched days with Tova so I could go to Vermont with my folks, to see the foliage."

"Nice."

"Have you ever been? It's soooo gorgeous. We go every year."

"I've seen pictures."

That was as close as I ever wanted to get to New England in the fall. I could just see myself, mind-blown by the cosmic beauty, the dividing line between me and the sublime Oneness of All Things eroding, and next thing I know I'm launching myself like a bird off the top of a neon tree.

"You are so irresistibly clueless." She was gazing at me with longing, with misty brimming eyes and totally undeserved tenderness. It was annoying.

"I'm hungry, is what I am." I looked down at the menu again. All that tenderness drew away from me like an outgoing tide.

"Oh silly me. You came in to eat, not to chat . . ." She sounded so hurt I wouldn't have been surprised to see black and blue marks erupt like stigmata on her buttermilk skin. "Your usual?"

"No, I'm going for the French toast this morning. And bacon. And scrambled eggs for Einstein. Tea though."

She wrote down my order, pressed so hard with her pen she tore through the thin paper of the order pad. She cursed under her breath.

"Arwen . . ." I could still see it, in my mind's eye. Her tenderness.

"What!?" Clipped, angry. In other words, *If you're not going to tell me you love me, then just shut up.* She moved away.

"Arwen . . ."

And then I did something I didn't understand. I touched her. I reached out and trailed my fingers along her bent arm. She didn't stop, we didn't look at one another, but she hesitated and as my fingers trailed off her elbow into thin air, she reached behind her, found my fingers,

held them for the space of a heartbeat. It was a seamless maneuver, and felt so much like when Ella and I seemed to be dancing that my sense of time and space warped, or whatever it was that happened when something unmoored me and I found myself somewhere else for a while. And in this other place, I was also sitting at the Coronet early in the morning, but I hadn't been with Ella the night before. I'd been with Arwen; I was seeing Arwen. And across town Ella was with Alex, and Evan and Kaylee were making Tess's French toast for them all. And I could see how right that could be, absolutely right, except that it wasn't right, because Ella and I would still be incomplete beings in any reality that might exist, and need something from one another that no one else could give us. We were stuck on that string, on that oscillation, till the end, like flies on flypaper. We couldn't fly off to someone else.

I woke up to the sight of Arwen's swaying hips pushing through the swinging kitchen doors and the murmur of Brendan's drunken observations flitting around my head. About me and my clingy little chicklets. About Ella. I guess there really is *veritas* in *vino,* because he was right. Even when I didn't want to be with them anymore, at least I knew what I was with half-formed young girls like Arwen. But I didn't know what I was with Ella, a man or a child, in or out of control.

✳

I CALLED ELLA WHEN I got home.

"I wish you'd been here when I woke up. Come back, I already miss you."

"I miss you, too. But I think I'd better leave you guys alone today. I came downstairs and Evan was upset. He didn't want me there. You should be extra-special nice to him." There was commotion in the background, pots banging, kids giggling. "See how happy he sounds now I'm gone? What's going on there anyway?"

"I invited Evan's friend Kaylee over for a playdate. We're making French toast."

I strained to hear if there was an adult male voice in among the laughers. It was one thing to believe Ella and I belonged together while I was weirded out in another dimension of reality. Awake in this real life, not so much. "Oh right, Kaylee."

"And since you're dying to ask but won't—yes, Alex brought her, but he didn't stay."

Of course he didn't. Dr. Chase was a respectful man. "No, come on, I wasn't thinking that." And a clever, patient man. I saw the way he'd looked at Ella. He wasn't going anywhere.

"Good. You shouldn't. And as for Evan, he likes you, Jody. A lot. Probably a little more than he's comfortable with."

"Well, if you say so. But not this morning, I don't think."

"Yes, I'm sure even this morning. The problem wasn't you, it was Ronald."

"Ah, you know."

"Oh yes. It wasn't hard to get it out of him. I know when my son is miserable and I know why. It's bad enough Ronald breaks promises, but I hate that he manipulates Evan's loyalty. Are you sure you don't want to come back for breakfast? I think he'd like you to. And I imagine I could stand it." I could hear her smiling.

Of course I did. I wanted to be with them, in her kitchen eating Tess's French toast with her. I'd watch Evan play with Einstein in the backyard. Kaylee, too. I'd steal caresses and kisses from Ella right under the kids' noses, make us burn for each other all day, until we could be alone. But I didn't want to be another player in Evan's father's loyalty games, and I could do without running into Alex and his x-ray eyes again.

"No, I already ate. And me and two kids—hey, let's not push things. I'm going to go play ball."

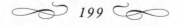

"Okay. Then come for dinner. I'm thinking lasagna. I read some-where that fake Poles like lasagna. You like lasagna, don't you, Jody?"

I'd fallen into a den of women who spoke in tongues, but amaz-ingly I could understand what they were saying. *You're at least part Ital-ian, aren't you, Jody? Just like Matt was?*

"Yes I do. It was a particular specialty of my Great-Aunt Marie's."

"Great-Aunt Marie Kowalczyk?"

"Yeah, right. No. Great-Aunt Marie Cannavarro, destined to be a Bride of Christ until her brother Sal's *puttana* wife ran off with some gangster wannabe and she was recruited for the thankless job of rais-ing the *puttana's* likewise *puttana* daughter—which would be my mother, Marian—and then the second-generation *puttana's* bastard son—which she had when she was fifteen, and which would be me."

There were an endless three seconds of silence on the line, during which infinite time I envisioned Ella on that cushy couch, eyes closed, head bowed, breathing deeply, revisiting the old truism that half an Italian does not a whole Matt Fischer make. It was also time enough to kill the inexplicable anger that had welled up in me during my equally unexpected *puttana* spiel. Like it had a few weeks before, when Tess asked me about my father. I'd been getting angry a lot lately—at Fern, and Ronald, people I barely knew, even at Arwen. I didn't know where it was coming from. I didn't get angry.

"Thank you for sharing that with me, Jody."

She didn't sound all that appalled. More sad, and like she really was glad I'd told her.

"You're welcome. No biggie really. You already know the Kowalczyks aren't my parents. You might as well know the rest."

"I'd like to know the rest. Little by little, when you want to tell me. So, that means once upon a time you were Jody Cannavarro. . . . Jody? Jody? Are you there?"

My silence was so complete she must have thought the line had gone dead. "Yeah, I'm here. No, I was never Jody Cannavarro. Once upon a time I was . . ." I didn't know why it was still so hard to say it, it was just a name. A name. "I was Christopher. Christopher Cannavarro."

"Ah. That's a lot to leave behind."

"Yeah, I guess. It was a long time ago, that's not who I am anymore."

"No, it's not. I'm sorry, but I've got to get back to Evan and Kaylee before they set the stove on fire. Should I expect you for dinner? Or would you prefer later, say nine, after Evan goes to bed?"

"Later." She knew when to stop, and that I wasn't going to be in the mood for lasagna. Just for her.

Man or child. In or out of control. Maybe somewhere, someone knew. But that someone wasn't me.

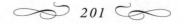

SHE TOLD ME TO STAND still. I moved only my eyes, watched her face as she peeled me naked. With every piece of me she uncovered, touched, kissed, every piece of my clothing she let drop to the floor, the heavy layers of her sad history seemed to fall away from her. I thought then I understood what she'd been ashamed of, that it wasn't so much wanting me, so much younger than her in body and so much less than her in all other ways, as her wanting to be young again herself, in the way she'd been with Matt. Young and passionate and shameless. Now she let it all go, my age and my classlessness and her shame. She still was that young girl, age had nothing to do with who you were inside. When she was done stripping us both bare, she stood in front of me and with that same deliberation took off her own clothes. She looked seventeen to me, and I told her so. She said she felt seventeen. Then she told me I could move if I wanted to.

I'd been right about her after all. She didn't wrench herself away from me this time. She fused to me, and together we traveled to a place where time slowed and light dimmed, where we were alone in

soundless velvet darkness, interchangeable, our molecules jumbled together and spread along the curvature of space as far as forever, the earth
a pulsing blue pinpoint, a sad prisoner of its sun. And for those blessed
breathless minutes before I fell asleep, wrapped up in her arms, I was
an astronaut.

I'd had a lot of sex in my life, enjoyed it in my way, despite it being
the loneliest activity I could imagine. I needed it, it taking me so far
from everything, out some far side of even myself. And I'd always assumed it was the same for everyone, isolating and solitary, but still we
were compelled to seek it out over and over and over because it felt so
much like it should be the answer to the greatest cosmic riddle: Where,
in all of the human experience, does one plus one equal one? Making
love with Ella made me doubt my assumptions, made me wonder if the
rules could be bent, mathematics defied, and, even if just for one high-
flying second, a person could truly be more than himself, could be not
alone. And that it wasn't about the physical act itself, but about finding
the right person to share it with, the person who sheltered the missing
part of you inside her. Making love with Ella made me ponder what
was really out there, if there were places one could go, a means of escape I'd never considered before.

✳

I WOKE UP ONE NEURON-FIRING step ahead of the dream,
its signature spine-numbing opening image sinking down into the bog
of my brain like the Loch Ness monster sliding back into its black
water lair. My heart pumped pure dread.

Ella's room was still new to me and so were the shadows in it. I
jerked upright, my eyes darted to the partially open doorway. Nothing.
No one. Ella turned onto her side, but didn't wake up, not even from
the noise and vibration of my heart. I wasn't planning on leaving, but
just in case I gathered up all my clothes. I put on my pants in the hall-

way while my eyes adjusted to the dark. I could hear the rhythmic sighing of Ella's breath, and then, as if they were breathing a two-part round, Evan's breath joined hers. They fit together perfectly. Mine was raggy, dissonant, off beat, off key.

I edged my way to Evan's door and peered in. He was asleep on his side, his bottom arm hyperextended, his hand near the pile of books on his night table. Up against the back wall was a long slab of plywood set on stacks of bricks, covered by a model train setup. In the light from the street I could make out little villages, the shapes and textures of hills and valleys, bridges and tunnels. It was a complicated setup, years of work had gone into it.

I'd never spent nights in a house with a sleeping child in it, unless that child was me. I'd never been the man leaving the bed of a sleeping woman and walking a hall full of shadows cast by trees outside second-floor windows, bypassing creaking stairs that led down to a room with a piano in it, all to stand by a kid's bedroom door while he slept, surrounded by his books and his toys and the worlds he made to take him away from the one he lived in. Until tonight. And even though tonight I wasn't the kid, and I knew I wasn't the kid, the kid I *had* been, the kid whose sleep was going to be broken into by the man standing in his doorway, came suddenly horribly alive in me. I was that kid again, but for the first time ever I was also the man in the doorway. And for the first time ever I tried to imagine why the man would go into the kid's room, what he felt when he did, what he felt when he took the kid's sleep, his peace, his body away from him. I wasn't aware that I'd so much as twitched a toe, but I was standing by Evan's bedside. I looked down at his pretty blond head on his pillow, at the outline of his defenseless body under a woven-cotton blanket, listened to the unsuspecting evenness of his breath, and I imagined the man would have felt the release of every excruciating thing pent up inside him, and with it a relief so strong and so sweet it defied any other emotion to come near it.

There was a thick ache in the hollow of my throat and a pricking in the cavities inside my head. I backed out of the room, into Einstein. I knelt down and put my arms around her neck. She rested her chin on my shoulder. When I got up and started down the stairs, I gestured for her to stay. I didn't know why, but I wanted her right there, at the entrance to Evan's room. She seemed to consider it, poked her nose into the room, looked around, but then she followed me down, and slept at my feet while I desecrated several of Evan's virgin ring-binder notebook pages with another of my stories for Tess.

For Tess

GAMES

December 7, 1977. It's still dark, but sleep's impossible, so he settles in to wait for the sounds of Scott waking up. School days, assuming he even slept at all, Scott gets up to get Christopher fed and on the bus. But weekends and holidays Christopher has to stay in his room and make no noise until Scott comes for him. During the day Scott can sleep like a bear in winter, Christopher can be pounding on the piano and Scott won't wake up till his drug-slowed blood thaws and starts running again. But late at night, once Marian's asleep and the house is still, he's awake as a vampire, stalking around downstairs in the remaining dark like he's starving mad for fresh blood. Marian's Rip Van Winkle, nothing wakes her up. Most school days Christopher doesn't see her at all.

It's a Wednesday, but it's his birthday and Scott's going to call him in sick, let him stay home from school. So officially, it's a holiday.

Even though it's his birthday, Christopher doesn't mind staying in his room. Over the last few months he's spent a lot of time there, healing up from his fall, and he's come to feel different about it than he used to, different than he's ever felt about any other place. It's <u>his</u> room. Everything in it is for him alone, even the air and the light. The quiet. The solitude. Marian never comes in, never did, and Scott doesn't much anymore. That just sort of happened, little by little, afterward, after Christopher started making his own bed, dusting his furniture and mopping his floor, doing his laundry in the basement, dressing himself, even while his arm was still in the cast. Now Scott'll hang by the door and watch him clean up, or with his Lincoln Logs and cars, with his books. They'll smile at each other, but Scott's eyes don't ask to come in and Christopher's don't invite him.

During those mornings of waiting in his room, he reads. He gets so deep into the words he can ignore his stomach growling, or having to pee, unless it's an emergency and for that he's WD40'd the window sash so he can slide it open without a sound and pee out his window. That morning, he grabs up the book he's been reading every day for the last six months. He's almost to the end. It's a big book, over four hundred pages, and meant for older kids, so it's been a tough haul, but he's going to read every word no matter how long it takes, and then he's going to read it again. There's something in the story he needs to understand, something meant just for him. The book was in one of the cartons left behind in his closet. It's old. On the page inside the cover is handwritten <u>This book is the property of</u> and below that are three names crossed out, then a fourth. When Christopher finishes the book and understands, it will belong to him, and he'll cross out that fourth name and write his own. He wants his name to be the last name ever written there.

The cover is a painting of a boy, older than Christopher but still young, with blond hair. He's a farm boy, from a time long ago. He's sitting facing you, cross-legged on an animal-skinned rug on a wooden floor, staring into the yellow light from an unseen fireplace, a rocking chair and table half in the dark behind him. Next to him is a deer, a fawn. The boy has his arms around the fawn's long neck, he's hugging the fawn to him, protecting it. The boy's got a scared, determined look on his pale face. The book is called <u>The Yearling</u>. The boy's name is Jody. Jody's mother doesn't love him, but his daddy does.

Around nine o'clock, Scott finally knocks on his door, sticks his head in and yells, Get your seven-year-old ass downstairs boy, laughs, and disappears down the hall.

Christopher didn't even hear Scott get up, because of the book, but now he catapults out of bed, dashes to the bathroom to empty his burning bladder, and races to the kitchen. Scott's already at the table, his jittery fingers drumming on the butcher-block top, a cigarette dangling from his mouth. He squints at Christopher through the thin gray smoke, grips the cigarette in his teeth, grins like the Cheshire Cat, and purrs, Why you standing there? Sit down, mongrel. Sit down. The cigarette bobs up and down.

Christopher can't sit down. There's a big bulky package on his chair. It's wrapped—sloppily, with uneven corners and tape sticking out all over, but still—in shiny colorful happy birthday balloons paper. Scott says, What's the problem, buddy? His voice is silly, like he's trying to pretend he doesn't know that Christopher can't sit down because there's this huge package on his chair. Christopher swims up to heaven, weightless as one of those birthday balloons. He loves when his daddy kids around with him like that, it makes him feel like the sun is shining inside him. He pretends back, like he's upset, and says, I can't sit down, Daddy, look, there's something on my chair! Scott leaps up, eyes wide now and all bursting with surprise, and shouts, No shit! Who'd do that? Let me see. Christopher points to the package and compresses his lips, so the laugh he's trying to keep from coming out of his mouth comes snorting out his nose instead. Scott pokes the package and says, Yeah, that's something all right. What do you think it is? Christopher shakes his head and throws up his hands. Scott high-fives him and says, Go on, mongrel. Open it.

Scott's bought him Stars of the NHL sheets and pillowcases, and a comforter, too, with Rangers number 7 Rod Gilbert smack in the middle. And hidden inside the comforter, Stars of the NHL flannel pajamas wrapped around a new pair of ice skates. Christopher practically swoons. Scott raps his knuckles on the table and says, Does your daddy know what you want, or what? Scott points at the skates. Winter's for hockey, am I right? We'll get you a new mitt for Easter. Christopher tramples the balloon paper to get to Scott, his arms can't wait to be around Scott's neck, his head on Scott's shoulder. Scott puts the cigarette on the table, the burning end hanging over the edge, and holds him tight. Scott kisses him on his temple, and says, real soft and right into his ear, I love you,

Chrissie, happy birthday. And then he asks, again, Everything's okay, right?

I fell off my bike. That's what Christopher said, to the nurse at the hospital, to Marian, to everyone on Superior Street, to the kids at school, to his first-grade teacher, Miss O'Reilly, who has red hair and freckles and a voice like music and who drew a flower on his cast and kissed his cheek and who he would never lie to. So it must be true. He remembers something else, but that only exists for him, and he tries not to think about it because then he gets confused, and it was a long time ago, and he knows that if he asks Scott does that memory maybe exist for him, too, he'll make Scott unhappy. And more than anything in the world, Christopher doesn't want to make Scott unhappy.

He lifts his head from Scott's shoulder, looks him in the eye, and says, again, Right. Everything's okay. I love you, too, Daddy.

Lennie comes over after aikido, and Christopher runs to meet him at the door. Even though it's only 8:30, and Scott won't send him to bed for hours, Christopher's been in his hockey star pajamas since after dinner. They're uncomfortably stiff, he's itchy and sweaty in the overheated living room, but there's no way in this world he's going to wait to put them on. He's ready to suffer for love. He hauls open the door and stands in front of Lennie, beaming up at him, saying nothing, bouncing, waiting. Lennie looks him over head to toe, nods his big round head and says, Whoa-ho, Mule Train, looking bad. Looking baaaaaad.

Lennie's brought him a couple of presents, a board game called Go and a single magazine in a clear plastic sleeve. It's the July 28, 1969, issue of Newsweek. The moon landing issue, a staticky photograph of Neil Armstrong standing on the surface of the moon on the cover. Scott watches through narrowed eyes as Christopher goggles at Lennie, his mouth wide open, nothing coming out. Lennie winks at him, gestures toward the stairs, says, Go put that in your hope chest, Mule Train. Then I'll teach you how to play the best game ever invented.

They play Go, black and white stones on the orange board, Christopher soaking up Lennie's instructions, his philosophies about patience and balance, concentration and discipline, beauty and intellect, as if his brain is a plot of dry summer dirt in a too-brief rainstorm. Scott sits on the couch smoking joints, snorting a little coke, flipping through a _Hustler_ and a pile of gun and combat magazines, glancing at the Go board every once in a while with an increasingly pissed-off look.

Two hours later Christopher packs up the game. As Lennie gets up to leave he smiles down at Christopher and says, _Si, si, mi muchacho._ A fine brain indeed. We'll play once a week, Mule Train, sound good? Scott puts down his magazine, says, Maybe I'll play with you, in between. Lennie hoots and snorts like that's the funniest thing he's ever heard. Man, that I'd like to see. Candyland's more your speed, Sundance. And speaking of candy, leave some for the customers, man. That's your boy's college tuition. Scott growls, Fuck you smartass. Lennie winks at Christopher, flashes a grin, says, Your dopey daddy's jealous 'cause you're smarter than he is. Christopher thinks it's all a riot, since he and Scott really do play Candyland, and Chutes & Ladders. He grins up at Lennie and quotes, Just keep thinkin' Butch, that's what you're good at. He's watched that movie with them a dozen times, he knows who's who. Scott rears up off the sofa, rocket throws a magazine at laughing Lennie, points a finger and shouts, Fuck you and the horse you rode in on, you fucking asshole. Christopher starts to giggle and doesn't stop until the door closes behind Lennie. Scott turns to him then, his face bleached white as bone with anger, and hisses, You better not be laughing at me, you stupid gook.

Christopher gurgles around his next giggle. He can't find enough air to breathe and he's gone cold in his new too warm pajamas. He stares up into Scott's eyes, hard icy-blue with an awful lifeless look in them, and he feels something skitter up his spine, like a blind hairy-legged insect, and start to probe and chew at the base of his skull. Scott says, You like games better than what I got you, huh, monkey? We can play a game. Ready? It's called war. Here are the rules. You hide. I find you. I blow your head off. Sounds like fun, right? Scott picks his gun off the coffee table and levels it at Christopher. Get going. Christopher's nailed to the floor, he's the weight of a planet, he can't move. Scott puts the barrel of the gun to Christopher's forehead. He says, I'm going to count to ten, you'd better fucking get going, little monkey.

Christopher's legs are as shaky as a newborn foal's, but he manages to clamber up the stairs, Scott's droning voice trailing after him, nipping at his seven-year-old birthday ass. There's light coming from his bedroom, where he left his sailboat lamp on, but he still can't see too well. There's a weird purple film over his eyes. He gains the upstairs landing. Five! It's a small house, and there isn't a lot of furniture in it. It's not like there are a ton of places to hide. Six! He hears his breath like a dog panting, he feels the beating of his heart inside his sticky pajamas. Seven! He runs into his room, his baby foal knees buckle at the threshold and he falls. Eight! He thinks, Scott doesn't like coming in here anymore, maybe he won't. Nine! He scrambles across the floor, aiming for the closet but he's afraid he won't make it so he shinnies under the bed, reaches up, and pulls on his new comforter until part of it touches the floor and he balls himself up behind that red, white, and blue curtain. Ten!

It's not like Scott doesn't know from the get-go where Christopher is. But he crashes around first in his and Marian's room, in the bathroom, bellowing like a bull, Where are you, you yellow mother fucker! The sounds mix with the deafening insect buzz in Christopher's ears. He senses Scott's bulk in his doorway like a massive cloud over the moon. Scott backs into the hall, pulls down the ladder to the attic, and yells up, Are you hiding up there, monkey? As much time as Christopher's been alive, that's how long it feels before Scott finds him. Probably actually ten minutes. Scott flips the comforter back onto the bed and thrusts his head forward like a striking snake. Everything in Christopher's life dissolves into a dream and all that's real is Scott's flushed twisted face, his teeth bared in a death grin. The shine of the gun in his hand. The blood singing in Christopher's ears.

Scott hauls Christopher from under the bed, pushes him onto the floor on his back, straddles him, puts the barrel of the gun at his lips. Lie still and open your mouth, monkey boy. Here comes the fun part. Here's where I blow your head off. Christopher lies as still as a corpse, except for his teeth, clenched in terror, uppers rattling against lowers. Scott pushes the gun between his lips. Don't make me break your nice new teeth. Open your mouth. Something happens then, and Christopher slips through the floor under his back. He knows he must still be lying there, but he's beneath the floor too, looking up through the plywood and carpeting at Scott and Christopher playing. It's so strange, but it's peaceful and he's not afraid there under the floor. He's not anything at all.

Christopher opens his mouth and the six-inch stainless steel barrel of Scott's prized Colt Python .357 Magnum scrapes past his teeth, down his throat. He can't breathe, the air has turned into the taste of steel and oil. Christopher pees himself, hot liquid soaks into his new pjs, spreads into the carpet underneath him. He's so scared, scared that Scott will see and know he's a coward. Under-the-floor Christopher doesn't feel scared, but he's scared for the other Christopher, who's crying, the tears rolling into his mouth, taking up whatever room is left. He's choking, but there's nothing under-the-floor Christopher can do except float in the nothingness of where he is and wait. Scott bears down on Christopher and says,

Don't cry. Did the gooks cry? No they didn't. Is my kid more yellow than a gook? No he isn't. Don't cry. I mean it. Do…not…cry. You'll spoil the game. Under-the-floor Christopher squeezes his mind with all his might and thinks, be brave, stop crying, and the other Christopher blinks a few times and stops crying, just like that. Scott blinks a few times, then he smiles and says, Okay, tonight you live. He laughs. His eyes, his face, all of him relaxes, like the strings being let go on a marionette. The hand holding the gun falls away and the gun is jerked out of Christopher's mouth. The protruding top slide slices the flesh at the left corner and now there's blood in his mouth and it tastes metallic, just like the gun.

Scott climbs off Christopher, leans against the bed. Good game, huh, mongrel? Exciting, not like that boring Go shit. Fucking brainiac Cardoza. You really got into it. We'll do it again. He lays the gun on the floor, peers over at Christopher. Are you bleeding, man? He probes at the cut. That's pretty deep. Stay here, I'll get my stuff. Then you got to go to bed. It's late. Scott leaves the room and Christopher becomes one again. Now he can feel his scorched throat, the side of his mouth pulsing with pain. Scott returns, cleans and tapes the cut, tucks Christopher into his new sheets, kisses him on the forehead, then draws back, puts a hand on Christopher's cheek, looks down at him. For a minute again Christopher sees Jesus on the cross in his old bedroom, that sad love. Scott says, The things we do here, Chrissie, don't tell anyone. They wouldn't understand. I'm the only one loves you enough to teach you the hard stuff. It's okay if you don't get it now. You will, later. Trust me. Scott gives him a red pill. Take this, it'll make that cut stop hurting. Scott turns off the sailboat lamp. He comes to stand over him again and out of the dark he says, Tomorrow we'll go to the rink, break in those skates, okay, buddy? He starts to go, but turns at the door. Next time, you tell Lennie you don't want to play that asshole game again. You're my kid, you play games with me. Christopher feels a rushing, a dropping sensation in his head, like water being pulled down a dark drain. He doesn't say anything. Scott says, I want you to tell him. He waits, a tall black shadow against the hall light. From somewhere in the sewer, Christopher says, Okay. Okay, Daddy. I'll tell him. I didn't like it anyway. Really. I didn't.

He can't suck his thumb, he can't pray for what he wants, now he can't cry. It's nighttime, he can't go out and run or bike or skate or throw a ball. He's got a whole colony of frantic ants trapped in his head, he can't read. Suddenly, the ants go berserk, hurtling around behind his eyes so furiously that for a minute he can't see a thing. What if Scott doesn't like that he's reading grown-up books, tells him to stop? _The Yearling_ is on the dresser, right next to the sailboat lamp. His legs are wobbly again, but he makes it there, rescues the book. There aren't many more places to hide it than there are to hide him, so he puts it back deep in the carton in the closet. He puts Neil Armstrong in there, too. Just in case. He leaves an alphabet book from school on the dresser as a decoy.

The ants won't settle down. Christopher knows the red pills put people to sleep. Fast and silent as a wraith he's at Marian's night table, gets another one from the bag there, and forces it through the fire in his throat. Back in his room he strips off his pajamas, tops and bottoms, and lays them over the wet spot on the carpet. He'll wash everything tomorrow.

Naked and cold, Christopher curls himself around a pillow, pulls a second one over his head. He begins to count backward from a hundred, saying each number slowly and clearly in his mind, and before too long the ants are finally quiet.

Christopher thinks he does already understand what Scott's teaching him—how not to be bad, how not to do things he'll be punished for. Although if he tries to see the pattern in Scott's love, like he sees in music, or letters, or in arithmetic, nothing holds, everything scatters into formlessness. So he despairs of ever making Scott proud, because how is he ever going to learn all of what Scott's trying to teach him if he can't see the pattern, if he can't get clear <u>what</u> those bad things are that he does, if he doesn't feel the badness in him until it's too late, until his punishment has already started?

He absolutely learns one thing that night, though. He learns to be afraid of Scott. He learns to recognize a certain look in Scott's eyes and set to his face that warns of punishment coming. And since he never does learn how to tell when that's going to happen, when he's about to be bad, Christopher learns to be afraid of Scott all the time. Even while he's loving him. Even when there's nothing to be afraid of.

That little piece of knowledge is a better gift even than the sheets, the comforter, the pajamas, the skates, his second big-boy scar, a doozy at the side of his mouth to match the one on his left arm. It isn't the kind of gift he'll grow bored with, or too big for in a year. It's the kind he'll keep for a lifetime. Like the scars, he'll see his fear every time he looks in a mirror, and he'll be reminded each time of how much Scott loves him. Bicycles become too small and sheets fade, but scars and fear are indestructible. They're like diamonds, like time. They're forever.

Oh, and no, in case you're curious, he doesn't get anything from Marian, not even a bologna sandwich. A few days later she half-heartedly tries to pretend the NHL stuff was from her, too, and when Scott apologizes for her Christopher curls his taped-up lip and says, Like I give a shit— clearly he's been paying sharp attention at the Scott and Lennie school of descriptive conversation, although he doesn't actually get what making doody has to do with caring about something—to which Scott replies, That's my boy! and laughs for ten minutes. In any case, that's what he says, although privately he's waiting for her to pull something out of her bag or her bathrobe pocket when she clomps downstairs at lunchtime, or to look at him across the kitchen table and say something about the cut on his mouth. He holds out for about another week, until his hoping starts to cut at him worse than Scott's gun and he remembers what he told himself about wanting things after he killed his aunt Marie. Never again. The only thing safe to kill, he finally realizes, is hope itself.

Fourteen

I CAME CLOSE TO BURNING those pages myself.
     I didn't know what to do with them, I just knew I didn't
     want to pollute Ella's house, so I snuck outside and stashed the
folded bundle under the stairs, in the wooden bin that held the building's garbage cans. When I turned from relocking the outer door, Ella
was at the door to the apartment, a sapphire-blue silk robe belted
around her. I'd been quiet, but I should've known that even asleep she
was connected to her son, attuned to the danger signals of someone
moving around her house, doors opening and closing at three thirty in
the morning.

She closed and locked her door, tilted her head, and looked the
question at me.

I attempted what I think is called a guileless look in return. "I
needed a little air."

She eyed me, head to toe, nothing on but my pants. "And that is
why God invented windows."

I smiled, chuckled, didn't say anything.

"Not going to tell me why you've been up since a quarter to two,
huh?"

"I'm sorry. I didn't mean to wake you, I thought you were asleep."

"No. I was waiting for you to calm down and come back to bed. I

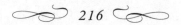

respect your privacy, but when I heard the door open I thought you were leaving."

I glanced down at my bare feet. "I wasn't leaving. I just needed to step outside for a second."

"Okay. Because I wouldn't let you." She moved closer. "I'd come after you, you know."

I played with the ends of her silk belt. "Really?" It was banter. Easy to say. She'd come after Evan, sure, but she was just flirting with me.

"Yes, really." She put her hands on my chest, moved them slowly, her eyes following everywhere they went. After a few minutes she held my head between her hands and looked into my eyes. "I'm going to say the words, and I want you to let yourself hear them."

"That's okay, I heard them." I had, she'd written them with her hands and eyes and when it was her saying them, that way, I could nearly stand to hear them.

"That's not good enough. I'm going to say them. Out loud. Prepare yourself . . . You. Are. So. Incredibly. Beautiful."

I tried to turn my head away but she was one strong woman.

"Okay okay I heard it thank you so are you." That was so not the way I'd wanted to tell her how beautiful she was, I actually groaned with regret.

"Jody, somewhere in your heart you have to know it's true. You don't need to be afraid of it, or apologize for it. Your looks were not why . . . why somebody hurt you."

"That's got nothing to do with it. *I* think I'm weird-looking is all."

No, it wasn't why someone shoved guns down my throat, put cigarettes out on my ass, et cetera, et cetera, and no, Scott's hands and eyes had never said what Ella's did. But how could anyone ever be sure about that, about the things he did that didn't leave scars. How could anyone say absolutely that it wasn't true, or that if I'd been ugly to begin with, Scott would have made me beautiful, and not the other way around.

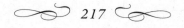

"Who was it, Jody? Your grandfather, Sal?"

"Sal was definitely less fun than, say, a barrel of monkeys, but no, it wasn't him. It was some guy named Scott that my mother lived with for a while."

"How long a while?" Her voice was petal soft and her right hand strayed to Scott's handiwork on my left shoulder.

"Four years." I ambushed her hand and put it somewhere better. "I really don't want to talk about him right now."

I pulled the belt open and the edges of her slinky robe fell apart. "It's you. You're the beautiful one." I slid my hands beneath the silk, kissed her mouth, her throat, her breasts, crouched down before her. An entire universe of freckled constellations shone in the Milky Way of her skin, all with secret shapes and meanings I had yet to uncover.

She moaned. "Oh, God, what am I going to do with you."

Her head fell forward, her hair fell around my shoulders and bent head. I looked up into her face through the threads of a red-gold curtain.

"You could show me how comfortable that couch is."

Fifteen

IRETRIEVED THE PAGES IN the morning, on my way home. It was hard to touch them, and not because they were clammy from the night air and the seeping of wet garbage. If I'd had my lighter with me—tick season was over so it was in the glove compartment of my car—maybe I'd have torched the thing right there. But probably not. I was no bigger a believer in the truth setting you free as I was in love conquering all, and I was just peachy with lies of the sin of omission rather than commission variety, but bald-faced lying to Tess just wasn't possible for me. Even thinking of doing it left me feeling like there was an enormous air bubble filling my lungs.

I put the story in the desk drawer before I showered and changed clothes for work. Big mistake. It took me ten days to touch it again, to leave it for her, and another two days to face her. I mean, it was bad, even I could see that, and it was possible she might have something to say this time. It was not, of course, as bad as if I'd kept going, to a night a few months later. But I wasn't about to go there. Not even with Tess. *There* was what lies of omission were created for. If there was even a snowball's chance in hell that she actually thought I was the reincarnation of her son or some such, better she didn't know everything he'd signed on for this time around. Likely death by land mine or bayonet was bad enough.

It was twelve days later when I finally knocked on her door.

"Come."

She was standing in the middle of her tiny living room, staring at the door, at me, her hands to her throat, my story crumpled under her fingers. I had the disturbing impression she'd been standing there like that for most of those two days. She looked a hundred years old.

"I'm sorry."

"Stop that. Who are you apologizing to?"

"I don't know. You. You never asked for these, I shouldn't bother you with them."

"I did ask for them. I want them. That doesn't mean it's easy to read them. Come here." I obeyed. She pried a hand loose and touched the scar at my mouth. "Does it hurt?"

"No. It's just cuts and bruises, you know, it heals, the pain goes away. None of it hurts anymore. Anyway, it was another life."

"It was this life, and pain doesn't go away. Cuts and bruises heal, but the pain of them stays. You carry it somewhere deep, forever. But we carry joy the same way, don't we, *caro?*"

She looked at me with a pointed sort of hopefulness as she asked that. That was why she wanted me and Ella together. Ella and Matt had brought joy to each other, so why not Ella and me, why not this time enough joy to balance out the pain, enough to keep me from doing something stupid and fucking it all up the way Matt had. She was giving me way too much credit, of course, and her mind had gotten loose in its aging wishfulness, she'd forgotten that pain and joy aren't always on opposite sides of the scale, that when they're meted out just right, by someone whose scale only had one side to begin with, you end up not being able to tell one from the other.

"We do, sure. Thank goodness, right? So, did Ella tell you that thing about my birthday . . . about it being the same as Matt's?"

"Yes, she told me. It confused her, I don't know why. When else should you have been born?" Matter of fact, her eyes childlike orbs of innocent certainty. Her connection to that world beyond was so solid, so real to her.

"So it's true then. You think I'm Matt, that he's in me somehow?"

I had trouble holding her eye. Not because it felt loony to ask her. Nothing felt loony with Tess. It was that bringing it up with her was such a killer Moment of Truth. But I had to know. Did she really think I was her son? Did she think that Matt's shredded soul had been so traumatized that it couldn't see where it was going and he missed the path of white light and plummeted back into darkness, screaming blind into a three-month-old fetus conceived in sin and empty of a soul of its own, or with a soul that had already oopsed to its viciously bad choice of womb and was scouring the ether for someone to hold his plasmatic digits while his soul got shredded, too? Because if she did believe it then maybe somewhere in there lay the answer to the unanswerable Why? of my life, past present and future.

She shook her head and waved a hand, as if to dismiss the wrong-headed simplicity of my question.

"This is what I know. Every time I see you, I see him, I feel him near me just as you are near me. To think of either of you is to think of you both. You and Matt are linked, Jody, I am sure of it. You have been searching for me, and for Ella, since the day your souls met. You have been seeking your peace together."

Not peace itself, but a heavy peaceful feeling came over me, like when I was little and Scott would wrap me up in the orange-and-brown blanket he kept on the couch to cover up the rips in the upholstery, and I'd know that the Bad Thing was over and I was loved and not alone, and I could go to sleep now. I think I must have closed my eyes right there on my feet, because Tess's hand was gripping my arm and she was saying, "Jody. I know you're tired, but it's not time. We have to deal with this."

She waved the pages under my nose like they were smelling salts. The breeze and musty odor worked like a charm. My eyes popped open.

"Right." I was prepared as a Boy Scout, had the Zippo with me. I reached into my pocket for it, but didn't take it out. Something felt wrong. The same as when I knew I had to get the story out of Ella's house. "Not here. There isn't enough room. Let's go into the park."

"The park, yes. And then we can sit and talk until dinner? If you have time?"

We burned it into the ground, on a patch of powdery dirt between the roots of a massive oak tree. I found a sharp-edged rock and worked the patch over until the ashes were blended into the dirt. Then we sat on a bench, making easy talk for a little while. She told me a cute story about Evan turning down her offer of a five dollar loan to buy a present for Ella's upcoming birthday—it clearly tickled her like mad when he announced that he didn't "believe in accruing debt"—and I found out that Ella's birthday was November 14.

Her chuckles died away. It wasn't Evan she wanted to talk about, it was Matt.

She took my hand, held it on her lap, and told me hard things about him, how much she'd feared for him in this world, because he was too much like her, but with his father's unexpectedly fragile core, nothing in him steely and sure enough to navigate a steady path through the pains of life. And how from the time he was a little boy he was able to feel down to where the pain of *her* lost life had lodged in her, and it hurt him, and although she reassured him that she was not unhappy, he couldn't accept the present, he was too seized by the past and worried about the future, so he took on the responsibility for her discontent, and for his father's optimistic dreams, and ended up believing that he'd failed them both, that he would always fail the people he loved most. He lived life too intensely for someone so young, and if he'd been an adolescent today, someone would surely have suggested one of those new drugs, Zoloft, or Prozac, to reset his wiring, make things easier for him. I listened, those two photos of him vivid in my mind, his eager face and haunted eyes, and I began to see more clearly the pattern in what linked us, why he'd picked my destiny to hitch a ride on.

We sat quietly for a few more minutes, then Tess said, "When the time comes, when your peace comes, you'll both know how wrong you were, and that you never failed. And you'll know how much you were loved." She stroked my hand. "It will be soon now."

Oddly enough, I didn't entirely disbelieve her, and that heavy peaceful feeling stole over me again.

O N AN UNSEASONABLY CHILLY NIGHT in early April of 1978, Scott, having recently and successfully inducted Christopher into the realm of war games, properly balances things out by inducting him into the realm of love games.

Scott and Marian have a screamer of a fight, Marian takes a sleeping pill and kicks Scott out of the bedroom, Scott starts downstairs to sleep on the couch. Nothing new. He glances into the open doorway of Christopher's room on his way down the hall, sees the kid lying on his side, sucking away on the corner of his sheet, his eyes and ears covered with his pillow. Again, nothing new. What's new is that Scott doesn't have to swallow crap from anyone anymore. He has someone he can spit it all out on to.

Marian's put the lights out, she's down till noon, but he goes back and closes the door anyway. Then he goes into Christopher's room, sits at the edge of Christopher's bed.

"It's okay, Chrissie, we're done fighting." He pulls the pillow and sheet away from Christopher's face and runs his fingers through the boy's luxuriant hair. "You're upset, though. How about I curl up with you for a while before I go downstairs?"

"Oh yeah, Daddy." Fear and vigilance have been his constant companions since the day of his birthday and nothing else bad happened. There's no punishing look in Scott's eyes now. The prospect of falling asleep in his own bed cuddled with his daddy is almost more bliss than he can stand. "Here, I'll make room." He shifts on the single bed, puts his back against the wall and makes himself as thin and small as he can, the little mouse seeking to find his way inside Scott's love again.

Scott climbs in, sets his back to Christopher. "Snuggle up." He reaches behind him, finds Christopher's hand and sets it on his hip. Christopher sighs and nestles his small body into the contours of Scott's long frame. Scott waits a couple of minutes, then takes Christopher's hand again and says, "You want to touch me?"

"What do you mean?" Christopher's muscles tense in confusion.

"We love each other, right?"

"Yes."

"Okay then. I'm going to show you how you touch someone when you really love them. Pay attention." Scott pulls on Christopher's hand, guides it through the opening in his briefs and puts it on his penis.

※

THE PATTERN IS SOON CEMENTED in place. Christopher never complains or reveals any signs of distress. Rather, he becomes every day more loving, more obedient, more loyal to Scott. Christopher's devotion and displays of physical affection put more pressure on Scott's belief in his own unworthiness than Scott can tolerate. Ultimately, Christopher's loving behavior engenders an abusive reaction of one sort—sexual, physical, emotional—from Scott, who then, out of shame and guilt at his own weakness, rains one of the other sorts of abuse down on Christopher as punishment for having provoked the previous one by being too pretty, too stupid, too smart, too vulnerable, too reticent, too available, et cetera, et cetera. Christopher understands that it's his fault that Scott has to express his love this way, a love that Christopher never questions. He doesn't understand what his fault is, but clearly there is something very wrong with him and Scott is trying hard to fix it.

On the heels of nearly every episode, Scott tells Christopher how much he loves him and takes him out to play ball or skate or bike or run, is tender and patient with him for hours, compliments him on every move he makes, buys him ice cream. So it's possible that Christopher does unconsciously seek out Scott's abuse, if not provoke it. Not by deserving it, not by *being* any one unacceptable thing, but because his constant terror at the anticipation of it warps his behavior, and because he comes to crave the reward that follows the same way Scott craves his drugs, with an insatiable gnawing hunger. Like an ant on a Möbius strip, Christopher is suspended in a permanent state of disorientation, crawling along an endless loop of punishment and reward, love and pain, fear and joy, confusion and more confusion, the one thing leading inevitably to the other to the other to the other. On and on and on.

School becomes a bewildering place, and he can't remember that or why he squirmed with excitement on the bus each morning. Everything he loves about school threatens his life with Scott, its specialness, its glorious isolation. And so, a quick student, he teaches himself not to love school anymore. Like an inversion of nature, a butterfly metamorphosing back into a caterpillar, Christopher, one of the liveliest and smartest kids in his elementary school, morphs into yet another disappointing uncommunicative little boy who can't pay attention. He has no friends. He can't let anyone see the way he lives, and Scott can't let him see the way other people live.

Marian knows what's happening but chooses to ignore it, as she's chosen to ignore everything about Christopher since the night he was conceived. As for everyone else—Lennie, neighbors, schoolmates, teachers—you'd think the devastations to Christopher's mind and soul, not to mention the scars and broken bones, would be apparent even with the collusive pains Christopher and Scott take to hide them. Incredibly enough, however, for over three years nobody manages to notice one goddamned single solitary suspicious thing.

Sixteen

HALLOWEEN. THE DARK INVADES THE world of light, monsters roam the streets, mischief is expected. It was Scott's favorite holiday. For two days before, Scott, Lennie, and I would bundle candy instead of pills and money. The neighborhood around Superior Street was lousy with trick-or-treating kids. I was not among them. Scott had to be home to dole out candy bundles + I couldn't go out without Scott = Mule Train renamed Doler Train for the night, the skeleton's assistant. That was Scott's permanent costume, although he barely needed one to look the part. He'd buy me something scary, rubbery, and sweltering and we'd hang by our door dropping candy into bags until the streets were empty of everything but splattered eggs, toilet paper, and sweet puke. Then we'd close and lock the door, keep our costumes on, and let the real fun begin. In three years I was infused with enough Halloween spirit to last me several lifetimes.

That night never ceased to work its magic on me. The charged and uncontrolled energy in the atmosphere, all those costumed people, their egos abandoned, ids on display, gleefully playing at crossing the line between good and evil. It came around, year after year, and I never found a way to filter it out, to not be blown backward by it into a storm of memories. I devolved like a werewolf under a full moon, so I stayed off the streets and enjoyed All Hallow's Eve shut up in my own room, bombarding myself with music, books, movies to try and ward off the shakes and keep the worst of the dark from finding me. There hadn't yet been a power on earth able to pry me loose, not even Ella's invitation to go trick-or-treating with her and Evan "Harry Potter" Landreth. Not even my paranoia that they'd go with the good doctor and Kaylee instead.

I was going to have only four more Saturdays off—we'd be done at Parkside by Thanksgiving, starting an office renovation after the holiday—so I lingered at Ella's, playing cards and Monopoly with Evan while Ella gave her lessons, grabbing time with her in between. She had a legitimate student in my old slot, and gave me lessons late in the evening—despite my original nonmusical motivation I'd come to like being at the piano again. But the best was afterward, when we'd lie on the floor with closed eyes, our bodies touching, and listen to the music she loved, pianos violins cellos shivering and soaring, dissolving the walls and ceiling, and the floor beneath our backs, spinning us out among the stars.

That morning of Halloween I taught Evan how to play blackjack and he taught me how to play *quidditch*. Well, theoretically that is, it not being real, but something from Harry Potter, a flying broomstick pololike sport. Whatever. I didn't listen too carefully to his description of the rules, it was a kid's fantasy. I was more interested in how juiced up he got talking about it, how he wanted to be a Seeker. Details of the position escaped me but clearly it came with the dream glory of a World Cup MVP. I decided right then that he needed to learn to be good at something that used his undersized body and not his oversized brain, so he wouldn't always feel like a wimp inside himself. Or in front of his father. Ten minutes later I'd gotten him to agree to let me teach him to Rollerblade. I have to say, I amazed myself with my kid-savvy cleverness in this matter. I let him win a hand and then said, "Hey, your mom's birthday is in a couple of weeks, right?"

He moaned, squirmed as if I'd goosed him with a hot wire. "Oh no, don't remind me! It's two weeks from tomorrow and I have *no* idea what to get her! There's a bracelet she likes, in the window of the Tibetan Bazaar, you know, that store on Bleecker? But it costs *ten dollars!!!*" He went rag-doll, arms and legs dangling off the chair, head back, his pleading face aimed straight at heaven.

The basics of this, of course, I already knew. And that he wasn't angling for a loan, but for someone to pull him out of the depths of his gift doodoo.

"Yikes. She's got expensive taste."

"Tell me about it." The pleading butterscotch eyes turned toward me.

I appeared to mull over his dilemma with supreme gravity. I took my time. Then I made like a lightbulb had gone off in my head, I may even have raised an index finger, and said, "I have an idea . . ."

"What? What?"

"Well, sometimes, the best presents are things money can't buy." True, although I'd already bought something for Ella in the event that wasn't her philosophy. And because I couldn't wait to see how she'd look in it, before I teased it off her. "How about *doing* something for her, something new, something she'd never think you could do, really surprise her."

He looked dubious, and confused, until he got where I was going, and then he looked scared and skeptical. "Oh, gosh, I don't know . . . Like, like what?"

I shrugged. "Oh, I don't know . . . like . . . I teach you to Rollerblade and the morning of her birthday you come zooming down the block with a dozen roses in your hand. They only cost five simoleons at the mini-market on Sixth. You have five simoleons, don't you?"

He snickered. He turned a pure shade of pink. "You'd do that? You'd teach me?"

"Sure. You, me, and Tess are hanging out next Saturday while your mom goes to that school conference? We could start then. Tess won't tell. We could sneak away a bit on Sunday, too. You'll pick it up fast—I saw the way you dove over that couch—you'll be a natural."

Pink to crimson. "Okay. I guess we could try. It'd be a cool gift, I think she'd like it. I mean, you're really good, and if *I* got really good . . ."

He could make his father proud into the bargain.

"You will. You'll show everybody, mark my words."

I saw a smile start, down in Evan's toes, burble through his bloodstream, and get bigger and lighter as it rose. He wrestled it down to a cynical twitch when it hit his mouth, but I knew what he was really feeling, and a blast of pleasure flooded my brain. Similar physically, but in no other conceivable way the same as all the times Scott wedged a straw up my nose, pushed my head down over the coke mirror and ordered me to inhale.

✳

I ENDED UP LINGERING TOO long. By midafternoon the Village—east and west—was Halloween madness ground zero. I put on my sunglasses and pulled my baseball cap down tight, then let Einstein lead me across town as if I were sightless, as if blindness guaranteed invisibility. You'd think I'd know better.

The streets were mayhem. It was impossible to walk five steps without being jostled, or smacked by a sweaty body part or devil's pitchfork or mermaid's tail . . . or a skeleton. The corner of my street was overrun by a coven of wild-wigged Goliath trannies, their hairless skin and buffed pecs and biceps bulging out of skintight dresses. I tried to go around them, but they broke ranks and circled me. *Ooooooo, aren't you the pretty one. Why don't you take off those glasses? Oh, honey, he should take off everything. Girlfriend, I'm tying this one up and taking him home. Hmm-mmm.* They moved close, laughing, plucking at me like parrots-gone-bad with bright acrylic-nailed fingers. I was half a block from my building, all I wanted was to get there. In my mind I saw myself yelling out, pushing them away, but I couldn't access the connection between my brain and body. My range of vision shrunk, I couldn't see where Einstein was and I got panicky, all I could see were painted faces ringed around me. Then one of the faces, long and bony with pale stubble beneath the thick makeup, grinned, a mean slash of thin red lips, and long bony fingers pressed into my crotch. The red lips touched my ear. They were wet. "What do you say, pretty boy? You like?" The fingers tightened around my balls. An electric jolt ran up my spine and exploded through the back of my head.

"Get the fuck *off me!!"*

I twisted the trannie's arm high and hard behind his back. I pushed and kicked him. He lurched on his stilettos, tumbled into two of the others. My body wanted to follow him, to push and kick until he was helpless on the ground, but there was a tug at my wrist, a fleeting memory of being pulled off someone crying under me, a freckled young face framed in red hair looking at me in horror. The trannie's red mouth opened, I felt the sound waves of his angry yell, but all I heard through the misty silence was Einstein barking. The handle of her leash was tangled around my wrist. An opening appeared in the circle and she drew me through it.

I LOCKED THE DOOR, LOWERED and shut the blinds. Put a Radiohead disk into my Walkman, inserted the earplugs, cranked up the volume, and lay down in the middle of the living room floor. On my back, eyes glued to the ceiling. The floor wouldn't stop rocking. I rolled into the corner. It was calmer there. I curled into a ball with my back against the wall. Einstein lay near me. When the last of the light around the edges of the blinds was finally gone, I led her into the kitchen and in the dark I put food in her bowl. I sat on the floor while she ate. I didn't eat.

At some point I was going to have to take Einstein out. Not far, only across the street to Tompkins Square Park, and she'd know to be quick, no walk tonight. She was such a good girl, so patient with me. We watched *Apollo 13*. Then it was time to go.

The park was heaving with people so we stayed just outside it, opposite my building. I put my back to the park entrance while Einstein peed, tensed and held my breath when someone with a light quick tread came out of the park and brushed by behind me. Whoever it was didn't slow or stop. I let the breath go. Einstein let me know she was done, we headed back home. My key was in the front door lock when I felt a presence behind and then beside me, silent and menacing as a ghost. My heart tripped over itself, my knees went weak. I forced myself to turn my head. Her tiny frame was stiff inside a long black raincoat, her round eyes sucked at mine like miniature black holes. At that moment, with my defenses shorted out until the dawn of a new day, an actual ghost, even Scott's, would have been a less frightening sight than her.

"What are you doing here?"

"Brendan told me you never go out on Halloween . . . it brings back bad memories . . ."

I bent down to get a good peek at her. She didn't look well. Paler than ever.

"Right. That's what *I'm* doing here. What are *you* doing here?"

"Brendan is at—"

"I know where he is." Brendan and some college frat friends organized a Halloween bash every year at Windows on the World, at the top of the World Trade Center, where they all worked. It was their talisman against growing old, they'd done it every year since they'd graduated, they'd do it until they were all dead. "Why aren't you with him?"

"I told him to go without me. He knows I don't like parties." Her voice was bewildered, awe-filled, like a sleepwalker, her mind unaware of what her body was doing. She looked away for a second. I thought the shock of the seedy surroundings might wake her up, but when she looked back at me her eyes were still bottomless, turned inward.

"I was thinking about memories . . . bad memories . . ."

She didn't touch me, but still I felt her, her scrambled energy, like a tropical hurricane whirling around me, pelting me with drops of unreasoning need. If she didn't know what she was doing or why she was there, I did. I guess I'd known this moment was coming since the day we'd met. I'd been a coward, or a fool, and pretended it wasn't true. Now it was here and it was too late, I wasn't prepared. Even unconscious, she'd been able to follow the dots. . . . I'd be home, I'd be alone, I'd be in bad shape. I'd be vulnerable. I had to make her leave.

"It's a bad night for me, Fern. I need to be alone. Go away. Go home."

Any bite my words might have had blew away in a gust of that hot wind coming off her. A part of me was melting down into something primordial.

"Please let me come upstairs, just for a little while." She hugged her coat to her body. "It's cold." It was, at the coldest, sixty-five degrees. "Please."

The dire pleading, the raw pain in those eyes of hers, in her voice—
it was wicked.

She followed me up the stairs. Into my apartment. She stalled just
across the threshold, I had to reach around her and slam the door shut.
Her head jerked, a thin mewl of fear leaked from her. First-time girls
almost always felt compelled to remark on how peculiarly nice, clean,
and neat my place was for a single guy, but Fern was too out of it to
actually see anything. She looked around, didn't say a word. Then she
noticed my computer, a new desktop. The sight of it, a known artifact
of the modern world she inhabited rather than the prehistoric one she
undoubtedly pictured me living in, snapped her out of her trance. She
strolled into the living room, played her fingers over the computer's
keyboard. It was shut down, the monitor screen black. She turned. The
haughty expression she reserved for me was on her face again.

"Do you actually use this for anything besides trolling for pornog-
raphy?"

I stepped into the room, slouched against the wall. "I'm not interested in porn."

"No. Of course you're not. You like the *news*. You must have seen
that fascinating study on AOL then. The Inseminator Male vs. Provider
Male: Partner Selection Patterns in the Human Female? You should
contact the group that did the study, really, offer yourself up. You're
the iconic inseminator poster boy, the man with more testosterone in
his blood than brains in his head . . ."

"Sounds like a plan. Should I offer up Brendan as the provider
poster boy while I'm at it, give them two for the price of one?"

The apartment was suffused with shadows. The only light I'd left
on was the low-watt ceiling fixture in the entry. I might have feigned
mortal insult, told her to go fuck herself, shoved her out the door, except for how badly it hurt to be near her, to feel the radiation storm of

her caged sexuality, to see her mocking mask disintegrate as we stared at one another through the dark dusty air.

I choked out a humorless laugh. "Jesus, Fern. Go home."

She seemed to collapse inside her coat. Her face burned hot, reflected whatever light there was. From across the room, in the dimness, she looked like a little girl who'd been slapped for no reason, stunned and shamed. She stood for a moment, rigid, then started for the door. She was going to have to walk by me to get there. I could have edged along the wall, further into the room, out of her way. But I didn't. She was moving slowly but steadily, aiming for the entry, and then, with the precision of a preprogrammed machine she veered and stopped in front of me. Her arms drifted to her sides, the coat, a wraparound thing without buttons, fell open. Her arms lifted. Her hands settled on my stomach, below my ribs, then swept over my sides and chest. Her eyes lifted. Her hunger was a naked animal crouching in the wide black pupils. I couldn't leave her starving like that. Even an animal deserved to be put out of such misery.

It would have been easy to blame Brendan for what I was about to do—he was too good and too happy to understand her, or me, to understand that some people were searching for a place where they didn't have to be alone with their badness, where they could be punished for their sins; he should have told Fern he had no brother—but I could never blame him for anything. You were either the safe place for someone, or you were the dangerous place. You couldn't be both. Brendan was Fern's safe place, and as near to my safe place as I'd ever found.

I moved a little away from the wall, the width of a shin, put my hands inside her coat, took her by her waist and lifted her off the floor. Her legs twined around my hips, her arms around my neck. I put one hand on her back, the other on her ass, under her flimsy rucked-up skirt. She arched upward to kiss me. I moved the hand on her back into her hair and pulled her head gently away.

"No." I didn't want to kiss her. This wasn't that kind of love. It was the other kind, the necessary kind that brings relief. "You hate me, remember?"

"I don't."

"Are you going to marry my brother?"

"Yes."

"Then you'll have to hate me."

"All right. I'll hate you. I'll hate you . . ." Her lips were parted. She pulled herself closer to me. Her sharp hipbones dug into the pad of muscle over my pelvis. I wanted the pain, there was no desire or excitement in me for her, I needed to feel something.

Her ass was hard, muscular, the cheek a perfect fit in the palm of my hand. I moved aside the lacy material of her thong and carefully worked two fingers inside her. I found her clit with my thumb. She was wet and swollen. Panting. Her entire body was shaking. Heat mottled her face and throat and her eyes lost their focus, her lids fluttered and began to close.

"Open your eyes. Look at me."

Her eyes flew open and fixed on mine while I stroked and massaged her. She came, with soft cries, her inner muscles clenching and releasing my fingers, her arms and legs clutching my torso. She came over and over as I kept at her, as if to make up for all the gone years that she'd lived without this, and for all the years ahead when she'd have to live without it again.

＊

I PUT HER ON HER feet when I thought she could stand. She was still lost in the aftermath, weak and wobbly, and I turned her, let her lean her back into me. We stood like that for I don't know how long, both of us semihypnotized by the cadence of her hard breathing, and me at least numbed by self-disgust. Then, out of that strange and otherworldly silence, she spoke. Her words were catches of sound between gasps, and seemed to come through her from someone or somewhere else.

"Do you ever wonder why you're still alive, Jody? What keeps you going? It's not happiness. Or hope. I know that. It's guilt. Isn't it? The same as me. It's guilt. Guilt for your very life. Your undeserved life."

Her hands wandered, came to rest on my thighs.

"You're so hard. You're like iron. Brendan is soft. He doesn't know anything about pain. Not like you. You know everything. I could take a pick and chisel my family's pain into you and you wouldn't break, would you? Nothing would break you. But I could punish you. And you could punish me. Don't you want that? Wouldn't that bring you peace? Wouldn't that bring you relief, Jody? From your guilt, from your rage and confusion, your pathetic helplessness? From all the questions you'll never find answers to? Ella and Brendan can't give us that. But we could give it to one another." She tilted her head back, tried to turn herself into me. "We're both set to self-destruct, buttons pushed a long time ago. You know what I'm talking about. *Chris . . . to . . . pher.*"

My name floated from her mouth like a summons from the underworld. I took her hands in mine, wrapped her arms across her body, held her immobile inside a straightjacket grip. "Don't move. Don't look up. Don't look at me."

"Jody! I can't breathe."

I thought I'd only been imagining tightening my hold, squeezing her out of existence, crushing her to ash like one of my stories, like all those other ghosts that had been rising up to haunt me since the day I met Tess. Fern's feather-light body was suddenly a crushing weight on me. I was pinned to the wall by it.

Fern wanted what I'd given her, but that was just the tip of the iceberg. The vastness below her surface wanted something deeper and darker. She wanted to be wrecked. And she believed I had all the knowledge anyone needed to do the job properly. Whether she was right or wrong about my breakability, and whether she gave a damn about where my knowledge came from, she was a thousand percent right that I had it, and that I could hurt her as bad as she wanted to get hurt. So bad she'd never recover, never know herself again or how to live on the same planet with other humans. It wasn't brain surgery. Scott was no rocket scientist and he knew what to do to me.

All I'd have to do to her was take her into my bedroom and strip her of what was left of her precious self-control, and then, when she thought we were done, get down to it for real and strip her of her illusions that she was in control of fucking anything. It took Scott a couple of years with me, but I was a stupid kid, and kids can't think about what's happening to them while it's happening so their illusions die slowly, and I held on to my Groundhog Day belief that each Bad Thing was the first, and the last, that there was no pile-up squashing me to pulp, that the good days were what was real. But I could knock Fern out of her phony reality in a matter of a few secret sweaty screaming hours. I'd make her need me more than she needed air and more deliriously than she wanted her illusions back, and then I'd kick her out. And then drag her back and fuck the shit out of her and tell her I loved her and then kick her out and remind her constantly what a sorry useless slut she was, and do it over and over, and hit her now and then out of the blue. I'd keep hurting her in the same place she thought I loved her, again and again, until she couldn't tell the difference between love and pain. I'd scramble her brain for good, turn her into someone who'd spend the rest of her life trying to make sense of it, trying to understand why I did that to her. How I could do that to her. How anyone could do that to someone else.

The hundred-pound body of a royally fucked-up woman wasn't what had me pinned to the wall. It was the brutal sting with which, at that moment, I itched to drag her down the hall and ruin both our lives, and my abject fear that I was more fucked-up than she'd ever be but she was smarter and more honest than I'd ever be, and she was right. That doing what I instinctively knew I was capable of would give me the kind of peace she knew I craved as much as she craved it for herself. I saw myself standing outside Evan's bedroom, and I felt again the scratching burrowing animal relief I imagined Scott felt when he did things to me, when he loved me the way he had to, after *his* self-destruct countdown hit zero, and my brain began to fry.

I came off the wall, released Fern but didn't let her turn around. I kept her back to me, held her by her upper arms, dug my fingers into the thin muscles until she grunted in pain. I pushed her ahead of me, marched us both out of the room. My front door was at my left, the hall that led to the rest of the apartment, to my bedroom, was at my right. I stopped there, in the entry, and I swear I didn't know which way to turn. And then she said, "Brendan doesn't ever have to know."

And I remembered who she was. My brother's fiancée, the lucky woman he loved and was going to marry and cherish and keep safe from herself and from nightmares like me. Maybe, maybe, maybe, I'd have been capable of ruining her life, and mine, if she'd been anyone else. But I could never ruin Brendan's.

I held on to her with my right hand, pulled open the door with my left, and threw her out.

"Don't ever come here again. You're marrying my brother, for Christ's sake."

She staggered toward the stairwell, then righted herself and whirled to face me. She stood ramrod upright and her eyes were burning again, not with the heat of desire anymore, but with humiliation and loathing.

"You idiot, this has nothing to do with him, are you too stupid to understand that?"

"No. And are you too stupid to understand that for me it has everything to do with him?"

She smiled, a canny tic of the lips and narrowing of the eyes. "Oh, yes, I understand. I understand that I can still punish *you*, Jody. Maybe I'll do that, as a return favor."

It was a good thing I hadn't eaten any dinner. I would have thrown it up all over her. I smiled back through a mouth full of nausea. "You *could* just say thank you."

Her hateful expression solidified. Her eyes went steely. Then she blinked, inhaled a sharp breath like a cardiac arrest patient after a paddling, and her eyes filled with tears.

"Thank you."

"Don't marry him, Fern. Leave him alone."

She shook her head. "I love him. I do." She lunged forward and kissed me on the mouth. "We're not done, Jody."

She turned, then ran down the five flights of stairs with the speed and grace of a hunted gazelle. Before the feel of her lips could even fire my nerve endings, my ears registered the building's heavy door slamming against the inside wall, then slamming shut.

※

THERE WERE NO SHADES OR blinds over the kitchen window. The blade of the knife was cool against my wrist and pulsed with thin silver-blue streetlight. I leaned back against the sink, next to the open cutlery drawer. I was curious, would my blood pulse a thin cool silver-blue, or pump a thick warm red? I swished the long blade slowly back and forth across the tangle of scars and the stretches of smooth skin as though I were sharpening it on my flesh. The steel vibrated in its eagerness to be used, sent a line of gooseflesh like a message up my arm, from the fingers that still held Fern's smell straight to the top of my skull.

I didn't know where Einstein had gotten to during Fern's visit, probably as far from her disappointment in me as she could, but she was with me now, on her feet, every inch of her pointed at me, tail tucked under her, following the movements of the knife with unblinking eyes and a steady rumble in her throat. As I'd ended up doing the handful of times before, I put the knife back, closed the drawer. It was seductive to contemplate, but it still wasn't up to me to choose my own punishment.

"It's okay, Einstein. I'm not going to slit my wrists. Not today."

Besides, I'd promised to teach Evan to Rollerblade.

Einstein snorted, shook herself, turned and left the room. I stayed very still, mainlined the narcotic sounds of her trotting into the living room, the creak and brush of the sofa as she settled herself in her corner, the retort of three quick barks. *Movie time, Jody.* I laughed out loud. Maybe I'd go to sleep one night and wake up on a planet circling Sirius, the Dog Star of Canis Major, only canines allowed, no people anywhere in sight.

The telephone rang. The answering machine picked up after five rings.

"Jody, it's Ella." She sounded tired. "Evan's gone to bed with a belly-ache. And I'm aching for you. I knew you wouldn't pick up the phone, but I hope you're listening to this message. Everything's going to be all right. This is going to be your last Halloween alone, I swear to you it is. Get some sleep. We'll see you tomorrow."

Ella can't give you peace . . . I threw Fern out. I told myself it had to prove that she was wrong, that I *could* find peace in the places normal people did.

I got my pad and a pen from my desk, joined Einstein, and we ripped through four more movies, Einstein mostly snoring through them, me mostly writing through them, this time a story Tess would never see. I fell asleep at dawn, in the middle of *Gladiator,* the pad and pen fallen into the crack between two cushions, and slept there on the couch all the way till seven frigging thirty.

BABY BEE BEHAVES BADLY

The three bees of the Bonkers Beehive inside 113 Superior Street are in a tizzy that September of 1978. Baby Bee's back in school. He's loopy from having to pretend again that he knows how to buzz the same way all the other bees in that huge alien hive do. And with Baby Bee not around to veer into as needed, the Queen and the Drone crash into each other constantly. Sparks fly.

That month, the Queen polishes her angry bird screeching technique and slams a lot of bedroom doors; the Drone experiments with yet new ways to compromise the integrity of 113's forty-year-old plasterboard walls and the marginally more durable seven-year-old flesh of Baby Bee; and Baby Bee, anxious to bring order back to the hive, works hard to perfect _his_ current specialty, namely his Can-Do attitude toward the Drone's increasingly frequent requests for affection. He still sometimes misses the bull's-eye on that, shows himself less avid than he ought to be, but over the summer he did totally perfect his 24/7 hyper-adrenalized synapse technique and his thousand-yard stare—you know, the one that's frozen on the outside and molten on the inside?—so he doesn't need to work on <u>those</u> anymore. Phew. Thank our Lord Jesus for little gifts.

Baby Bee doesn't eat well that month. The infusion of semen into his mucus membranes makes everything feel slimy and taste salty and bitter. Even though a dozen times a day he rinses and brushes, and brushes and rinses, and snorts water in and out of his nose until his snot runs hot down the back of his throat and makes him retch. He's afraid to open his mouth on the school bus, or in Mrs. Rauch's third-grade classroom, or during recess for fear that everyone will smell him. He's in a panic that the school janitors will swat him down and sweep him out into the sewer, because little by little Baby Bee feels himself filling with garbage, everything that was once baby soft and honey sweet inside him slowly rotting and stinking.

One day in the schoolyard after lunch, model-of-good-behavior Christopher stuns everybody, especially himself, by sending Artie Toomey to the emergency room.

Christopher and a bunch of older boys are kicking a soccer ball back and forth. It's a warm day, but he's in a long-sleeved sports jersey. Everyone's used to him wearing them at odd times, his dumb little boy devotion to his sports heroes is just so adorable. Miss O'Reilly of the red hair and musical voice is watching from over by the fence. He loves Miss O'Reilly. He aches for her attention. He steals the ball from Artie, maneuvers it across the yard, swerves to pass nearer to her, all fancy with his feet. She smiles and gives him two thumbs-up as he goes by and deep in his belly, where her smile always swells him with secret imaginings, he knots up in fury.

Artie catches up with him, tries to trip him, hisses in his ear, Your stepdaddy's a junkie and you're a fucking runt retard, throws his arm around Christopher's neck from behind, and locks a choke hold on him. The next thing Christopher knows he's got a male teacher on each arm, his legs are kicking at the air, his right hand is throbbing and covered with blood, he's screaming some unintelligible threat with the word kill in it, Artie is lying on the cement crying and bleeding, and Miss O'Reilly is giving him her undivided attention, staring at him with her hands over her mouth. He's taken to the principal's office, where he sits in a daze waiting for Scott to come, breathing unsteadily through his mouth, offering no explanation, trying not to think about how good it felt to smash his fist into Artie's face. Or to see Miss O'Reilly watching him like in one more second she might get it.

Scott delivers a somber smile and a bullshit story about Christopher being upset because his beloved hamster, Whiskers, dropped dead on its wheel that morning, right in front of the poor kid's eyes. Chrissie, honey? You think that's maybe why? And you're sorry, aren't you, lovey? Teary-eyed, Christopher nods. Everybody buys it, they have no time for disbelief and anyway it's his first offense. They tell Scott to take him home and give him a good talking to. Whiskers, now there's one unlucky imaginary hamster.

"You can't do shit like that, mongrel."

Christopher's perched on the couch, Scott's squatting in front of him. Scott's eyes are windows into the soul of fatherly concern, his hand rests lightly on Christopher's knee. He's calm. He's almost smiling. He's not angry. It would be reassuring except that there's no warmth or love or forgiveness in Scott's calm concern. Christopher sends out all his feelers, searches and searches, but he can't find anything in Scott to hook on to. He's been disconnected. Even when Scott does things to him, Christopher always feels <u>something</u>, some emotion between them that makes it okay. Now he feels nothing, and that <u>nothing</u> is realer and heavier and denser than any <u>something</u>. He's finally done something too bad to be forgiven for, and now he's more frightened than he's ever been.

"You hear me? You can't do shit like that, mongrel, get everybody looking at you all squinty brained. I'm not angry, man, but you know what will happen if you do anything like that ever again, right? Make somebody ask me crap about you, about me? You know, right?"

He doesn't know what will happen the next time, he doesn't even know what happened this time, why he did what he did. He's so totally at sea that he can't even begin to imagine what's coming. He's so scared he can barely see. There's a big black void opening up all around him. He shakes his head.

Scott's entire forehead lifts in surprise. "No? It's obvious. Come on, man, take a guess."

Scott smiles encouragingly. Christopher whispers, "You'll have to punish me?"

Scott smiles pityingly. "Oh, no, we'd be way beyond that, mongrel. You do shit like that just one more time, outside or in this house, and I'll have to get rid of you."

"No!" Christopher screams. The void is sucking at him like Scott's Car-Vac at a Fruit Loop on the back seat. He's getting pulled in. He grabs Scott's hand with both of his, clings to it, lifts it from his knee toward his mouth to kiss it, but Scott pulls his hand free and leans away, back onto his heels.

"Yes sir. I'd have to get rid of you, and really man, where in the fucking world are you going to go? Who wants you? Your mom?" Scott snickers. "Like she'd leave me for you. Your grandfather? Yeah, I send you to Florida, he cuts you into small pieces and uses you for tarpon bait." He leans forward again, puts his palms on Christopher's cheeks. "I want you, Chrissie. I know you're the best kid there is. But I'm the only one. So you have to be good. Don't make me have to cut you loose. I don't care how upset or pissed off you get, you behave. You be good and nice to everybody, you be like fucking Jesus, man, you be that good, or I'm done with you."

Scott tilts his head and waves a finger in Christopher's face. "You asked me once, man, remember? I said no, but don't think it couldn't happen. It could. It could definitely happen. You could go into the garbage and nobody on this earth would miss you."

For the next few months, Christopher's caught between a rock and a hard place, because as blindingly bad as Scott's threat is, he's getting picked on at school and that fury in his belly keeps coming back, and the memory of the power that exploded out of him when he hit Artie. But before he loses his balance all together, Scott comes to his rescue again, breaks Christopher's right femur with a well-placed blow from the barrel of his AK47 on a particularly creative game night in January and puts him out of action for most of the spring.

Baby Bee behaves badly only one more time after that, and not until more than a year later. Afterward, as promised, Scott is as done with him as done can be. Baby Bee thus learns the hard way that Scott was telling the God's honest truth that time—he really can't do shit like that.

Part Three

THE SPEED OF LIGHT

The speed at which impeded light travels will vary depending on what stands in its way. However, the speed at which light travels in a vacuum is a physical constant [c], 299,792,458 meters per second, or (approximately) 186,282 miles per second, and is unaffected by the motion of the source of the light, or by the motion of the observer.

c is believed to be the finite speed at which any and all matter, energy, or information in the universe can travel . . . And, given its inextricable relation to time and space, there abides within us the romantic notion that if one could only attain the speed of light on one's journey, then, relative to the world the traveler will have left behind, time, within the infinity of space, would all . . . but . . . stop.

Seventeen

THE FIRST SATURDAY IN NOVEMBER was overcast and chilly, one of those days that warned you in no uncertain terms that winter was breathing down your warm exposed neck. I'd been staying at Ella's Friday night through Sunday, and I'd expected that's where we'd spend the afternoon without her, but Tess and Evan pecked at me about wanting to see where I lived. I'd worked hard over the years to keep the accumulation of human energy in my space to a minimum—the Kowalczyks, a few women who'd left more of a mark than others, now Fern's indelible spoor—but I hadn't been able to think of any legitimate reason to say no. The building even had heat.

"Jody?"

I was squatting in my entryway, helping Evan on with the all-body-parts pads I'd rented for him, along with a good pair of skates and a state-of-the-art helmet. I thought Tess had gone into the kitchen with Einstein, where I'd deposited the bags of groceries she'd brought, but her summoning voice came from the wrong direction. I raised my head, looked both ways. Einstein was lying across the threshold of the kitchen, observing, but Tess had stepped into the living room and was staring at the wall, at the spot where for a week I'd been seeing the sooty hunched outline of me and Fern burned into the paint, the incinerated atomic residue of our fusion. Tess turned to briefly glance at me. There was a perplexed and unhappy expression on her face, a perfect fit with the tone of her voice. My stomach knotted. I forced my attention back to Evan. A line of nervous sweat had erupted on his forehead.

"Hey, you're going to do great, don't worry. Here, put on this other knee pad. I'll get Tess set up in the kitchen and then we're good to go."

TESS WAS EXAMINING THAT DAMNING wall with shiny eyes and an almost religious intensity. Seeing her like that threw me into a vivid memory of being brought by my aunt Marie to a gathering of the neighborhood *nonna*s behind the local supermarket. Someone had reported a sighting of the Blessed Virgin Mary. I remembered watching Father Assface—Marian's typically respectful name for our parish priest and the only name I could ever remember him by—studying the streaks left on the stucco wall by wet garbage overflowing the dumpsters with an avidity that even at four years old I knew had more to do with money than miracles. There was nothing there but a projection of the semihysterical hive-mind of a bunch of aging Catholic women. But what Tess was seeing, or feeling, emanating from my wall was real.

I came up beside her. She turned to me. Loose wisps of snowy hair fell over her ears.

"Why do I feel that girl here, the dark one? She doesn't belong here. I told you to be careful of her, *caro*."

It didn't occur to me to deny that Fern had been there. I thought about that night, all the things that had gone through my head. "Yeah, you did. You were right. I may not know where I want to go, but it's not there."

Tess took hold of my hands. The joints of her fingers were inflamed. "*I* know where you want to go. Somewhere light, not dark. You're on your way, don't get lost."

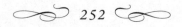

She left me there with my own hands tingling and went to admire Evan's munchkin urban gladiator outfit.

"Look at you! All wrapped up like the best birthday present ever!" She kissed the tip of his nose, about the only spot that wasn't covered up. "It looks like it might rain any minute. You brave boys had better get going."

Evan lifted his arms and pumped them like Mr. Universe. He beamed at her. Like the touch of an eternal white-winged angel, her kiss removed all mortal fear.

A COLD WET WIND WAS swirling through Tompkins Square Park. I found a sheltered stretch of smooth pavement, cleared away the plastic bags and stained food containers left from Friday night's party crowd. At least there were no used condoms or blood-rusted needles. We got in a half hour lesson before the skies opened up, but in that short time, even though he fell twice and shed a few tears I didn't let on I saw, the kid mastered the basics. When we made our mad dash out of the park in the pouring rain, he negotiated the turns and curbs like a champ and managed to stop without having to use me as his crash pillow.

We took off our skates and helmets in the lobby, dripping water onto the chipped marble floor. Pride plumped up Evan's scrawny muscles, straightened his back. His head was in constant motion, up and down, he was trying to grab my eyes, to share the moment with me. Only Yoda-like souls and surly misanthropes could tolerate being that happy alone, the rest of us needed to see our happiness reflected in someone else before we could be sure it was real. I kept my eyes averted from his giddy face, his eyes shining at me like a pair of bright yellow high beams. I remembered wearing that face, with Scott, when he played with me. I remembered seeing my happiness reflected in him. I remembered the moment I knew it was all a lie.

"Ready, buddy? Come on then, let's go see what Tess and Einstein are up to."

I stood at the base of the stairs and made a gesture for him to climb on up ahead of me. The light was gone from his eyes. He slung his skates over his shoulder, hooked the helmet over a wrist. His knees and elbows were still enveloped in their pads. He hauled himself up a couple of steps. It was my inattention, not his gear, that was so heavy, pressing all that precious happiness out of every cell of his tired, exhilarated body. *He could use some kinder men in his life,* Ella had said. Not another Ronald.

I stopped him with a hand on his shoulder, turned him to face me.

"You did good. Really good. You're going to be totally awesome." I looked into his eyes, smiled my crooked smile.

Evan grew two inches on the spot. His arms snaked around my waist. He hugged me. I stiffened and lifted my arms, jerked back against the stairwell wall. He looked up, ready to shrivel again. Suddenly, I wanted more than anything to make that yellow light come on in his soft taffy eyes. I reached out a cautious hand, brushed aside his damp hair. Then I leaned over and kissed his forehead. The light from Evan's eyes and face when he smiled up at me put the sun back in the sunless sky. He sighed, rested his head against my chest, right over my heart, and hugged me harder. I slipped my fingers under his hair and cupped his head in my hand. We hung there for a few minutes, puddles of dirty rainwater soaking our socks.

﹡

A FAMILIAR AROMA PERMEATED MY apartment. There was a pot of soup simmering on my stove. On my table a fat loaf of Italian bread, pointed end sticking out of a paper sleeve. When I was little, my aunt Marie would break off one of those crusty ends, dip it in thick green olive oil, then my soup bowl, blow on it a couple of times, put it in my mouth in bite-sized pieces.

Tess was dozing on the sofa, her sketchbook on her lap, a drawing pencil in her hand. Einstein was on the floor nearby, one of my red napkins loosely tied around her neck. Tess must have anointed her sous-chef. When Evan saw them, he pulled an exaggerated *shhhh* face, eyes wide, finger to his pursed lips. I nodded and pointed up the hall. I stole a few quick deep breaths of that smell—minestrone, the one thing that could keep my mother in the house for dinner—then we tiptoed to the bathroom, leaving a trail of footprints on the wood floor. We shed our rain slickers, pads, and wet socks and left them in the tub with the curtain drawn so Ella wouldn't see them. I wrapped Evan's feet in a towel, rubbed them warm, then took him into my bedroom. When I turned from my dresser with a pair of dry socks for him to flop around in, he was by my bookcase with one of my books in his hands, his mouth hanging open.

"Did you read this?"

It was the book I'd been reading the day I met Tess. The book I'd had to put down for a week before I could read again. It was called *Cryptonomicon*. A brilliant epic novel about code-breaking during World War II, the invention of the computer, binary number theory, buried Nazi gold, Japanese kamikaze pilots, half-breed wreck divers, doomed lovers, Time, Fate, Chaos, and Reason . . . It was about everything in heaven and hell, and whatever lay between them.

"Yeah, I read it. It's pretty amazing."

"Wow!" He turned it around and around in his hands. "Holy cow! It *looks* amazing. Absolutely everyone in the AP science and math classes at my school is reading this. I mean, it's all they talk about, like it's their Bible or something! I can't wait to be old enough to read it. I'm thinking two years. Wow! I cannot believe you read it!" Totally incredulous, like he was sure I hadn't, or couldn't, given how obviously stupid I was—good at sports, nice enough, fun to have around, but not smart, not like his friends or parents or the other adults he knew.

I sat on the bed, said nothing. Just watched him. He put the book back next to my copy of *The Yearling,* a book actually meant for someone with the brains of a nine-year-old, which he ignored. He bent down to see the shelves below. My science fiction and science stuff. Wells. Asimov, Heinlein, Bradbury, and Clarke. Gibson, Dick, Aldiss, Zindell. Einstein, Hawking, Gould, Sagan. And my DVDs. *Apollo 13. The Usual Suspects. Gladiator. Blade Runner.*

After a few minutes he backed up toward the bed, eyes still on the bookcase, plopped himself next to me. His mouth was hanging open again. He put his hands between his thighs. He looked up at me like a shy girl on a first date.

"You've read all those books?"

I nodded. "Lots of others, too."

"So . . . What are you, a secret genius or something? I thought you just liked to skate and play ball and stuff, and that you only came for piano lessons so you could date my mom." He leaned into my arm and laughed, a small *don't be angry* laugh.

"That *is* why I came for lessons. But don't tell her." I grinned at him. He shrieked and turned red, ducked his head into my ribs and giggled himself nearly off the bed. I hauled him up by his shirt. "Easy, big boy. Anyway, I'm no genius, but yeah, I like to read. Not the kind of stuff your mom reads . . ."—books about people's lives and feelings made my brain hurt, go blank, like I was trapped in a burning house and couldn't see anything through the smoke—". . . I like books that are like reading music, the words pure as notes, but you get pictures in your head instead of sounds. Pictures of things so far outside us but also so deep down inside us that it's all beyond words or feelings, and you can see how we're all made of the same stuff as the universe, everything moving and looping through time and space together." That's why Brendan made up that nickname for me, Idiot Genius, because of what I read. "Know what I mean?"

Evan looked like I'd dumped a bucket of icy water over his head. What the hell was I thinking talking like that, and to him?

He blinked like an owl. Slow and thoughtful. "I know *exactly* what you mean, Jody. You have to read *Harry Potter and the Sorcerer's Stone.* I'm going to lend it to you. You've *got* to read it. We've got to talk."

"Okay then." I turned my head away so he wouldn't think I was laughing at him.

"Could we watch a movie? You've got one I'm dying to see."

"Which one?"

He leapt up, came back with *Blade Runner.* The kid was uncanny.

"Whoa. That's my favorite movie of all time, it's great, but I don't know . . ."

He groaned. "Oh come on! Don't be like my mom, she thinks I'm still a baby. I have friends who've seen it, I've seen the trailer, I know what it's about. It'll be okay. Please, Jody."

"Hey, I don't think you're a baby. But if it gives you nightmares, your mother will kill me. I don't know. Maybe we should watch something Tess would like, too."

"*Terminator* didn't give me nightmares, it was cool." He gave me the DVD. "I bet Aunt Tess'll like it. She's not like other old people, you know. Anyway, my mother would never kill you."

I really wanted to follow up on that last statement, but thought better of it.

"Okay. If Tess wants to see it, and if she thinks it's okay for you, we'll do it. Wait here."

Tess was up, reading a magazine. The sketchpad was lying open on the couch and I could see the drawing she'd done of Evan in his skating gear.

"Wow. That's great. You're good."

"Why, thank you. I'm going to give that to Ella." She closed the pad and moved it aside.

I'd brought three ibuprofen and a glass of water for her. "For your hands."

She closed the magazine. "Thank you, darling. At least I can still hold a pencil. And how was the skating lesson?"

"Terrific. Ella's going to flip out. Um, Tess, I need some advice . . ."

"I heard." She reached for the DVD. "How old were you when you saw it?"

"Twelve. Brendan took me. I'd have been fine even if I'd been Evan's age, but he's not me. I don't know what's appropriate for him. He's pretty grown-up for a nine-year-old, but he's not me." The skin of that movie wouldn't fit him like a custom-made glove, the way it did me.

"There's violence in it, I see. Is it frightening?" She looked at the photos on the DVD box, read the copy. "Is there sex?"

"No, no sex. And less violence than *Terminator,* which he thinks was 'cool.' But it's realer . . . I don't think it's frightening, though. It's . . . intense. Because of the reasons, though, not the violence itself."

"Well . . . I'd like to know why it's your favorite movie. Let's try it. We can always stop."

Evan didn't make a peep or move a muscle. During a few scenes I was sure we'd made a huge mistake letting him see it, but he was okay, sitting cross-legged on the floor next to me in front of the couch looking like I remembered feeling the first time I'd seen it. Leaning forward, eyes wide, mouth open, barely breathing he was so connected to that world.

When it was over, and I mean totally blank screen over, final credits faded to black, he turned to me in slow motion, face fierce with how serious he was, and said, "Thank you. That was absolutely the *best* movie I have *ever* seen in my *entire . . . life.*"

His *entire life.* He was nine for shit sake. On the other hand, nine *was* his entire life. And the fact was, it was possible for a person to have lived their entire life by the time they were nine, in that even if they actually lived to be a hundred, the last ninety-one years would be nothing more than marching in place. I'm not saying that's what I imagined or would ever want for Evan, I'm just saying a life can work out that way.

"I *loved* it, Jody. But it was so sad, that the replicants had to die, that there was no way to fix the way they'd been made. They just wanted to live a little longer."

"It is sad. But Roy, he's different, right? He wants to live, but at the end, when he knows it's over and there are no answers, he sees that even though it was too short, his life was ... unique ... and special, and it was his, he'd made his *own* memories. And then he stops fighting and just lets go."

"Right! He's not even angry at Deckard for trying to kill him anymore—he saves his life!"

I ejected the disc. "Go put it back on my shelf."

Evan went, holding the DVD to his chest. I sat down on the sofa next to Tess. She put her hand on my back. I'd been more aware of her behind me than of Evan, of what she was seeing of me in the movie, the story of an artificial man whose life and memories don't belong to him, who came into the world with his future already written.

"Jody. You are not someone else's creation, destined to burn out without ever knowing why or how you were created. I can see why you'd take comfort in reducing yourself to that. But you mustn't. You are so much more."

"It's just a movie, Tess."

"That's right. And don't you forget it. And that the replicant girl, Rachael ... Maybe she *will* live."

Evan padded in, wriggled onto the couch. Einstein moved so Evan could use her as a foot rest. He had *The Yearling* with him.

"This looks like something you've had since you were a kid. Is it okay if I look at it?"

I nodded. He opened it up and read the jacket copy. His head came up, fast, and swung at me. "The boy's name is Jody! Was this your mother's favorite book or something? Were you named after him?"

"No, I don't think so. I found the book, in a house where we were living. Just a coincidence." I reached over and closed the cover partway. "Like how the picture of the boy here kind of looks like you."

"Wow, it does! Your name, my face!"

He gave me a sideways glance from under the edges of his Harry Potter glasses, another shy smile. He slid the too-large socks back and forth on Einstein's belly. I got that prickly feeling inside my head again, that ache in my throat.

"It's a good book. I'll lend it to you in exchange for the Potter."

"Deal. I'm going to start it right now." He turned back the cover again. "Hey, look. This is who owned it before. Why didn't you cross out the last name and write yours in?" The last name on the list was Christopher Cannavarro.

"I don't know. Maybe it was never meant to be my book."

"But it *is* your book." And he gave me a *you're strange but I like you anyway* scowl and settled in to read.

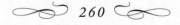

TESS STOPPED TO KISS MY cheek on our way to the kitchen. "Evan is blooming. You are so good with him."

I looked back at him, nose in *The Yearling,* feet on Einstein's side. "He's a great kid. Look at the two of them. Boy, if I ever couldn't keep Einstein, she's definitely found her new master."

Tess kissed my other cheek. "I know how hard all of this is for you. But you know you couldn't stay alone forever, Jody."

"Oh, I don't know. I was *that* close to pulling it off until you showed up." Her lips curved up a smidgen. "So, did you ever meet that guy Ella was dating, Alan, or something?"

"Alex. Yes. A very fine man. Why?"

I set the table while Tess went at the soup with the salt shaker then threw together a salad.

"Don't you think he'd be good for her?"

"Perhaps. But not now."

"Oh man. Would it have killed you to say no?"

She laughed, wiped her hands on a dishcloth. "You know, for a replicant, you are quite witty. There's a time for everything, *caro,* and this is your time. Take it. Because later, who knows." She cocked her head. "Ah. She's here."

The downstairs buzzer buzzed. The announcement of Ella's arrival reverberated throughout the apartment. She wasn't even at my door yet, but she'd already obliterated whatever space I thought I could keep for myself.

It would have been different if what would linger of them—the smell of Tess's soup, the bounce of Evan's body on my couch, the hot green glow of Ella's eyes in the dusk of my bedroom where I held her captive in my arms and kissed her until Tess called us to dinner—if any of those ethereal traces, even Arwen's, even Fern's, served to keep any of them with me. But instead, they slipped through the holes Scott had bored in me. I'd been his human voodoo doll, punctured by his love, his rage, his guns, his cigarettes, his needles, his knives, his prick, until I was star stuff, a thing made of cosmic dust and airless space, nothing left of me solid enough for that lingering evidence of my life among humans to attach to. It could only crowd out the places where I'd momentarily been.

Eighteen

FERN WAS A WOMAN OF her word. It would be a cold day in hell before I'd return the messages she'd left for me during the week, but she jumped right on returning the favor I'd done her. When I got home from Ella's Sunday evening, Brendan was waiting for me on my stoop, sitting on the top step, tucked into his jacket, his head in his hands. I didn't know how long he'd been there, but he was shivering in the last of the weekend's raw wind.

"Hey."

The effort to look up seemed to take all the energy he had, none left for a response. But there was none necessary, his pinched and baffled face said it all, told me I'd just run out of the last of my safe places. But I plowed ahead, hoping I was wrong, that she'd done something to wound him, but didn't mention me, and he was here for advice, for comfort.

"Hey, Brendan. What's wrong?" I tied Einstein's leash to the stair rail and told her to sit, be quiet. I started up the stairs, to sit next to him, put my arm around his shoulder, but as soon as I began to move he reared up as fast and strong as a bear disturbed from sleep. I stopped, one foot on the first step, one on the sidewalk.

"What did you do?" He started down, picking up speed as he came. I backed up. "What happened. Tell me what happened."

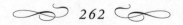

"No, you tell *me* what happened!" he yelled and rushed me, got behind me, and got me in a half nelson. "What did you do to her, you fucking freak?!"

Einstein was barking but I could barely hear her for the blood filling my head. All I could think was that I had to get free. The heel of my shoe connected with Brendan's shin, and my elbow with his ribs. He howled and let me go. I moved out of his reach, held up my hands.

"Brendan, come on, calm down. We can talk this out. I'm not going to fight with you."

"Calm down? She left me, you fucker. She gave me back my ring. Why, Jody? Why would she do that, huh? Come on, hot shot, you're so smart about women, tell me, why would she do that?"

To see if I was breakable after all. To see if it would bring me to my knees to cause Brendan this kind of pain, then capsize me completely when I lost his love and his trust to her. Because once he'd cast me out, she'd be back to him for that ring, all apologies and tears. I'd have bet his life on it.

"I don't know, Brendan. What did she say?" I was playing for time. I knew Brendan, and if I could come up with an out here, he'd take it.

He looked like he wanted to pulverize me, but he stayed where he was, fists clenched, chest heaving.

"She tried to tell me she wasn't good enough for me, that . . ." He stopped, his fists opened and his hands dropped to his sides. His mouth began to tremble and his eyes misted up. "Oh, man, why am I bothering . . . I had to force it out of her, she didn't want to have to tell me, that's the kind of person she is. But I could see she was scared of something, and I made her tell me. Even then, all she'd say is that it was because of you . . . but the way she said it . . ." He looked at me like he'd never seen me before. "Twenty years, and I don't know who you are. So come on, Jody, Christopher, whatever your name is, tell the truth for once in your miserable life. What kind of a monster are you, really? What did you do to her?"

My mind was still frantically trying to think of some fantasy I could spin that he'd buy, some way we could put things back together, but I looked into his eyes and knew there wasn't enough glue in the world for that. Blood was thicker than water for people like Brendan, but at the end of the day I wasn't blood, whereas hers was already flowing through his heart. It was okay. Because like I'd said to Irene, all I wanted was for Brendan to be happy. And for that he needed Fern. And she and I couldn't be near one another. I'd been right about her needing me out of Brendan's life, we'd just both misunderstood the reason.

I looked at my brother, my protector, for the bit of time it took to put every line and contour of his face and twenty years of his friendship in a box, then did what I had to do. I smiled and said, "Oh, you know. I can't let a pretty woman go to waste. I made a pass at her, let her know I was watching her."

Brendan turned purple. He came at me again, swung a big fist at my face. He was a good wrestler, but no street fighter. I could have gotten clear of the blow but I moved into it, let it catch me on my cheekbone. I staggered backward.

"Fight me! Fight me, you goddamned coward!"

"I'm not going to fight you, Brendan. I love you. Come on, beat the shit out of me." I raised my arms out to the sides.

That worked. He went apoplectic. He roared and came at me again, this time landed a flurry of fury-fueled punches to my middle. I felt a rib move, maybe break. The breath went out of me. I grunted, doubled over, and sank to my knees. I hoped he might keep going, take a kick at me, but he managed to control himself. He stood over me, his breath audible over Einstein's frantic barking.

"I don't want to know you anymore. I don't want to see you anymore. I'll leave it to you to tell the folks why you won't be there for

Thanksgiving, or Christmas, or ever again. You're not my brother. You're no one."

＊

I COULDN'T GO UPSTAIRS. ALL those lingering traces filled every room, there was no space left for me.

I couldn't go back to Ella's. Sunday night was get ready for school and work night. Possibly breachable, but I'd have to tell her why I was there, why I was sprouting a black eye and swollen cheek, why I was cringing from the weight of her body on top of me. Why we wouldn't be seeing much of Brendan and Fern for a while. I was usually a whiz at fashioning lies that had enough truth to them to not fall apart when looked at with two good eyes, that I could defend with conviction. But for the moment, Brendan had beaten all the cleverness out of me.

I didn't need to go to the ER. I'd had more than a little experience with broken ribs, I knew there was nothing to do for them but leave them alone and let them heal.

I could only think of one place to go. I quieted Einstein down, sat on the stairs with her for a little while, and then we walked over to the Coronet.

＊

"OH MY GOD!! WHAT HAPPENED to you!"

"I got into a little, shall we say, altercation with a drunk jerk in the park who was throwing rocks at Einstein." The fable rolled off my tongue like it was greased, sounded one hundred percent feasible, even to me.

Arwen put a firm hand on my elbow and steered me away from the door. "That booth by the kitchen just opened up. Go, I'm going to bring you an ice pack and some tea. Do you want something to eat?"

"No." I wasn't hungry, I was sick to my stomach. "I just . . . I didn't

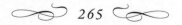

feel like going home. I'm going to sit and watch you work and try to think nice thoughts." I smiled.

"You're making fun of me."

"No, I'm not. You're the nicest person I know." She blushed, but I could tell from the sad set of her mouth she knew I wasn't flirting with her. It was a simple statement of fact.

It was a little after eight, the place was crowded. I iced my cheek. I drank my tea. Einstein had snuck up onto the seat, between me and the wall. I let her stay there, the warmth of her heavy head on my thigh slowly seeping through me. My head grew heavy. I pushed aside the teapot and mug and put my arms on the table, my good cheek on my arms. Just for a minute.

Someone was shaking me. I bolted upright, flailed out with a hand, hit something.

"Ouch! I'm sorry. I didn't mean to startle you." Arwen rubbed her arm where I'd hit her. "Jody, it's ten thirty . . . Oh, gosh, you don't look good. Maybe you should go to the hospital."

I shook my head to clear it from the deep sleep I'd fallen into. "No, I'm fine. I'm tired, that's all. I . . . I need to go home. I'm really tired."

I was. So, so tired I didn't think I could stand. Still half-asleep, I rested my head against the banquette's high back and stared at her, my despair and confusion and pain leaking out of my pores. If I'd been more awake I'd never have been that unfair to her.

She held my eyes with the fixity of a hypnosis victim. "Jody. I can't leave early. But . . ."

I pulled myself out of the booth, to my feet. "No, no but." I tucked a loose strand of her hair behind her ear. "Thanks for the TLC. I'll see you around."

Nelson, his dreads looking a little unkempt, was behind the bar, as always. I didn't think the man ever went home. He waved me over as I made my aching way out. He slipped a tiny manila envelope across the scarred wood. "Jody, my friend, you look like you could use these—some high-octane Oxy for the pain, and some reds to put out the lights. No charge." He grinned, perfect white teeth against cocoa skin. "Take care of yourself, man."

Two eighty-milligram OxyContin, two one-hundred-milligram Seconal. The Oxys were dull-looking gray-green tablets. But the Seconal . . . so red-bright and shiny in the palm of my hand. I didn't take anything. But I didn't flush them, either. I put them in my night table and lay awake, my face and side throbbing with heat and pain, listening to their siren's song leech from the drawer like the strains of a long-ago lullaby.

✳

IN THE END, I TOLD Ella what I'd told Arwen. Any tale that involved a falling-out with Brendan led to Fern, which led to nothing good, and I'd still be lying to her. I let her assume I was in touch with Brendan, but that he and Fern were laid low with millennium fever until the new year. Maybe the world *would* implode by then, and none of this would matter anyway.

Nineteen

THE WEEKEND OF ELLA'S BIRTHDAY was mild and cloudy, the air soft on the skin. T-shirt weather, perfect for Rollerblading.

We had a little more work to do before the curtain went up on Evan's debut performance on Sunday. Ella saw students until three on Saturday. Our cover story was I was taking Evan to lunch and to see *Star Wars: The Phantom Menace* for the second time while it was still around, which made her so happy it was criminal. Evan was so excited, and so bad at keeping secrets from his mother, that he'd been acting all week like we were in fact planning to rob a bank. I of course gave away squat, but I could tell from her curious scrutiny of her son's guilty goofball behavior, his shirt on inside out, mumbling and casting furtive looks at me when she asked what time the movie let out, that she knew we were up to something.

The whole thing *was* sort of like a heist caper. I'd stashed my car in a garage on Thirteenth Street with the gear in it. I'd checked the route from the mini-mart to the brownstone for possible security risks—curbs, potholes, cracks. I'd concocted our diversion—we'd order Ella to wait like a receiving princess on her stoop while her slaves, two-legged and four, ventured out to Murray's Bagels for her favorite Scottish salmon and cream cheese on an everything bagel. It was a flawless plan.

I bought me and Evan humongous drippy burgers at the Corner Bistro on West Fourth and, fortified with enough fat, protein, and iron to get us through the winter, we skated to the river. Evan had taken to Rollerblading like a pig to mud, wallowing in the undreamed-of prospect of him being athletically possible at all. And he was in love with speed. I warned him to slow down until he was a little more skilled, but I'd hatched a little preppie maniac. Every time his momentum threatened to tip him forward over his toes I had to make a mad grab for his arm.

We were having such a good time that we lost track of it. It was almost four when we finally made it back to Eleventh Street. Ella was watching for us through the long windows, Einstein alert at her side, her hand nervously tapping Einstein's head, her neck and shoulders stiff with tension. I waved. She relaxed and smiled, waved back a little too furiously. Evan didn't wave, he was too busy fighting down his high, trying to sober up before we went inside.

"Okay. Act natural. Don't overdo the nonchalant thing. Your mother's got a nose for bullsh . . . for balderdash." There was that nine-year-old giggle again.

"I'm good. I'm good. Oh, this is going to be *so cool!*"

"Yeah, you're good. *Not.* You're a jumping bean. Let me do the talking. And stop laughing." I mock-cuffed him on the back of his head. He laughed.

Ella met us at the door. "I was getting worried!"

I hugged her. "Sorry. I should've called. We stopped for ice cream after the movie."

She took Evan's hand as we moved into the room. "Did you have a good time?"

Evan had sailed past nonchalant to robotic. He couldn't hold her eye. He kept glancing at me, his lips stuck together. "Mm-mmm."

She gave me a playful look, transferred it to Evan, and then all of a sudden her expression faltered. Her gaze was laser-trained on his arm. On the bruises that had formed there, unnoticed by either of us, from the repeated clamping of my terrified fingers on his tender skin.

Ella put her other hand on Evan's shoulder. Her eyes flicked from the bruises to my hands, to the bruises, to my eyes. It came and went so fast, that snake-strike of doubt, of distrust and fear. But it had been there, in her eyes, when she'd looked at me.

The floor swayed beneath my feet. "*Ella!*"

She blanched. "Jody, Jody, no, no, Jody. Oh my God, I'm sorry, I didn't ..."

I tried to say something, I don't even know what, maybe just her name again, or fuck or shit or Jesus, but nothing came out, I couldn't speak.

"Jody, please! It was just a stupid knee-jerk reaction. I *never* thought ..."

Words emerged like wisps of smoke. "You did. I saw it. You did. Jesus. Ella."

"I *didn't!*"

"What? What? Mom??? Jody???" Evan started to cry.

Ella pulled him to her. "Nothing, nothing. Everything's all right." Her voice broke, her breath wavered. She stared at me with imploring eyes and mouthed, "*I'm sorry ...*"

I groped Einstein's leash off the coat stand and fled.

※

I WALKED. FOR HOURS. WITHOUT any awareness of where I was going, or where I was, dimly conscious of the comfort of Einstein walking steadily, uncomplaining, next to me. My brain was seared. The distrust in Ella's eyes had planted a seed in me, and as I walked and walked it grew into a sequoia of doubt about whether I'd really *had* to grab Evan hard enough to bruise him, or whether I'd *wanted* to, and by the time I peeked out from the pit of my confusion I was way uptown, in Riverside Park, somewhere past the Seventy-ninth Street boat basin, the lights of the George Washington Bridge like distant strands of diamonds in a dark misty sky, and I still didn't trust myself to know the answer.

My side was killing me, but it was a long way home so I pushed the pain and the growing cold away and kept walking. The minute I closed the apartment door, the pain and cold slammed me, and the exhaustion, worse than the night at the Coronet. My legs wouldn't hold me. I slid to the floor, my back against the door, slithered into the bedroom. All I wanted was to sleep, but voices were murmuring all around me. I fumbled in the drawer of my night table and found them, the Seconal, their shape and texture as recognizable to my fingers as though no time had passed since I'd last fumbled for them, so tired and blinded by a different kind of darkness. I took them both. Shed my sneakers and windbreaker, got under the covers with the rest of my clothes still on, Einstein tunneling in after me. I pulled a pillow over my head, and started counting backward from a hundred.

I'm a puppy, perfect and pure in the way all new creatures are perfect and pure. What kind of puppy is unimportant, because I know what I am, deep down, in my essence. I may look like a puppy, but what I truly am is love, which has no bounds and no form. I am formless boundless love, and the desire to please and to be loved. Nothing more and nothing less.

I'm on my haunches by the open kitchen door. My mistress is at the sink. My tail thumps the floor. My head is lifted toward her, but she is looking out the window. We'll be going out to play soon. My body quivers in anticipation and my throat tightens around a bark of joy. The windows are open, it's summer, it's warm, there's sunlight everywhere. She turns to me, smiles, says, "Come." My bark explodes. I follow her.

We are in the middle of an enormous field of tall grass and wildflowers. It's beautiful. The house is far away, a speck at the edge of the field. I'm playing for her, every trick and game I know. At last, she tells me to sit. I sit for her. I'm panting, my puppy heart beats a million miles an hour. I please her. I sit, waiting for my reward. But instead of a bologna sandwich, she puts her palm against my nose. Stay! A terrible pain spears through my rocketing heart. I don't like stay, it's the game where she leaves and it fills me with fear, but I do it for her, always, the best I can. I do it now, my head shaking, whinnies of misery trapped in my throat, but I don't move. Oh so slowly, she backs away from me. After every ten steps she holds out her palm again. Stay!

Then she's gone, and the house is gone, and the sun is gone, and I'm alone in a field that has become as boundless as my love. And I wait. I wait. I wait. She told me to stay and I will stay. I will die for her, of thirst and starvation, of loneliness and heartbreak, if that's what she wants of me. I lie down in the dark and cold, dwarfed by the tall grass, invisible. An unseen animal is feeding on my shoulder. I'm trembling and choking on grief, my heartbeat is a gong, each strike tears another piece of my heart away, and still I wait...

Einstein was awakened by a violent shaking and a wet, ripping sound, like a towering rain cloud being sundered by lightning. Her ears flattened against her head, she began to tremble and whine in terror. She half rose, making ready to creep off the exposed surface of Jody's bed to gain the shelter of the darkness underneath. A storm, a terrible storm was approaching. She stopped in her crouch, Jody's back still touching hers. The storm was already here. It was inside him, the wind of it tossing his body like a dry leaf, the thunder leaking from his throat and the rain from his eyes. She tried to blot the salty water with her tongue, but it flowed too fast. She took his shoulder in her mouth and held him in her jaws, gently, firmly, so that the storm would not sunder him like a cloud.

I WOKE UP IN A fetal position, quaking, my arms and legs curled tight around the pillow. The pillowcase was wet beneath my face. After twenty years, I'd finally remembered a different dream. And I didn't wake up screaming, my throat raw and my mouth stuffed with the remembered bitter tastes of guns and Scott. I woke up sobbing, the first tears I'd shed since I was nine years old, feeling like that dog, lying alone in darkness, waiting to die.

LITTLE BY LITTLE, THE DREAM let go its possession of me. I stopped shaking, stopped crying. The animal gnawing on my shoulder was Einstein. She released me and I rolled onto my back. I was awake, but not alert, woozy, my head muddy from the pills. I looked at my watch. It was 1:10 a.m. The phone rang, the sound like the heartbeat gong of my dream. *Ella.* The caller hung up one ring before the answering machine would have clicked on. I got up and checked it. She'd called a dozen times, left one message. "This is me coming after you, the only way I can right now—I have no one to stay with Evan . . . I'm sorry. Forgive me, I didn't mean it. I trust you. I'm waiting up for you. Come back."

I'd forgiven her hours ago. I splashed water on my face, put on my shoes, my jacket. We were halfway out the door when her message got through to me. And her trust.

I ran away. And she came after me.

Maybe the dream and the drugs hadn't fully left me, because

grown-up tough guy that I was, I suddenly felt small and weak as a puppy, and I remembered the day I'd wanted to read *The Runaway Bunny* for Marian. I'd been leveled then by the same awful overwhelming loneliness as the dream, and it spread through me again, sickening me. But I wasn't going to cry anymore. I wasn't a puppy. Or a child. I wasn't a runaway bunny and Ella wasn't my mother. That's not what we were to one another.

I went back inside and called her. She must have been sitting by the phone. I told her to leave the key in the window box and go to bed, that I needed another hour or two, there was something I had to do, but I'd be there before the sun came up on her birthday.

For Tess

THE DEEP-DOWN

Christopher reads <u>The Yearling</u> over and over. He's never not reading it. It takes him almost a year the first time, but after that it goes faster and by the time he's eight he's been through it beginning to end three times. He reads other things, too, and likes them, but <u>The Yearling</u> is different. He doesn't just read it, he lives in it. He lives in the ending, where both Jody's parents love him, but he goes back to the beginning and reads it all again, every time, because he's near desperate to make sense of how they get there, how and why Jody's mother, Ora, comes to love him when she didn't all along.

The ending, where Jody runs away, reminds him at first of <u>The Runaway Bunny</u>, but then real quick he sees the difference. Runaway bunny knows it's safe to run away. It's just a game of pretend. He runs away <u>because he knows</u> his mother loves him, <u>because he knows</u> she'll come after him. But when Jody runs away, he does it even though it's not safe, probably <u>because</u> it's not safe. Because believing that his mother doesn't love him, doesn't care if he lives or dies, is more than he can stand.

Christopher once was stupid enough to think he might be a runaway bunny, with a rabbit mommy. Now he wants to be a runaway boy. Like Jody Baxter. A boy whose mother doesn't <u>act</u> like she loves him, doesn't <u>want</u> to love him, but ends up realizing she does. A boy whose mother comes after him even when he thinks she never will.

The more he tries to make sense of Ora, the more confused Christopher gets about what Marian might be. He knows she's not a rabbit mommy, but what if she's a secret Ora mommy! What if she doesn't <u>want</u> to love Christopher, what if she's <u>afraid</u> to in case something bad happens to him, but actually she does, somewhere so deep down that even she doesn't know it exists? Because Marian treats Christopher a lot like Ora treats Jody, cold and heartless like. But before he moves to verify that, Christopher needs to figure out why Ora changes, what Jody does to bring her love alive, so that he can be ready to do the same thing with Marian. He decides it has to be one of two things. It's either Jody's running away, so Ora fears he's dead and realizes how much more terrible that fear is than her fear of loving him. Or his doing the One Right Thing that she's waiting for him to do, which is finally killing his pet fawn, who he loves more than anything, who she already wounded, to show her that he forgives her, and that he loves her even more.

So once he confirms what kind of mommy Marian is, Christopher will have to do one of two things. Either make Scott hurt him bad enough that Marian can't pretend not to see it or that she doesn't care, or find a way to make it look like he's stopped loving Scott even though Scott still loves him, like Marian already has, which would prove his allegiance, prove him deserving of her secret love.

Once he's got that straight, he starts watching her. When Scott gets up to take his shower, Christopher sneaks into the bedroom and studies her while she sleeps, confused at how she looks so young, like the teenager she practically still is, her skin smooth and clean and her lids masking her hard dark ancient eyes. He follows her around the house during the hours in the afternoon when she's awake and old again, before she leaves for work. He's got to get this right or he'll just screw everything up, because if he goes ahead with one of his plans and it turns out she's not a rabbit mommy _or_ an Ora mommy, but her own thing, a Marian mommy with no deep-down, he'll end up dead, or worse, with no love at all. He doesn't get very far in this important research, however, because after a few weeks of stalking her, Marian whirls around when he sidles up behind her one afternoon, smacks him with her fist on the side of his head and screams at him, *Knock it off you cockroach! What the hell's with you? Jesus Christ. Stay the fuck away from me!* So he never does figure out what kind of mommy she is, and if there might have been something he could've done to change the way she feels about him.

And as for Jody's father, Penny. Christopher can't even begin to comprehend him, why he never hurts Jody, even when he's angry, how there could be so much love between them if there's no fear or pain to make it real. He dreams of himself being Jody, but when he imagines being treated that way, all the time with kindness and patience, Christopher's head gets light and heavy at the same time, he gets dizzy and scared, and even though his mind knows that Penny is the father a boy should have, his knotted gut knows that he couldn't live that way, in a world so big and lonely, he'd always be standing at the edge with shaking legs, peering over, looking for a familiar sign on a sharp rock, for solid bodily proof that he was really loved.

Twenty

THE KEY WAS DOWN IN the dirt of the geraniums. I let myself in. Lamplight led me into the back room. Ella was asleep on the sofa, a light quilt over her feet and legs, a book fallen to her side. I pictured her reading, determined to wait for me, but being pulled down into sleep by the dissipating tension of a better end to a bad night. I sat by her feet, put my hands on her ankles. Her eyes opened. We looked at each other for a while, not speaking.

"I'm so sorry." Her voice was hushed.

"It's okay. I understand. Distrust is really the only reasonable thing to feel."

"No, it was an irrational thing to feel, and . . ."

I wiggled her feet. "Forget it." I stood up and held out my hand. "I had a . . . weird dream before. I don't think I've shaken it off yet. Can we go upstairs? Just lie down together?"

Today Ella turned forty-eight. She was four years older than Marian. I'd hidden her birthday present in the overstuffed linen closet, but it didn't feel like the right time for birthday wishes or sexy lingerie.

<hr/>

I WITHDREW A SECTION OF the sheet from over her abdomen, traced the stretch marks on her exposed hip bone with my fingertips.

They were beautiful, silvery and smooth. I licked them, then pulled my tongue across her soft pale skin, through downy golden fuzz, and slowly pushed the tip into the well of her navel. She gasped, grabbed my head as though to move it away, but held me there instead.

"I feel you," she whispered.

I wanted to be there, where she was feeling me. I wanted to be inside her, everywhere, even there beneath my tongue, where Evan had been, be one with her, not just from the outside, the way we'd already been, but from the inside, a tiny possible me, soft and curled like a sightless, innocent caterpillar in the cocoon of her womb.

I removed my tongue and lifted my head. I put the flat of my hand on the raised curve of her belly just below her navel. She closed her eyes, put her hand over mine.

"Did you ever read *The Runaway Bunny* to Evan when he was little?"

She smiled, remembering. "Maybe a hundred times. It was one of his favorites."

"Mine, too." I kissed her sleepy eyelids. "Ella . . . I ran away and you came after me."

"Hmmm. Didn't I tell you I would? I'm not giving up on you, Jody." She shook her head, drew in a breath. "I'm not giving up on you."

I kissed her nose. "The day she left, my mother told me she'd wanted to abort me. She would never come after me. That dream I had tonight . . . I don't want to be a child to you. I don't want to feel like one when I'm with you."

She made an indescribable sound, from deep in her throat, a mournful hum, then was quiet. Her eyes remained closed, but I could see them moving behind the lids, I could see her digesting what I'd said, thinking about all the things it meant. After a moment, she inhaled a long breath and opened her eyes. As she exhaled, she caressed my face and head, drew me down and kissed me.

"Your mother brought a radiant, wise, and poetic soul into the world, despite herself. And the world brought you to me. You're not a child to me, Jody, but the difference in our years does mean something, to both of us. It can't not. But *whatever* we are together . . . it's what we're meant to be."

Her hand was still atop mine, on her stomach. I thought I felt something move under my palm. My mind went slack with the longing to believe her, that we were what we were meant to be together, and I could be everything with her, the boy she'd loved in her past, the man she might love now, and every so often, I could even let her touch the child I'd been before I knew her. That *this* was the peace I needed and wanted, not what Fern offered me. Not the horror of what Ella unconsciously feared I'd done to Evan. But I just didn't know. I didn't know if I could survive feeling like a child ever again.

"Maybe you're right. I don't know."

"I *am* right, Jody. Try to believe me."

"I'll try." I peeled away the rest of the sheet and recovered her with my body. My mouth was at her ear. "Happy birthday."

ELLA'S BIRTHDAY SURPRISE WENT OFF without a hitch. Evan hadn't given it away. Turned out, it being an unfortunate truth that kids these days were warned all about predators and child abuse from the time they could walk and talk, that as soon as Ella started trying to explain why I'd run out, he'd looked at her and said, "Jody didn't hurt me, mommy. Jody would never hurt me. You worry too much."

Evan skated like a pro. Ella loved it, went nuts when it hit her that it was her scaredy-cat bookworm son bombing down the block with a bunch of roses in his raised hand. They were both so out-of-their-minds thrilled, I didn't even care when Doctor Chase dropped by with Kaylee to wish Ella a happy birthday, or when his shrink's eyes seemed to remain on me longer than was necessary and made me wonder whether Ella had called him in between calls to me last night to ask his professional opinion on what the odds actually were that I might be dangerous. For the moment, it was Evan's judgment she'd clearly chosen to accept.

Since that night at Brendan's, overhearing Fern on the balcony, and after what happened with me and her, I'd thought about it, a lot, how dangerous I might be. There were times I looked at Evan and saw how little he was, how weak. How his bones were like a bird's. I'd think about how he'd come to love me, and how much power that gave me over him. I was sure I hadn't meant to hurt him when I grabbed his arm. But I knew Scott never meant to hurt me, either. So if my self-destruct clock was set to run down when I turned twenty-nine, if I was set to turn into Scott, what difference would it make whether I meant to hurt someone or not, if not meaning to couldn't stop me from doing it?

SCOTT TAKES CHRISTOPHER TO MASON'S toy store in downtown Bay Shore every few weeks and tells him to pick out ten dollars worth of stuff for his LEGOS and Lincoln Logs setups. Christopher examines everything, breathing gingerly, his deep-set eyes stretched wide like he was seeing it all for the first time, and loads a plastic basket with his careful choices. He notes the price of each item, keeps a tally in his head. When he's done, he hands the basket to Scott and Scott lifts it onto the high counter to pay. The total is always within twenty-five cents of ten dollars. If it's under, Scott says, "Go get something else." If it's over, he doesn't say boo. Sometimes, when he sees Christopher touch some special thing, some one thing that costs nearly, or more than ten dollars all on its own, and then leave it on the shelf, Scott goes back the next day and buys it for him, puts it in his room while he's at school.

Christopher builds forts and castles and villages, rocket ships and spaceships and alien cities. He builds all sorts of things, plays in them a while, then takes them down to build the next thing. When he finishes reading *The Yearling* for the second time, he demolishes whatever it was he's been working on and begins creating a meticulous replica of Jody Baxter's long-ago world. The things he's collected that he doesn't need get put away. Whatever he needs that he can't buy, he makes. Little by little, he replicates the hardscrabble farm in the lonely interior of northern Florida with its log house, barn, slat and split-rail fences, its fields of corn, cotton, and tobacco; the pine and cedar woods, swamps, creeks, and rivers; the roads and bridges and train tracks; the town of Volusia a few miles away. The snakes and deer and bears and bobcats. The people. Flag, the devoted but destructive fawn.

Within six months, Christopher covers a third of his bedroom floor. The replica is complete, nothing missing, but this isn't one of his normal setups, an inanimate concoction to ultimately be torn down and replaced with another. This is a living world, a place for Christopher to dwell, to tend and rearrange according to the pre-ordained happenings he knows so well, a place that will shift again and again through the seasons, through time and space itself, to its inevitable happy conclusion, and transport Christopher with it.

SCOTT AND CHRISTOPHER USED TO have fun building things together. Lately, on the occasions when Scott ambles upstairs to ask, "Hey, that's looking major complicated. Need some help?" Christopher keeps his head down and says no.

Scott isn't comfortable being shut out of any part of Christopher's life. One afternoon he goes up to Christopher's room to put an end to it.

"You've had this here for over a year, man. Aren't you tired of it?" Scott prods the edge of the model with the pointed toe of his cowboy boot. "What the hell is it, anyway?"

"I've told you, it's nothing special, just a plain old boring farm." Christopher kneels on the floor. He maneuvers himself into Scott's path. "Don't get so close. Don't touch it."

Scott's ears prick up. "Come on, mongrel. You never let me near this thing. It's nothing special? So let's have some fun with it. Where's half the shit I bought for you? You're not even using it anymore." He strides over to Christopher's closet. "The stuff in here?"

Christopher's eyes follow Scott. "No! Stop! I'll use everything next time, I promise, Daddy. I like this the way it is. Just leave it alone, okay?"

Scott hears the unmistakable tremor of anxiety beneath Christopher's plea. Scott doesn't want Christopher to be afraid of him.

He wants Christopher to love him. But he knows that if he lets the kid run free out in the world, beyond the one they inhabit alone together, he'll find a million people better than Scott to love.

"Well, I don't like it the way it is. We're going to add something." He peers into the closet. "Where's the rest of the stuff I bought you?"

Christopher gets to his feet. He doesn't answer, just stands and stares at Scott.

"Don't fuck around with me, mongrel. Where's the stuff?"

"Daddy, please." Christopher's voice shakes. "Please, leave it alone. It doesn't need anything else."

"Yeah, well I think it does. Tell me where that stuff is." Scott walks back to the setup and lifts a foot.

Christopher begins to breathe hard, his hands clenched into fists at his sides. "No, please. Pleeeease." His begging eyes dart toward his bed.

Scott grins and lowers his foot to the floor. "Nice try, buddy. Okay. We're going to add a doghouse . . ." he points to a spot near the house ". . . here." He gestures toward the bed. "Go get what we need from under there."

"No! No doghouse! It's not supposed to have a doghouse, you'll ruin it!" Christopher jumps up and down, his hands fly to his head to pull at his hair. "Why can't you just leave it alone! It's mine! Don't touch it! It's mine!"

Scott grabs Christopher's arm, digs his fingers into the tender spot above the elbow, where his own father used to grab him. "Nothing is yours, you ungrateful piece of shit! It's mine! Everything in this fucking house is mine, including you, and I'll do whatever I want with it. Now go get what we need to make a doghouse." He pushes Christopher toward the bed.

"*No!*" Christopher throws himself at Scott and shoves him in the stomach. "I hate you! Get out! Get out! Leave it alone!" He shoves Scott twice more, moves him a couple of feet in the direction of the door, before Scott recovers from his surprise and pins Christopher's arms behind his back.

"Oh, that was a big mistake, little buddy."

Scott stares down and watches the fight bleed out of Christopher's eyes, watches as fear and surrender fall over them like a veil. He smiles without humor. "A big mistake."

He drags Christopher over to the meticulous replica of Jody Baxter's world, flings him down on top of it, then steps over his unmoving body and methodically kicks the rest to smithereens.

"Didn't want a doghouse, huh? Tough noogies, man. You're getting one."

Scott yanks Christopher up by the arm, nearly dislocating it from its socket, and carts him unresisting down the stairs, through the house, out the kitchen door, to the rotting doghouse in the corner of the backyard. He takes off his leather belt, loops it around Christopher's neck, orders him to crawl inside and lie down, then places a symbolic stone on the trailing end of the belt.

"You're going to stay here until you learn that you always—always—do what I tell you. And you're not going to move. If I come back and that stone isn't exactly where it is now, you're toast."

It's around four in the afternoon. It's late spring. It stays warm for a bunch more hours, but after the sun goes down it gets pretty cool. Christopher lies in the dirt and watches stars appear in the patches of sky visible through the holes in the doghouse. He lies without moving except for his eyes, and the shivers he can't control, and when Scott comes back for him, the stone is exactly where Scott placed it.

Scott props Christopher on his hip and carries him back to the house. Christopher shrinks against him and cries without making a sound. Scott doesn't order him to stop. He sweeps Christopher's sweaty clumped hair off his forehead.

"You're okay, Chrissie. You're one tough cookie. And I'm sorry, man. I'm really sorry. But what can you do, right?"

Christopher nuzzles his head into the crook of Scott's neck. "It's all right, Daddy." His voice is wet and wobbly, deeply apologetic. "It's okay. What can you do?"

Scott laughs and kisses the top of Christopher's head. "I'll help you rebuild it, buddy. Okay?"

"No. I don't want it anymore. It was no good, it was all wrong."

They go inside and Scott rustles them up some Hamburger Helper, makes sure Christopher eats his whole plateful and drinks a glass of milk. They sit on the couch together and watch an episode of *Happy Days*, everyone's favorite show. Scott bundles Christopher up in an orange and brown afghan Lennie's girlfriend Monique crocheted, and Christopher, snug and full and forgiven once more for his constant mistakes, goes horizontal with his head in Scott's lap, Scott's hand on his head. Within minutes he's asleep, lulled by the soft hum of the Cunninghams' warm and loving bygone world.

Twenty-one

I DIDN'T HAVE TO MAKE up a story for Karl and Irene about why I wasn't joining the family for Thanksgiving. The truth—that I was spending the holiday with a very special woman I'd met a few months earlier, a divorcée named Ella whose young son was with his father for the weekend—went over gangbusters, better than any fib I could've invented. Brendan was the one who lied— Irene mentioned what a disappointment it was that Fern had to go to relatives upstate—and I wanted to think he'd done it for his own sake, to hide the wounds Fern and I had inflicted on him, but knowing Brendan he probably did it for me and his parents.

Tess was with us for Thanksgiving Day. Every time I caught her looking at me and Ella, I heard her telling me that *this* was our time, mine and Ella's, and I should take it. Saturday afternoon was winding down and except to walk Einstein neither of us had left the brownstone since I'd driven Tess back to Brooklyn Thursday night. We'd cooked, eaten, listened to music, made music. Devoted many industrious hours to perfecting the how and where of putting on and taking off her birthday present, which we somehow hadn't quite mastered yet. Marveled at the suspicious longevity and spray-paint-crimson color of Evan's five-dollar roses, in a vase on the dining room table. The phone had gone unanswered. There was no sound or movement from the basement or third-floor apartments—the other tenants were away. We felt as though we'd banished the world.

We were sitting in her back garden after finishing off the last of the turkey for lunch, sunk into side-by-side webbed lawn chairs and a three-day tryptophan and dopamine stupor. The air was cool, but in the garden, sheltered by the parallel rows of low buildings that lined Tenth and Eleventh Streets, there was no wind and the sun was steady and warm. We were both in T-shirts and bare feet, limp as eels in our chairs. Not talking. Not looking at one another. Lazily playing with each other's fingers, feeling each other's thereness.

My head was back, my eyes on the trees above me, on the clear blue sky beyond the branches and late-clinging leaves. Birds chirped and flitted, bursts of song in the stillness, flashes of gray and brown and red against the blue. I rolled my head to the side and snuck a heavy-lidded peek at Ella. Her eyes were closed, she had a smile on her face, her fingers continued to move in and out of mine. The mass of her hair shone like a second sun. I looked at her for a hundred years, then rolled my head back to center and let my eyes close. My body felt rooted, not into the chair but into the earth itself, my mind empty and calm. I drifted, tethered by Ella's hand, now unmoving in mine as she dozed. New sounds rose up behind the rush and trill of the birds—insects and squirrels rustling in the dry fallen leaves, Einstein's sleeping breath from under the deck, and then, from my right, from a fenced-off garden at the end of the block, the faint far-off sounds of children squealing, adults laughing and calling out. And the *brrrrrnnng brrrrrnnng* of a metal bike bell.

A feeling took hold of me. As though I were expanding, out beyond the border of my own skin, into a state of absolute harmony with each and every cosmic vibration, immediate and distant, with the nearest blade of grass and the farthest galaxy all at once. Like every single creature in the universe, I was exactly who and where I was meant to be.

It was alien and unfamiliar at first, but I quickly recognized the feeling as one I'd had before. That same blissful certainty of my own existence. Once before. With the sun warm on my face and arms, the *brrrrnnng* of a bike bell ringing in the air, and the person I loved more than any other sleeping near me. On another Saturday afternoon long ago, in the driveway of 113 Superior Street, before the sun went out. And that I hadn't known who I was or where I belonged or why I was here for the twenty-two years since.

I'm happy.

"That's good. I want you to be happy, here with me."

I'd spoken aloud without knowing it. Her fingers were moving again. I opened my eyes and turned my head. Ella was looking at me, smiling.

"I am. I am happy here with you."

Now. I was happy now. But even as the feeling overtook me, and the words were out of my mouth, I knew it wouldn't last. The assassin of my happiness was already riding in from the past. I could feel the thrum of his approach, deep in the ground where I'd just spread my roots.

＊

"YOU HAVE SO MANY SCARS. Visible ones. Invisible ones. Talk to me, Jody. Tell me something else. Can you do that? One other thing?"

It had been dark for hours but the bedroom was mellow with candlelight. My birthday present was a sheer black crumple on the floor. I was sitting naked at the edge of the bed, Ella behind me, her legs hooked over my thighs, her breasts pressed into my back. I reached for her hips, pulled her closer to me.

Her right hand wove itself between my arm and her leg and came to rest on the ugly nickel-sized burn above the crease of my right thigh, on the hairless skin between my hip and genitals. Round, raised, and shiny, latticed with a unique pattern of white lines. Its twin was on the meat of my right buttock. Both cleverly placed so that underwear or a swimsuit would cover them. I took her hand away, raised it to my lips and kissed her fingers. I did want to tell her something else, but the thrilling tale of Branding Night was not it.

She trailed her left hand down my arm, from shoulder to wrist. "This poor arm of yours has certainly taken a beating."

"Took a lickin' and kept on tickin'."

I did a quick mental inventory. Puckered scar on the front of my shoulder: kitchen knife target practice; long pale scar on the bone ridge of my forearm: knocked off my bike; sloppy saw marks on the inside of my wrist: incompetent use of dull razor; permanent dents below misshapen nails on my index and middle fingers: . . . yeah, I could tell her about that.

"How about I tell you about me and the piano."

"Okay." She wrapped both arms around my middle and leaned her head on my shoulder.

"Right, so . . . I learned to play in my grandfather's house. From my aunt Marie. I'd sit on her lap, and she'd put her hands over mine and we'd play together. The way little girls dance with their fathers, standing on their feet, holding on, their dads making them feel like they're really dancing, you know? But she taught me to read music, too, and we'd pick out the notes of songs we liked . . .

"She died when I was five. My grandfather moved away. I went to live with my mother and Scott. My grandfather wanted to sell everything, but Marian wanted that piano. It'd been her mother's. She hated her mother, I don't know why she wanted it, she never touched it. I was the only one who ever played it. Anyway, one day, I was picking out a song. I was concentrating so hard I didn't hear Scott sneak up on me. He was a tall guy, over six feet, but he was skinny and . . . slinky. He could do that, sneak up so you'd never hear him. So I'm playing, and then, boom, he slams the lid down on my hands." I held up my left hand, wiggled the offending digits. "Broke two fingers. Screwed up the nail beds. I didn't play the piano anymore after that."

She didn't say anything. She just held me tight and breathed against my spine.

"I'm so fucked it isn't even funny." I laughed.

"No. It's not funny. But look what happened. You told me something, something real and awful about yourself. And you're still alive. It didn't kill you. Jody, maybe you should go talk to someone. Someone who specializes in trauma. Things can change. Broken things can be fixed."

I lowered my head so she'd know I was listening with earnest attention. And I was, really. I heard her. I understood what she was saying. It was the majority opinion after all, I'd heard it plenty of times before and had even considered, in an objective sort of way, that there might be some truth to it. And because it was her saying it now, I tried to make my understanding go deeper, to not lay so light and inconsequential on my mind. But every way down was blocked and sealed, like the entrances to a decades-old mine disaster.

"You're not going to do that, are you?"

"No. I'm not going to do that." You could mend broken things so that they'd perform, do what they were supposed to do, but you couldn't fix them. Like a banged-up car or a broken bone, the underlying weakness would always be there. I took her hand and guided it back to the burn. "Put your hand there again. That's all the therapy I need."

She softly grunted her disagreement, but cupped the scar like it was a precious jewel. She rested her chin on my shoulder and said, "You're safe here with me."

I softly grunted my disagreement, but I turned my head and kissed her in appreciation of the sentiment.

✳

I WOKE UP IN THE middle of the night, freezing. Even in sleep, Ella had had the instinctive good sense to get under the covers, but not me, my nakedness was enjoying the cryogenic chill that had tiptoed down from Canada while we slept. I pulled half the blanket over me, waited until I'd warmed up enough so that my touch wouldn't turn her to ice, then curled up behind her and let her heat warm me the rest of the way.

I didn't want Ella to save me. I didn't want her to fix me. I didn't want her to convince me that I was smart or beautiful or talented. I didn't want her to undo what'd been done to me. None of that was possible, and besides, in the final scheme of things none of it mattered. Whatever had happened, it was all right, and whatever was going to happen would be all right, too, because I'd just lived through one perfect day, and I knew it, and really, how many people ever get that lucky?

Twenty-two

THIS TIME, SHE CALLED FIRST. Late one night the week after Thanksgiving. She said she had to talk to me in person, she needed ten minutes of my time. Cloaked in the armor of my recent days with Ella, I told her to come over.

But still, I waited for her downstairs, in the lobby. When a taxi pulled up, I opened the building door halfway and looked out. I saw a slice of Fern's face like a crescent winter moon in the rear window of the cab, her black eyes searching for and catching sight of me. Her face vanished and the rear door opened. Her legs emerged, spread slightly, her coat open and her skirt hiked, the tops of black stockings and the tendrils of a black lace garter belt clearly visible, along with an almost metallic gleam of hard white flesh. She stayed like that, exposed to me, the rest of her inside the taxi, while she paid the fare. That blade-sharp blackness, that metallic gleam of her intent, went clean through my armor and skewered me. I couldn't look away.

I'd told Tess I didn't want to go where Fern's demons wanted me to take her, but I hadn't spoken the whole truth. Wanting was more complicated, more tenacious than I'd ever admitted it could be. I remembered now, how wanting could fountain up from underground springs I'd thought drained dry, create a thirst for something I'd never even drunk before, or had and knew was poison. My mother's love, Scott's love. I remembered how I could want and not want a thing with equal agony of yearning, and that I'd never known whether you were meant to act on the wanting or on the not wanting, or to not act at all but let yourself be acted upon, let the thing come to you or not. I understood that Fern was a test, and of the sort I'd never known the answer to. Do I push her back into the cab and send her home? Do I take her tiny wrist captive in my fingers and take her upstairs? Do I stand in my doorway and wait for her to dismantle me?

I went out onto the street and as soon as she was out of the taxi I pulled her into the park.

"What are you doing? It's freezing. You're not wearing a jacket."

"I'm fine for ten minutes. Say what you have to say."

"No, not here. I want to go inside." My hand was tight around her upper arm. She looked up at me and her eyes brimmed with the same pain she'd brought to me on Halloween, that honed pick of her pain chiseling away at mine. "Take me inside."

I pulled her across the street and into the lobby, away from the door, under the stairs where the heat was. Heat, but no light, the back bulb having burned out over the summer and everyone in the building content to live off the memory of its illumination. I let go of her arm and we listed toward one another like drunks. I stepped back, out from under the stairs. My heart was beating too fast.

"What did you need to talk to me about."

Fern's lips were parted. Her underdeveloped chest rose and fell rapidly beneath her coat.

"I . . . I wanted you to know that I've spoken to Brendan. I'm seeing him over the weekend, I'm going to make up with him, get my ring back."

"What a surprise."

She pursed her mouth in a strained shaky attempt at a smile. "You see how we understand each other? How alike we are? You know I only broke up with him to make him angry at you. To hurt you. For not being willing to treat me badly." She laughed, a dry, hacking sound. "I'd broken up with him twice before. He's used to my quirks, he understands my resistance to being treated with such . . . kindness and patience."

I guess I should have hated her, but I couldn't. We were soul mates of the worst sort, identical to one another as my mirror-image burns.

"Yeah, being treated like a human being . . . it's definitely a bitch."

"Yes. This is so much easier, isn't it, Jody? Like slipping into a warm bath."

She moved deeper under the stairs, into the corner. She arched her head back against the wall and her hips out toward me. The small space got smaller, and darker, and the air got denser and harder to breathe. She kept her eyes on my face but forced mine down, to where she was slowly pulling up her skirt, one inch at a time. The dark hem rose up her thighs, I saw the stocking tops and garters again, her white flesh, and then my eyes ricocheted off the sight of a thatch of black hair. She wasn't wearing any panties.

"Oh, fuck!"

"Jody. Please. You can do whatever you want with me . . ."

Her voice and eyes were heavier and steamier than our little alcove and this time I felt a response to her, a visceral desire that was more than the desire to explore several levels of hell with her, though it was still a dark desire, a mess of pity, recognition, and a rekindled hatred for her and for myself, for what we were and for everyone who'd made us what we were.

I closed my eyes for a moment, and imagined Ella, in all her golden-ness, wrapping herself around me, telling me I was safe with her.

I went to Fern, pulled her skirt out of her hands and over her knees. I took her delicate face in my hands.

"We'd end up killing each other."

She laid her hands over mine. "It would be a good way to die."

"No, it wouldn't. Trust me, pain isn't romantic, and not all games are fun. You should pray to die of old age, in a rocking chair next to Brendan, on a porch with a view of the sea. Think about it. *That* would be a good way to die. You're right, this is easier, but easier isn't better, and you know it. That's why you keep going back to Brendan."

She shuddered and let out a moan. Brendan, her rock, her teddy bear, her safe place. I slid my hands out from under hers and her hands flew up to cover her face. When she finally brought them down, she looked at me as if my words had been the pronouncement of her impending death, a shiv between her ribs that had found her heart.

"I don't know anything."

"You know he loves you. Do you love him?"

Her breath caught in her throat, but she nodded.

"Then go back to him and try to let him make you happy. And stay away from me."

"No, I can fix this. I don't know what you told him, but I can fix it. I can turn you into a hero. He loves you and . . ."

"No. Don't do anything. Don't try and fix it." Fern really had done me a return favor. She'd relieved me of the burden of Brendan's love. "Just go back to him. He doesn't need me. He needs you, and he needs to be sure of you, and if I'm around he never will be. He's worried about you already, and yeah he does love me, but he thinks I'm not quite fit for the company he keeps. And even if you paint me a saint, he's not an idiot, Fern, he's got eyes. I mean, Jesus. Look at us. Look what happens when we're together."

I moved out toward the door, to put some distance between us.

"Don't hurt him, Fern. He doesn't deserve that. He's too good a person."

We looked at each other, and then we both smiled. *Unlike you. Unlike me.*

I GOT EINSTEIN, AND A jacket, and me and my girl went for a walk in the biting cold, down through Chinatown, over the Manhattan Bridge into Brooklyn and back. The wind had picked up. It tore at my uncovered hands and face, throat, and neck, stripped away the last couple of hours, stripped away Fern, stripped away Brendan, time and people shed like layers of dead skin. It felt good to be scoured clean. It felt necessary.

I crossed East Houston. Essex Street turned into Avenue A. I continued north toward home. At the corner of Ninth Street, I stopped. A half block ahead, a wide rectangle of rose-tinged light spilled onto the sidewalk out in front of the Coronet. It was time to shed Arwen, too, for real, let her shed me. I hadn't meant to, but I'd kept her dangling—further evidence of the ineffectiveness of my intentions. I didn't want to make her cry anymore and I didn't want to feel myself sucker-punched by the false hope of her relentless sunniness, wondering again and again if there might actually be elf-magic in this leaden world that could make a matter/antimatter union produce a stable whole instead of an obliterating explosion.

I caught up with her just as she was getting ready to go home. The way she lit up when she saw me come through the door would have shaken the resolve of a lesser misfit than I.

She hurried over to me, touched my cheek.

"You're all healed."

"It never really got that bad. Arwen, let's sit for a minute, I've got to talk to you."

The place was quiet. I steered us to a table in the back, out of sight of the bar and the few late-night eaters by the windows. I sat her down, sat myself across from her. Her eyes followed my every movement.

"Arwen, listen. The last few times I was in here, I was not in the

best shape, and I . . . it felt good, letting you take care of me, and I want you to know I appreciated it, a lot, but I don't want you hoping that anything's going to change between us, because it isn't."

She smiled, an eager open smile, put her hands on my forearms. "But I've never stopped hoping. And I know I'm right, because I saw the way you looked at me, Jody."

"I know, I'm sorry, I shouldn't have done that. It had nothing to do with you, it didn't mean anything."

Her smile fell apart. Her hands fell away. I took hold of them, tight enough to make her wince, and pulled her toward me across the table. I leaned my head close to hers and hardened my eyes. I spoke very quietly, delivered each word into her lovesick face.

"Arwen, I don't want your love." Her hands jerked in mine. Her head drew back and she turned the color of chalk. I leaned further across the table. "Don't pull away. Listen to me. Loving me would be like trying to survive a famine. You'd feed me your love so I could live, but I wouldn't give you anything. I don't have anything. I would starve you to death."

Her head whipped back and forth. "I don't believe that."

"I don't care what you believe. It only matters what I believe. And what I believe is that love is an illusion that pops like a balloon the first time you poke it."

"You're lying! I make you feel good, I know I do, that's not an illusion. Why are you saying these things?"

"Because you're gorgeous and good and forgiving and it would be easy to convince myself that I loved you, and my punishment for that would be to watch the Coronet's elf-girl become mortal and die."

I'd made her cry again, but I hoped it was for the last time. I brought a wad of napkins to the table, and sat with her while she went through them. I asked her if she'd like me to go somewhere else for my tea and toast fixes from now on, and through dripping eyes and sorrow-puckered mouth she summoned up a look as if to say, *Get over yourself, dude.* Those elves were a tough breed. With their indestructible faith in the inevitable triumph of Good over Evil, it was no wonder they lived forever.

I cared what she believed. I cared that for however long I'd be in her thoughts, I'd be there not as the guy who'd dumped her, but as the poor shlump who maybe actually did love her but was too damaged to feel it, or to let her love him.

And it wasn't as if it didn't occur to me that maybe I was shooting myself in the foot, blasting Arwen and Brendan out of my life. But the gun felt so good in my hand. And my finger on the trigger . . . it was just like playing the piano with Aunt Marie, I was playing but there was something else guiding me, stronger wiser fingers over mine, making sure I found the right notes, found my aim and squeezed.

JULY 6, 1980, THE SUNDAY OF July 4th weekend, 4:00 a.m. In the stillest bleakest blackest hour before dawn, Scott Hanson is wide awake and alight with malevolent energy. He's positively radioactive. He hasn't slept in twenty-six hours. The previous afternoon, he went to the movies, alone. He finally went to see *The Deer Hunter*. If he'd been able to reach Lennie, Lennie would've talked him out of seeing it, like he'd talked Scott out of seeing it since it first came out over a year ago, like he'd talked him out of seeing all the other Vietnam films that had come out over the last couple of years. But Lennie never returned Scott's call. Marian's been gone five months. Left to make a decision on his own, Scott, born dumb and blind to even the basics of cause and effect, made a typically unwise one. He declared his independence, he went to the movies.

He doesn't miss Marian, he's incapable of appreciating how she propped him up. With her oozing contempt for him, his utter failure to find a way into her heart, his having to scheme and grovel for sex, she kept him tottering yet at least on his mental toes. She was the corresponding bookend to Lennie's inadmissible guardianship. Both bookends having lately fallen away, the rational, civilized part of Scott's brain, which is supposed to maintain control over the wild, primitive part, has been overrun by the enemy. Tonight, it's surrendered altogether and lain down its puny weapons.

Scott's sitting on the couch in his living room snorting cocaine, drinking beer, smoking pot, and replaying scenes from the film in his head, particularly the one at the end where the Christopher Walken character blows his brains to kingdom come. He's been sitting there doing all that since midnight, when the heroin torpor started letting go and he made another bad decision—to leave the torpor for another day and go full-out for maximum voltage. In four hours he's sucked up eight lines of high-grade coke, smoked a similar number of joints, and drunk a six pack of Pabst. His nose is bleeding, his hands are twitching, he's seeing things out of the corners of his vibrating chemically propelled eyeballs, and the living room walls, which he is about to start bouncing off, are moving. So Scott's a bit hazy as to where or when the fuck he is, because while he sort of knows he's in his living room in Bay Shore, he feels like he's in a combat zone, gearing up to go into battle again. He's for sure prepped to mess somebody up. One way or another, he knows something bad's going to get done today.

Scott thrusts his head against the back of the couch and glares up at the ceiling. Something's up there. He can't see or hear it, but he senses the disturbance. There's somebody up there. His mind grinds on the problem and then on goes the zillion-watt light bulb. He's got a Christopher right here in the house! The coincidence boggles him for a moment—coincidence or *message?* Is he supposed to sneak up there and blow Christopher's brains out once and for all, no more fooling around? Is that the mission? He hopes not, because good riddance to the arrogant, selfish cunt but the kid is a whole other story. But what if that's his purpose, the Deed he's meant to perform, the sacrifice he's meant to make? To release Christopher from the unrelenting pain of life, to unselfishly let go of the one thing he truly loves. Only one way to find out. Scott takes the gun, the Smith & Wesson .357 Magnum tonight, and pads upstairs.

＊

CHRISTOPHER DREAMS OF SWIMMING IN warm water, all alone in the night in a big heated pool like the one at the town rec center, except this one is outside, on the top of a high green mountain. Above him are the pinpoint lights of a million stars, dancing now on the surface of the water, twinkling in the past in the heavens far away. Like the starlight, he is now and then, here and there.

He is light and limber and as elemental as the first fish that ever swam the ocean. He inhales and exhales water sweeter than air. He wriggles his hips and kicks his feet, glides effortlessly through warmth, through darkness and silence as deep and endless as the dark spaces between the glittering stars. He swims and swims and peace courses all through him, as though peace has replaced his blood, his nerves, his breath. Then, from out of the depths he sees a dark shadow moving toward him. The shadow takes the form of a shark, moving fast, already coming up alongside him. He tries to swim away, but the shark is too fast for him. It turns to face him, its jaws wide, and begins to gnaw on his side. He opens his mouth to scream, and his mouth fills with water. Christopher wakes, flailing and gasping, to a jabbing pain, into the onset of the familiar nightmare. Scott is looming over him, poking him with the barrel of one of his guns.

"Get up, mongrel. It's time to play."

THE SIGHT OF CHRISTOPHER'S FEAR-FILLED eyes and pliant mouth brings Scott back down to cruising altitude, reminds him he and the kid have a reality of their own, nothing to do with the movie, nothing to do with anyone or anything else. All those deep space questions about purpose and Deeds and sacrifice are neatly incinerated in the fire of his reentry. He's still imbued with the film's raging violence, but he's no longer considering whether he's supposed to blow this Christopher's brains out. That doesn't prevent him from aiming the barrel of the S&W smack at the center of Christopher's forehead. To get him to pay attention, to stay with the game. Because lately the kid seems otherwise engaged, so to speak, like he's not paying attention, and Scott doesn't like that, it leaves him feeling lonely, no matter what they do together.

Scott rousts Christopher and marches him down the hall into his sty of a room. Rooting around earlier in the fun-filled night for the right gun and the right drugs has left the dust-laden sparsely furnished space looking like a criminal-activity-shitbomb went off in it. The bed, floor, chair, tops of night tables and dressers, all are strewn with bags of pills and powders, handguns and rifles, clothes, beer cans, sheets and pillows. It's so bad it offends even Scott's tolerance for chaos. And he vaguely perceives that it's probably not such a smart thing to have all that stuff out in the open like that. He pushes Christopher into the mess, points the gun at him.

"Clean it up, monkey."

Christopher stands in place, his eyes lunging all over the room. "I don't know where it all goes, Daddy," he pleads.

"What are you, pretending to be stupid?"

"No."

"If you're not pretending, that means you *are* stupid. Is that it? You're a stupid yellow monkey and you can't even clean up this fucking room? Hey! Look at me when I talk to you, dirtbag!"

The kid's head whips around. His eyes are impossibly huge and blue-black with fear. His mouth is open, his breath audible. "I'm sorry, Daddy. I'm sorry. I'm sorry."

And here it comes again. Scott's lifelong rage at his own victimization, his own helplessness, comes bubbling up like precious oil from the pulverized remains of his own life. It flows out to engulf Christopher, to draw him closer to Scott's helpless soul than anyone's ever been, close enough for Scott's hopeless helplessness to get lost for a little while in the greater magnitude of Christopher's hopeless helplessness. The power of the game is revving up inside him and his manhood is starting to tingle. He makes a come-hither gesture with the revolver and works at the zipper of his jeans with his free hand.

"Your words mean shit. Get over here and use that big mouth to apologize the right way."

He's so coked up he can't keep an erection, but he trained the kid well and it feels good so he zones out and lets the kid work at it a nice long time before pushing him away. "That's enough." Christopher falls against the bed. "Christ, you're fucking drooling." Scott peels Christopher's pajama top off, wipes his mouth with it, and pitches it at the headboard.

"I'm gonna go pee. Then we'll play war." Scott's thoughts of cleaning up the room have gone wherever his thoughts of shooting Christopher in the head went. He's on to better things. "This time you stay here and count to . . . count to like a hundred, but slow. I'm going to turn out all the lights and close all the blinds. Then you try to get to the kitchen. But I'll be out there, somewhere, waiting for you. Think you'll make it, little monkey?"

※

SCOTT IS AN ECLIPSE OF the sun and Christopher is consumed by his shadow, near to immobilized in his wake. When Scott leaves the room, Christopher drags himself through the debris to the triangular space behind the open door. He turns his body and sits on the floor with his naked back flush against the wall, his knees tucked up tight under his chin, his fingers wrapped around his ankles, his head down. It's hard to breathe, the air is heavy. And hot. He feels its heat on his skin, but beneath that flimsy layer of protection the chill of darkness is spreading. He hears Scott coming back from the bathroom. He stares at his bare feet and imagines driving his body through the paint and plasterboard into that other world. He doesn't need to look up to see, he can feel Scott's crazy glazey eyes boring through the top of his head and he starts there, at the top of his head, and from there down to his toes he forces himself to go still. Frozen tundra still, petrified forest still. End of the world still. From inside he pushes down on every tiny motion, down, down, until he's all numb and can't feel any of himself anymore and he closes his eyes and prays that maybe somehow Scott can't see him now. Yes, he's started praying again, he doesn't care what the price might be. He doesn't care if Scott dies. He doesn't care if either one of them dies. He just wants this not to happen again, whatever it's going to be this time. He drains himself into the floor, into the wall. He's camouflaging himself in blindness, in stillness, like a dumb deer in the forest who should bolt but stands scared shitless, like a statue, and fools itself into believing that ugly two-legged thing with a rifle can't see it. He does all he can, but it's not enough. It's never enough. Scott is right. He's stupid, as stupid as the deer. Every time, there's one breach in his cloak of invisibility that he forgets about until it's too late: he's still breathing. He can't not. He's panting, open-mouthed, lungs working like bellows, his breath swift and shallow and wavering in his throat, and the sound, even though he tries so hard to keep it soft, is loud as thunder and booms into the farthest corners of the cosmos where anyone can hear it. Even if he can't see Christopher, Scott's doped-out, radar rabbit ears can hear him.

Christopher doesn't make it to the other side. Scott grabs his arm and hauls him up before he can find his way through.

※

WHEN SCOTT SNAPS TO AND finds himself sitting at the kitchen table with his tongue probing the insides of an empty Baggie for coke fluff, he figures he's had enough for the day. He lights a joint and pops the last unopened can of beer. Church bells peal in the distance. The clock on the wall reads eight. He and the mongrel have been playing games for hours. Scott finishes the joint. He swivels in his chair and gazes at Christopher, who is curled up on his side on the rag rug in front of the sink. The kid is so still he could be sleeping, except his eyes are open. He's looking straight ahead of him, at nothing.

Scott's eight-hour high is fizzling out. He's coming down, the cocaine clarity giving way to melancholy, anxiety, and confusion. He rolls and lights another joint. He leans forward, his arms on his knees, and stares at Christopher while he slowly smokes it. On the floor in front of where the boy is lying is a patch of sunlight. It reflects off the linoleum and lights up Christopher's unreadable face, his arms and torso. Scott is awestruck anew by how beautiful the kid is. How unusual and strong his features, how perfectly formed his little body, how extraordinary the deep blended color of his silky skin, the luminescent violet blue of his eyes against the dense charcoal blackness of his hair and lashes. Scott inhales, and stares, and all at once the bright slanting light and unmoving young boy give way in Scott's cooling brain to still, muted images of death and destruction, memories of Vietnam and scenes from *The Deer Hunter*. The beauty of the boy on the floor in sunlight and the images of violence conflate in his mind. He sees the beauty that can exist in violence, and the violence that is a part of such extreme beauty as Christopher's. And he realizes, finally, what the mission is, what the movie is telling him to do. He is meant to meld the two into one, to perform an act that will fuse its inherent beauty to its inherent violence, thus creating something at once violently beautiful, and beautifully violent.

Scott picks Christopher off the floor and carries him to the kitchen chair. He sits down with the boy in his lap, puts his arms around him. Christopher leans limply against his chest. "Chrissie, we're going to do one more thing. Something really special. And after that, we'll go to sleep." He kisses the top of Christopher's head. "I love you. Now stand up."

※

SCOTT TURNS CHRISTOPHER SO HE'S facing the table, pushes his torso down onto the tabletop, tugs at the waistband of his pajamas. Christopher's feet no longer reach the floor, he dangles there, ungrounded, disoriented, and feels a shock of warm air on his now bare bottom. He struggles to flip himself over but Scott's body is pressing against the backs of his legs and one of Scott's hands is on his shoulder. The other is fumbling between the cheeks of his butt. A fearsome tremor ripples through him, he struggles harder and involuntarily yells out, "Daddy, stop!!" Scott whispers, "Stay still, Chrissie. Relax. It'll be easier if you relax." His hand slides from Christopher's shoulder, lovingly strokes the back of his neck. "Just relax." Christopher absorbs the caress and releases a small whimper, tries to turn his head to look up at Scott, but Scott's hand instructs him to not move. Christopher can't disobey Scott. He stops moving on the outside, he can do that, but inside he is contracting like a dying star before it explodes, his body clenched around the roiling cauldron of his uncomprehending terror. He wants to be brave for Scott, so he bites down on his terror, bites down on his lips as Scott thrusts between his cheeks and forces himself inside. He bites so hard he draws blood, but the hurt is unbearable, worse than when Scott burned him with the cigar, worse than anything he's ever endured. A torrent of scalding tears gushes from his eyes and he shrieks in pain. Scott's hand moves quickly from the back of Christopher's neck to cover his mouth. "Shhh. Be quiet. Listen to me. You're the only one who loves me and, man, I need some love right now. You're the only one I could ever do this with, Chrissie, you know that." Christopher whimpers again, his salty wet lips tremble against the sweaty skin of Scott's palm. "Just this once, mongrel, okay? For love, man. Just this once and I promise, I'll never touch you again, not even the other thing. It won't be so bad." It is. Scott lied. The pain keeps growing, blooming inside him like a raging fire. Christopher closes his eyes, stretches his arms out past his head and frantically sweeps his palms over the tabletop until he finds it, the right spot, the wormhole in the solid surface, and he pushes and pushes against the hard scarred wood and he's through it, he's finally falling through the void on the other side of the fear-pain wall.

＊

SCOTT IS SAYING SOMETHING. HE'S telling Christopher to open his eyes and look at him. Christopher can do that, it doesn't matter if his eyes are open or shut, because he's behind the wall now, where he can see and hear but not feel, where time moves so fast it stops, then inches past itself so that when Christopher goes back, to the other side, it's before again.

Somehow he's gotten turned around, his feet are on the floor, his face is cradled in Scott's spidery fingers. Scott's mouth is moving and his voice is a faraway echo saying, "I'm sorry, man, I know that hurt. But it'll be better next time. Hang here while I get some more beer." Scott takes his hands away and Christopher slowly sinks to his knees. His bunched pajamas land in a pool of something wet. His head falls forward and he vomits onto his thighs and the floor.

It takes a few seconds for Scott's words to get through the noise in the pulsing air around Christopher's head, to pierce through all that null space he's encased himself in. *It'll be better next time.* He'd said, *Just this once and then I'll never touch you again.* He'd said, *I prom-*

ise, and Christopher believed him. He'd said I promise and Christopher believed that if he let Scott do this thing to him, showed Scott how much he loves him, *proved* it to him, Scott wouldn't have to hurt him anymore. He'd find a different way to love him. *It'll be better next time.* His promise was nothing but another lie.

The words shove Christopher through the wall of numbness, back into the kitchen, into the inescapable present. His bottom burns, deep inside, as though he's been stuffed with hot coals. He can smell himself, a nauseating stench of years of blood, sweat, beer, saliva, tears, vomit, semen. He's kneeling in a pool of his own filth. He *is* garbage. Scott lied to him about that, too, he lied from the very beginning. Christopher lifts his head and sees Scott staggering toward the door to the basement, his blood-streaked penis swaying between his legs. Everything Scott's ever said has been a lie. Christopher's not his son. Scott doesn't love him.

Nobody loves you. He hears her careless, brittle voice in his head. Scott doesn't love him, and this will never stop, no matter what he does. *Or you could kill him.* His mind and body ignite in a white-hot amalgam of hatred and fury that he can not bear to feel, and so he buries it under panic of an intensity he's never known before. Adrenaline floods his every synapse. All pain disappears as his heart rate blasts into the stratosphere. He is no longer human. He's a desperate animal wrapped around a pounding heart. Christopher launches himself up, runs across the room with the unnatural speed of a puma, and pushes Scott down the basement stairs.

※

SCOTT'S LYING ON THE CEMENT floor. He's not moving. Even with his penis exposed he looks harmless now. One arm is out-flung, the hand lying open, palm up, and Christopher remembers the feel of that hand soft in his hair, on the back of his neck.

The relentless panic threatens to pop his eyeballs, push his heart out through his mouth. He swiftly shuts the basement door and turns away. Marian is standing in the middle of the room, smiling at him, and in a flash he understands everything. He sees so clearly where he went wrong before, what he should have done to make her stay, to make her see that it was her he'd always loved best. Always. What he has to do now to make her love him. It's not too late. She hasn't been gone that long. If he gets it right this time, she'll come back.

Ora didn't come to love Jody from him doing just one of two possible things. Being deserving of that kind of love requires more of a person. It had to be that he did *both* things, that he killed the thing Ora believed Jody loved more than her, and that he showed her he was ready to die, knew he *should* die, if she couldn't love him.

Christopher stumbles back to the kitchen table. He doesn't pull up his pajamas, which are pasted to the backs of his thighs. He doesn't wipe his face. He's afraid to touch himself, he's an abomination. A walking cesspool. He picks the razor off the powder-coated mirror and jabs and slashes at his left wrist. Blood drips from the wounds, but the blade is rusted and dull, it won't slice cleanly through his flesh. He drops it. There's a bag of red pills on the table. The ones that put you to sleep best of all. Scott gave him one, before, but he's not even tired from it anymore. He needs to take more. He needs to take enough to put him to sleep for long enough for her to find him. He knows that can work because he's read stories like that, where someone goes to sleep and time stops for them, and they wake up far in the future and everything's different.

He swallows pills with the beer dregs in the cans on the table, proud of every one he gets down, thinking that if she were really there, he'd be saying, *Mommy, look, look at me, look what I'm doing!* and she'd be watching and smiling. He swallows as many as he can before he feels himself wanting to vomit again. He's going to wait for her outside, but first there's one more thing he needs to do. He needs to get her boots from his closet. As he tucks them against his bare chest, he begins to hear a murmur in the air around his head, a soft hissing that moves as he moves and will stay with him until the end, until he falls asleep. It's a comforting sound. He's not aware that it's his own whispered chant. *Please Mommy please Mommy please Mommy.* Back in the kitchen, he takes the pills from the table and trips his way out the back door, across the yard. He drops to his knees and crawls through the doghouse's splintered arched opening. He falls on his face. He loses his grip on the bag and pills spill out. He lifts his head and tries to eat a few more right off the dirt, but they tumble out of his mouth. He's starting to feel sick and his feverish energy is draining away. He doesn't need to count, his mind is already getting fuzzy, and he thinks he sees, out the corner of his eye, a golden thread lowering itself through the air outside the doghouse doorway, descending slowly from high above the sky, from the red gold ball of the sun. A trail for her to follow. His last thought is that he's done it, he's done it all, and now she'll come back for him, her runaway bunny. He'll wake up in the future, somewhere else, and she'll be there.

✳

"CHRISTOPHER? CAN YOU HEAR ME?"

He is bathed in clean white light. His eyes are still closed, but he can feel it all around him. There is sweetness on his mouth. Milk and honey. He wonders if he's in heaven. If that's where she'd gone when she left and she's brought him to be with her. "Christopher?" His nose pricks with incipient tears and his sluggish heart, so very tired in his aching chest, begins to wake up. His sweet mouth forms a smile as he turns his head toward the sound of her voice. He slowly opens his eyes. A plump matronly face hovers over him. Bright blue eyes, a little pointed cap on her curly graying hair. A caring smile. It's not her. Not his mommy. Harsh white light stabs at his eyes. He jerks his head to the side, away from the strange face, closes his eyes again.

"Don't be frightened, sweetheart. I'm Irene, I'm your nurse. You're in the hospital, you've been asleep for a few days, but you're going to be all right. Everything's going to be all right now. Can you look at me, Christopher?"

Jupiter-force gravity pins his body to the bed, his head to the pillow. He couldn't look at her even if he wanted to.

"I'm going to put a little more ointment on your mouth. It will feel good on your lips and the sores, I promise. Okay, Christopher?"

He doesn't move or speak. After a moment, he feels her coated finger slowly tracing the shape of his parched mouth, the deep bowed contour of his lips, their despised fullness, finding its way inside. He pushes his head more deeply into the pillow but he can't escape her finger, it follows him down into the soft foam. The sweet thick ointment does feel good, and her touch is so gentle it fills him with an infinite despair. Tears snake from beneath his lids.

"There. That wasn't so bad, was it?" Irene Kowalczyk rests the back of her hand against his cheek, as though to catch his tears. "Christopher. Can you open your eyes and look at me? Do you think you could stay awake and talk to me for a little while? Christopher?"

She doesn't take her hand away, just lets it lie lightly on his face. She waits.

"Christopher?"

"That's not my name." His voice is a nearly inaudible croak, his throat is raw and feels long-unused. He doesn't want to talk to her, but he has to let her know so she'll stop saying it.

Irene doesn't miss a beat. "Oh, I'm sorry, sweetheart. That's what it says on your chart here. I guess someone made a mistake?"

He turns his head a fraction, takes a fleeting peek at her. There's nothing but kindness in her face. He looks her in the eye and nods.

She nods with him. "Well. We can't have that. Will you tell me your name, so we can fix it?"

He can't be Christopher anymore; Christopher is a bad, bad boy who killed his daddy and has to stay in the doghouse until his mommy comes back and makes him good again. There's nothing more anyone can do for him.

"I'm Jody. My name is Jody."

Twenty-three

"**J**ODY! JODY! WATCH ME! WATCH how fast I can go!! Jody!!"

"I'm watching! Slow down, I had a hard week, I'm tired, I can't keep up with you!"

I let Evan pass and race ahead of me up Tenth Street toward Avenue B. He'd decided that the East Village was "like totally awesome," so that afternoon, the Sunday after Thanksgiving weekend, we'd gone skating in East River Park, which ran south from Twelfth Street down to Montgomery, on the river side of the stretch of housing projects east of Avenue D. The park was a work in progress, crummier, of course, in both amenities and clientele than its cousin along the Hudson, but it had some good stretches to skate or bike, and amazing views of Brooklyn, Queens, and downtown Manhattan, and of the east side bridges. Evan loved it.

The sun had been behind heavy clouds all day and at four o'clock the day's gray sky was fast turning to black. I'd promised Ella I'd have us back to her before dark. We were making for my apartment to drop our gear, pick up Einstein, and beat it across town. I didn't want to do anything that could possibly make her nervous, make her look at me like that again when I brought Evan home.

"Evan, stop at the corner!" I yelled out to him from half a block behind. "Don't cross without me!"

Either he didn't hear me, or didn't want to. He didn't even slow down, just gave a quick look in both directions and slalomed around the other people crossing Avenue B against the light like he'd invented Frogger. He didn't stop on the far corner, or continue up the block toward my building. Instead, he turned and flashed me a grin that made my heart lurch—a sassy, see-no-evil grin exactly like the grin I'd given Scott the day he came out of the house to watch me on my bike in the driveway. Then he darted left, heading for the avenue entrance to Tompkins Square Park.

I lost sight of him behind the Tenth Street buildings. When I reached the corner a few seconds later, Evan was already nearing the park entry in the middle of the block, arms and legs pumping, oblivious to everything around him. Closer to Ninth Street, a black SUV, a massive blinged-out Lincoln Navigator, was double-parked and idling and three punks were dropping out of its high cab like a SWAT team on a covert black-ops mission. One punk pointed at Evan, at his helmet and skates, snickered silently, then gestured for the other two to follow him. My chest seized up.

A chewed-up sofa and two scarred wooden kitchen chairs lay discarded on the sidewalk. I backed up, stomped on one of the chairs with my skate and freed a leg. I went into a sprint and got myself between the punks and Evan just as he made his turn into the park.

I could hear the noises of dogs and their owners from inside the park. I called out, "Evan, meet me at the dog run! I'll just be a minute—ran into some neighborhood pals!"

Evan looked back over his shoulder, took in the scene, me on the sidewalk, three guys standing in the street. His innocent eyes couldn't see the already boiling blood, the swirling red haze that would soon engulf me and my pals. I didn't want Evan to ever have eyes to see such things. He raised his arms over his head and gave me two thumbs-up. "Okay, Jody!" He disappeared.

"So, *mis amigos*." I turned and gave them my full attention. Kept the splintered but sturdy chair leg hidden along the length of my leg.

Huey, Dewey, and Louie were a matching trio of Puerto Rican punks, probably from the projects we'd just skated through. If they were a day over fifteen I was a duck's uncle. They sported leather jackets, duck-billed baseball caps, expensive sneakers. Identical phony ear-to-ear smiles split their smooth brown baby faces, and three sets of wide nostrils set in flat noses flared in anger. The pupils in their narrow black eyes had dilated down to pinpoints and their squat stocky bodies twitched in excitement. It wasn't hard to figure that they'd been snorting meth in the SUV while keeping watch for an easy victim to jump on.

I'd pissed on their fun and they were not happy about it. Huey, the snickerer, made a show of his slow head-to-toe scan of me. His eyes reduced themselves to slits of malice and greed. His intention to take me down and take my gear home in payment for getting in their way was clear as a bell. I brought the chair leg out where they could see it.

Huey took a cautious step toward me while Dewey and Louie came up behind and on either side of him, shit-eating grins glued in place.

"*¡Calma, pappy! ¡Calma!* You no wanna use that thing . . ."

"*Yo no soy tu papá* and I'll take it easy when I see your backs."

"*¡Que hablar bien español!*" Huey showed me his pearly teeth, then glanced in the direction of Evan's escape. "What's he to you, man? Little honky boy. Why you no let us mess with him a little, heh? His daddy buy him new crap, right? You one of us. *Conozco un hermano cuando veo uno.*"

"Get your eyes checked, *chico*. I'm not your brother, either. You and your friends waddle on home now." He was trying to get me to let my guard down. Being "one of them," a "brother," wasn't worth the DNA analysis to prove it as far as offering me protection from them. They'd steal from their own sainted mothers. I brought my makeshift weapon up in front of me like a bat.

Number One Duck didn't flinch. An expression of twisted joy darted across his features. "You know, *mi hermano,* I like you stuff. Is better than little honky . . ." His eyes slid side to side, a message to ducks two and three to get set. "How 'bout we take it off you?"

"You can try." I brandished the chair leg. "Come on, Huey. Give me a reason . . ." I took a step closer.

Teeth and smile disappeared, there was a flick of his wrist, a glint of metal in the waning light, and a Saturday night special hidden in his jacket cuff was pointed at my face.

"I wouldn't be doin' that. We gonna take you helmet and skates, and you wallet, *lo entiendes?* Any of that shit worth dyin' for *pappy?* 'Cause *madre de dios* I swear I shove this gun down you throat and I blow your head off. Let your pretty honky lover-boy find you."

✳

THAT HEAVY SKY CAME DOWN all the way, blanketing my head in a cloud of evil memories. In my vision there were no streets or buildings, no park no cars no trees, just the round black opening of the gun grown to the size of a manhole cover, the nail-bitten finger on the trigger a tensed extension of the anger and violence in the brown face and black eyes behind it. My gut took control of me, shut down all thought and feeling. My head and heart were eyes and muscle. Gut, eyes, muscle. That's all there was to me. Gut, eyes, muscle, and volcanic fury.

I swung the chair leg with all my might. So fast it blurred the air and caught the underside of Huey's hand before he registered any sign that he saw it coming. A bone cracked and he let out a screech of pain. His arm jerked up and to the side. The gun clattered into the street. I swung down and he collapsed with another shriek, clutching his knee. My vision began to expand. I saw Dewey wake up and think about going for the gun, but he was flesh and I was a wave. I got to it before the thought exited his brain.

The chair leg was in my left hand now, the gun in my right. I aimed it at Louie.

Then at Dewey.

Then down at Huey.

"If you three roaches are not gone in ten seconds I'm going to blow his head off. *¿Está claro? Uno, dos, tres . . .*"

My voice sounded like gravel. My eyes felt like they'd been propped open with toothpicks. Dewey and Louie didn't want to get any nearer, their fear of me was stinking up the fresh winter air, but they hustled Huey to his feet and dragged him toward the Navigator. I followed them. My arm was straight as a rod, the gun steady in my hand. Huey swiveled his torso, forced the trio to a momentary halt, and glared at me over his shoulder. He wasn't scared. He was fifteen going on hard time. I took another step, put the barrel of the gun to the middle of his forehead and said, "Keep going, little duck." Then I moved back. Huey's eyes bulged with rage. He pointed at my chest with his broken hand, his thumb and index finger imitating the gun pointing at him, so cold with anger and vengefulness and the excruciating longing to inflict pain that he felt none himself, so cold that for a second it was Scott's ice-blue eyes I saw in Huey's hot black sockets.

It had been a lifetime since I'd felt the concrete comfort of his half-crazed eyes on me, blazing with love and his need to hurt me. A lifetime since I'd let myself remember how much I loved him.

"*Usted es un hombre muerto.* Jody." You're a dead man.

I lowered the gun to my side.

"*Esto es cierto.* Huey." This is true.

I smiled, so grateful for Huey's blue-black rage, my rage all gone, washed away by the elation that soared through me from my feet, solid on the ground, to my head. Like air bubbles trapped in mud under the weight of the ocean, moving in the opposite direction of the joy that once infused me from my head to my feet, the first time Scott's hand touched my hair, every time Scott's hand touched my hair. Canceling it out.

"Why you smile at me like that, fool?" Huey yelled. He thrust his pointing finger at me to the limit of his reach, mimicked the sound of a muffled gunshot, notched his finger, and jerked his hand upward like from a recoil. "*Diez.*" Ten. "*Ahora es mi turno para contar, hombre muerto.*" Now it's my turn to count, dead man. Then he smiled back at me and quacked. Hey, he may have lost his humanity along with his morality, but at least he hadn't lost his love of cartoons or his sense of humor.

The three ducks climbed into the SUV. It pealed out with a squeal of fat tires, took the corner of Eighth Street without braking, and sped east.

There was a sewer grate at the curb. I removed the magazine from the gun, pulled my shirt free of my pants and wiped the gun and magazine clean of prints, kneeled, and shoved them both through the grate with the chair leg. Then I bent over and vomited up the contents and lining of my stomach.

Four twenty on a Sunday afternoon. Nobody stops to help, nobody sees anything, nobody says anything. You had to love the East Village. People there really knew how to mind their own business. I mean, honestly, why would I want to live anywhere else?

*

I WIPED MY MOUTH WITH the already-soiled bottom of my shirt, neatened myself up, and skated into the park. The chair leg got dumped into a garbage can. Evan had listened to me this time, and was waiting on a bench by the dog run. I dropped down next to him, took off his helmet so the cool air could dry up the sweat trapped underneath the polystyrene and plastic. I put my arm around him. He leaned into the crook of my shoulder. I looked down at the top of his head. I reached to tousle his hair, but my fingers had a mind of their own.

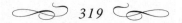

They eased themselves into the thick blond mass and moved, slowly and gently, across his scalp. Evan sighed with contentment and tilted his head up so he could see me. It wasn't until our eyes met that I realized I was watching him in a way that could only confuse him. I tried to smile, but it came up wrong.

"What's the matter, Jody? You're all pale. Are you sick?"

I wasn't going to say I was fine, nothing was the matter. It really messed with kids' minds when adults lied to them like that, saying everything was okay when it clearly wasn't.

"No, I'm not sick. I'm just . . . a little upset, I guess."

Now he turned pale. "You're angry with me. I didn't listen to you."

"No, that's not it. I'm not angry with you. I mean, yeah, maybe next time please don't cross a street without me? But you were skating really great, I was watching. So no, I'm not angry with you. No. It's something I heard from one of those guys . . ." I tossed my head in the direction of Avenue B.

"One of your friends? What was it?"

Evan had no idea about any part of what had really happened just then, and it was going to stay that way. But I had to warn him, somehow, I had to make him understand that he had to be careful. Always, everywhere. Careful, careful, careful.

"His kid brother got mugged, in the projects, where they live. They stole his bike, roughed him up a little. Mostly just scared him, but still . . ." I put my hand under Evan's chin, held his head still. "Evan. Listen to me . . . If something or somebody ever scares you . . . ? I mean . . . Look, being scared isn't always a bad thing, it can be an alarm going off inside you, it's not always about something you want to push through, like being afraid of Rollerblading. Sometimes it's . . . a warning, it's telling you . . . you're someplace you don't want to be. Then it's a good thing. So if anybody ever scares you, *anybody*, and I'm . . . and you're alone? . . . Even if they tell you it's okay, if you're scared, you scream. You scream bloody murder, and you hit, you bite, you kick, you run, you don't let anybody hurt you. Don't ever let anybody hurt you. You hear me?"

I wanted him to understand what I meant, but still it wasn't easy to see the teary confirmation in those gooey amber eyes of his that he did. That he knew it wasn't just the danger of another street mugging I was warning him about.

I held his face, and he held my eye, and then he nodded into my hand, said, "I hear you, Jody," and gave me a smile that nearly made me cry for the second time in twenty years.

"Jody?"

"Yeah?"

"What do you think is going to happen at midnight on December thirty-first?"

I put my hands on his shoulders. "Aw, shit." He snorted and giggled. "I mean, oh darn, now *I've* scared you. Listen up. Nothing. Absolutely nothing is going to happen. A bunch of idiots are going to party like it's the end of the world, and wake up embarrassed as all hell the next morning."

"You really think so?"

"I know so. Nothing bad is going to happen."

"You promise?"

And just like that, I understood at least one reason why people made promises they had no power to keep. "I promise."

"And you'll be there, when I wake up the next morning?"

In for a penny, in for a pound. "I'll be there. I promise."

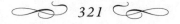

"WHAT ARE YOU, A SQUIRREL storing up acorns for winter? You're going to see me in two days," Ella teased, but she nestled into me and returned the latest of my endless kisses.

The elation had been swelling in me all evening, and with it an impatience to be gone, to at long last start down the final road. So it was harder than I thought it would be, saying goodnight to Ella, acting as though nothing could change the plans we'd made. I kept leaving, then turning back for one more kiss, one more moving picture of her face, one more feel of her body to take away with me.

"Two days is a long time for a cold hungry squirrel."

"Well, I'll make sure the cold hungry squirrel gets a very special treat for his birthday. Something to keep him warm and fed until the weekend. You're going to stay over on Tuesday, I want you in my arms at eleven-oh-eight, at the moment you were born. I'm going to make you feel like you're being born again, into a better world this time . . ." She blushed at her own boldness, or her corniness, except I didn't think it was corny, it was profound and beautiful and I had to kiss her again.

"And at eleven thirty-three. Just in case."

She peered at me to make sure I wasn't joking with her. I wasn't.

"Jody. It's *your* birthday, you're the one I—"

"No, you can say yes, it's okay. It doesn't take away from this, from you and me. It's his birthday, too, and . . . I don't know, I don't think it's so crazy that maybe he's here, somehow." I put my hands over my heart. "I mean, *something* guided me to you and Tess. Something that's not *me,* that already knows you. So, better safe than sorry, right? Because if he *is* here, he wants to be with you, too."

She hid her face against my shoulder. When she lifted her head, her cheeks were wet. "I love you, Jody."

"We love you, too."

She laughed and kissed me. Now I could say goodnight. Today she loved me.

※

I WALKED BY MY BUILDING and circled the park, letting Einstein take her time identifying the scent of every dog that had ever peed on any piece of cement or clod of dirt. After the third pass I held up on the top step, at the door to my building, and gazed out over the street for long enough for anyone nearby, on foot or in a black SUV, to get a good look at me.

Rounding the corner and seeing Evan in danger ... and that gun in my face. It sparked a white rage that Evan never learn the things I'd been taught by his age, never know the astronomical heights of cruelty and fear that people could scale. And that rage for him flipped on me, became *my* rage, and it sent me somewhere I believed I would never go, into the one memory I'd hacked into a million pieces and buried across a million scattered synapses so I would never see it whole again. My memory of the night Scott died. Of the games he'd played and the heights of my terror. Of the lies he'd told and my moment of rage that led to my sin. And of my other sin, my failure to die with him. It was *that* rage I felt, the rage to kill or die, it hardly mattered which, but to one way or another put an end to a situation I couldn't bear to live inside of anymore.

The rage and fear were gone, they were of no use to me anymore. I only needed my memories, intact and undeniable, and this elation. They reverberated inside me, like the expanding aftershocks of a powerful impact, of having finally hurtled, head on and at full speed, into the wall I'd been racing toward my whole life, into *my* Cambodia. Tonight I got to take my foot off the pedal.

There was one more thing I had to write before it was too late. No one was ever going to read it. This one was just for me. *WHY HER LOVE WILL DIE.*

Twenty-four

MONDAY MORNING. THE BAREST GLIMMER of dawn in the sky. My building was in the middle of the block, and in winter, when the trees were leafless, the view from my living room took in all of Tenth Street and the park, and parts of Seventh Street and both avenues. I could even see the rosy lights of the Coronet. I stood by the window, just another shadow in the murky gloom, watching the wee-hour activity on the streets; not that much, all of it moving slowly. In particular, I watched a blinged-out black Navigator inch up Avenue A, turn onto Tenth, and creep slowly east past my building. The Duckmobile, hunting for the ragged chunk of bread I'd tossed at Huey's mindless appetite. I wasn't a fan of SUVs, but this one was a beautiful sight to my eyes. It turned north onto B, its row of demon-eye-red taillights winking out as it disappeared around the corner.

I stayed dumbly at the window as the advancing daylight gradually leached all the softness and mystery from the darkened city and the pace of movement below me began to accelerate. The Navigator was long gone, but I imagined I could still see its superheated trail encircling the park, writing its early-hour message to me in the thin chilly morning air. Huey was a hothead, and cocky, but he wasn't stupid.

He'd be back, but not before day's end, not until darkness fell again; like I said, I had always seen this happening in the cold and the dark. I had a day of work left, time to see Tess afterward.

I turned into the room, went to my desk, and picked up the phone. Tess would be awake. She'd told me she started her days at first light, sitting in the chair by her bedroom window, looking out over the tree-tops in the park. Using the quiet time to think about her dreams and visions, listen for their messages. If she'd dreamt about me last night, I wanted it to have been a happy dream, nothing about me and a black SUV and juvenile Puerto Rican thugs. I wanted her to get the gift of the message, that was all.

There was a phone by her bed. She answered on the second ring.

"Hey, Tess."

"Oh, what do you know. I was just about to call you."

"Great minds, et cetera. How come?"

She gave a soft swift laugh. "Well . . . I'm not going to see you to-morrow, on your birthday, and I have something for you, so I was hop-ing I might be able to see you tonight . . . ?"

"Incredibly great minds. That's actually why I'm calling. I wanted to come by for a short visit after work. Around seven thirty?"

"Perfect. I'll be in my room."

There was a giveaway in her voice, a hesitant sort of joyfulness, more than the bestowing of a birthday present called for, unless she'd maybe bought me a Ferrari or something. She'd had a good dream.

"Okay then. Uhhmm, is there anything else? You sound like the cat that's swallowed the canary."

A small silence, then she said, "Matt came to me last night. He's been with me all morning. He's at peace. That's why I want to see you today."

Impossibly, the bubble of elation I'd been in since yesterday afternoon swelled further, to ridiculous proportions. Tess had gotten the gift of the message. And, as I'd hoped, it'd come to her from her own historic plane of existence rather than mine. I had to trust now that when it happened, when my peace came, she would recognize it; she would think of Matt the way he was with her now, me the way she'd feel me tonight, and she would know how pointless it would be to dwell on the ugliness of the gift's wrapping.

※

BEFORE I LEFT FOR WORK, I retrieved the pages I'd written the night before, folded them up, and put them into my jacket's inside pocket.

Evan had accidentally left *The Yearling* on my desk in yesterday's shook-up frenzy to get home. I told him I'd bring it for him when I came the next day. I carried it to the window and turned back the cover, looked at my name, my childish handwriting. I had to smile, re-membering the day I'd printed it there, claimed the book for my own, believing I understood what Jody had done to make Ora love him. I'd made it way too complicated when really it was simple. Ora and Penny were normal humans. Like Tess and Ella and Alex were normal hu-mans. Normal humans love their children and don't hurt them. Sal, Marian, Scott—even Marie—they were all something else. Fragments of Darkness, drawn like magnets to my karma, driven to break me into dark pieces like themselves, turn me into something else, too.

I got a pen from the desk, crossed out my name, wrote *Jody Kowal-czyk*. That was for Evan, because he didn't know that Jody Kowalczyk was nothing more than Christopher Cannavarro with some pieces re-arranged, like a cell with those jumping genes that cut and paste them-selves into a different spot on a chromosome in the hopes that a new configuration will code for survival. And that for twenty years—while he thought he was living a life of his own choosing, with his sports and muscle-powered job and serial girlfriends, and reading smart books in secret at night—all Jody was really doing was running in place, trying to keep the pieces from transferring back to where they'd come from. Clearly, that hadn't worked out too well.

I crossed out *Jody Kowalczyk* and wrote *Evan Landreth*. I put the book next to the computer.

The phone rang again just as I was heading for the door. The caller ID showed Brendan's name. I didn't pick it up, but I waited and listened to the message he left.

"Jody, it's me. Oh shit, I don't even know what to say. Just call me, please. Fern's back, and she told me it *wasn't* you, that you didn't *do* anything. Jody, damn it, why did you lie to me like that? I don't understand. I know I've been nuts with her, but what, do you think I can't still love you, too? Oh man, I'm sorry . . . You still need me, tough guy. So call me. Please. Call."

Even if this were an ordinary day, I wouldn't have called him. Even if I thought Fern would ever do what I asked, leave it alone, I wouldn't have called him. It's not that his message didn't tug at me, stir up my wishes for what might have been, but it was irrelevant now, like a weeks' old transmission from Mission Control back on Earth ordering me to turn around when I'd already rocketed past Jupiter, not enough fuel left to get home.

AT SIX THIRTY I LEFT Einstein—who'd been disturbingly subdued all day, like when I'd first found her, as if my preternatural calm was not to be trusted—with the car-service Israelis and set out for Brooklyn.

I hadn't been inside Parkside since I drove Tess back there on

Thanksgiving. Only a couple of weeks, so it was probably me, seeing everything differently now, but although I recognized that it was a supernice place given what it was, that night it didn't look so nice. Not even with the Christmas lights strung around the outside awning and front doors, a tree up and trimmed in the lobby, cheery gas fireplaces in the public rooms. You could feel the strain of how hard the place was trying, and you knew it could never replace the real homes these people had left behind.

I climbed the stairs to Tess's floor, knocked on her door. She let me in and we stood for a moment, smiling at one another. That soft light beneath her skin was glowing. It illuminated and warmed the air between us, turned the room into a hushed space that only she and I were meant to occupy. Like the first time I'd seen her, in the hallway, three months and a lifetime ago.

I reached out and took her hands in mine. Tess drew in a sharp breath, then her smile spread across her entire face.

"Oh, my," she said. "Oh, my. I think I'm still dreaming."

"No. You're awake as anything." I kissed her cheek. "Come on, tell me about Matt."

She cocked her head and squinted up into my eyes, like she might find the source of my tranquillity in them. "Should we be talking about *you?*"

"Matt, me. Same thing, right? I'm just dumb and happy. Matt's the man with the message. Come on."

I steered her to the couch. Her sketchbook was in the middle of the coffee table. A couple of loose pages were peeking out beyond the edges. Tess casually moved the pad nearer to her side.

"Perhaps there's nothing more that needs to be said." She looked at me for a moment, then touched charcoal-stained fingers to my cheek. "In all this time, I have never sensed Matt with me as strongly as he has been since the day I met you. After so many years of feeling him wandering, distraught, unable to find where he was supposed to go, every-thing changed. He was no longer aimless or lost. Because of you, Jody. You had found him, you had found each other. I know, you must be tired of hearing me say this . . . I'm sorry I repeat myself, but this will be the last time." She stroked my cheek again, then let her hands fall into her lap. "Last night, Matt came to tell me that together you had found the path home. That he was finally all right and ready to say good-bye. And I think you have found your way home, too." She clasped her hands and brought them up to her heart. "I feel so certain of this, but God knows what you really think."

One thing *I* was certain of was that Tess could never be at peace until she believed Matt to be. I was as sure of that as Tess was about Matt and me. This was what she'd been waiting for, for nearly thirty years: Matt's transformation, now mine. And her own release. There was no way I was going to deny her any of it.

"Well, if He does know what I think, I wish He'd tell me." I'd got-ten her to smile again. "I know that I'm happier than I've been maybe ever in my life, and here you dream about Matt finally being at peace, so . . . What I really think is, who am I to question it? Life is nothing but one mystery after another, anyway."

"You're happy with Ella. With Ella and Evan."

I shrugged. "You know . . . Yesterday was a good day. Today was a good day. Right now, I'm happy. I'm not thinking about anything more." I raised my eyebrows. "Except maybe what you got me for my birth-day?" With my lifelong lying skills having rusted out pretty damn thoroughly recently, I wasn't going to let the conversation come around to me.

Her smile became indulgent. She shook her head gently, then placed a hand protectively on the cover of her sketch pad.

"Don't get too excited. I didn't get you a pony. But I hope you'll like it." She opened the pad to where the loose pages were, removed them, and stacked two drawings on the table in front of me. "I did them early this morning, before we spoke."

On top was a portrait of me and Ella seated on my sofa, turned toward one another, Evan leaning forward between us, his hands resting on our knees. It was a simple drawing, but somehow Tess had imbued it, and us, with contentment, excitement, anticipation—all those hopeful emotions we'd surrendered to that day in my apartment.

I didn't remember being on the couch with them like that, but Evan had put a hand on my leg, Ella and I *had* looked at one another that way. I remembered what the whole of that rainy afternoon had felt like. I raised my head and turned to her.

"This is beautiful, Tess. Really beautiful. I love it."

"I'm so glad. The scene appeared in my mind as I was waking up. It came to me with such feeling . . ."

"Yeah, I can see that. I can feel it."

She reached over my leg and slid the top drawing away.

"And what do you see in this one?"

I smiled. I looked down. Everything around me was instantly sucked away by a rushing scouring tide of memory. Nothing left but the drawing—and my wanting to *be* there one final time, at that moment when the possibility of being the family we should have been, could have been, still existed. Before the high wire we were balancing on snapped, before we fell.

"How . . . how did you do this?" My voice sounded hollow. I felt Tess's hand between my shoulder blades. The world slowly returned. I didn't look up. I couldn't.

"You wrote about them so vividly, and about those nights . . . I have been seeing them in my mind's eye, but this, this image came to me this morning, after the other. You remember me telling you that when the time came, you would know that you hadn't failed, know how much you were loved? I believe this drawing is their message for you, Jody."

Scott and Marian in a room, side by side on a tattered sofa. Hands entwined. Heads back, loose and relaxed against the couch, their eyes on the ceiling. Unhurried, unworried smiles on their faces. The palest gray fog in the air. Above them, above the ceiling, another room, and Christopher, me, on a bed, one arm and my head over the side reaching down. My fingers outstretched, tips just touching the floor, touching the gazes reaching up toward me. No ripples disturb the unspoken intimacy. There's no fear in the fog. There's love. In the before time.

"Jody?"

I wrenched myself from the past, ripped myself from those rooms and bulled my way back into the one I was physically in. There was no way to tell her what I saw in this one. I just nodded and said, "Okay, I'm okay." And then I was able to look away, look at Tess and smile.

"Yes, you are." Tess squeezed my knee, then pushed herself up off the couch and headed for the kitchen corner. "I'll get you something to take these home in."

She came back with a plastic bag. I put the drawing of me, Ella, and Evan over the other one and put them both in the bag. I stood up.

"I should go pick up Einstein and head home."

"Of course. You have a big day ahead."

She walked with me to the entrance lobby. "Come, let me take another look at you before you go." She cupped my jaw and cheeks. "Those angel eyes." There were things her hands couldn't do anymore, but they could still make someone feel loved. "Have a very, very happy birthday tomorrow."

"Thanks. I have a feeling it's going to be a special one. And . . . I love my present. Way better than a pony." I put my arms around her bony back, felt hers encircle my waist. "I love you, Tess."

"I love you, too."

She held me tight for another minute, and then we let each other go.

*

I'D PARKED ON THE OTHER side of Prospect Park West. It had gotten colder and windier. I hustled to the car, started it up, turned the heater to blast. I shook the sketches out of the bag and laid them side by side on the passenger seat. Stared down at them in the cold ghostly illumination of the streetlights.

I shifted the car into gear, but before I pulled out, I turned my head and looked back across the street. Tess was still standing inside the Parkside's double doors, palms pressed to the glass on either side of her peering face, like a worried child looking out for her father, late coming home. I kept my foot on the brake and put my palms to my window as though to touch hers through the glass. I looked at her one last time across the divide, and I remembered what I'd thought coming here the first time, to do the estimate, how the people living there were going to die there, how sad that felt to me. I didn't want Tess to live and die there, not without ever seeing her real home again. The vineyards outside her childhood bedroom window. Teo's family's barn. Whatever and whoever remained of what had formed her. All those things you couldn't leave behind, no matter what you told yourself. Going back, going straight through the pain of it and out the other side, that's how you filled in the spaces, how you made your life whole at the end.

When I couldn't see her anymore through the fog my warm breath left on the cold glass, I pulled out and drove back to Manhattan. I parked my car in the rear of Citywide's garage. I took the Zippo out of the glove compartment, took the pages from inside my jacket and burned them in the car's ashtray. I picked up Tess's drawing of Scott, Marian, and me, folded it into quarters and put that into my inside jacket pocket. It was stiff against my chest. I left the car unlocked, keys in the cup holder, the way I always did, in case someone needed to move the car. I left Ella and Evan and me on the passenger seat.

※

"I TRIED SEDUCE HER," AVI said, his Hebrew accent thicker than the rejected Snausages he waved under Einstein's disinterested nose. "She have none of me. A loyal woman is hard to find. You are lucky man." He laughed and roughed up Einstein's ears.

Now that I was there, she softened, let Avi manhandle her before attaching herself to my side.

"Thanks for watching her."

"A most excellent dog. Anytime you need."

"Okay if I make a quick call before I head out?"

He gestured to the phone on the desk behind his.

I put my back to him and called Ella. It was nearly nine, I knew she had to be home, but she must have been doing something with Evan because I got her answering machine. Leaving a message wasn't what I'd expected to do. I'd wanted to hear her voice, and to breathe with her for the seconds of tender silence that would follow my telling her I loved her, before she told me she loved me, too. But it was probably better this way. I didn't want her to worry, I didn't want her to hear anything creep into my voice as we talked. I wanted her to be happy for as long as possible even if it meant another dislocation in time for her at the end, like when she'd been told about Matt after weeks of believing him alive, dreaming about him and imagining him dreaming of her, because every minute of happiness was worth the price we paid for it. So I took a breath when the *beep* sounded, put a smile on my face and in my tone, and said, "Hey, it's me. I just came from seeing Tess, and you know what I think would be great? If you took her back to Italy in the spring, for her birthday maybe. You should talk to her about it. Anyway, that's not the real reason why I called. I called to say

I love you. The little guy, too. You don't have to call back, I'm still at the warehouse and I may catch a late movie. I'll see you tomorrow." One, two, three heartbeats. "I love you."

＊

I WALKED HOME. I TOOK my time. The temperature had been dropping steadily, people were bundled up in winter gear. I'd left the house that morning in a lightweight jacket, but I wasn't cold. There was heat inside me, not the heat of old fear, but this new stoked furnace of anticipation. I went a block further west on Houston than I needed to, so I could walk up Avenue A instead of B. Einstein stayed close while we walked, no exploring. Every so often she'd stop and look up at me and I'd hold her head against my leg for a minute. I'd made sure her ID was secure on her collar, Brendan's number as emergency contact clear and readable.

I took my time, but it wasn't all that far and soon enough I was at the corner of Avenue A and Seventh Street, Tompkins Square Park stretching away before me, and as I kept to my leisurely pace heading toward Tenth, I looked slowly and carefully all around me. Through the trees, I made out the hulking shape of an SUV, not far off the corner of Tenth and A, in the NO STANDING space by the fire hydrant. Engine off, lights out, blending into the night.

I eased into the Coronet and waited while Nelson drew a perfect leaf design in the foam of a cappuccino and put the cup in front of a young woman sitting alone, looking at herself in the fake antique mirror that covered the wall behind the bar. I didn't see Arwen.

"Hey, Jody man, good to see you. What can I do you for?"

"Hey, Nelson. I'm an idiot, but listen, could I leave Einstein with you for a minute while I run back up to my apartment? I forgot my wallet."

"No problem." He lifted a hinged section of the side counter. "Bring her back here where I can keep an eye on her."

I led her behind the bar and knelt down in front of her. I stroked her head, then kissed her between her ears and whispered, "I'm sorry. I have to go now." Then I pulled back, put my palm against her nose, and said, "Sit. Stay." She gave me a look that carved out a hole in my chest, but she sat. And she stayed.

At the door, I hesitated, turned and looked around the familiar room. I could stay, too. I closed my eyes and imagined myself at my corner booth, my chamomile tea and English muffin on the table. They didn't hold any appeal for me anymore. I pushed open the door.

I turned onto Tenth Street. It wasn't until I was a car's length beyond the Navigator that it came to life with a throaty cough, its high headlights streaming down the street, streaming over me. I didn't look back. I didn't see it move, but its beams swerved to aim into the park, then straightened to aim down the street, and I felt the heavy machine pull away from the curb and crawl down the block, matching my slow and steady steps. I reached my building, climbed the stoop to my front door. I put my hand in my pocket and felt my keys. The headlights swept over me, and the immense shadow of the SUV cast by the street-lights crept onto the face of my building, inching toward me. I heard Huey cry out, *"Feliz fin de su mundo"*—Happy end of your world, very clever for a duck—*"hombre muerto! Vaya con Dios, motherfucker!"*

I turned my head. A weightless sensation ballooned in my chest and spread outward into my limbs, to my toes and fingers, as gravity let go its earthbound hold on me. Sound waves broke and scattered around me. All of teeming life's howling and screeching grew quiet while the throaty purr of the Navigator's V8 engine and the rubber hiss of its tires on the tarry road grew louder and louder. Time and energy became visible, sheeting and luminous and vast, a crawl of particles moving so slowly you could drive a Lincoln Navigator through the spaces between each and every infinitesimal element. Huey's round baby face loomed in the open window behind the Navigator's driver's seat, his black eyes hard and reflective as marbles, his left hand steadying the instrument of my deliverance, a hunting issue eight-gauge double-barreled sawed-off shotgun, his right hand, in a white cast that left his itchy fingers free, at the trigger.

They say that when you know you're about to die, the whole of your life flashes before your eyes. I guess I'd seen my past life flash before my eyes so often already there wasn't any novelty in it anymore so my jokester brain came up with a final new way to screw with me. Instead of my past, it flashed me snippets of a perfect future, where there was a place for me in the lives of everyone I loved and we were all safe. My insides went cold and eely with doubt. Because there was, after all, a subtle difference between not wanting to live as opposed to wanting to be dead, and for a horrible time-stopped second I wasn't sure I wanted to be dead, and I had to wonder what would have happened if I *had* tried harder, if I'd forced myself to trust even one person enough to ask for help. If I hadn't pushed Huey, but backed off and let him take the meaningless stuff and forget about me. I mean, all things considered, I guess I'd have preferred to live. My keys were in my hand, I was being given one last chance. All I had to do was take them out of my pocket, unlock the front door, and walk into the vestibule. I guess I'd have preferred to live, but not like this. It wasn't good enough, throwing myself endlessly against the bars of a cage and never finding an opening, the one bar that finally softens and bends enough to let me out. So I'd done what I'd done and there I was, not at the whim of Fate again, like I'd always been, but making my own Fate for once. There was nothing left but to face it. I let go of the keys and turned around. Scott and Marian crackled inside my jacket, right over my heart.

✳

THE NAVIGATOR DRIFTS PAST ME, the rifle swivels and lifts, Huey's head bends low over the stock, his finger completes the pull.

Two sharp cracks reverberate in the chilly air. There's an instant of searing pain as a fearsome pressure pushes into and through my abdomen, but it's over quickly and then I feel nothing. I sense the thud of something falling hard, me, falling, against the door and onto the ground. My back meets the cold concrete and I think, it's happened, it's really happened, and my doubts take flight like doves let loose from their coop, a commotion of white feathers all around me and then gone. I'm going to be safe soon. And so is everyone I love. We're all going to be safe from the terrible things love—the pain of having more of it than we can handle and the fear of there never being enough, never, never enough—can make us do.

I let go of everything and it's then I see Ella's face, through a tangle of lush vines and fronds, her hair and eyes like the sun and the trees, and I know I'm seeing her with Matt's eyes, just as he saw her the moment he let it all go, her face looking down at him as his blood soaks into the steaming earth at his back, as mine spreads over the icy cement, her face when she kissed us and told us she loved us. I did the right thing. I made sure that she would always love me the way she loves me now, at the moment I'm leaving, the way she still loves Matt, with an unfinished love that will never diminish or desert her. It will remain an open wound, like my love for Scott and my mother, and she will know me when she sees me again, when the wound suddenly begins to throb.

I hear screams, and running footfalls, and then, finally, I hear the tick of Einstein's nails on the ground, that sound I love so much, galloping toward me, closer and closer. Her breath is on my face, and her paw, and she pushes my face to the side and the hot metallic taste that chokes me flows from my mouth like liquid, like lava. I feel her stretch out on the ground by my side, her head comes to rest on my shoulder, and it's good because except for the lava I'm so cold inside the dream and she's so warm. I try to touch her, to pet her, but I can't make my arm move. Ella's face dissolves into a silent explosion of white above my head and the whiteness rains its silence down on me, as pure and gentle and peaceful as snow, and it wraps me like a blanket. I'm not cold any longer. I can sleep now. I don't need to wake up. The dream is over.

Why Her Love Will Die

When I was nine, I killed my mother's boyfriend. He'd been my daddy for four and a half years and I loved him even though he hurt me. Sometimes it was hard, but mostly it was all right, because I knew he loved me, too, and only hurt me because he had to. But one day he hurt me so bad that for a minute the pain flared so hot and high it burned right through my flesh and set my heart on fire, burned away all the love. And in that one minute of weakness, when I let the pain betray his love, I did the unforgivable thing.

I didn't know, feel, or hear anything until the silent bubble burst and time started moving again, and all the love came back. But by then it was too late, because there I am, standing at the top of the basement steps, and there is Scott, lying at the bottom. Only then do I feel the slap of the cool floor on my bare soles as I run at him, his damp heat through his shirt on my palms. Hear the thuds and the crack as he tumbles and lands. Myself screaming, my fists at my mouth, screaming so hard my throat rips, just like the other end of me. My entire body becomes a heart, beating and sparking like thunder and lightning, beating harder and faster than any heart should ever beat.

I believed I'd killed my aunt Marie, too, with my wishing and praying to get away from my grandfather's house. And maybe I did kill her, I don't know, that's a question only God—whatever God is—can answer, whether I bear the same weight of responsibility for both sins. But even if they're not equal, I must have sinned bad in that house, with my ungratefulness and my wanting what I couldn't have, and brought worse sins with me from the past, because what was Scott if not my punishment? What other explanation could there be? I needed to know punishment, and Scott needed to punish someone.

The first day we met we knew we belonged together. He saw what I already was, born in sin, born carrying sin. He saw the sins I was yet to commit. That's how he knew to love me, because I'd been born judged and guilty and he could do whatever he had to with me. I saw my savior and I loved him because I knew he would teach me what no one else would be able to, that love, fear, and pain cannot be separated, they are One, the single greatest experience of human existence, and when I'd learned that I'd be washed clean.

That is how I've lived, until now. Loving Ella has changed me, changed my ideas about what life is for. I don't think anymore that it's a race to outrun annihilation, or a simple balancing act between sin and punishment. Tonight I'm thinking that the Buddhists might have it right after all, and that life is a recurring journey along the road to Peace, and we get to take as many trips as we need to shed our karmic load and reach it. Now that I know what happiness is, how precious and ephemeral, and how you can't appreciate it unless you also know its absence, it makes a lot of sense. I guess I was meant to take a very long time getting there, but if I've learned so much this time, traveled so far, maybe it's because I'm nearing the end.

So maybe there's hope for me. I mean, not now—this life can't be redeemed, and I'm tired—but the next time around. I've loved her before, maybe last time as Matt, who knows, and I'm going to love her again, so next time, if we're allowed to find each other maybe we'll also be allowed to keep each other. Suffering can't be life's permanent default setting. It can't. There has to come a time when we find our way to the other side, when we live in the opposite of suffering.

And if I still have it wrong, and it is a sin to be born, then what is death if not forgiveness?

Part Four

INFINITY

∞

I N THE FALL OF 1980, Jody Kowalczyk entered fifth grade. He lived in a different area of Bay Shore from where Christopher Cannavarro had once lived, and attended a different school from the one Christopher had attended. And so he never crossed paths with the boy whose name and life might have been his. Roberto Rivera, called Bobby, a cherubic little boy with warm brown skin, dark blue eyes, and full lips who began kindergarten at Christopher's old school that same September. If Christopher had seen him one day, in the schoolyard perhaps or in the cafeteria, he would not have talked to him but he would have stared at him, studied his face like he studied his own in the mirror. He would have concluded, having searched for so long for someone who looked like him, that Bobby Rivera's father was his father, too, that maybe Sal had actually known something when he'd called him a spic brat. Bobby's family moved away at the end of that school year. With the boy gone from sight, Christopher would have let the idea go as well, dismissed it as childish foolishness and never known that he was correct, and that if it weren't for an oft-occurring, ages-old, sometimes catastrophic bit of casual ignorance neither Christopher Cannavarro nor Jody Kowalczyk would ever have had to exist.

Seventeen-year-old Angel Rivera was ignorant of the fact that due to a faulty condom—a purple one plucked from a bowlful on the host's living room table—he'd impregnated the pretty sky-high Italian girl who'd claimed to be eighteen and looked it and who'd heedlessly lain down in a hot bedroom with him and two of his buddies at a party on a cold night in March of 1970. Angel was a typically randy teenage stud, but he was also an atypically decent randy teenage stud and, unlike his buddies, had tried to talk to her, told her his name, tried to please her, although there was no way for him to know if he had.

Angel was not only innately decent, he was also a God-loving

Catholic from a good, loving family. When, again accidentally but this time knowingly, he impregnated his pretty Puerto Rican girlfriend four years later, he did the right thing and married her, and named his first-born son Roberto, after his beloved grandfather. Angel took great pride in his son, who looked just like him. He didn't know that his powerful genes, a smoothly blended cocktail of Puerto Rican, Spanish, North African Berber, and just a dash of pre-Columbian native Caribbean Taino, had once before created a boy who looked just like him, who had his eyes and lips and skin and build, as well as the full and kind heart that beat beneath his macho Latino exterior. If he'd known, if there'd been someone, anyone, to tell him, if the karmic wheel of the life that was about to begin had not been so burdened, everything might have spun differently.

Nothing would have stopped Angel from taking his son from that dead-eyed girl and her crude cruel family. The boy would have been named Roberto, called Bobby, and been smothered with love by Angel's parents, fussed over like the beautiful doll he was by Angel's pubescent sisters. When Angel married, Bobby would become the son of his wife. The boy would never know she wasn't his real mother; he and his younger brother Luis might have been twins, that's how alike they looked. When Bobby was ten, Angel, hard-working and skilled with his hands, would land a job with a construction company in Manhattan. The family would move to a cramped but bright apartment on the southern fringes of Spanish Harlem. In the neighborhood's austere schoolyard and on the primitive ball field hacked out of a vacant lot, Bobby would be spotted by a scout for the Atlanta Braves. After graduating City College in the top quarter of his class, he would be signed by the Braves to their AAA farm team, be brought to Atlanta a year later to play third base, be voted Rookie of the Year. The great Roberto "Bobby" Rivera, future Hall of Famer, would play for the Braves for eighteen seasons, retiring in 2009 after earning eight Gold Gloves, playing in thirteen All Star games and five World Series, taking home the 1995 championship ring and the dream glory title of World Series MVP.

But the karmic wheel was too heavy, and did not turn that way. Angel Rivera's first-born son remained an unknown boy named Christopher Cannavarro who became an unknown boy named Jody Kowalczyk who bled his stillborn life away on a grimy New York City stoop, his dog the witness to his death, on the night before the day he turned twenty-nine.

As for Angel Rivera . . . If he had ever discovered that he'd fathered a child that night, and learned what had happened to that child, his full and kind heart would have shattered into a million pieces, never to be mended.

LENNIE CARDOZA HASN'T BEEN SPENDING as many evenings at his buddy Scott's house as he used to. In fact, it's been a couple of weeks since Lennie saw Scott at all and for the past few days he's even been avoiding Scott's calls. He feels really bad about it. Cowardly almost, an unfamiliar and unpleasant feeling for Lennie. He made up his mind to pull the plug on their partnership months ago, when things with him and Monique got serious, but he hasn't done it yet, hasn't figured out how to tell Scott. The problem is, he can't see any way that Scott is going to survive without him.

Lennie has always been the thinker on their two-man team, the planner. The analytical Butch Cassidy to Scott's impulsive Sundance Kid. They reveled in that, it was so fucking cool, even called themselves Butch and Sundance for a few years after they got back to civilization in 1970 and saw the movie. Lennie, dark and square-built, was no Paul Newman, for sure, but Scott even looked a little like Redford back then with his wavy blond hair, sparking blue eyes, jungle-tanned and toughened body, quick grin. That was before Lennie set them up in the drug business, before Scott started using the shit they sold, way more than he'd ever used in 'Nam, before that shit started thinning him out, fading him out, making him translucent, like a balloon blown up too full. No, Scott has never been the sensible one, and whatever sense he might have been born with has long since leached right out of his undisciplined brain.

He knows he has to do it, but it isn't easy for Lennie to think about cutting Scott loose. They go back a lifetime, the two of them, to an afternoon when they both were six and separately had the idea to go foraging for something gleaming and dangerous in the weedy, excrement-nourished, litter-filled lot on the corner of their block, the ironically named Superior Street. One of the shittiest blocks in one of the shittiest neighborhoods in northwest Bay Shore, upon whose shoals their respective families had washed up and bot-tomed out that past summer. They were just kids, but old enough to understand what alienation felt like even though neither one of them could have spelled it. Old enough to be made desperate by boredom and the need to get out of their houses. Lennie found a bloody syringe; Scott a few jellyfish-like used condoms. Quite the haul. They formed a partnership on the spot, pooled their loot, stashed it inside a discarded minifridge that they then dragged to the back of the lot and camouflaged beneath a pile of uncategoriz-able debris. They knew the stuff was worthless crap. It was just some-thing to do. There wasn't much else available.

Stunned and confused, young Lennie and Scott may have been, but together they made a successful team. Lennie was quiet, thought-ful, and trustworthy, and Scott was his charming, willing, loyal fol-lower. They were a pair of smiling desperadoes who figured that any place had to be better than their alcohol-saturated homes and anyone safer than their drunken, violent parents. They gave school a shot, but by eighth grade they concluded that nothing they were being taught was the least bit helpful in real life. They began devot-ing their time and wiles to something more useful—ingratiating themselves into the local community of guys who understood what the world was really like, what was important. Guys who stayed under the radar and did their business out of the nicotine-drenched pool halls or ravaged streets between Main and Union. Old guys, in their twenties and thirties, guys who'd been around, been to jail, been to Korea; some blacks, some Puerto Ricans even. Tough, fuck you over as soon as look at you guys. Guys who understood what freedom meant.

One night when they were thirteen, Scott and Lennie sliced open the tips of their middle fingers with a Puerto Rican drug dealer's borrowed switchblade, pressed their fingers together, and mingled their blood, swore to be friends forever, to always watch out for the other's back, to protect the other from all the bad in the world. And they'd done it. They'd stuck together all through school; got laid, got gonorrhea for the first time the night of Scott's fifteenth birthday, Lennie's present to his blood-brother: a street-walker up against the scuzzy tile wall of a pool hall bathroom with one impatiently bobbing foot in a red vinyl stiletto-heeled shoe balanced on the stained sink, twenty-five dollars for the two of them. They enlisted in the Army as soon as they both turned nineteen. Trained to be medics, served five years of their required six on active duty in Vietnam and Cambodia together. Saved each other's lives more than once. Came back to Bay Shore and the smokey pool halls and shadowed streets, joined the community of tough guys, went into business—Lennie the sharp calm entrepreneur handling their suppliers and their profits, Scott the charming street kid sniffing out clients, moving the stuff, collecting the money. Doing it together. Always together.

But you know how it goes. Things change. People change. Lennie changed, Scott didn't. Lennie could see it so clearly lately. Selling dope, it was no good, there was no future in it for your honest local dealer anymore. There was too much of it going on now, too many people with too little conscience and too much greed. He'd been careful, and Scott'd been lucky, and they'd stayed alive and out of jail for nearly a decade, but it was time to stop. It had been a means to an end, that's all.

Lennie has plenty of money now. And a sweet respectable girl who believes he's a sweet respectable guy. Lennie's idea of what constitutes real life has taken a U-turn. He made a deal with old Hanagawa for the aikido dojo, it's his now, he can let the street kids in for free, give them an alternative to the empty lots, the decaying pool halls. He's ready for it, the move from the dark to the light. The nice house, the reportable income. A wife, a couple of kids of his own; he'll father himself a superfine boy like Mule Train and raise him clean and right. No drugs, no booze, no beatings. But Scott. Man, Scott doesn't get it at all. He thinks this shit *is* the end. He's nothing but a walking dead man, an upright zombie waiting to greet the reaper.

※

SUNDAY MORNING, JULY 6, 1980, LENNIE Cardoza bites the bullet and drives once again to the once-shittiest block in the once-shittiest neighborhood of Bay Shore, to the house that Scott's parents had the unexpected sobriety and intelligence to deed to their son before they died of acute alcoholism.

Like many others throughout fast-growing eastern Long Island, Scott and Lennie's old neighborhood had changed for the better in the decades since World War II, had risen from spectacularly bad to ignorably ordinary. The demographics of Superior Street had changed, too, from hard-living down-at-the-heels whites to hard-working lower-middle-class blacks and Hispanics. By 1976, when Scott brought that trashy young woman and her cowed little boy to live with him, he had already been the last white homeowner standing for a few years. That suited Scott and Lennie. Scott's neighbors were, to a man, woman, and child, distrustful-of-authority types who soundly minded their own business. Most of them knew what Scott did for a living. Some were occasional customers and the rest didn't care one way or another. Scott plied his trade away from the street, and he didn't sell to children. He kept to himself, was polite, respectful. And if there was a little more door slamming and grown-up yelling going on behind the walls of number 113 than from some other houses, and if the kid didn't talk much and rarely played with the other kids on the block, well, that was no one else's business either.

✳

LENNIE PARKS AT THE CURB. Church bells are ringing out from up on Union Boulevard. Ten o'clock in the morning, the sun is already merciless in a cloudless sky. Lennie starts sweating in the hot wind the second he hoists himself out of his air-conditioned Mercury Cougar. There isn't much activity on the street, just the regular Sunday morning sight of the block's teenaged rebels, the church-shunning Dee-Boyz—Duquan, Damar, and Diego—shooting hoops in Damar's driveway, braving the heat and the wrath of both God and parents. Lennie waves and calls out, *"¡Hola, muchachos! ¿Qué pasa?"* They call out, *"¡Hola,* Señor Cardoza!" without breaking stride. They're okay kids.

Lennie picks his way along the path from the street to Scott's front door, a cautious twenty-foot trip. You want to avoid the cracks that snake through the old flagstones; the world was a perilous and inexplicable place, so why look for trouble. He rings the bell and while he waits on the stoop for probably Mule Train to come to the door, what with Marian long gone and Scott most likely still out cold, Lennie rehearses his presentation in his head one more time. His mouth moves silently.

Last night he realized he can't move on without at least trying to take Scott with him. Not after all this time. Not after everything they've been through together. He's going to offer Scott a deal: clean up, stay clean six months, then come work at the dojo. Monique didn't want him to do it, said Scott couldn't stay clean even if you put a full-body lead condom on him. And he doesn't necessarily think she's wrong, but he said to her that after twenty-six years you've got to show faith in your blood-brother. You've got to help him, let him see you believe in him, give him some of your faith. Scott had grit, maybe he could stay clean if Lennie gave him a reason to. Monique still didn't want him to do it, but she kissed him and took him to bed without another word because she loved him so much at that moment for being someone who could say, who could feel, something like that.

In the middle of the night, lying next to her and dreaming about the kids they'd have soon, it came to Lennie like a lightning strike that Scott already *had* a reason, the best in the world. He had Mule Train. Man, Scott loved that kid. How many times had Scott said the kid was the best thing that ever happened to him? He'd do anything for him. He'd get straight. He'd stay straight, maybe go back to being a PA again. For Mule Train. For the kid.

Thinking all those good thoughts, it takes a minute to register that Mule Train hasn't come to the door. Lennie rings the bell again and waits some more. He watches the hoopsters; Duquan has soft hands and quick feet, he can play. No one comes to the door. A little strange. Scott's Mustang is in the driveway. Lennie has a key, but he doesn't like walking into someone else's house like that. He rings the bell three times in a row, fast, opens the screen door, listens with a cauliflower ear to the hollow wooden front door. Nothing. Definitely strange. Mule Train would be up for hours by now. Lennie takes out his key and lets himself in.

The door swings shut behind him, pushed by an invisible power. For a brief, dizzying instant Lennie is overtaken by the surreal sensation of having walked through a space/time portal rather than a normal door. Of having crossed Scott's threshold and jumped back a dozen years and across the world, from the lethargic steaming streets of 1980 Bay Shore, Long Island, to the paralyzing steaming jungles of 1968 Southeast Asia.

It's the roaring silence, a deadly silence so wet and heavy it fills his mouth and nose and lungs when he breathes. And then the sudden shocking return of a chaos of mundane sounds—a ticking clock, a leaking faucet, a staticky radio, a buzzing cicada, a banging gate, a humming refrigerator, a leather ball on concrete—none of them human. And a rectangle of sunlight, and a hot breeze falling on his face where there shouldn't be any light or breeze; a wrong brightness and a wrong movement of air coming toward him up the narrow hallway, from the far end of the kitchen where the back door stands open when it should be shut.

The malign wind carries the sour smell of beer and something worse. The acrid smell of violence and fear. Lennie's heart starts to race and the hairs on his arms and the back of his neck stand up off his skin.

His first thought might have been: a robbery, an invasion, one of their users finally gone rabid from a bad habit and a bad temper. But he knows that's not what happened. The only energy traces in the house belong to Scott and Mule Train. If anyone else had been there recently, he'd feel it. Lennie glances to his right, at the stairs leading to the second floor. He gallops up them, eyes trained on the upstairs hallway. Maybe he's crazy, suffering a doozy little brain cramp like he'd get sometimes during those first years home after 'Nam. They were still asleep, that's all. Or they were at the park playing ball. They'd opened the back door for the heat. Forgot to close it.

He peers into Mule Train's and then Scott's bedrooms. Mule Train's room is as neat as ever, except for a little-boy-rumpled bed, small creases in the kid's cherished Stars of the NHL sheets. Scott's room is a fucking mess. A disaster. Stained bedding half on the floor, a couple cans of beer on a night table. Closet doors and night table drawers ajar, everything out in the open. M1 Carbine hanging over the top of the dresser, Colt Python .357 Magnum on the bed next to bags of grass, coke, and packets of heroin. Open bags of pills, the tranqs and barbiturates—Seconal, quaaludes, Nembutal, Valium—some of each strewn like M&Ms over the mattress. Mule Train's pajama top a misplaced hummock of material near the headboard.

Lennie doesn't touch a thing. He doesn't enter the room. He just turns and slowly retraces his steps. When he reaches the bottom of the stairs, he hesitates at the door to the street. He wishes he'd gone to church with Monique, or to the dojo, or just stayed in bed. Into his brain pops the cosmic riddle—does a tree falling in the forest make a noise if there's no one there to hear it—and he wishes to God he knew the answer because if it was no, and he turned around right now and left, if he wasn't here to witness the bad thing that he knows has happened, it wouldn't have happened. Nothing was real until you saw, felt, or heard it. Until you were a part of it.

But then he realizes his error. Even if it makes no noise without someone there to hear it when it rips out of the earth and hits the ground, the tree still falls.

✳

THERE ARE SOME SMALL MOIST patches along the scuffed wood floor of the hall. At the far end of the kitchen, the inner door to the backyard is flung open and lies against the back wall; in the breeze, the warped screen door bangs lightly against the doorframe. On the table, amid a half dozen crumpled beer cans and some dirty dishes, are the Smith & Wesson, its safety on, a small spill of Seconal, two bags of cocaine, a mirror, a short straw, a razor blade. One of the coke bags is empty, nothing but a coating of white dust inside. There are wide, clear rivulets in the dust where Scott lapped at the last of it with his tongue. The other bag is sealed, but only half full. If Scott snorted as much coke as it looked like he had, he ought to be caroming around the house like an electron in a particle accelerator. So where the fuck was he? And where was Mule Train?

Lennie leans over and examines the mirror and the razor. A coke fuzz clings to the mirror's surface, to the edge of the blade. There are dark smears of blood in with the remnants of white powder on the blade, drops of blood on the table and mirror. His heart in his throat, Lennie squats down and examines a small reeking pool of sticky fluid on the floor by a table leg. Vomit, blood, beer. Semen. Scott's jeans are jammed under the table, against the wall. Lennie's eyes close for a second, his heart hurts so bad he has to put a hand on the table's edge to steady himself. Rage and hopelessness want to bloom inside him, but he doesn't allow it. He has to be all business now. Heart rate slow and steady, mind clear and calm. Once it was real, you were no good freaking out.

He stands up. His eyes follow a smeary trail of small footprints leading from the noxious pool to the closed door to the basement, on the right side wall, next to the humming refrigerator, and back again. Then another, from the table to the back door, the slimy tracks growing faint, but the path marked by a sporadic dribble of red Seconal capsules. Keeping to the side of the wet prints, Lennie follows the trail to the basement door, opens it, and looks down into the underground dimness.

Scott is sprawled face-up at the bottom of the stairs, head and torso on the concrete floor, legs on the wooden steps. His shirt is open, the hairless skin of his chest and belly glisten wetly in the light that spills down the stairs. His flaccid penis hangs outside his blood-spattered briefs. While Lennie stands and stares at him, Scott groans, then begins to snore steadily. Lennie doesn't feel surprise or fear or sadness. He doesn't feel anything. He hears Monique's voice in his head saying, "What did I tell you, baby?" From where he stands, there's no telling if Mule Train is somewhere in the thick darkness beyond Scott's head. The only other thing he can see are cases of beer stacked against the wall near Scott's outflung arm.

He's about to start down the stairs when a speck in the periphery of his vision draws his eyes to his left, out toward the yard. Through the angled mesh of the screen, he sees the derelict doghouse, and a bare brown foot extending from it, the tender sole exposed to the burning sun. Lennie's head swivels from side to side. *Two buddies down!* This time, Lennie doesn't have to ask himself who to help first. Fear and sorrow explode like a bomb inside him and he runs.

Out the back door, through the high stalky grass, the sharp tips of burnt-out blades pricking at his bare ankles like thorny tropical vines, an equatorially hot sun pounding down on his head, intricate thready cobwebs lit by the sun glinting between the trees. It was 'Nam all over again, nothing ever changed in this fucking world, another superfine young boy on the ground and Lennie asking himself as he ran, *Is this one going home in a body bag? Or is he just going to wish he had?*

HALF-NAKED, UNCONSCIOUS NINE-YEAR-OLD BOY LYING head-in on his stomach on the dirt floor of disintegrating doghouse. Pair of cracked white vinyl boots wedged underneath him. Pale green polyester pajama bottoms dragged down to his knees, the back waistband and seat damp and stained with blood and semen. Blood, semen, and dirt smudged all over his bare bottom and the backs of his legs. Blood still slowly welling from an inept razor cut across the inside of the left wrist. Head twisted harshly to the right. Bag of Seconal near his clenched right hand, pills on the ground near his mouth. Lacerated bleeding lips. Bottom half of his face covered with a stinking, hardening mix of vomit, beer, blood, saliva, semen. Layer of dust on smooth-skinned cheeks criss-crossed with clear lines of shed tears. Some moisture still trapped in dense black eyelashes. Thick dark hair matted with filth. Small new cut in the corner of the mouth, near the scar of an older one. Old nickel-sized burn on the upper meaty part of the right buttock. Narrow circle-sliver of dark blue iris surrounding distended pupil. Thready, decelerated pulse. Clammy skin. Shallow depressed respiration. Unresponsive to all stimuli. Comatose.

✳

LENNIE MAKES A COOL, DETACHED assessment. There's nothing he can do for Mule Train on-site; the kid needs to be evacuated to a hospital ASAP. Lennie's brain gives the order for him to stand up and make that happen, go inside and call 911. But his body rebels. His massive legs won't lift him, his head is too heavy for his thick neck to support, and he can't stop his hand from shaking as it wraps itself around Mule Train's slim, limp ankle. He hangs there for a moment, nauseated with guilt and disbelief, stunned by a torrent of memories of things his eyes had seen but his heart and mind had not—graceful, athletic Mule Train's inexplicable accidents; the broken bones, the cuts and bruises; the slow decay of his noise and energy, his contagious good humor, his eager curiosity; the filmy curtain gradually descending over his perceptive, penetrating cobalt-blue eyes. The recent tenacity of his grip when he hugged Lennie good-bye. Lennie knows it will haunt him, that this happened in front of him yet he'd been blind to it, but he has no time for that now.

✳

SCOTT'S PULSE IS STRONG. ONE arm is bent under him, probably broken, and a lump the size of a golf ball has risen on the back of his skull. Lennie squats by his best buddy of twenty-six years, his blood-brother. He rocks on his heels and watches Scott's placid face, listens to the throaty, knocked-out snorts and snores, looking and listening for some expression of torment, of remorse, to emerge from him. After a long disappointing moment, Lennie shakes his head and sighs.

"Scott, you sorry piece of shit pervert, you really stepped over the line this time. But Lennie's going to take care of you, just like always. Jail's not a good place for child molesters, man, not a lot of forgiveness there, you know what I'm saying?"

Then, ever decisive, ever the leader, he takes Scott's head in his well-trained hands, says a short prayer for both their souls, and in one smooth swift motion, Lennie Cardoza breaks Scott Hanson's neck.

✳

IT'S 10:15. LENNIE SITS AT the kitchen table, listening to the thunderous ticking of the cheap wall clock behind his head. He is waiting for that one tick whose sound will tell him that Time has reached a perfect place of balance between enough of it left to save Mule Train's life and enough of it gone so that the cops won't think to suspect Lennie of finishing Scott off. He'll never know exactly what happened, all the whens and whats and hows, but as his eyes make another slow sweep of the scene, follow the lines of footprints again, and then again, he knows one thing for sure: Mule Train'd had all he could take. He'd had enough and he'd run from the table, where Scott had raped him and then left him to go get more beer, and pushed Scott down the stairs. He'd done what he had to do, but he was too scared, too young and inexperienced to go down after Scott and make sure the mission was a success. Instead, he'd closed the basement door as though to undo the reality of what he'd done. Lennie is as sure of that as he has ever been of anything in his life.

But the one thing Lennie can't be sure of is the most important thing: when did it happen? *When* did Mule Train push Scott, cut his own wrist, take the Seconal, and go out to the doghouse to die?

Lennie was a good medic. He knows that Seconal is the deadliest barbiturate of them all, that as few as ten pretty red pills would kill a nine-year-old child in three to four hours; he'd stop breathing, his heart would fail. Lennie has no doubt the boy downed at least that many. But when? How much time does he have? He considers the evidence of the fluids on the floor, the footprints, deduces how quickly they might thicken and dry in the heat, and the current rate of Mule Train's pulse and breathing. He concludes the kid has less than an hour. Lennie knows he's walking the tightrope, but he's going to need some of that time.

Lennie doesn't want the cops looking to him for anything here, and he doesn't want them looking to the kid, either. If he makes it appear most likely that Scott left the boy outside and then, drunk as a skunk and high/low as a kite, took a fatal tumble down the stairs sometime later, everyone would be in the clear. He's already left the basement door open. Now he has to get rid of the footprints. He gets a mop out of the garage, swabs the damning trails out of existence with scalding water and Lysol. In the hot breeze from the back door, the floor is dry before he puts the mop away.

One more *tick,* and the time is now. Lennie uses the phone in the living room to call 911. He goes and sits on the concrete steps of the front stoop, watches the Dee-Boyz dribble and shoot. The ambulance arrives ahead of the cops. Lennie decides not to wait around any longer. He hurries down the walkway to intercept the beefy EMT hurrying up it. He says, "The guy in the basement's dead. Go get the kid. Straight through the house, out back, in the doghouse." Lennie reads the man's name tag. Karl Kowalczyk. Lennie looks into Karl's soft brown eyes and allows himself an instant of hope. Karl Kowalczyk isn't young, and he has the smart, no-nonsense, dedicated eyes of a retired cop, or an ex-soldier. A good one. "His name's Christopher. He's a great kid. You take good care of him, Karl. You give him his life back, you understand?"

Karl Kowalczyk grunts an assent and bolts into the house. The Dee-Boyz are sprinting like racehorses toward number 113. Lennie gets into his Cougar, pulls out into the street. He and Duquan exchange a fleeting glance as they glide by one another. Duquan's eyes are miserable with silent apology and a promise to keep his mouth shut. Lennie likes Duquan, but at that moment he wants to leap out of the car and bash the teen's clean, unscarred face into the pavement. Instead, he steels himself against the commotion rising like a tidal wave behind him, presses down hard on the gas pedal and removes himself from Superior Street as surely as he's removed Scott, with a finality no less absolute than death.

Only Mule Train will remain, owned by his past, trapped in that basement where Scott died. Lennie's instinctive act of merciful justice will lock the boy behind the bars of a diamond-hard cage of guilt, his unbearable feelings and the possibility of one day coming to bear them always beyond his reach, and ensure that no matter where the boy goes, or what he calls himself, or who wants and loves him, he will live forever and die alone behind the walls of 113 Superior Street.

Epilogue

THE MULTIVERSE

*Physicists, cosmologists, philosophers, and writers
have long posited the possibility –
nay, likelihood – of a cosmos comprised of a
multitude of universes,
all coexisting with the one we know and inhabit,
while remaining, so far at least,
beyond the limits of our perception. These multiple
universes are often referred to as
parallel universes, or alternate realities . . .*

Contemplating the existence of The Multiverse *leads
us to wonder: Do other versions of ourselves exist in
these parallel universes? And might other versions of
ourselves in an alternate reality walk through other
doors, choose other paths? Does, indeed, that place
exist where our lives might turn out differently?*

IT'S LATE ON A FRIDAY afternoon in August of 2007. Seventeen-year-old Evan Landreth is working as a barista at the Starbucks in the student union on the campus of Long Island's Stony Brook University. He is expertly crafting a venti decaf soy mocha, no whip, for the Goth geek girl who comes in every afternoon around this time, near the end of his shift. She wears four-inch platform boots and short skirts, has a pierced eyebrow and a rose tattoo at the nape of her neck. She has spiked tangerine hair and turquoise eyes. Evan has recently come to think that tangerine and turquoise is the most beautiful color combination in the world. He accidentally splashes the hot soy milk on his hand and groans, "Ow!" but too quietly for her to hear.

This is Evan's final day of work. Once the fall semester of his sophomore year begins, he won't have time for much else besides school. He's carrying a full load of classes. He's premed, with a major in psychology. He's going to be a psychiatrist. He wants to help people who have been so damaged by the world that they've forgotten the possibility of happiness. In particular, Evan wants to help children. It's been his dream ever since he was ten.

Classes begin in two weeks and Evan is going to spend the break back in the city, at home in his mother's brownstone in the Village, hanging out, sleeping in his own bed, eating home-cooked meals. It will probably be his last chance to do that until Thanksgiving. He hasn't told his mother yet, but he's decided that he's going to take his dog back to school with him. She's getting old, and now that he's living off-campus and can have a pet, he wants her with him. His mother will miss her, but Evan misses her, too.

Evan makes his last drink of the summer. He cleans up his station, says good-bye to his work buddies, and heads out to the parking lot. When he opens the door of his car, the aroma permeating the warm, trapped air makes him salivate. He knows it was insane, but he drove all the way down to the south shore and back early this morning, to Marley's in Bay Shore, to buy a bag of doughnuts to take back to the city. Nobody doesn't like a Marley's doughnut.

It's a gorgeous evening. Evan puts the top down on the gently used three-year-old BMW convertible his father, Ronald, bought for him in lieu of saying *I'm proud of you* when Evan announced his intention to become an MD. Evan doesn't care; his father's coldness doesn't bother him anymore and he loves the car. He delays getting on the expressway and drives west toward the city on a winding, dappled back road, the warm wind tossing his long caramel-colored hair around his face.

Miraculously, he finds a parking spot on West Eleventh Street, practically in front of the brownstone. By the time he's got the top up and the trunk open, Alex is there, hugging him, hauling his bags of books and clothes out of the trunk and up the steps, calling out toward the open door, "Ella, Kaylee, Evan's home!" Evan grabs the doughnuts, locks the car, and runs after him. "Dad! Leave the stuff in the hall, I'll take it upstairs later."

He walks into the living room and his mouth drops open in surprise. Everyone is there. Mom, Alex, Kaylee. Aunt Tess. Aunt Irene and Uncle Karl. Brendan and Fern and their four-year-old twins. Like a trained chorus, they shout out, "Welcome home, Evan!" They swarm around him, laughing at his surprise and their own excitement, and he hugs and kisses each and every one.

Einstein barrels through the crowd from beneath the piano where she was napping. Her snout is more white than black and she pushes it, hard, into Evan's hand and licks him, quivering with joy. Evan kneels and puts his arms around her, turns his face into the fur of her shoulder so no one will see the sudden tears in his eyes.

He's a teenager, such childish feelings are embarrassing, but he is absurdly happy to be exactly where he is, and he can't deny to himself that there are days, like this, when life simply can't get any better.